RED RIGHT HAND

ALSO BY CHRIS TULLBANE

Red Right Hand

CHRIS TULLBANE

GHOST FALLS PRESS

First published by Ghost Falls Press 2020
Red Right Hand. Copyright © 2020 by Chris Tullbane.

GHOST FALLS PRESS

Publisher's Cataloging-in-Publication Data
provided by Five Rainbows Cataloging Services

Names: Tullbane, Chris, author.
Title: Red right hand / Chris Tullbane.
Description: Henderson, NV : Ghost Falls Press, 2020. | Series: Murder of crows, bk. 2. | Also available in audiobook format.
Identifiers: ISBN 978-1-7334824-7-9 (paperback) | ISBN 978-1-7334824-6-2 (ebook)
Subjects: LCSH: Superheroes--Fiction. | Conspiracies--Fiction. | Self-actualization (Psychology)--Fiction. | Bildungsromans. | Fantasy fiction. | Science fiction. | BISAC: FICTION / Superheroes. | FICTION / Coming of Age. | FICTION / Fantasy / Action & Adventure. | FICTION / Science Fiction / Action & Adventure. | GSAFD: Fantasy fiction. | Science fiction. | Bildungsromans.
Classification: LCC PS3620.U45 R43 2020 (print) | LCC PS3620.U45 (ebook) | DDC 813/.6--dc23.

Book cover design by ebooklaunch.com

FIRST EDITION

For Nami,
the reason for everything

ACKNOWLEDGMENTS

This book would not be what it is without the support of a number of wonderful people:

Nami, my angel-wife. The power on the throne and the secret to my success.

Johanna, my whisky buddy. I told her how this whole thing would end… and then she forgot.

Jamie, protector of the free world, who remains both the best and the only brother I've ever had.

Keith and Shawn, who listen to my book-related monologues every day and have yet to unsubscribe.

Simon, poet and friend, whose words create worlds.

Kerri, who read this whole book on her phone and didn't try to kill me afterward.

And last but not least, my mother and father; great people and even better parents.

Thank you all.

The Class of 76

Given Name	Cape Name	Power Class
Alan Jackson	The Manimal	Beast Shifter
Caleb Mikkazi	Supersonic	Jitterbug/Flyboy
Damian Banach	Walker	Crow
Erik Thorsson	The Viking	Titan
Erin Pearson	Cyclone	Wind Dancer
Evelyn Mandelhoff	Wormhole	Teleporter
Frederic Ficus	Muse	Switch
Ishmae Naser	Phoenix	Pyromancer
Jason Abara	Nug	Hydromancer
Jeremiah Jones	Stonewall	Mineral Shifter
Johannes Callum	Prince	Siren
Kayleigh Watai	Vibe	Empath
London Sullivan	Ember	Pyromancer
Matthew Strich	Paladin	Stalwart
Nadia Kahale	Orca	Stalwart
Olympia Kennedy	Spectra	Lightbringer
Orson Douglas	Oscuro	Shadecaster
Patricia O'Connor	Makara	Hydromancer
Penelope Von Pell	Winter	Weather Witch/Wind Dancer
Rebecca Wells	Static	Spark
Santiago Tomayo	El Bosque	Druid
Shane Stevenson	Unicorn	Healer
Sofia Black	Silt	Earthshaker
Tessa McShane	Poltergeist	Telekinetic

CHAPTER 1

My father murdered my mom when I was five.

Thirteen years later, I quit superhero school to return the favor.

I'd say that's when everything went to hell, but that would be a lie. Hell is seeing your mom's blood spread across the kitchen floor. Everything that comes after is just life. You either survive it or you don't.

I'm a survivor.

Survived Mom's murder. Survived more than a decade at Mama Rawlins' House for Unwanted Brats. Survived a year at the Academy as the school's only necromancer student. Even survived that mess out at the Hole, where a lot of other people died. Better people, mostly. If life's taught me anything, it's that you scrap and claw for every moment you can get. And if you're a Crow like me, you don't let a little thing like dying get in your way.

My name is Damian, but most people call me Walker.

○○○

In Los Angeles, cold is something that happens to other people… to the sad sacks who live up north or inland. Bakersfield, where I was born, abandoned, and sort of raised, has its own brand of winter—fog, fog, and more fog—but it's not until you get into the Badlands, to the scattering of tiny towns disappearing by the year, that you learn what real cold is; ice and snow, limbs turning blue, and pieces of you dropping off like you're a mindless walker some asshole Crow raised.

In L.A., the land of sunshine and balmy ocean breezes, Winter is just the name of one of my more annoying classmates.

I was sitting on a stone bench in the clearing on the west side of campus, watching ghosts flicker in and out of existence around me. After a year of school, I still didn't understand what ghosts really were. Fragments of people, maybe. Echoes of what was, pulled into the orbit of my power. Most of them silent, most unaware I was even there.

There were exceptions, of course.

A few months back, Mom's ghost had hit me with a vision of her own death, revealing that I'd been my dad's intended target. And then she'd gone right back to humming her silent song, a mindless specter in a yellow sundress, smiling blankly into space. No explanation. No words. Not even a shared glance.

Dad's ghost was newer. Not even a month old and clear as daylight, shuffling aimlessly through the trees around me. I hadn't been the one who killed him, but he'd followed me back to the Academy just the same. Part of me hoped he had his own vision to share— something to explain why he'd wanted to kill me and murdered Mom instead—but most of me just wanted his translucent ass gone for good.

He'd been a Crow, back when he was alive. One of too damn many things we had in common. Everyone assumed that's why he'd gone bad—just another necromancer succumbing to madness—but before his death at the Hole, he'd told me otherwise. Told me Sally Cemetery, herself long dead, had come and made him remember.

Remember what?

No fucking clue. Sally was as infamous a Crow and Black Hat as there'd ever been, and somehow, death hadn't kept her from appearing to my dad and destroying my life. It also hadn't kept her from showing up on the Academy grounds thirteen years later and saving that same life, right when I was on the precipice of madness.

Damned if I could understand why she'd done either.

If all that wasn't enough of a mindfuck, I'd stumbled across another shocker while awaiting the results of my expulsion hearing. The Finder who'd come to Bakersfield just before my eighteenth birthday, who'd somehow gotten me enrolled in the prestigious Academy of Heroes? The mysterious Mr. Grey, who was as bland as his name except for two eyes that shined like copper pennies? He was number nine on the Security Council's most wanted list, a Black Hat known to the Free States as Tyrant.

I'd been sent to hero school by one of the worst villains in the country, and I had no idea why.

Shit on the left of me, shit on the right, and a whole mess of dead bodies behind. The only path was forward. Another year at the Academy. One last chance to prove I could be a Cape. If I flamed out a second time, I was fucked.

But that's life too, isn't it?

We're all survivors right up until the day we aren't.

CHAPTER 2

As I left the woods, the sound of orientation hit me like a Titan's fist; music and cheering and a godawful number of eighteen-year-olds relishing their first day away from Mommy and Daddy. For the normals who formed the bulk of the Academy's student body, it was a day of celebration.

The Powers who made up the incoming class of first-years weren't getting a party. They were in an auditorium near the center of campus, where Dean Bard was telling them they were all going to die. Welcome to life as a Cape in the only democracy left in North America. Shit's not easy. Even making it to graduation isn't a guarantee.

As if the thought had summoned him, I saw Shane's ghost in the distance; a teenage ginger named Unicorn who'd had dreams of healing the world. He'd died in our first semester. Wish I could say his death had been for something. Wish I could say seeing him didn't still hurt. Wish I could say a lot of things, but wish is just another word for dream, and ever since the Break, Dr. Nowhere's dream is the only one that matters.

I met Unicorn's vacant eyes, unleashed some of that emptiness that makes me a Crow, and watched my friend's ghost fade away.

ooo

If you're a first-year, Orientation gets you a seat in the auditorium and the dubious pleasure of Dean Bard's one and only speech. If you're a second-year, all you get is a note on your Glass, telling you what sub-dorm you've been assigned to. See, that initial year at the Academy is about testing future Capes as individuals; seeing who has what it takes to not snap under the pressure.

Can't say I handled it all that well, given I'd quit school and run off to murder my dad, but the expulsion board had seen fit to give me another chance anyway.

By second-year, the Academy was done testing us as individuals. Now, it was time to see how we performed in teams. That's where the sub-dorm thing came in. Second-years lived with their teammates in one of ten smaller buildings on the east side of campus. Four bedrooms, one bathroom, and a common area for me and three people who, chances were, hated my guts.

Knowing my luck, I'd be stuck with Wormhole, Supersonic and Paladin. Or worse... I'd share a bedroom wall with Santiago like I had as a first-year. Another year forced to listen to him and London having sex would drive me crazy faster than my power ever could.

I checked my Glass one last time before sliding it into the bag that held my possessions; underwear and toiletries, a half-dozen sets of Academy grey sweats that matched the ones I was currently wearing, a faded t-shirt with the adult Paladin's logo across the chest, and a glossy black card with a single-use net address in raised lettering.

I'd already used the card, making it little more than a reminder of the woman who'd given it to me, the leather-clad Shifter mercenary known to me as Her Majesty and to the Free States as the Queen of Smiles. I now knew she'd been hired by Tyrant to get me to the Academy. What I didn't know was why she'd helped me afterwards, bringing me the gun I'd smuggled into the Hole to kill my Dad.

Had all of that been part of Tyrant's plan too? Hell if I knew, but I was tired of feeling like a pawn.

Only five of the ten sub-dorms were in use. The Academy had been built to house hundreds of potential Capes, but those numbers had yet to materialize. To hear Bard talk, the Capes of the Free States were fighting a war of attrition... and losing.

My home for the year was distinguished from the other sub-dorms by a V on its door. That's the Roman numeral five, for you lucky bastards who never had to sit through a full year of pre-Break history. Loud and angry voices were already coming from inside. Fights were kind of a staple of our class—from Supersonic coming after me at Unicorn's funeral to the brawl at the Liquid Hero that had made us all famous as first-years—but I wasn't used to having them start without me.

The door opened on a small common room with a couch, a vid screen, two easy chairs, and a pair of furiously arguing women. One of the women had dark hair, shoulder-length and curly, while the other had silken white hair to her waist and a nose almost as crooked as mine.

Tessa McShane and Penelope Von Pell. Better known to our class as Poltergeist and Winter.

Because *of course* I'd get stuck on a team with both.

Fuck my fucking life.

Both women turned as I entered. I watched the emotions parade across their faces, terminating in what could only be described as disappointment.

"You've got to be kidding." For once, Winter had her hair down instead of up in one of the ridiculous styles she favored. It might have softened the narrow planes of her face if she hadn't been so busy frowning.

"*Of course* it would be you." Poltergeist scowled.

"That's my line." They weren't my *least* favorite people in the class, but it wasn't for lack of trying. "Is it just the three of us? I don't know if I can deal with you two by myself for an entire year."

"What's that supposed to mean?" demanded Winter.

"Our fourth is in his room," said Poltergeist, nodding to the hallway and the one door off of it that was closed. "Sleeping."

"With the noise you two were making? Yeah, right."

"*Sleeping*," she repeated, this time adding air quotes. "He was drunk when I got here."

"Shit." There was only one person I could think of who would already be drunk before school even started. Frederic Ficus, sometimes called Freddy, but mostly referred to by his Cape name. "Muse?"

"If he pukes, I'm not cleaning it up." Winter wrinkled her long nose and sighed. "I guess it could have been worse. None of us like each other—" For some reason, she gave me the side-eye. "—but powers-wise, we're going to be tough to handle."

"You've got to be kidding." Poltergeist shook her head. "This team is a disaster!"

Winter pulled herself up to her full height and looked scornfully at the other woman. "You're a Low Four, I'm amazing, we have the class' only Switch, and Damian…"

"What about me?" I couldn't wait to see where Winter went with this.

"You're a jerk, but you fought at the Hole and killed Carnage with a touch. Who in our class can stand up to that?"

"Anyone with ranged abilities," Tessa and I said at the same time. The dark-haired woman shot me an irritated look, then continued. "Do you really think the Academy will let the Crow just start killing our classmates?"

"I have a name, Poltergeist."

"Whatever. *Damian.*"

"I meant my Cape name."

"I'm not calling you Walker. Bad enough that the Academy has a Crow student. You don't need to rub what you are in everyone's face."

"Nobody died and made you the boss of Cape names, Tessa," interjected Penelope.

"Winter's right, for once," I said. From the twin glares shot my way, neither woman appreciated my contribution. "Anyway, Dominion didn't have a problem with the name, and I value his opinion a lot more than either of yours."

That ended the debate, like I'd hoped it would. As the country's only Full-Five, Dominion had been the very first Cape and remained far and away our greatest.

"Fine. Whatever. *Walker.*" If Poltergeist's tone hadn't already communicated how she still felt about my name, her rolled eyes would have done so. "My point stands. The teachers aren't going to let you kill our classmates, even if you do somehow get your hands on them.

That makes you useless as a front-line fighter. And once Muse amplifies us, he's basically just a normal."

"So what?" argued Winter. "We'll be the only boosted Powers on the field. Even if there are only three of us actually fighting, that should be plenty."

"Unless we're in a situation where numbers matter."

"Right." It was Penelope's turn to roll her eyes. "This is why I should be team leader. We need someone with ideas instead of excuses!"

Normally, I'd have sat back and let the two go at it—better they attack each other than me, after all—but after a month of near-isolation on campus, all the noise was giving me a headache. I opened myself to my power, letting emptiness drown out the dull throb, and interrupted the argument.

"Team leader?"

Poltergeist scowled. "Every team needs to pick one tonight. Bard wants the leaders in his office tomorrow morning."

"*That's* what you two were fighting about?"

Winter's scowl mirrored Tessa's. "We weren't fighting. Just... discussing."

"I could hear your discussion all the way down the quad." I glanced down the hallway to the one bedroom whose door remained shut. "Let's just wake up Muse and put it to a vote."

"He said he didn't care who was leader, as long as it wasn't him." Winter's sigh was long and exasperated. "I'm the obvious choice. My grades as a first-year put all of yours to shame."

"How do you know that?" I'd flunked my last semester, of course, but I was pretty sure grades weren't public knowledge.

Poltergeist shook her head. "She's the only person in class who got straight A's... which would matter if we were supposed to debate the other teams. Otherwise, it's as meaningful as Muse's ability to identify beers blindfolded."

"So she thinks she should lead because she's the smartest—" Classic Winter. "—and you think you should lead because...?"

"I'm the only Four on the team. And one of only two in our whole class. Strength matters."

"Sounds like the sort of thing a Four would say."

She rolled her eyes. "I guess we'll have to wake up Muse anyway so he can break the tie."

"What tie?"

"Winter's voting for herself, I'm voting for myself, and you——"

"Wouldn't be team leader if you fucking paid me."

That was a lie, actually. Given that I'd left my last six dollars on a store counter in Ludlow, there were a lot of things I'd do if it meant getting paid. But still…

"Why don't you want to be leader?" Winter looked offended for some reason.

"With this team? Way too much work."

Now they both looked annoyed.

"Besides, it should be someone who can actually benefit from the experience."

"And that's not you because you're——"

"Never going to be a team leader in the real world." After a year of my Empath friend, Vibe, interrupting me every other sentence, it was actually kind of fun to do the same to Poltergeist. "Who would willingly follow a Crow?"

"Oh."

"You think I'm wrong?"

"No. I'm just surprised you realize it."

I gritted my teeth and continued. "So if Muse isn't campaigning for the role and you two are literally the only remaining options——"

"You're enjoying this, aren't you?"

"——then I guess my vote goes to Poltergeist."

"What?" I couldn't tell which of the women was more shocked.

"Why her?" demanded Penelope.

"Why not her?" I shrugged. "Everyone knows I'm not Tessa's biggest fan. She's been a pain in my ass since day one——"

"I'm right fucking here," muttered the dark-haired Telekinetic.

"——but she's right. Strength matters. And if we have to elect a leader, I want someone who also acknowledges our weaknesses. Anything else will just get us killed."

Poltergeist looked torn between confusion and irritation, but she shrugged both emotions away. "Fine. That's two votes for me, one for Winter, and one drunken abstention… unless you want to try waking up Muse, Penelope?"

The Weather Witch shook her head. "I'm not going near him until he sobers up. And showers. And maybe not even then."

"Then it's settled. I'll report to Bard's office tomorrow, while the rest of you head to Nikolai's."

"Wait… what?"

"It's the first day of school," said Winter, the words as frosty as her name. "Time for our physical evaluations."

Meaning all the non-leaders would be beating each other senseless in the fighting pits of Nikolai Tsarnaev's concrete bunker.

No wonder they'd both wanted command.

CHAPTER 3

There wasn't much to our sub-dorm. A small kitchen was just past the common room, while four bedrooms and a bathroom were off the long hall.

One bathroom, and a small one at that. Growing up at Mama Rawlins' orphanage told me *that* was going to be annoying.

I was halfway to the empty bedroom next to Muse's, when Winter cleared her throat, sounding like a cartoon cat trying to cough up a hairball. I politely ignored the disgusting noise, but she made it again. This time, she also stepped into my path.

"What do you want, Winter?"

"We're going to be living together for a year," she said, reedy voice firm, "so I think we need to take care of the elephant in the room."

I'd never seen an elephant, but I was pretty sure she was being metaphorical.

"I know you like me." The look she sent my way was almost pitying. "And I suppose I should be flattered, but I really don't—"

"What are you talking about?" I interrupted.

"You don't have to pretend, Damian. Or Walker, if you prefer. We all saw how you tried to defend my honor against Backstreet."

"Defend your honor?" Backstreet was one of the San Francisco Capes who had been down at the Academy for the Graduation Games. He'd been drunk and set on making an ass of himself. "This isn't a vid, Penelope."

"When he insulted me, you got in his face."

I shrugged. "I don't like bullies."

"Uh huh."

"Seriously. I'd have stood up for anyone in our class. Even Poltergeist, for fuck's sake."

Tessa, who'd been halfway down the hall to the bathroom, stopped, looking less than pleased. Women made no damn sense sometimes.

"If that's how you want to play this, then fine," said Winter. "I just wanted to make things clear. I'm here to train and to learn. I won't be another Vibe."

"What?"

"Kayleigh? The pink-haired Empath you asked to the Remembrance Day dance and then stood up?!" said Poltergeist, coming back down the hall. Apparently, we were all having this conversation now.

"I know who Vibe is..." I trailed off. "*Pink*-haired?"

"She changed it over the break."

"Why?"

"I have no idea. Stop changing the subject."

I rolled my eyes. "I didn't stand Kayleigh up. Not really. I just had to be elsewhere. Besides, I asked Matthew to take her instead. Or did he not show up?" If so, I was going to kick that blonde automaton's ass. After dosing his water with stim-weed, anyway... as a Stalwart, he was a much better fighter than I was.

"Paladin showed up in a tux with flowers. That's not the point."

"It's totally the point! Vibe got to go to the dance. Matthew got to pretend to be human. And I almost died at the Hole. Everyone won."

"Kayleigh's right," said Winter. "You really are a selfish jerk."

"*Vibe* said that?" The little Japanese Empath was one of the few friends I had at the Academy. What I hadn't realized until far too late was that she also had a crush on me. Apparently, that crush was over. "I'll talk to her tomorrow and get things straightened out."

"I don't think she wants anything to do with you," said Poltergeist. "Especially now that she and Matthew are dating."

"They're what?!" Nothing about this conversation was making sense. "There were only two days left in the school year when I left. How the fuck did everything go crazy?"

"You didn't just miss a few days of school. You missed a *dance*." Tessa said it like it should mean something, but I'd been an orphan for most of my life. The only dances I'd ever seen had been in vids.

And honestly, they'd seemed pretty dull.

"Whatever." I shook my head. "Vibe can date whoever she wants." I turned to Winter. "I'm as happy to keep things professional as you are, so let's never, ever talk about this again." I looked to Tessa. "And I need to take a leak, so you should either use the bathroom or get out of my way."

Winter disappeared into her bedroom with a huff and Tessa did the same into the bathroom at the end of the hall. With them gone, I could now clearly hear the loud snores coming from Muse's bedroom.

It'd be a miracle if I made it through second-year without murdering my teammates.

○○○

The next morning, as Tessa and the other team leaders met Dean Bard for coffee and donuts, the rest of us headed to the concrete bunker that Professor Nikolai Tsarnaev called a classroom, and most students simply referred to as Hell.

As far as I could tell, the other teams traveled as units. Team Five went as three separate units of one.

Winter was first, nose in the air as if she wasn't wearing the same grey sweats as everyone else, her long hair braided and tied back from her face. She'd monopolized the bathroom, exiting only after I threatened to kick down the door, and that had left Muse and me less than fifteen minutes to get ready.

Not that Freddy had taken advantage of that time. He was a small guy, but that morning, his smell was anything but. It was like every pore in his body was leaking alcohol.

I'd waited for him to leave and then opened all the windows in our sub-dorm in the hopes of airing the place out before we returned. Winter's room was spotless, the bed made with military precision, and all of her possessions neatly put away in their proper place. Tessa's was a bit of a mess, not unlike mine, although she had four times as much stuff as I did.

The less said about Muse's room, the better.

When we'd been first-years, we'd gotten breakfast before our first class with Nikolai. This year, nobody bothered. As good as the food tasted going down, it wasn't worth having it all come right back up again. Whenever the fights—and resulting Healings—were done, we'd be able to migrate over to the cafeteria… especially since our second class wasn't until nine.

Between Winter's monopolization of the bathroom and Muse's sub-dorm funk, I barely made it to class on time. The other second-years were already seated on the old metal bleachers at the back wall of the bunker. Opposite them, standing in front of the glass wall that gave an overhead view of the fighting pits, was the man himself.

Nikolai was a Titan, with all the size and strength that power type suggested. Our own Titan, Erik the Viking, was six and a half feet tall, but the professor still topped him by a head. His beady eyes flickered over to me on my entry, and the familiar sadist's smile spread across his broad face.

"Now that we're all here—"

"What do you mean all?" That was Winter. Because *of course* it would be. "There's only fifteen of us."

"The five team leaders are at Bard's office," said a sharp voice behind me, "or did your team not get the memo?"

I turned to find a sneering Caleb Mikkazi, two rows behind me and still every inch the spiky-haired asshole.

"That makes twenty, Supersonic," shot back Winter. "There were twenty-one of us at the end of last year. Twenty-two if you count Damian."

Given that I was there in the fucking room, I wasn't sure why I wouldn't be counted.

"Jason and Becky didn't come back," said Olympia, the silver-eyed Lightbringer who went by Spectra.

"Guess they couldn't cut it."

"Not everyone can, Supersonic." Nikolai's voice was a baritone rumble. "Better to realize it now than on the battlefield, where they might get their teammates killed."

"So… they're just going to forget about being Capes?" That was Muse, sitting in his own circle of space on the top row of the bleachers, and sounding every bit as rough as he looked. It was the first time I'd ever heard him speak in class without being specifically called upon.

"I heard they were transferred to one of the vocational colleges," said Spectra. "Jason will work at one of the hydro-electric plants, while Becky—"

"Will likewise be trained for a job suited to her power," finished Nikolai. "If you want to know more, I'm sure Dean Bard will be happy to answer your questions. But for the next ninety minutes, you're mine." He glowered at Winter. "Interrupt me again and you'll spend every minute of it in the pits."

For once, Winter swallowed her retort.

The older Titan shook his massive head. "You all know the drill from last year. When your name is called, head to your assigned pit. Fight and fight hard, or I will make you go again." He paused. "You have a question, El Bosque?"

Santiago Tomayo, our resident Druid, was near the top of the bleachers, wearing his Academy greys like they were a three-piece suit. For some reason, his girlfriend, London, was several rows away. "Yeah. What about the Crow? If the news reports on the battle at the Hole were true…"

"Walker will fight last," said Nikolai, "and the dampeners will be turned up to full to make sure he doesn't accidentally kill anyone."

"It wasn't a fucking accident," I announced to the suddenly quiet room. Which was a lie, as most of you already know. I didn't know how I'd killed Carnage, an unstoppable, damn-near invulnerable Black Hat, but it sure as hell hadn't been on purpose. I was also pretty sure it had had something to do with the sheer number of dead people on the battlefield around me, making a repeat occurrence unlikely, but I wasn't going to tell anyone that either. "But whatever makes you all feel safe, I guess."

"I wasn't asking permission." Nikolai shook his head a second time. "Goddamn second-years."

ooo

This year, nobody protested when their name was called. Not even Spectra. After a year of training, even the ranged Powers were comfortable with hand-to-hand combat.

Which wasn't to say they were all good at it, although Nikolai did his best to keep the matchups as even as possible. The Stalwarts and Titans were paired up against one another, each able to partially draw upon their abilities at the dampeners' current setting. The remaining students, whose more active powers were blocked by those same dampeners, were ranked and paired off according to their respective capabilities as mundane fighters.

In the first group of fights, Winter faced off with Spectra. For all her bravado, it was my teammate who ended up on the floor. Olympia had one knee in Penelope's back and torqued the other woman's arm until she banged the stone floor in frustrated submission. Muse didn't fare much better against the somehow still-chubby Prince.

One pit over, Santi and Caleb fought, reprising their matchup as first-years, but this time Caleb gave as good as he got. Both men were bleeding and wobbly by the time El Bosque finally managed to put Supersonic down. Meanwhile, my old roommate, Jeremiah, again had the misfortune of being paired with Alan-fucking-Jackson. Both were Shifters, but even without access to their powers, that was where the similarities ended. At the end of the match, the Healers scraped Jeremiah off the floor and onto a gurney, rolling him down the underground tunnel to the med ward.

As I watched fight after fight, one truth was unmistakable. After a year of training, we were all in drastically better shape. Even the worst of us—Muse and Prince—were starting to move like they knew what they were doing. As much as I hated to admit it, Nikolai's psychotic training methods were actually working. I'd seen that much out at the Hole.

I'd also seen just how far we all still had to go before we could stand as real Capes.

Vibe was nowhere to be found, which meant she'd been picked as a team leader. Six months ago, when her empathic powers still made interaction almost impossible, that would've been unthinkable. I'd expected Paladin to take on a leadership role, given that his dad was the leader of the Defenders, but Kayleigh's new boyfriend was down in the pits instead, giving the Viking a thrashing that was eerily reminiscent of their first fight.

By process of elimination, I figured out the other team leads. Silt and Wormhole were both absent, which meant the former roommates were not only on different teams, but were also leaders of their respective teams. Last but not at all least was Nadia, known as Orca, a Stalwart who could outfight Paladin with one hand tied behind her back.

Orca and Silt both made sense to me as leaders. Even Kayleigh had shown on multiple occasions that she was a Cape to the core. But Wormhole? She just didn't seem like leadership material.

Then again, I'd voted for Poltergeist as Team Five's leader. Who was I to throw stones?

CHAPTER 4

With only fifteen second-years present, it didn't take long to get through the fights. I was the odd man out; lucky number fifteen. Other than Jeremiah, who remained in the med ward, the second-years had all cycled back into the viewing room after their respective Healings. Nikolai let the silence and anticipation build, that smile still wide on his square-jawed face.

"Paladin," he finally barked. "You're up."

Paladin vs. Walker.

Again.

Guess we all saw that one coming.

I marched to the fifth pit, where Matthew and I had fought for the very first time as first-years. That had been the one and only time I'd 'beaten' Paladin... when he'd surrendered because he couldn't figure out how to stop me without killing me.

The pit was fifteen feet in diameter and just as deep, rough stone dark from years of blood soaking into its surface. High above, a vid screen captured every detail in excruciating detail for those few second-years who weren't crowded against the viewing room window. I couldn't see the dampeners installed along the rim of the high ceiling, but I knew Nikolai had already turned them up to maximum intensity. The emptiness that always lurked within me, that hole at the center of my being, was inaccessible.

The dampeners finally being at full strength meant Paladin was just as much a normal as I was. Unfortunately, he was also the son of the Free States' most popular Cape, and had been trained by the best instructors the private sector had to offer. My instruction had come at the hands of kids like Fat Joey, Dingus, and Tiny… older boys at Mama Rawlins' House of Unwanted Brats who saw a little boy crying for his dead mommy and stomped on that weakness until it bled. A year at the Academy had taught me the limitations of their training. I'd gotten better, yeah, but there's no catching a Stalwart who already has a head start.

Even after his fight with the Viking, Paladin looked like he'd stepped out of a recruitment poster. Blonde hair, blue eyes, square jaw, and spotless Academy greys. Matthew wasn't my arch nemesis like I'd originally thought, but damn if it wasn't easy to hate the fucker sometimes.

As we awaited Nikolai's command, I breathed in the smell of the pit, that stench of blood that always made me think of apple pie and Mom on the day of her death. Matthew said something, but I couldn't parse his words over the sudden buzzing in my ears, the formless howling of a wind that wasn't there, and the heartbeat that pounded like a steel drum.

Then, Nikolai gave the order, and the time for talking was done.

ooo

Paladin and I had fought literally dozens of times as first-years. We'd long since moved beyond the feeling-out stage, but this match was different. Maybe it was the dampeners. Maybe it was what had happened out at the Hole. We circled the pit for a few seconds. Without his powers, Matthew was slower, weaker, and halfway vulnerable, but he still moved like the trained fighter he was. He'd use that training to control the distance and pick me apart, and this time, my power wouldn't be there to let me ignore the pain.

As usual, I had to ugly things up.

We both moved at the same time. He dodged past my left jab, stepping forward at an angle to avoid a follow-up cross that never came. Instead, I pulled my jab back to my chest and spun out with an elbow.

Even without powers, he was too damn fast. Somehow, he got a hand up to block the strike. He winced at the contact, but he'd bladed his arm perfectly, catching me up by the shoulder and sapping my blow of the majority of its force.

Still… it had hurt him more than it had me, and that was a first. I almost smiled.

Then his free hand blasted into my kidney and my entire body locked up.

It only took a second to shake off the effects of the kidney punch, but that's an eternity in a fight, and Paladin took advantage. Before I knew it, he had my left arm rotated and locked, using it like a lever to lift me onto my toes. As I flailed for balance, he drove a foot into my calf and dropped his weight. I fell to my knees and he rotated that same tortured arm, now using my own limb to hold me down.

I wasn't flat on my belly, but it was otherwise eerily similar to what Spectra had done to Winter in their fight.

No powers, no mobility, and Paladin in a position of overwhelming strength. Maybe that should've been the end of it. Even a few months earlier, it probably would've been. But out in the Mojave, as my blood soaked into the desert soil, as I watched Carnage kill the White Knight and Fallout prepare to bring down Tempest, I'd made myself a promise. Four words I repeated every night as I lay awake in the early hours of the morning, waiting for the nightmares to come.

Fuck going out easy.

Leverage is only as good as the lever being used, so I took Paladin's away from him. His grip tightened as I spun into the arm lock, doing the exact opposite of the escapes Nikolai had trained us in. I kept going even as the pain whited out my vision, as I heard something pop and then something else crack.

A broken arm hurts like hell. A dislocated shoulder can be even worse. But add the two together, and Matthew was left holding a piece of meat that no longer gave him any leverage at all.

Before he could adjust, I punched out with my other arm. On my knees, my choice of targets was limited, but I could have aimed for a leg or thigh.

Instead, I went for his balls.

Paladin grunted, but held on anyway, so I followed up the punch by grabbing him between the legs and squeezing.

That got him to let go. He went up on his toes, yelling something I still couldn't hear, and I powered to my feet, driving a shoulder into his washboard abs and toppling him to the stone floor. There, I climbed him like one of those cartoon monkeys you see in vids, dropping a knee into his already tortured groin on the way.

I ended up on his chest, that same knee now buried in his sternum as my other one pinned an arm to the ground by its sleeve. Face purple, he tried to buck me off. I hooked a thumb into his eye socket, tilting his head back to expose his throat.

"Enough!" Nikolai's voice boomed out. I froze, part of me still trying to solve the mechanics of finishing off Paladin when—thanks to my own actions—I lacked a second hand to punch his throat with. "Walker wins."

Adrenaline drained out of me, and the sounds of the arena trickled back in. The murmurs of the other second-years high above us. The hum of the dampeners. The squeaking of wheels as gurneys raced down the tunnel toward our pit.

Beneath me, Matthew was perfectly still. "Could you take your thumb out of my eye, Damian?"

Whoops. I coughed and did just that, taking care to avoid damaging the eyeball on the way out. In a life or death struggle, I'd have driven my thumb straight through his eye, but the school Healers could only do so much. Instead, I'd used his socket to get my own little bit of leverage.

I rolled off Paladin and choked back a scream as my mangled arm flopped to the floor. Next to me, Matthew was still on his back, but his hands had dropped below his waist, fluttering around—but not quite touching—his groin.

It was the most human thing I'd seen him do in twelve months.

He coughed. From the look on his face, even that hurt.

"I take it you heard Kayleigh and I are dating."

○○○

As Twos, Gladys and the other school Healer were a far cry from what Unicorn would have become if he'd lived, but the damage Paladin and I had taken was well within their capabilities. Twenty minutes later, we were back with the rest of the class.

"Not bad," Nikolai was saying. "The progress you've all made since last year is gratifying, but there is a very, very long way to go." He folded his massive arms across his chest and nodded in my direction. "Now that Walker and Paladin are back, who wants to explain what happened in their fight?"

"Paladin lost again," volunteered Caleb. "And may now be incapable of having children."

"Why?"

"Because that psycho went for his nuts? We're not all Titans… some of us are vulnerable down there."

"I wasn't asking about your delicate little man bits, Supersonic." Behind me, someone tittered. "I was asking why Paladin lost the fight. Anyone else?"

"Because you turned the dampeners all the way up," guessed Spectra.

"So without powers, you think Walker is the better fighter of the two?"

"Well, I mean… it kind of looked like it." She shot the blonde Stalwart an apologetic look. "Sorry, Matthew."

"Is that what you think, Paladin?" asked Nikolai.

"Not really." Matthew studied the floor. "He was faster than I remember—or I was slower without my powers—but I still should have had him."

"So why didn't you?"

"Experience." Alan Jackson's contributions were rare and almost always unwelcome. At least this time he wasn't suggesting I be decapitated.

"Explain."

"The Crow's seen real battle. Life or death stakes. It changes your mindset. He didn't treat this like a sparring match."

"Exactly." Nikolai turned to me. "You're one of the few second-years who has participated in a true battle between Powers. What was your take on it?"

"It sucked."

Someone laughed.

"Perhaps you could elaborate?"

"Total chaos. Shit happening on all sides, bullets flying, people falling out of the sky…" I swallowed. "Everyone was faster and stronger than I expected."

"Then how did you survive when so many others didn't?" That was Patty, our class' one remaining Hydromancer, and Vibe's former roommate. It was the first time she had ever spoken to me.

"A lot of luck, the intervention of the White Knight, and…" I shook my head.

"And?"

"Fuck if I know. I was trying to stop Fallout and save Tempest—"

"Epic fail on both counts," muttered Supersonic.

"—and just kept pushing forward. What else was I going to do, lie down and die?"

"Like I said," rumbled Alan Jackson, "life or death stakes."

"Yeah." I shared a look with the Shifter. All I knew about him was that a Finder had brought him in from the Badlands. If anyone knew about real stakes, it was probably him.

Come to think of it, that might explain why he was such a nightmare to fight.

"In real battle," said Nikolai, once again addressing the class as a whole, "some of the people you fight will be like Walker."

"Black Hat asshole Crows? Yeah… no kidding."

The look the professor sent Supersonic's way was chilling. "Survivors. People who will break their own arm rather than be trapped by it."

"Then why did we spend months learning joint locks?" demanded London.

"Because they're useful." Nikolai shook his head. "The vast majority of the time, anyway. As Capes, you'll need to learn to make that judgement on the fly. Sometimes, an arm lock will take the fight out of your opponent. Other times, knocking them out or choking them unconscious will do. And still other times—"

"Rip his head off."

It had taken Alan a while, but he'd finally gotten back to his favorite subject.

CHAPTER 5

Sitting on the bench on the west side of campus, eyes closed as I listened to the distant sounds of the ocean, I felt as much as heard her approach. Heavy steps, no pause as she cleared the tree line and found me sitting there, not even a sigh as she came and dropped onto the bench next to me.

"Hey Silt. Welcome back."

"You know, if you keep coming out here to stare at the edge of the world, people are going to talk."

"Oh yeah?" I finally opened my eyes. Sofia was short and almost as wide as she was tall, built like a tree stump with legs. A year at the Academy had only made her more formidable. She was a mix of brown shades… dark brown hair, golden brown skin, and eyes as warm as fresh baked bread. Those eyes were dancing.

"That Crow's gone wet between the ears," she quoted in a cracked falsetto. *"Thinks he's a damn Hydromancer or something."*

"I like the ocean. Doesn't mean I'm going to jump the wall and go for a swim. Besides, the Pacific's hardly the edge of the world. Japan and the rest of Asia are out there somewhere."

"On the other side of a continent-sized storm, sure. A storm that never ends and which even Dominion can't fly around or through."

"Do you believe the legend?"

"That it's actually a Full-Five Weather Witch, marooned on an island and gone insane?" She frowned. "Maybe. That wouldn't explain all the other horrors living in the ocean though. I'm pretty sure Dr. Nowhere's dream did more than just give the world superpowers."

"Scary fucking thought." I looked out across the Pacific, watching the sun flicker on distant waves. It looked peaceful from this far away, but even Hydromancers were wary when it came to open water. "Anyway, I wasn't staring at the ocean. I was meditating."

"You didn't get enough of that in Control class today?"

"The new guy does seem a bit obsessed with getting back to the basics, doesn't he?" Given Gabriella Stein's role in Shane's death and Ishmae's departure, the Academy had decided to bring in a new professor of Control. Gabriella's replacement was bald, ancient, and hard as nails. After he'd split us into groups, we'd spent the entire class in silent, powers-free meditation. Nobody had enjoyed it. "It's different out here, away from the dampeners."

"If you say so." We sat in silence for all of twenty seconds. "So. Team Five, huh? What on earth made you all decide to put *Poltergeist* in charge?"

"Sometimes, there are no good choices. Now if I'd been on a team with a certain Earthshaker..."

"Wouldn't that have been nice?"

"A whole lot better than Tessa, Winter, and Muse. How's your team looking? Already ruling your minions with an iron fist?"

"Hell yeah. I've got things to do after graduation. I figure the more I know about leadership and tactics, the better my odds."

"Brownsville?" Silt was from a small town in Texas, the former state that was now one part Badlands and two parts warlords engaged in bloody civil wars. I wasn't sure what had forced her to leave, but whatever it was, it was apparently a long way from over.

"Damn right."

"Well, seeing as how Bard saw fit to make me a second-year, you can count me back in for that trip."

"Already done. Assuming Evie doesn't kill you first." She grinned and waved her hand. In front of us a statue of Wormhole formed out of the dirt. Even the simulacrum's glare was a perfect likeness. "Never saw the little Teleporter so mad as when she heard you'd come back. What did you say to her out in the desert?"

"Promised I wouldn't. Come back, I mean." I sighed. "That was before all the shit happened at the Hole."

"Ah." The statue crumbled, returning to the earth. "Well, she'll get over it. Or she'll teleport you to the far side of the moon and leave you there. One or the other."

"Funny."

"And speaking of pocket-sized women…" Sofia gave me the side-eye from beneath surprisingly long lashes. "Did you hear about Vibe?"

"Her and Paladin? Yeah. Winter told me before I'd even made it to my new bedroom."

"Is that why you—" She mimed squeezing something in her hand. Or two somethings. Apparently, the story had already spread.

"Is that what you think?"

"You did tell the class you'd murder the world for her last year."

I shook my head. I was never going to live that down. "Kayleigh's an adult. She can make her own decisions."

"Yeah. Maybe you should remember that next time you decide to set her up on a date."

This was the second time in two days someone was giving me shit about my behavior toward Vibe. It hit a little bit harder coming from Silt. "You think she would've wanted to just stay in her dorm room after I stood her up?"

"I think she'd have preferred not being stood up at all." She waved down my objections. "I know. You had places to go, and that's fair. But instead of telling her so, you bugged out, and picked a replacement date for her."

"And now they're a couple. Which means it all worked out! Why's everyone busting my balls over this?"

"Everyone?"

"You, Poltergeist, and Winter."

"Huh. Maybe you being stuck with those two won't be a total disaster." Silt's voice softened. "You know I'm on Team Skeletor, right?"

I still didn't know who or what Skeletor was, other than one of Sofia's many nicknames for me. I also hadn't known I had my own team, but I nodded anyway.

"Good. Then take this as constructive feedback from someone who wants to see you happy and not so horribly undersexed. We're Powers, not gods. We don't get to make people's choices for them. And yeah," she allowed, "Matthew and Kayleigh are dating now. Maybe it'll even end up being a long-term thing, although relationships in our class seem to have the life expectancies of fruit flies. But somewhere at the back of their minds, they're both going to remember that you were Vibe's first choice, and that Paladin was just the replacement you assigned her. And that sucks."

Constructive feedback or not, I had a shitload of angry replies on the tip of my tongue. Problem was, Silt didn't deserve any of them. So I opened myself up to the hole in my center and let the emptiness chase away my irritation. What was left behind was cold logic, hard as steel rails. And that logic told me...

"Shit."

"Shit?"

"You're right."

"Boneboy, I'm always right! It's one of my superpowers." Silt's grin was wide. "Just something to think about for the future."

"Which part? That we're not gods or that you're always right?"

"Both, obviously. Things seems to have worked out with Vibe and Paladin, but—"

"But I still owe her an apology."

"That's your call, not mine, but it wouldn't hurt."

Fuck. I hated apologizing almost as much as I hated being in someone's debt.

"Anyway," Silt continued, "we were all pretty surprised when those two became a couple, but I guess someone had to fill the vacuum left by Santi and London."

"What? They broke up?"

"Combusted, really. At the dance, no less."

"After almost a year of going at it on the other side of my room's paper-thin walls? What is it with you people and dances?"

"I think it was less about the dance and more about the pregnancy scare that came right before."

"Oh." Teen pregnancies were fairly common, helped by both the government's push for repopulation and the exorbitant price of birth control, but I couldn't even fathom being a father at nineteen.

Not that I'd had a great experience with family.

Or fathers.

"Turns out El Bosque wants kids, while Ember is… less enthused. Especially seeing as how pregnancy would get in the way of her becoming a Cape."

"I can't blame her for that."

"No kidding. It's a whole lot safer playing on my side of the fence."

"You and Debbie are still together though, right?"

She winced.

"Sorry to hear it. She seemed nice."

"Too nice for someone like me, I think." Sofia made a show of shrugging it off. "Anyway, there are lots of fish in the dating pool, and I've got skills and a net. I'm not worried."

"If you can't find a date—"

"Have we met? Once I put the word out, women will be lined up outside my team's sub-dorm."

"—then we could always go to next year's dance. As friends." The words were eerily similar to when Vibe had asked me out as a first-year. "*Actual* friends, I mean… not 'I'm-secretly-into-you-but-will-date-the-guy-you-sent-as-a-replacement' friends."

"Hmm." Silt shot me a thoughtful look.

"What?"

"Just trying to figure out what sort of dress you should wear. Pink would pair nicely with your eyes."

"Hilarity is definitely not one of your powers."

"My adoring public disagrees. Anyway, I thought you hated dances?"

"I've never actually been to one. I just assumed from last year's endless dress discussions that they'd be boring. High on the dancing, low on the drama. Clearly, I was way off base."

"Relationship meltdowns aside, it was still just a dance. Nothing like what you were dealing with out at the Hole."

"That's a good thing. Trust me."

"Was it as bad as the vids made it out to be?"

"I haven't watched the vids but…" I sighed. "It wasn't fun."

Except for the killing Carnage part. That bit I was still pretty okay with.

"Did you even get to see your Dad?"

"I was across the table from him when everything went down." I carefully avoided looking at his ghost, standing just a few feet away. "He was one of the first people Fallout killed."

"Shit. I'm sorry, Damian."

I was quiet for a long moment. "I don't know if I am."

Rather than reply, she reached over and gave my hand a squeeze. Her fingers were warm and soft, even with the calluses.

It was the first time someone had voluntarily touched me since the Hole.

Kill one unstoppable asshole with a touch and people get paranoid.

"I know how you get about sharing, but… it might help to talk it over with someone."

"Is that the voice of experience?"

"Unfortunately." For a moment, her warm brown eyes were a thousand years old. "Maybe have a chat with Shrink Spooky?"

That was Silt's name for Alexa, one-time Cape and current psychologist for the Academy's only Crow.

"That's the plan on Sunday. Assuming she'll even see me." I met her look with a shrug. "I've made my peace with Bard for leaving school early, but Alexa was gone all break."

"Well, if that doesn't work out, come on over to Team Three. I'm not a professional, but I can listen. As long as you don't mind the occasional brilliant insight."

"Ha." It was a weird thing to admit, even to myself, but I'd really missed Silt. I'd had almost a month to myself on campus, but this was the first time it had really felt like home again. "Actually…"

She had thick eyebrows and knew how to use them. "Yeah?"

"My dad had some weird things to say when I saw him." I hadn't planned to share details of that conversation with anyone, even Sofia, but it suddenly felt stupid to keep it a secret. Especially when I needed help getting answers. "Things about my mom, me and... Sally Cemetery, of all people. I don't know how much of it was him being totally fucked-in-the-head insane, but—"

"You could use somebody to talk it over with? Somebody who's not faculty?"

"Not just talk it over. Dig into it. Find out how much of it was real. I'm tired of not knowing what's going on with my life."

"Well, shit, Boneboy... that sounds like research," drawled Silt. "What do you think this is? Some kind of university?" She grinned. "I've got your back. Pretty sure I can even talk Vibe into helping, since she's better at this sort of thing. Anyone else you want involved?"

"Maybe Stonewall?" My old roommate, Jeremiah, had been part of a group project bent on digging into my own shitty life story. I still wasn't happy about that, but at least I knew his research skills were solid. If anyone could find the connection between Sally and my dad, it would be him.

"Alright. I'll gather the posse. You want to meet back out here this coming weekend? Saturday afternoon?"

"Can we do Sunday instead? After my session with Alexa? I've got tutors and work all day Saturday." I rolled my eyes. "Part of my punishment."

"The Academy always gets its pound of flesh."

"In my case, I think they want the whole package."

"And who can blame them; a sexy-ass skeleton like you?" She snickered. "Sunday then. That gives you six days to think of a team name for our little cabal. The Four Musketeers or something."

"Thank you, Sofia." Gratitude didn't come easy for me, but the battle out in the desert had taught me my solo act was a quick road to an early death.

"Of course. Truthfully, I'm just banking some credit for when you and your undead legions of doom take over the world."

"You do remember I can't actually raise the dead, right?"

"A month ago, you couldn't kill Black Hats with a touch either." She slapped me on the back. "I'm hedging my bets. It's called strategy, and it's just one of the many reasons my team is going straight to the top of the rankings." Silt grinned and rose to her feet. "Speaking of which, *your* team is having a meeting at the moment. Pretty sure Poltergeist's pissed that you're AWOL."

"What?"

"Or so I gathered when I stopped by your sub-dorm looking for you. Should've known you'd be out here and not in there with them. Anyway, you should probably head back at some point. I can't imagine your fearless new leader is any happier now than she was fifteen minutes ago."

One day into Tessa's reign and she was scheduling meetings.

I was already regretting my vote.

CHAPTER 6

I'd barely made it through the door before Poltergeist started in on me.

"What the hell, Damian? Where have you been?"

There are really only two ways to respond to an interrogation like that. I went with the less helpful one.

"Not here, obviously. What do you care?"

Invisible bands of telekinetic force wrapped around me like the world's least comfortable blanket, and just like that, Tessa was in my face. "I care because our team meeting was supposed to start a half-hour ago, you asshole!"

"I know this whole leadership thing is new for you, but if you want people to show up, maybe you should tell them the fucking meeting is happening?"

"She did." That was Muse, sitting opposite Winter in one of the common room chairs. The little Switch looked like hell... a sure sign that he'd stopped drinking long enough to get a hangover. "Sent out a group message and everything."

"Oh." My attempt at a shrug was foiled by Poltergeist's iron telekinetic grip. "My Glass is in my room, so I didn't get the message."

"Why would you leave your Glass behind?" asked Winter, caught between suspicion and outrage. She'd showered since her beating in Nikolai's pits and had for some reason decided that two white pigtails to her waist *wasn't* a totally ridiculous looking hairstyle.

"Unlike you and Poltergeist, I don't have a purse… and it's way too big to fit in a pocket."

"I use a backpack," said Muse.

"Very helpful." I couldn't move my head, but I let my eyes drift back over to Poltergeist. "If I'd known there was a meeting, I'd have been here. Maybe give some advance warning next time?"

"Fine. Whatever." Tessa rolled her eyes and retreated to the couch. "You're here, finally, so let's just get on with it."

"Uhm."

"Oh, right." Tessa made a gesture and my invisible bonds fell away. I stumbled slightly as I became responsible for my own stability again.

Winter's eyes went wide. "We're not supposed to use our powers outside of class!"

"Like you're not pulling humidity out of the air to keep your hair from frizzing?" Tessa's dark curls bounced as she shot the other woman a glare.

"That's different!"

"Poltergeist has a thing for manhandling me. At least this time, she didn't threaten to rip out my pubes with her teeth." The only seat left was on the couch with Tessa, so I went and leaned against the opposite wall, next to the vid screen. "I assume you're here to fill us in on your meeting with Bard?"

For some reason, Tessa had gone bright red, but she gathered herself and gave a firm nod. "It's pretty much what we expected. Team versus team battles at the end of every month. It'll be a big part of our grade for the year."

"More time in the pits?" Muse looked like he was going to be sick, but it was hard to tell if that was the hangover or the subject matter.

"No." Tessa and I had answered at the same time. When she raised an imperious eyebrow in my direction, I shrugged. "They aren't large enough for team battles."

"And wouldn't let us utilize the group tactics we're supposed to learn in class," she agreed. "Bard wouldn't say where the contests were going to take place, but he did say we'd have full access to our powers."

"Even the Crow?"

"For fuck's sake, Penelope, I have a name. Two of them, even!"

"They're going to let *Walker* run around death-touching other second-years?"

"Hardcore," muttered Muse.

"Obviously not." Poltergeist frowned. "At least, I don't think so. Bard said it wouldn't be a problem."

"Well as long as Bard said so…" I yawned. "What could go wrong?"

"So when's our training session?" asked Winter.

"Tomorrow." Poltergeist shot the other woman a confused look. "In Group Tactics. I figured you would have already memorized our course schedule."

"Group Tactics is just a class. We should be training outside of class too."

"The hell with that." Muse shuddered. "Free time is rare enough as it is."

"I agree with Freddy," said Tessa. "Especially since, as second-years, we have new responsibilities."

"Like what?"

"Like the Liquid Hero," she said, referring to the on-campus bar. "Our class will be responsible for running the place when it opens at the end of the month."

"Shit. So much for sleep." Between nights at the Liquid Hero, my school-mandated counseling sessions, meeting with my cadre of academic tutors, *and* the job Bard had given me as punishment, my weekends were going to be busier than my weekdays. And that was fucking ridiculous.

"I'm working on a schedule with the other team leaders. We'll figure it out."

"Or flunk." It almost sounded like Muse would prefer that outcome.

"I've never failed anything in my life," declared Winter, "and I'm not starting now, even if I have to drag your dead weight behind me."

"There's that team spirit you're famous for."

"Nobody asked you, *Walker*." She turned back to Poltergeist. "So our first battle is at the end of the month? Do we have the rosters for the other teams yet?"

"Yeah."

"And?"

"And we're kind of screwed."

○○○

Poltergeist wasn't kidding.

"How did Vibe get Paladin, Supersonic, *and* Spectra on her team?" demanded Winter. "I guess it pays to be dating a famous Cape's son."

That almost went without saying. Everyone knew politics had a role in the professional teams. Why should it be any different at the Academy?

"Team One is the least of our concerns," said Tessa. "Look at Team Three."

I did and immediately wished I hadn't. "Silt told me her team was strong, but that's ridiculous. Alan Jackson, Cyclone and... wait, who's Oscuro?"

"Orson," supplied Freddy. "He chose the name over break."

Not sure if I've mentioned Orson Douglas to this point. Tall, dark, and just a bit weird, he'd kept a low profile as a first year. Which sort of fit, given his powers. "So Sofia's team has an Earthshaker, a Low-Four Shifter, a Wind Dancer, *and* a Shadecaster?"

"Erin won't be much of a problem," said Winter. "She might be a High-Three, but she doesn't have any Weather Witch powers at all. I'll blow her out of the sky."

"Before or after she throws Alan-fucking-Jackson at us?"

"The Manimal's mine." Tessa cracked her knuckles ostentatiously.

"You sure?" I asked.

"I kind of have to be. What are the chances of you taking him down before he tears your head off?"

"Not great." I'd spent more time in the med ward than the rest of the class combined, and a large part of that was from sparring with Alan Jackson. Orca was the only fighter in our class who could even keep up with him.

"Exactly. He and I are the only Fours left in the class. I always knew we'd end up facing each other. At least I can do it from a distance."

"Assuming you see him coming," said Winter, "which isn't a guarantee with Oscuro on the team."

"In other words, Team Three is a problem," I summarized.

"Team Four too." Poltergeist settled back on the couch, legs curled up beneath her. "Wormhole gives them mobility, the Viking gives them a meat shield, El Bosque is as versatile as I am in the right environment, and Makara—"

"Makara?"

"That's the Cape name Patty decided to go with." Winter wrinkled her long nose. "Apparently, it means something in one of the few languages even I don't speak."

I took a moment to admire the sheer amount of ego Penelope had packed into that sentence. Any minute now, she'd pull out her elementary school report cards.

Assuming elementary schools still gave report cards, anyway. Thanks to my stay at Mama Rawlins' Home for Unwanted Brats, I'd avoided the whole experience.

"Teleporter, Titan, Druid, and Hydromancer." Tessa ticked them off on her fingers. "Like I said… they'll be tough."

"Team Two's no picnic either." It was my turn to scowl. "I don't know what Prince brings to the table as a Siren, but they've got *both* Orca and Stonewall, which means hand-to-hand is a shitty idea. And Ember might not be anywhere near as strong as Ishmae was, but she's still a Pyro. They're nightmares in a real fight."

I knew that from all-too-recent experience.

"You guys are assuming we actually have to fight," pointed out Muse. "For all we know, Bard's idea of battle is a competitive eating contest."

"Then pray we don't get matched up with Team Four. You've seen the Viking eat."

"I've seen way too much of him in general," he agreed. The only good thing about moving to sub-dorms was that he and I would no longer be subjected to a mostly-naked Erik Thorsson roaming the men's wing.

"It's not going to be an eating contest, you idiots," argued Winter. "You saw the Graduation Games. We're going to be fighting."

"Then I'd say we're fucked."

There was a moment of silence as we considered Muse's words. I glanced over at Tessa, but she was avoiding eye contact with everyone.

Finally, Winter shook her head, making her absurdly long pigtails sway. "How did I get matched up with you losers? It's not about what those other teams can do! It's about what we can do! I may not be a Low-Four like *some people*, but my power gives us air superiority. That's worth the Viking's weight in gold."

"Yes, Penelope. We all know you think you're the best thing to happen to the Free States since Dominion."

Spots of color gathered in Winter's cheeks, all the more noticeable against her snow-white hair. "I'm pointing out one of our team's tactical advantages, *Tessa*. Someone has to, since our so-called leader has already given up. You all need to stop whining like babies and do something!"

Muse rose to his feet. "I'm going to bed."

"It's not even seven!"

The Switch shrugged. "You said do something. I'm doing it."

"Fine. Then I'm getting dinner at the cafeteria." And then, despite the fact that neither Poltergeist nor I had made a move to join her, Winter added, in a voice of chilled frost, "*Alone.*"

Two doors banged shut in near synchrony.

"Great meeting, Poltergeist." I took Winter's vacated seat— which no doubt smelled a shit-ton better than the one Muse had been sitting in—and flicked on the vid screen. "Truly inspirational. I'm just thankful I was here for it."

"Screw you, Walker."

And that was Team Five for you, ladies and gentlemen of the dead.

Team-fucking-Five.

CHAPTER 7

If you were here for the start of my story—if you didn't just now stop to see what all the fuss was about—you already know what my first week at the Academy as a first-year was like. Being a second-year didn't improve things any. In fact, having a team almost made it worse.

Outside of that one shitshow of a meeting, the only time Team Five spent together that week was in Group Tactics, a class that seemed to involve more reading and discussion than actual tactics. Or groups. Outside of class, we all did our own thing and exchanged as few words as possible.

Friday night was more of the same. Muse stayed sequestered in his room, Tessa avoided the sub-dorm entirely, and the one time I saw Winter, she had her crooked nose high in the air, as if calling out our team's dysfunction would somehow save her from being ranked with the rest of us.

Before I knew it, it was Saturday afternoon and time for my first day on the job that Dean Bard had assigned me as punishment.

Damian Banach, Low-Three Crow, black sheep of his class, and now…. undergraduate mentor to first-years.

I shit you not.

The idea of having second-years serve as mentors to the first-years wasn't a new one. Life at the Academy was hard, intentionally so, and the grind took its toll on all first-years. The university had professional counselors to help, but few of the students made use of them. A psychology degree didn't count for much in terms of street cred with Capes-in-training. Second-years, on the other hand, were peers who had just survived the grind the first-years would be currently experiencing.

Like I said, the idea wasn't a new one, but this was the first year it was actually being put into practice. You didn't have to be a genius to know that what happened with Shane and Ishmae had a lot to do with it.

As a first-hand witness to Unicorn's death and Phoenix's meltdown, that all made sense to me. Designate a few of the more responsible and empathetic students to help with the incoming first-years' transition, answer class-related questions the counselors wouldn't know a damn thing about, and ensure tragedies like that never happened again.

What didn't make sense was me being one of those second-years. I couldn't think of a single thing I'd done as a first-year that suggested I'd be a good candidate for the role. Punishments didn't always have to make sense, but it was shitty luck for the first-years who'd been dumped in my lap. Whoever the other mentors were, they had to be better than the school's one and only baby Crow.

I made my way to the first-year dorm, the wide one-story where I'd spent most of my time the previous year. The door was shut but I could hear excited conversation from the common room inside. That conversation didn't so much shut off as slowly peter out when I pulled open the door and stepped inside.

"Nobody but first-years is allowed in here." The kid who approached was clearly a Titan, tall and wide as The Viking, but he looked soft and moved all wrong, someone still used to his size being all that mattered in a fight.

Nikolai's pits would change that fast.

"I'm aware." I didn't know who he was and I didn't really care either.

"Then you should leave before I throw you out." With the room now quiet, the Titan was ready to put on a show.

Fucking eighteen-year-olds. We were all that dumb once. I ignored the implied threat and scanned my Glass. Bard had sent me a list of students and a time to come get them, but I hadn't expected the whole thing to turn into theater. Or for the common room to have almost twenty people cluttering its many couches and chairs.

"I warned you." Apparently, I hadn't been paying Junior Titan enough attention. He took one long step and reached for my arm.

I took a half-step to the side, leaving him grasping nothing but air, and finally turned in his direction. "You don't want to touch me," I said, unconsciously paraphrasing Sally Cemetery's own words from almost eight months earlier. "And I don't want to be touched."

Something in my face gave him pause, and before he could rally, one of the other first-years spoke up.

"He's in Academy greys, Chase." The speaker was one of the many teenagers sprawled out on the nearest couch, his voice laconic. "I'm guessing he's one of the second-years Bard said would be coming by today."

"So?" Chase was about as smart as the Viking too.

"So you should probably back off before he boils you alive or does whatever it is he can do."

"I can handle myself, Vijay."

"You won one fight in the pits. Don't let it go to your head."

Neither guy was on my list which meant I could officially ignore them both. I shook my head and addressed the room. "Like Vijay said, I'm a second-year. Apparently, I'm also the first second-year Bard decided to send over. Fucking story of my life. If I read your name, please get up and come to the door. If someone I call isn't here, I'll need one of you to go get them."

"This is our whole class." That was a redhead who'd been leaning against the wall, arms crossed in front of her.

"Sorry to hear that." My class had started with twenty-four and was down to twenty after a single year. If they were starting with only eighteen, it meant their graduating class was going to be miniscule. I called out names. "Lucy David, Francisco Diaz, Jacinda Elman, Shawn Elman, Lynn Ostovich, and Reid Spielman."

"Paco," said one of the first-years I'd called.

"What?"

"I go by Paco, not Francisco."

"That's a weird Cape name." And as someone who'd initially wanted to be Baron Boner, I knew weird Cape names.

"It's a nickname. I haven't picked my Cape name yet." Paco was a wiry Latino who looked like he'd fallen out of the ugly tree and hit every single branch on his way down.

El Bosque he definitely wasn't.

"Fair enough." I waited as the others reached us. The Elmans were easy to identify, two skinny black teenagers with an obvious familial resemblance. Fraternal twins, I guessed. One of either Lucy or Lynn was a Titan, with the other girl being considerably smaller. That left only Reid, dark-haired and dressed like the Liquid Hero had opened early. He moved with the unconscious grace unique to Stalwarts.

"Hey," I told them all, once they'd gathered, "I'm part of a new program Bard set up to help with the whole first-year adjustment process. Let's take a walk and get to know each other."

"You could start by telling us your name." Jacinda looked me up and down and scowled, unimpressed.

"Right." If I ever actually became a Cape, I was going to give my eventual team's public relations rep fits. I opened the door and started to wave them through. "I'm Damian, but you can call me Walker."

Even after the door shut behind us, the common room stayed quiet.

ooo

"You're Walker? *The* Walker?"

That was Jacinda again. Of the two siblings, she seemed to do all the talking.

"Only one on record as far as I could see." The official registry held names of all of the licensed Capes, as well as known Black Hats both in and out of the country. It was a convenient way to keep from having three-dozen wanna-be Dominions running around and confusing everyone, but it also led to a mad rush whenever a particularly popular name came back open for licensing. Winter must have been stalking her name online for months before her predecessor finally died. "Why?"

"You killed Carnage."

"Yeah."

"You're a fucking Crow!" I couldn't tell if Paco was impressed or horrified.

"That too." I led the six down one of the paths that wound their way across campus until we reached a rare spot with multiple benches. It was a gray day for Los Angeles, but still nicer than any other place I'd been.

Not that Bakersfield or the goddamn Mojave were fantastic points of comparison.

Once everyone was seated, I cleared my throat. I had a bit of experience with younger kids, thanks to my time at Mama Rawlins', but for the most part, those had been actual children. I wasn't nearly as used to dealing with—let alone being some sort of Crows-fucked mentor for—people close to my age.

Little Nyah, five years old and cute as could be, had been a joy even when she was bugging the shit out of all of us. Eighteen-year-old Powers though?

Deep inside, I just knew this was all going to go to hell.

"Like I said, I'm Walker. And yes, I'm a Crow, and yes, I was involved in that shit-storm out at the Hole, but that's not important."

For some reason, that seemed to irritate the smaller of the two unnamed women.

"What matters is that I was a first-year, like you are now. I survived everything you're going to be dealing with over the next year. Because of—" I cleared my throat again, deciding at the last minute not to bring up Unicorn. "—stuff that happened last year, Bard thought it'd be a good idea for first-years to have someone to talk to in a less official capacity. You six were unlucky enough to get me. I'd say sorry, but that's the Academy for you. You roll with the punches or they scrape you off the floor."

The Titan went as pale as the blonde hair she'd pulled back into a ponytail.

"Before we get into all that, why don't you introduce yourselves and your powers? For those of you who didn't already know, I'm a Low-Three Crow."

"How does a Low-Three anything kill Carnage?" Reid was sprawled out on his bench like it was a lounge chair instead of rough stone. The smirk on his face told me he was definitely higher than a Low-Three.

"Extenuating circumstances."

"Meaning?"

"Hundreds of dead fucking people." I met his gaze and watched the smirk slide right off. "Let's start with you, Reid."

"You already know my name, and I'm guessing my power, but sure. Reid, High-Three Stalwart."

Next to him, the Titan swallowed, her voice far too small for her hulking frame. "Lucy. Lucy David. Mid-Three Titan."

"I'm Jacinda and this is my brother, Shawn. I'm a Mid-Three Wind Dancer, and he's a Mid-Three Pyro."

"And does Shawn ever talk?"

"That's the problem with having a Wind Dancer twin," said the teenager in question, his grin lightning-quick. "She somehow never runs out of breath."

Jacinda's grin was a mirror of Shawn's.

"Lynn," said the smaller woman who shared their bench and had been giving me death glares ever since she sat down. "Low-Three Technomancer."

"And you want to be a Cape?" For most of us, that was the dream, a one-way ticket to stardom and riches that we'd never even be able to sniff otherwise, but Technomancers were usually the exception. For them, the private sector was every bit as lucrative and a shitload less fatal.

"I *will* be a Cape." If she'd been a Lightbringer, her stare would have burned right through me. Since I'd never met the girl before, I could only assume she was yet another member of the school's Crow-hating brigade.

Hard to blame her for that, honestly. I'd learned that lesson last year with Spectra, whose whole family had been killed by Crimson

Death out in Reno. People had a lot of reasons for hating Crows and most of those reasons were valid.

"And I'm Paco," said the ugly kid. "Low-Three Summoner."

"No shit?"

"No shit."

"How does a Summoner get enrolled at the Academy?" Part of the so-called Aberrant class of powers, Summoners were as rare as Crows. Maybe even more so. They didn't have quite as bad a reputation, but most still ended up as Black Hats.

"I was doing work in Compton when a Finder came hunting." The smallest of the six first-years, Paco nevertheless seemed older than any of them. Maybe it was the thousand yard stare. "Guess the Academy is taking whoever they can get."

"Your Finder... did he call himself Mr. Grey by any chance? Average-looking psychopath with eyes like pennies?"

"No. *She* was as wide as Lucy over there and half as tall. Face like an anvil and voice to match." His tone was suspicious. I liked the little shit already. "Why?"

"No reason." I swept my gaze across the whole group. "If you guys need me for some reason during the week, I'm living in the Team Five sub-dorm. Try not to irritate Winter or Poltergeist... they're both pretty high strung. Otherwise, we'll be meeting out here every Saturday through the end of the school year."

"To do what?" asked Jacinda.

"Whatever you guys want. Talk, mostly. I'm sure you all have questions or complaints. You could go to Dean Bard with them, but he's not a Power. He helped design the curriculum but he's never had to live through it. I have. I'm here to help make sure you all do too."

Which again made zero fucking sense, given that I'd flunked my second semester, illegally left campus, and then headed to the Hole to kill my own father. But nobody had asked my opinion.

"Anyway," I continued, "your first week is over. Thoughts?"

"Is it always going to be this hard?" That was Lucy, slouched on the bench as if trying to downplay her own size.

"For the first semester? Yeah. Second semester should be easier though." As long as they didn't get overloaded with Powers classes like

I had. "The thing to remember is that it's *supposed* to be hard. Three years is a short time for anyone to become a Cape. The Academy doesn't have the luxury of taking it easy on us."

"Why not just make it a four-year program?" asked Shawn.

"They don't have the luxury of time either. Twenty-three Capes died at the Hole. Four more down by the border when Tezcatlipoca made his move. Not to mention the seven who were killed over the course of the year."

"Bard already gave us the death speech," said Reid.

"I'm sure he did. My point is that February's graduating class was just a drop in the bucket compared to our losses. The country needs Capes as fast as it can get them. So yeah, school sucks, but there's a reason for it. Focus on that and on learning everything you can. Believe it or not, your teachers are trying to help."

"Even Ms. Ferra?" Apparently, Paco had already pegged the Ethics teacher as an asshole. Smart kid.

"I still don't get your issue with Isabel, Paco."

Reid, on the other hand, still had a lot to learn.

○○○

Saturday night passed as quietly as Friday. Muse drank, Winter studied in her room, and Poltergeist was nowhere to be found. I took advantage of having our sub-dorm's small common room to myself and watched hero vids. The couch was comfortable, the vid screen was practically new, and the company, or lack of company, was outstanding.

Three vids in though, the stream switched to one of Tempest's vids, and just like that, the fun was over. I'd watched all of the female Cape's vids a dozen times or more, and loved every damn minute of them, but it wasn't the same now that she was dead. Especially when I'd watched her die.

I closed my eyes, but my brain conjured up images of her plummeting from the sky, struck down by Fallout even after I'd stabbed the asshole in the back with the White Knight's broken sword.

Part of me wanted to knock on Muse's door and grab a bottle of whatever rotgut made his bedroom smell like sweat and burning rubber. Problem was, the last time I'd gotten drunk, Mom had hit me with the vision of her own murder. Fuck if I was going to go through something like *that* again.

Even worse, I now knew my Power wasn't actually a bust. Getting drunk didn't seem so safe anymore.

So instead, I shut down the vid screen, took a leak in our sub-dorm's only bathroom, and retreated back to my bedroom. Much as I hated to admit it, Winter had the right idea with studying.

I know… it surprised the hell out of me too.

CHAPTER 8

On Sunday morning, I waited for someone—probably Tessa, though I didn't see her leave—to get the hell out of the bathroom, then showered, and took my week's worth of clothes across campus to the laundromat. At that hour, the place was empty, which suited me just fine.

A few hours later, I was headed back across campus to the building that held the counselor's office. I'd actually spent most of February living in that same building, in one of the rooms reserved for special guests. Would've been pretty convenient to be able to just wander over and chat with Alexa, especially given everything that had gone down out at the Hole, but neither she nor the official school counselor had been around while school was out.

Another part of my non-expulsion agreement had been that all of Bard's rules were back in effect. I couldn't leave campus. I had to actually pass my classes. And last but not least, I needed to meet with Alexa every Sunday, so the monochromatic former Cape could make sure I was still sane.

Apparently, nobody had told Alexa that though. The door to the office she shared with Dr. Gibbings was locked when I arrived, and no amount of knocking changed that fact.

The doctor was *not* in.

Can't say whether I was happy or sad about that. The two of us had a bit of a complicated history, and I wasn't sure how our first meeting was going to go down. Even so, there were some things I needed to tell her.

Finally, I shrugged. Bard was off campus most weekends, but I'd check in with him on Monday and find out what was going on. In the meantime, I suddenly had an almost-free morning.

Even better, the Academy cafeteria was making black bean burgers for lunch.

ooo

"You came early." Silt marched out of the woods with all the subtlety of a tank. "Thought you'd still be talking to Shrink Spooky. She give you the all-clear on your mental health?"

"Apparently, I'm the sanest person she knows. She wants to have a talk with you though."

"Wait. Really?" As far as I knew, I was the only student on Alexa's patient list. Silt and Vibe only even knew she existed because of me.

"Of course not. She wasn't even there."

"Weird. Guess she had patients elsewhere or something."

"Or something." I was about ninety-five percent sure that, when not psychoanalyzing potentially insane Crows, the ex-Cape once known as Midnight did covert work for the government. As a Shadecaster, a little bit of espionage or even assassination would be right in her wheelhouse. "Anyway, after my third burger, I decided to come out and enjoy the day."

"By staring at the ocean?"

"More or less. Were you able to talk to Vibe and Stonewall?"

"Yeah. They'll both be here."

"Good." I'd tried to talk to the little Empath—who did, in fact, have pink hair now, instead of blue—but Matthew had been glued to her hip, and she'd seemed to go out of her way to avoid me. If nothing else, this little meeting would give me the chance to smooth things over.

As if on cue, Kayleigh stepped out into the clearing, but whatever words I'd had planned died when Paladin followed shortly after.

"What the fuck?" I asked Silt in a hiss.

"I didn't invite him," she told me. "Guess they're a package deal until they get past the whole honeymoon phase."

"Fantastic."

Other than her hair, Vibe hadn't changed much in the month she'd been gone. Still small, still Japanese-American, still delicate-seeming until you realized she had a core of solid steel.

Figuratively speaking.

Matthew was shorter than I was, but still towered over his diminutive girlfriend. Instead of holding hands, he had one arm around her waist. As always, he looked like he'd stepped right out of a vid, and when they moved in our direction, he did so without any sort of limp.

Maybe the Healers had done *too* good of a job patching him up after our match.

I rose to my feet and met them halfway.

"Walker."

"Paladin. I wasn't expecting you."

"Kayleigh—"

"Asked him to come," finished the Empath. Apparently, her habit of interrupting people hadn't changed either. "Is that going to be a problem?"

"What if I said yes?"

"Then Matthew and I would find something better to do with our Sunday." I opened my mouth, but the Empath beat me to the punch. "You asked for my help, although I'm not sure why. I'm here as a favor."

Vibe was one of the worst hand-to-hand fighters in our class, and her powers weren't offensive in any way, but I still knew when I was beaten. I held up both hands in surrender. "You're right. Thanks for coming."

With a nod and a hint of a smile, she was past me, joining Silt on the bench, and leaving me standing awkwardly with her boyfriend.

"I hear you're the other mentor," he said, something like approval in his voice. "Good for you."

"It sure as fuck wasn't my decision—" I started to say. "Wait, *other* mentor? Does that mean you're one too?"

"Yeah. Kayleigh and I each have six first-years. With her power, she's perfect for the role. I don't know what I really bring to the table, but... I wanted to help."

"Of course you did." Sometimes, Matthew was so squeaky clean he gave me stomach cramps. "Something tells me your first-years will be plenty happy being mentored by the son of the most popular Cape in the Free States."

"Maybe." For some reason, the adult Paladin—Matthew's dad—was a sore spot with my classmate. It was part of what had led to the previous year's brawl at the Liquid Hero. "Anyway, should we get started? Silt didn't tell Kayleigh what it was you needed. Some sort of research? Is this for school?"

"No, it's a personal thing. And we're waiting on one more person."

Except, as it turned out, that wasn't true either.

With her powers, Kayleigh was the first to sense Jeremiah coming our way, but we all could hear him soon after. My old roommate was many things, but light on his feet wasn't one of them. We'd all turned around, Kayleigh and Sofia on the bench, Matthew and I still standing, when the big Shifter entered the clearing.

He wasn't alone.

"You've got to be fucking kidding me."

Stonewall must not have heard me. He gave us all a wave and crossed over to the bench. And trailing behind him was...

"Poltergeist."

"Walker." My team leader's voice was cool, giving away nothing.

"What are you doing here?"

"I was wondering the same thing," she replied.

"I asked her to come," said Jeremiah.

"Why?"

"Silt said you needed researchers."

"And?"

"And Tessa's good at it." He shrugged his massive shoulders. Like the rest of us, Jeremiah had developed significantly since entering the Academy as a first-year. "Who do you think dug up all the stuff on you last year?"

"I thought that was you!" I'd been on my way to pay him back for that invasion of privacy when Shane's death turned the whole world upside down.

"Only the part that came from our talk at the Liquid Hero. The rest was all Tessa."

Of course it fucking was.

"I don't have to be here," said the Telekinetic, angrily shaking her curls. "There are plenty of other things I'd be happy to do with my time."

Surprisingly, it was Vibe who played the peacemaker. "I'm sure Damian's just surprised. Whatever convinced him to ask for help for once is probably way too important for him to let his temper screw things up."

I was starting to think Silt and even Winter had been right. Kayleigh was not happy with me.

"Vibe's right," I said. "This is personal, but I need all the help I can get."

Not sure who was more surprised to hear those words, them or me. Either way, Tessa lost her scowl.

"Okay then. What are we here for? What do you need?"

So I told them about my dad. About the vision I'd had of my mom's murder and what he'd said to me, down in the Hole, moments before his own.

I told them about Sally Cemetery.

ooo

"Wait. How did Sally Cemetery convince your dad to try to kill you?" asked Paladin. "She died before any of us were even born."

The problem with sharing secrets is that one leads to the next. This one wasn't my biggest secret, but I knew it'd still be a tough one for the others to swallow.

"Sally's ghost is still out there," I told him. "And not just a fragment of a personality either, as far as I can tell."

"How do you know that?"

"I've met her. Right here in this clearing."

My old roommate's deep baritone was a gentle rumble. "Damian, are you sure you're doing okay?"

"I'm not fucking crazy, Jeremiah! Not yet anyway."

"And as I recall, you've actually got Sally to thank for that," said Silt.

I nodded. "Yeah. She talked me off the ledge after Shane's death started my downward spiral. Which makes this all the more confusing."

Tessa looked from me to Silt and back again. "You knew about this, Sofia?"

"Yep."

"I did too," said Vibe. "Damian told us when we got back from summer break last year."

"So the ghost of Sally Cemetery told your dad to kill you... and then showed up a dozen years later to help you? How does that make any sense?"

"It doesn't." I shrugged. "Welcome to my life."

"So how are we supposed to help you?" I couldn't tell if Paladin was just so even-keeled that my confession hadn't troubled him at all or if his programming didn't allow for that sort of show of humanity. "Based on what you've said, you're the only one of us who can even see her."

"I don't need help with Sally," I said. Which was only true as long as the infamous Crow never came back for me. If it came down to a showdown... well, Sally had been at least a Four. Being a Low-Three was a handicap I wasn't going to be able to overcome. And that was before you added in the whole 'she's a ghost' part. "I need help figuring out what the hell happened. Did my dad know Sally before all of this? If not, what's their connection? He was a One or a Two, at best. As far as I can tell, neither he nor my Mom even knew he was a Crow until..."

"Until he snapped."

"Yeah." I swallowed past the lump in my throat. "All this time, I blamed him. Still do, really, but... he's dead now, and if there's more to the story, I need to know what it is."

The six of us talked it over a fair bit. Whatever I thought of Paladin and Poltergeist, the two seemed every bit as committed to the task as my actual friends. By the end of the hour, we all had our assignments.

"Thank you," I told them, amazed that the words were somehow not sticking in my throat. "Even with the school year just starting, I know you all have a lot on your plates without me adding my life story to it. This means a lot."

"Consider it payback for me getting you kicked out of Combat class," said Jeremiah.

"It beats Ethics homework," drawled Silt.

"Capes help people," said Tessa. "Isn't that right, Kayleigh? Besides," she continued, "the leaders from Team Two and Three are both pitching in and you're not even on their teams. How could I do any less?"

ooo

"Kayleigh, can I talk with you a second?"

"What is it?" The Empath paused on her way out of the clearing, Paladin's arm still about her waist.

"Alone?"

With a sigh, she disengaged from her boyfriend. "Go ahead. I'll meet you back at the sub-dorm."

We both waited for Paladin to leave, and then she turned to me, head cocked. With only the two of us left, the small clearing suddenly felt huge.

"What did you want to say, Damian?" For someone whose whole power revolved around sensing emotions, she did a lousy job of hiding hers. Assuming she was even trying.

"I haven't gotten a chance to talk to you all week."

"Things have been busy. What's up?"

"I just wanted to say I'm sorry."

"For what?" The way she asked made it clear she wasn't so much confused about why I was apologizing as she was curious as to exactly which of my fuck-ups I'd decided to apologize for.

It felt like a test.

Unfortunately, I sucked at tests. When given a multiple choice question, I almost always went with 'd': all of the above.

So that's what I did.

"For everything. For not telling you I was going to the Hole. For making you think we were going to the dance together. For asking Paladin to take you, instead of giving you a choice in the matter."

"I had a choice. I could have told Matthew no." It was hard to see the shattered, desperately isolated Empath I'd first met in the steely-eyed woman before me, and it wasn't just a question of hair dye. "As for the rest of it... I thought we were friends."

"We were. We still are, I hope."

"Then why'd you do it?"

"I just... I thought I was done. Flunking out of the Academy meant I wouldn't have a place to live, or a job, or anything to eat. And that meant this year's Reconciliation Day was the best—maybe the only—chance I had to get answers from my dad."

"Did you know I was talking to my parents about covering your tuition?"

"What? No, I had—"

"I *told* you to wait. I told you we'd figure something out. Even if you couldn't be a Cape, you could've had another year at the Academy as a normal student. It wasn't an all-or-nothing situation."

"I didn't know."

"Yeah." She sighed, looking away. "It's not a big deal, I guess. It was humiliating to find out that my date had left school and sent someone in his place, but Matthew is a good person, and I think we might have something. And you went off and nearly got yourself killed but came out of the whole thing with another year as a Cape student and a fresh new mystery to solve. So I guess everything worked out there too."

Her tone didn't really match her words, but I rolled with it anyway. "So... friends?"

"I don't know. Friends trust each other."

"I just trusted you with my dad's story."

"I was talking about me trusting you."

"Oh."

"Anyway, I should go." She was almost to the tree line when she stopped. Her voice was quiet. "I'm glad you're alive, Damian. And I'm sorry about your dad."

"Yeah." I watched her leave, my last words falling to the earth like pine needles from the surrounding trees. "Everyone but me seems to be."

CHAPTER 9

Contrary to expectations, the next few weeks were among the least hectic I'd had since first coming to the Academy. My course load had been reduced considerably. No more Projection, meaning the teachers had finally decided my powers didn't work that way. No more Mobility, because the higher-level classes were reserved for people who actually had mobility-based powers. No more Advanced Combat, because Nikolai Tsarnaev still had a steel beam up his ass, and the latest wrinkle in my powers wasn't enough for him to reconsider my dismissal from his class.

Maybe in some colleges, the seven classes I still had would've been a lot, especially with Control coming every single day. But in my last semester, I'd had six Powers classes *and* all the academic ones. Seven classes, total, was a stim-weed dream.

Saturdays were still a shitshow, between my many tutors and the weekly meeting with my first-year Junior Capes, but Sundays were weirdly empty. When I'd finally gotten hold of Bard, the dean had informed me that Alexa would be away from school for at least the next month, which meant my shrink sessions were temporarily suspended. Silt, Vibe, and the others had agreed to meet once a month to discuss whatever they'd found on my dad, if anything, and our second meeting was still a ways out. We had a week until the Liquid Hero's opening and our first group fight, both scheduled for the end of the month. All of that meant that, for the first time since I'd arrived at the Academy, I had a whole day every week with no responsibilities.

It should've been perfect.

Instead, I was bored out of my mind.

Maybe it's because we weren't fucking *doing* anything, even in our Powers classes. Group Tactics continued to consist of a lot of reading, film watching, and discussion. Endless hours of discussion. Run jointly by Nikolai and Jessica Strich, Matthew's older sister, it lacked the excitement and thrill of either of their individual courses. Meanwhile, Physical Training & Defense was just a continuation from the previous year; cardio, weights, and the occasional self defense technique judged harmless enough for us non-Advanced Combat students to attempt.

Weapons was one of the few remaining classes where we got to actually perform, but the thrill of shooting guns had paled somewhat after my time at the Hole. I'd already killed a man with a one-shot bullet that literally ate him in seconds. Plinking away at a down-range target didn't really get the blood flowing like it used to.

With my teammates still doing their best to avoid each other, my suddenly excessive free time was mostly spent out in the clearing on the west edge of campus. I wasn't eye-fucking the ocean, like Silt had most recently accused me of doing. I wasn't eye-fucking anything, given that my eyes were closed, but I couldn't deny that something about the water spoke to me.

We were too far away to actually hear the waves, but every now and then, the breeze shifted, bringing the smell of iodine, salt, and sulphur. That hill was as close as I'd ever been to the ocean—I sure as hell had never tried wading into it—but the body of water's presence, sound, and smell all centered me, in a way that Professor Chu's metronome and Emery Goldstein's monotonous voice never could.

Remember that, if you run across another Crow in the future, or some other Power that learns to speak with the dead. Tell them that even Walker had a soul.

Of course, I wasn't out there in the clearing to connect with the ocean and find enlightenment or any of that sort of shit. I wasn't even really meditating, like I'd told Silt each and every time she brought the subject up. I was focusing inward, on the emptiness at my core. Sally had told me that every Crow had a hole inside them, like a crack in their soul, and that was how the emptiness got in, slowly filling the metaphysical bucket of their power.

I still wasn't sure how much of what she'd told me I could trust, but that one piece of information rang true. When I'd been dying at the Hole, I'd seen the world, not as shapes or even colors, but as energy, life and death, light and dark. I'd let the energy from the battlefield's many casualties flow through me and into Carnage and that had been what killed the unkillable Black Hat.

Fuck if I understood how any of it worked, but after that, my power had gone distant, like a seed buried deep inside me, waiting for some signal to sprout again.

To get back to Sally's metaphor, my bucket was empty. Even of emptiness.

It had been more than a month now though, and I could feel that changing. I could feel the emptiness rising again. Still a far cry from what it had been in the Mojave, or even in the months before that, but rising and filling faster than it ever had before. It was as if the hole inside of me had torn wider and what had once been a slow drip was now a trickle.

Probably should've terrified me. Probably would've, but when I gave the emptiness free rein, fear was a distant thing, just like pain or emotion. All that was left was will and action. So I sat there for at least an hour every damn day, not looking at the ocean, but feeling its presence as I set my power free. I focused on eradicating any obstacle, mental or otherwise, that might be keeping that bucket from filling as fast as it could.

Professor Chu would probably have had something to say about all that, but the old man had a cushy job teaching Control in the safety and security of the Academy grounds. I had enemies waiting in the real world. Every damn one of them—from Fallout to Tyrant to Sally—was stronger than I was, but fuck if I was just going to roll over next time one of them came calling. I might not be able to death-touch anyone without a field of the dying and recently dead to supercharge me, but whoever came for me was still going to know they'd been in a fight.

So yeah, all that unexpected free time went to maximizing my limited potential, to getting back to whatever counted as a Low-Three Crow's best.

I don't know what the ocean thought of the whole affair. Something tells me it had seen this all before, and would see it all again, long after I was dust.

There's a comfort in that, I guess.

○○○

The end of the month finally brought an end to all that free time. Saturday morning was the long-awaited team competition. Saturday night was the opening of the Liquid Hero. Seemed like a shitty idea to do both on the same day, but nobody had consulted me when making the schedule.

The team leaders all had another meeting on Friday, while the rest of us were running laps on campus. We assumed they were given details on the nature of the competition that awaited us, and how exactly we were going to be able to let loose on each other without ending up with a whole lot of dead second-years.

I say *assumed* because Poltergeist never passed that information on to the rest of us. In fact, our fearless leader was a no-show on Friday night.

"This is on you, Walker," hissed Winter, when she finally gave up on pretending to read and headed off to begin the hour-long process of getting ready for bed. A process that meant the bathroom would be off limits to Muse and me for that entire time. "You're the one who voted for her."

"Maybe one of the other teams poisoned her." I shrugged. "If so, we can make you team leader. Assuming Freddy still doesn't want the job."

"Hell no," said the diminutive Switch.

Muse was still a bit of an enigma to me. Other than drinking—which he did a lot of, even by second-year standards—I couldn't really figure out what made him tick. He made it to every class but rarely participated, even in the academic courses. It was almost like he didn't want to be at the Academy at all… but if that were true, he'd have never made it to second-year.

"There you have it," I called down the hall to Winter's back. "Poltergeist dies and you get to be queen bee. Happy?"

The bathroom door slamming shut suggested the Weather Witch was not, in fact, happy.

Some people never are.

We didn't see Tessa until Saturday morning, when she swung by—still alive and healthy, by all appearances—for a shower and change of clothes. Muse was still groggy from waking up, but Winter let the dark-haired Telekinetic have it.

"What the hell, Tessa?" Penelope had both hands on her hips, her long white hair in a braid that fell all the way to her waist. "Our competition is in thirty minutes!"

"I know! That's why I'm here." Tessa emerged from the bathroom a few minutes later, fresh-faced and pulling on her Academy greys. "Are you all ready or what?"

"We were ready last night," growled Winter, "when you were supposed to tell us what we'd be getting into today. You know, like an actual team leader would."

"Sorry." Wonder of wonders, Poltergeist did look vaguely apologetic. "Something came up that I had to deal with. Luckily, there's not that much to tell about the team competitions."

"Who are we matched up against? And how?"

"We're facing Team One. It's going to be Capture the Flag."

The other two nodded, as if that meant something to them.

"What's Capture the Flag?"

"It's a game?" Poltergeist frowned. "How do you not know what it is? It's practically mandatory in high school."

"Some of us didn't fucking go to high school," I reminded her.

"Oh, right. Well—"

"Two teams," interrupted Winter. "Each has a flag that they can't move from their base. The object is to get the other team's flag back to your base while protecting your own."

That actually sounded kind of fun. But there was still a Crow-sized elephant in the room.

"And how do we do that without mass casualties?"

"It's virtual," said Tessa.

"Virtual? What does that mean?"

She shrugged. "Sort of like the Maze, I guess? I don't know… there was a lot of technical jargon in the info packet."

"We got an information packet?!?" Winter's voice went high, like the whistle of a boiling tea kettle. "Where is it and why haven't the rest of us gotten to read it?"

Poltergeist coughed. "I'll send it to you after our match. You can read it to your heart's content."

"So we're going to go put our lives in the hands of some sort of Technomancer's creation to play a game Walker's never heard of against a team we haven't planned for at all, with limited and probably faulty intelligence?" Muse's smile was bleak. "This is going to go great. Sure glad you were voted leader, Tessa."

"You were drunk, Freddy. You don't get to bitch about how things turned out!"

"Maybe he doesn't, but I do." Winter scowled. Despite what she'd said about not using powers, I could actually feel the temperature plummet. "What was so important that you couldn't be bothered to put together a plan of attack with us last night?"

"Look, I get it. This is a lot to take in," said Tessa, dodging the question, "but it's not a big deal. We won't find out the full details of the scenario until we get there anyway. As for the tactics? Those are easy. Muse powers us all up. I guard the flag, Winter scouts ahead, and Damian goes and kills everyone and retrieves the flag. Easy peasy."

When I'd voted for her to be team leader, it was at least partly because she'd seemed aware of our team's flaws and shortcomings. Yet here we were, a month later, and all she had for us was *easy peasy*?

To say I was regretting my vote was a bit of an understatement.

"I can only amplify two of you," said Freddy.

"What? How come?"

"Because that's how my power works."

"Why didn't you say that earlier?"

"Nobody asked."

"Fine. Whatever. Hit me and Winter then. Walker will just have to make do." She waved both hands toward the door, as if we were one of the few herds of livestock left in the Free States. "Let's go, team! We don't have all day."

Turns out we probably should've just stayed in the dorm and forfeited. It would've hurt a hell of a lot less.

CHAPTER 10

If nothing else, our fearless leader at least knew where to go. We marched across campus to one of the many buildings I'd never entered, and then around to its side, where a second door was secured by a biometric lock. With a smug glance at the rest of us, Poltergeist put her flat palm against the sensor. Moments later, we could all hear the door unlock.

"Does that work for all of us?"

"Team leaders only. Bard doesn't want anyone sneaking in here when they're not supposed to. Not after what happened with Ishmae."

'Here' turned out to be a small empty room with a steel door set in the far wall. When that door hissed open, revealing the interior of an elevator, I couldn't help but think back to the elevator at the Hole that had led down to the cell blocks.

It wasn't a comforting thought.

There was ample room for all of us in the elevator, and only three buttons on the panel. Freddy stabbed one of them with his index finger, but it refused to light up.

"This one's secured too," said Tessa, this time bringing her face up close to an opaque glass panel, like she was trying to terrify it. The verification process finished in seconds, and all three elevator buttons became active.

"G, CR or TG?" asked Muse.

"G is ground level... we're already there. CR is the Control Room. We want TG." She pressed the button in question, and the elevator immediately began to descend.

"Totally Great?" guessed the Switch.

"Training Grounds."

A few seconds later, the elevator doors opened on a short hall. At the end of that hall was a room, empty of furniture, with another hall leading away.

Vibe, Paladin, and the other two members of Team One were already in that first room, as were Bard, Nikolai, Jessica, and a handful of older men and women. As we filed in, Nikolai had us stand in a line facing the faculty, with our opponents in a similar line to our left.

"Welcome to the Training Grounds," said Bard, his voice smooth and compelling as ever. "As you have no doubt read, the Training Grounds were created a little over a decade ago, at the faculty's request. We needed a way to allow for large-scale group combat that wouldn't end with all of our students dead. This was Mr. Gage's solution. And his last creation."

More than a few heads turned at that. Gage was the Technomancer who had created the first device used for testing and classifying Powers. After that, he'd turned his abilities towards becoming the richest man in the Free States. Even with him dead, the company he'd founded still ran a lot of the country's infrastructure.

"The technical details, what little we've been able to translate to a language anybody understands, are in the information packets you were given. Suffice it to say that the Training Grounds allow us to create mock environments that you will be completely immersed in. In the real world, your powers will continue to be limited by dampeners, but in the Training Grounds, those limits will be gone. The faculty has spent the last year giving you all foundational instruction—how to move, how to defend yourselves, how to achieve control—but as Capes, you must know how to use your abilities to their fullest when lives are on the line. This is the start of that process."

"Having said that, we are not in the business of training kamikaze soldiers," continued Bard, his eyes for some reason coming to rest on me. "Combat has consequences. Poor tactics do too.

Because you will be operating in a virtual environment, your physical bodies will remain safe. However, getting hit in the Training Grounds hurts. Getting killed hurts even more. That pain being entirely in your head will not make it any less terrible. There's a reason we only hold these matches once a month."

Over on Team One, Supersonic just smirked, as if that promise of pain was going to be someone else's problem. Asshole probably couldn't imagine a world where he'd be the one getting killed.

"Pain is instructive," added Nikolai in his heavy accent. "It is there to make sure you do not treat this as a game. Fight like your lives depend upon it, because one day, they will."

"Thank you, professor." Bard nodded to the bigger man, and then gestured toward the hall behind him. "Down this hall are doors labeled 1-10. Inside the door that corresponds to your team's number, you will find a row of pods. The men and women behind me will make sure you are properly seated in your pods before we begin. Your teachers and I will be up in the control room, where we'll be able to initiate the simulation and observe your actions within."

He turned to Poltergeist. "I have Team One's list. Does Team Five have one of their own?"

Tessa shook her head.

"Very well. Then you may proceed to your respective rooms. Please be aware that you are being graded on your performances, both individually and as a team. These directly impact your class rankings and therefore the likelihood of you receiving an internship offer from an existing Cape team next year. Take this seriously."

With that, he, Nikolai, and Jessica all disappeared into the elevator. Team One was already halfway down the hall to their room before we got in gear. As we walked, Winter turned on Poltergeist.

"What list?"

"I have no idea," replied the Telekinetic. "I didn't see anything about a list."

"And you read the whole information packet?"

"More or less." Tessa coughed. "Don't worry about it, Penelope. Just stick to the plan and everything will work itself out."

Oh yeah. This was going to go great.

The fact that there were ten rooms off the hall once again spoke to the idea that the builders had assumed Academy classes would be vastly larger than they were. The pods in our room were oblong, raised beds with retractable covers. At one end, near the padding that was apparently supposed to serve as a pillow, was a copper wire basket. Thick cables connected that basket to ports on either side of the pod.

At the sight of the baskets, I felt a shiver go through me. The last time I'd seen something like that, it had been on a comatose Ishmae's head, when the Pyro stupidly tried to run the Maze as a first-year.

And we all knew how that had turned out.

"Pick a pod. Any pod," said the man who had led us in, a pot-bellied individual with a receding hairline. "We'll get you set up, and then wait for the Dean to initiate the sim."

"Are you all Technomancers?" asked Winter.

"Ha! I wish," said the man, shaking his head. "We're just technicians. It takes someone like Mr. Gage to create this sort of masterpiece, but anyone with the right training can maintain it."

I was already in my pod, staring up at a featureless ceiling, but from the far side of the room, I could hear Muse.

"Are you sure it's safe?"

"Of course it is. Think of it like a more complicated testing machine. You all came through that just fine, didn't you?"

"My machine exploded and nearly electrocuted me," I said.

"That's... not supposed to happen. And it definitely won't happen with the Training Grounds. We make certain of that."

One of the other technicians came and strapped me into the pod. They then placed the wire basket over my head, adjusted it so the nodes all made contact, and tightened the chin strap. I reached for my power, just to escape the sudden rush of panic, but the dampeners were already running and that emptiness remained elusive.

"I know it's uncomfortable," the first technician told us, "but in just a few seconds, you won't even feel it. Good luck. We'll see you back here in a bit."

With a loud hum that was echoed throughout the room, the lid on my pod began to close. And then, just like that, I was elsewhere.

○○○

For a moment, the flood of sensory data was overwhelming, but that rush of sensation quickly receded, and I was able to start making sense of my surroundings.

I'd been strapped into the pod, but now I was standing, the terrain under my worn sneakers less rigid than the reinforced concrete of the Academy. A breeze blew in from somewhere, and I opened my eyes to find that we were in a forest, far older and larger than the woods on the west side of campus. A blue sky was barely visible beyond the canopy of branches and leaves above us.

"Welcome, teams." Bard's voice was everywhere and nowhere, soft yet carrying easily even over the sounds of the forest. "As you're aware, today's sim is a simple game of capture the flag. If you look behind you, you'll find your team's flag."

Sure enough, just behind a wobbly Muse, a flag pole the length and width of a baton had been planted at the top of a low hill. The brightly colored flag unfurled in the breeze, displaying the number five.

"Your objective is simple." Jessica Strich spoke up for the first time. Her voice carried just as easily as Bard's. "Retrieve the other team's flag while defending your own. This is an active-powers scenario, meaning you can and should use your abilities to their fullest. Remember the tactics you've been learning, maximize your advantages, and victory will be yours."

It sounded easy when she said it.

We waited to see if Nikolai was going to add anything, but the teachers had gone silent.

"Okay," said Tessa. "Let's get this party started. Muse?"

"Yeah yeah." The little Switch touched Poltergeist's forehead with a sweaty finger, closed his eyes and shivered, then did the same with Winter. I couldn't see any difference at all, but Freddy looked drained afterward.

"Holy crap," said Tessa. "This is fantastic. What am I now? Mid-Four?"

"I can't amp you to a new ranking," he admitted. "I can only get you to the top of your existing ranking. So you're the highest of Low-Fours, and Winter—"

"Is ready to kick some butt," finished the Weather Witch in question, already taking to the air. "So I'll run reconnaissance, you two will stay with our flag, and Walker..."

"I'll start walking, I guess?" Behind the raised mound that held our flag, much larger foothills rose out of the forest to become mountains. They looked forbidding, as if intentionally designed to be impassable obstacles. Given that this was a sim, I decided to just go with it. I turned and pointed deeper into the forest. "That way."

"How will Winter signal you when she finds something?" asked Tessa.

"I have no idea."

"I can carry him in my wind stream." With the wind whipping about her, stirring up dirt from the forest floor, I couldn't actually see Penelope's smug look, but I could damn well hear it. "He's a Crow. It's time he learned to fly."

"You know Supersonic will be scouting too," I warned Tessa, as much to delay putting my life in Winter's hands as anything. "He'll make a grab for the flag as soon as he sees it. Can you make a bubble around it? Like a shield?"

"That's not how my telekinesis works. I can only grab and manipulate things."

"Shit. Well, Caleb still moves in straight lines," I told her, "so he should at least be predictable."

"I've got our defense handled. You worry about your end. Death-touch every opponent you can find."

It wasn't the most elegant of plans, but it would have to do.

"Head out," she continued. "Come back with the flag or not at all."

I was pretty sure she'd stolen that from a vid.

∘∘∘

Winter's wind stream picked me up as easily as if I was a sack of synth-rations, and with just as little care. I spun about for a bit before I discovered spreading my arms and legs gave me some measure of stability. By then, we were already above the forest's canopy.

Fuck if I'd ever tell Penelope, but before Mom's death, before I found out I'd gotten the one power nobody wants, I'd always wanted to fly. Wind Dancer or Flyboy… the how didn't matter as much as the end result; soaring through the sky.

For just a moment, with the sun shining down from a brilliant blue sky onto a living carpet of a thousand different shades of green, I gloried in the fulfillment of that childhood dream.

Winter waved a long-fingered hand, and we rocketed forward above the trees. She kept us low to avoid detection, mere feet above the tallest trees. Our zig zag flight path gave us a wide search area and some small measure of unpredictability, in the event that we were spotted.

If I'd been prone to motion sickness, I'd have hurled all over the pristine forest below. Thankfully, I was spared that indignity. I set the emptiness of my Power loose, killing extraneous thought or feeling. Going full-Walker, as Silt called it, was of limited value when I was stuck in Winter's wind stream, but it gave me a clarity of focus that might help in our search.

Sure enough, I saw something, moments later.

Problem was, it wasn't Team One's base.

"Look out!" I screamed, but Supersonic was already on us, his combination of Jitterbug and Flyboy powers rocketing him through the air like an arrow.

It was too late for Winter to dodge outright, but she used her wind stream to bat the other Cape to the side, diverting his trajectory just far enough that he blew right by her. It was a brilliant move, fast and instinctive, and it saved her life.

Unfortunately, if she was using her wind to defend herself, it meant she wasn't using it to keep us in the air.

I dropped like a stone, plunging into the trees below us.

With my power filling me, there was no place for fear or surprise. I measured the rapidly diminishing distance between me and the nearest branches, did my best to angle in the correct direction, and grabbed one as I fell past.

There was a loud crack. At first, I thought it might have been my arm, but despite the pain in my shoulders, it was the branch, splintering and giving way. I kept falling, a little bit slower than before that impact.

The branches thickened the further I descended. I was twenty feet above the ground when I was finally able to halt my plunge. The skin on my arms and hands was torn and bleeding, and there was a pain in my left shoulder that told me I'd done some serious damage, but the sensation was as distant as the fear. I didn't have full range of motion in that arm, but it still worked well enough that I'd be able to climb down to the forest floor.

And then? I had no fucking clue. Still no idea where Team One's base was, who was guarding it, or how I'd fight them all with only one hand. But I'd burn that bridge when I came to it.

I was five feet down the tree's knobby trunk when Spectra stepped into view. The Lightbringer's blonde hair was in a braid just like Winter's, and her silver eyes were already glowing.

I dropped the remaining fifteen feet, barely avoiding a blast of pure light that tore right through the tree I'd been climbing. That was the good news.

The bad news was that I landed on one of the gnarled roots at the tree's base, and my right ankle snapped like a toothpick, dropping me to the dirt.

I was struggling up onto my good ankle, using my single working arm to support me, when the next blast came; light and heat and energy that annihilated all in its path, including me.

Bard was right. Even with my power active, dying hurt like a motherfucker.

CHAPTER 11

I woke up to pain and the low hum of the pod room's dampeners. With them running, I couldn't unleash the emptiness that drowned out sensation. I was still strapped down too, the lid above me closed and locked, so I just lay there a while, letting the white-hot sensation run riot through my body as I took mental stock of the situation.

At least I wasn't dead. Maybe the Training Grounds *weren't* some sort of secret murder toy the faculty used to rid themselves of troublemakers.

Part of me had wondered.

As I carefully rotated the shoulder I'd torn in the sim, pain spiked, but the only impediment to my movement was the strap holding that arm down. That meant we didn't bring back the physical damage we suffered in the sim. Just the pain.

That would probably make the Healers happy. I'm sure Gladys and her counterpart had their hands full with the first-years.

As for the pain… no doubt one of the techs would tell us something about the mind making our pain real or some such bullshit. As Nikolai had said, that little fact would motivate us to all do our damnedest to avoid dying in the Training Grounds in the future.

Truth was, I didn't need a sim to teach me that dying sucked. I'd already come as close to real death as someone could without leaving forever.

The lid on my pod still hadn't retracted, so I could only assume the sim was still going on. With their powers amped up, maybe Poltergeist and Winter would be able to handle Supersonic, Spectra, and Paladin on their own. I'd find out soon enough, so there wasn't much point in wondering.

What I did wonder was how they'd found us so fast. Winter was a pain in the world's ass, but I couldn't see anything she'd done wrong in her approach. Yet Supersonic had come out of the trees like he knew exactly where we were. And Spectra had reached me before I'd even made it to the ground. Either we'd flown right above their base and been spotted, or…

Or Kayleigh had used her Empath powers to find us.

It wouldn't have even been hard. She was used to dealing with a campus of thousands. In an otherwise empty forest, my team's emotions must have been jumped out at her like bonfires.

I was the one exception to that—my power making me invisible to her abilities—but I'd been with Winter, and ended up getting caught in the trap they'd set for my teammate.

That said, I didn't understand how they'd coordinated the attack. Unless their base really had been right there, they'd have faced the same communication issues that led to Winter dragging me along in the first place.

One more question to ask whenever the sim finally ended.

As if that thought had been a trigger, the opaque glass lid above my pod finally started to retract. I blinked as the overhead lights came on. One of the technicians came over to remove the copper wire basket and my restraints.

Pain spiked briefly as I climbed out of the pod, then settled back into a dull roar that left my fingers and toes twitching. From the sounds emerging from the other three pods, I wasn't the only member of Team Five who'd gotten murdered in the Training Grounds.

Winter was second out of the pods. The Weather Witch took one step before she went almost as white as her hair. She'd have fallen if the tech who'd just released her hadn't been there to catch her.

A moment later, she was back on her feet, stalking over to Poltergeist's pod. The Telekinetic was still coming to when Winter got in her face.

"Great job, Tessa. Way to lead us right into an absolute disaster!"

"Could you shut up for like five seconds?" asked the other woman. "My head is killing me."

"It's not just *your* head," said Muse, now sitting up in his pod. "And," he continued, frowning, "it's not just my head either. Everything hurts, even though all the bones Paladin broke are healed again. Why am I hurting when I don't have any actual injuries?"

"Your bodies aren't impacted by damage taken in the Training Grounds," said the pot-bellied tech who had released me. "But your mind makes the pain you suffered real."

Just as I'd fucking predicted.

"Well, that sucks," said the diminutive Switch. "At least it's over."

"That's all you care about, Freddy?" Winter was in full warpath mode, clutching her braid like she was planning to strangle someone with it. "What about the fact that we just got our butts kicked by Team One?"

"Shit happens." He shrugged. "I did my best, but once Tessa went down, it's not like I was going to be able to hold off Paladin or anything."

"Supersonic and Spectra were facing off against Winter and I," I said, finally joining the conversation. "And I assume Vibe was with their team's flag. So how the hell did Paladin take out Poltergeist by himself?"

"I don't know." The curly-haired Telekinetic had finally made it to her feet, shoving Winter aside with a scowl. "One moment I was defending the flag... the next I was gone."

"He shot her," answered Muse. "With a crossbow, I think. Right in the face. Wish he'd done the same to me, but he settled for just breaking my arms and legs and taking the flag."

"Where the hell did Matthew get a crossbow from?"

"That's not the worst of it," said Winter. "Supersonic was wearing some sort of comm unit too."

I tried to think back to right before Spectra had liquefied my bones. Had there been something in her ear too?

Yeah. I was pretty sure there had been. Which answered my question about how they'd coordinated their attack. But it raised an even bigger question.

"How did they bring gear into the sim with them? And where did they get it in the first place?"

"It was probably on their requested equipment list," volunteered the technician. "There are limits to what the Training Grounds can provide, and the faculty adds their own restrictions on top of that, but comms and simple projectile weapons? Those are fairly standard requests."

"So we could have brought our own gear in," hissed Winter, looming over Poltergeist. "Only *you* didn't read the information package Bard gave you. Leaving us under-equipped and completely unprepared!"

With us all freed from the pods and a potential battle brewing, the techs beat a hasty retreat out the door. Muse followed after, the coward.

"Look—" began Tessa, bright spots of color in her cheeks.

"No! You look!" interrupted the Weather Witch. "This is my future at stake! I have plans for when I leave this school and they don't involve settling for some third-rate Cape team out on the border! Maybe reading an entire document is just too much for anyone to ask of you, but it shouldn't be! Heck, you could have left the packet for us to read! Except you never even came back to the sub-dorm last night! What was so damn important that you'd put my future plans in jeopardy?"

"London was having a rough night," the Telekinetic responded, her green eyes hard. "Santi's been working his way through a bunch of Cape-bunnies, and she just found out about it."

"Wait. She dumped him. El Bosque can do whatever he—"

"Shut up, Damian." Both women spoke in unison without even glancing in my direction.

"Boohoo for London," said Winter, her voice still hard. "So what?"

"So she's my friend! I know you don't have any of those, but when a friend is hurting, you try to fucking help them!"

If the dampeners hadn't been running, I was pretty sure Tessa would've been a scorch mark on the floor.

"Screw you, Tessa McShane." Winter's voice was as frosty as her name. "You're supposed to be our team leader. This team takes precedence. We have one contest a month. One opportunity! And you flushed ours right down the toilet." Grey eyes flicked over to me. "Great damn choice, Walker."

I waited for the door to slam shut behind her, and then cleared my throat. "I hate to ever agree with Penelope, but—"

"I hope you're happy, you asshole!"

"What? Why would I—"

"This is what you wanted all along, wasn't it?" The Telekinetic's eyes flashed. "Put Tessa in charge and watch her screw everything up! Won't that be a laugh?"

"You caught on to my diabolical plan even faster than I expected," I agreed, sarcasm oozing into every word. "It's gone so much better than I hoped!"

"Fuck you!"

"Don't be stupid, Poltergeist," I told her as she marched for the door. "I know what's waiting for me after graduation. So do you. You did the fucking research last year."

She paused, one hand on the handle.

"I still don't know if training is going to keep me from going mad," I continued, "but even if it does, I have way more to lose than any of you if our team shits the bed."

"What are you talking about?" Her voice had lost some of its edge. "You made it past first-year. Unless you snap like Ishmae, you're going to graduate."

"Sure… and how many teams are going to want to take a chance on a necromancer?"

"You killed Carnage."

"Crows kill all kinds of people. That's kind of the fucking problem."

"And?"

"I need to show I can succeed in a group. Even if we end up the top-ranked team in our class, it's going to be hard for me to earn an internship, let alone a full invite. If we're at the bottom? Shit. Even the Mission might not take me. So maybe you should fucking believe me when I say I didn't vote for you to be our team leader as some sort of plot to make you look bad." She was managing that much all on her own. "I thought you'd give us the best chance at succeeding."

There was a long pause. Just when I thought she was going to storm out anyway, she spoke again.

"Why?"

"You're smart, you're social, and you don't take shit from anyone."

"That's it?"

"To be fair, Winter was your only competition. I'm pretty sure I'd have murdered her by now if she'd been made leader."

"I'd help hide the body." Tessa was still turned away, but I saw her shoulders sag. "Fine. So I was the best of bad options. What now?"

"Fuck if I know. If I had any answers, I'd have voted for myself as team leader. After today, I'm pretty sure we're going to be at the bottom of the rankings, but that's life. We still have time to turn things around. But Tessa?"

"Yeah?"

"This team is a disaster. You and I both know it. Even Penelope knows it. We need someone to actually lead us. And that means you need to get your shit together."

ooo

When I made it back to the sub-dorms, Winter and Poltergeist were nowhere to be found, and Muse's door was shut. That gave me sole claim to the bathroom, and I took advantage of that fact with an extra-long shower. It did nothing to help with the pain—with that pain entirely in my mind, the only thing that seemed to help was my power—but just getting clean again was an achievement of its own. I tossed my Academy greys into my laundry basket and pulled out a fresh pair. Even though the Training Grounds were virtual, our physical bodies had managed to sweat up a storm.

If this kept up, I was going to need to arrange another trip to the med ward. Between the muscle I'd put on since first-year and the rate I was going through my greys, I needed to steal a few more sets of clothes from under Gladys' nose.

I grabbed my Glass and headed to meet with my tutors. Ethics and History were my only remaining academic courses, but I still had tutors in a variety of other subjects. Math. Philosophy. Statistics. English. And now Political Science, whatever the hell that was. Apparently, flunking my way through first-year had convinced Bard to continue my education outside the scope of the usual curriculum.

Lucky me.

Four fucking hours later, I hit the cafeteria for a late lunch, and then swung back by the sub-dorm to drop off my Glass. Poltergeist was seated on the couch, her own Glass in her hands. Muse's door was still shut. And… was Winter in the kitchen?

"What's that smell?"

"I have no idea," said Tessa. "Penelope has been back there since I came in. But now that you're here, we should have a team meeting."

"I can't. Sorry. I've got to be somewhere in ten minutes."

"You've already been gone for hours! Where were you all morning?"

"I have tutors on Saturday."

"Tutors?"

"Yeah. Remember that whole 'never went to high school' thing? Apparently, there are gaps in my education, and God forbid I be unable to quote Shakespeare while trying to kill a Black Hat."

Shakespeare, for those of you who've been here all along, was some pre-Break writer. And also the 'real Bard' that the dean had mentioned way back when we first met. I'd just been assigned five of his sonnets as reading homework.

Have I mentioned how much I hated my tutors?

"We don't have English class anymore," she pointed out.

"Yeah, well… tell that to Bard. This was one of the requirements for me coming back as a second-year."

"Fine. So you met with your tutors this morning, after… you know. And now?"

"Now, I have to go meet my first-years and make sure none of them are doing something stupid that will get them killed. At least not while they're students," I amended.

"What?"

I couldn't tell exactly what part of that was unclear. Luckily, she saved me from asking.

"You're one of the mentors? How does that make any sense?"

I shrugged. "It sure as fuck wasn't my idea."

"But why you, of all people?"

"As a cautionary tale, maybe? How the hell would I know? When I survived my expulsion hearing, Bard said one of his punishments would be giving me a job. And apparently this was it."

Tessa sank back onto the couch, shaking her head. "This was not how I expected today to go."

"Yeah, well." I waved my Glass. "I'm just here to drop this off and then head out to meet with them. So if that's it?"

"Yeah. Whatever." She was still shaking her head. "Can you come back afterward? We do need to have that team meeting, especially before tonight's opening of the Liquid Hero."

"I'll be here." It'd have been nice to have some time to myself, but I wasn't going to complain that Tessa was finally trying to step up as a team leader.

And at least I wouldn't be bored.

I paused on my way to the hall, as the banging of pans came from the kitchen. Whatever Winter was doing, it smelled surprisingly good.

CHAPTER 12

When I walked back in an hour later, the kitchen was quiet, but the sub-dorm smelled amazing. At the end of the hall, the bathroom door was shut, light seeping out from underneath, and in the common room, Poltergeist was still on the couch. She looked up as soon as I came in. Oddly, her gaze went straight to my hands.

"What?"

"Just looking for blood," she said. "But I guess you're getting along with your first-years better than you did when you were one yourself."

"Funny. Actually, there's no blood when I death-touch someone. Just dust. It makes cleanup way the hell easier." I scowled at the look on her face. "It was a joke, Tessa. My kids are a pain in the ass, but nothing's reached the *violent confrontation* stage just yet."

"It's the *yet* I'm worried about."

"Don't be. They're annoying, but it's not like there are any brewing blood feuds. For the most part, they're a hell of a lot better adjusted than we were."

With the exception of Lynn, who still seemed to hate my guts for some reason. And Lucy, who'd made eye contact all of once in all our meetings. And Paco, who...

I stopped and gave a mental shrug. Actually, I didn't have any concerns about Paco. Kid was a born survivor. And way better at blending into the background than me.

"Speak for yourself," said Tessa. "I was perfectly prepared for being a first-year."

"Really?" I shrugged. "Must have been some other Telekinetic that kept getting drunk and dancing on tables then."

"How did you—?" Tessa scowled. "Was it Kayleigh or Sofia that told you?"

Before I could reply, the bathroom door opened. Winter marched out, one towel wrapped around her long frame, the other piled atop her head like she was some sort of sultaness from the vids.

She stopped when she saw both Poltergeist and I had turned to look. "Don't be pervs. It's bad enough we only have one bathroom."

"Nobody wants to see your bony—"

"Now that Walker is back, I'm calling a team meeting," interjected Tessa. "Can you join us when you're dressed?"

"Oh *now* you're worried about team stuff?" Winter rolled her eyes. "Fine. One of you can comb my hair."

Her bedroom door slammed shut behind her, leaving Poltergeist and I to share a look.

"That sounds like a team leader sort of responsibility," I told her.

"I think I'll delegate it to one of my minions," she shot back.

"Shit. I'd better wake up Muse then."

ooo

Despite her threats, Winter seemed content to comb her own hair, sitting in one of the two recliners. With her long white hair wrapped around to the front so she could reach the ends and her equally long legs curled up underneath her, she looked like a hairball with eyes.

A sleepy Muse was in the other recliner, which left me on the couch with Poltergeist. It was an arrangement that didn't suit either of us particularly well.

"We're here," declared Winter, just when the silence was starting to get obnoxious. "What did you want to talk about, Ms. Team Leader?"

"We need to go over schedules and responsibilities for tonight's opening," said the dark-haired Telekinetic, "but first, I wanted to talk about this morning's—"

"Debacle?"

"Yeah." Tessa swallowed. "I fucked up. I'm sorry."

"They've posted the new rankings already," said Winter. "We're not the only team that lost, of course, but they still put us right at the bottom."

"We're not going to stay there." Tessa flicked the screen of her Glass. "I've sent you all the information packet I received on the Training Grounds. We all need to read it so we're prepared for next month."

"Also," she continued, "we need to pick a time we can all meet each week to practice some of what we're being taught in Group Tactics."

"More homework?" sighed Muse.

"We aren't going to work as a team without training, Freddy. We have exactly one month until our next fight, and I want to use it to make sure today's *debacle* doesn't repeat itself."

She looked over to Winter and the Weather Witch gave back a grudging nod. Both women turned to me and I shrugged.

"Dying sucks, even when it's purely virtual. And it's not like I have anything else to do with my nights."

"I do," muttered Muse, "but getting my arms and legs broken wasn't fun either. I can spare one night a week. What about Wednesday?"

"I have tutoring," said Winter.

"You need tutoring?"

She shot me a look of utter scorn. "I'm the tutor, you jerk."

Because of course she was. I sent up a silent prayer of thanks to the God I didn't believe in that Bard hadn't made her one of mine.

"Tuesday then?" Poltergeist waited for our nods. "Okay. On to tonight and the official opening of the Liquid Hero then. Our team and Team Four have the late shift."

"How are we even ready to open?" asked Winter. "Aren't there like a hundred things that need to be done first?"

"Like inventory and cleaning and job training?" Tessa nodded. "Except for the last part, it's all taken care of. What do you think the team leaders have been doing for the last month?"

I had a few answers ready to go, but recognized a rhetorical question when I heard it.

"Evelyn's handling inventory and supply orders. She's used to that sort of thing because her parents have a storefront in East Los Angeles."

"Really? They own a store?"

For some reason, the Telekinetic shot me a glare. "There's nothing wrong with being a small business owner. Not every family can be rich like Kayleigh's."

"I didn't even know Kayleigh's family *was* rich. How can you tell?"

"They have their own chef!"

"Oh." I shrugged. "You all seem pretty damn well off to me."

"My parents are professors," said Winter. "Everyone knows that knowledge is the best kind of wealth."

She colored under the looks we all sent her way.

"What? It is."

"I need a drink," announced our Switch.

"Sorry, Freddy," said Tessa. "Tonight, you're bussing tables. I'm not sure anyone trusts you behind the bar just yet."

At the other man's shrug, she turned to Winter. "You, on the other hand... how are you at mixing?"

"I don't drink alcohol."

"How do you feel about chilling drinks once Santi and I have mixed them, then?"

"Wait," protested Freddy. "Why do you and he get to play bartender?"

"Economics," I guessed.

My team all turned to me. "What's that supposed to mean?" demanded Winter.

"The more drinks we sell, the better for the bar, right?" I shrugged. "Who do you think guys would rather buy drinks from?

Freddy? Me? Or Tessa? I'm guessing it works the same with the women and El Bosque."

For some reason, Tessa went beet red. I swear… I never knew what was going to set her off.

"Actually, I *could* learn to tend bar," decided Winter. "For the good of the team."

Clearly, she hadn't gotten my point.

"What am I doing?" I asked our team leader. "Let me guess? Toilet cleaning?"

"Makara and the Viking are tackling clean-up, actually."

Makara made a bit of sense. As a Hydromancer, Patty could wash things down without much effort. But the Viking? This was the problem with the team leaders all being women. None of them had seen the utter wasteland Erik had turned the men's bathroom into on a regular basis as a first-year.

"Damian, you and Alan Jackson are going to be bouncers. You work the door while he handles security inside."

Alan Jackson on security would have people pissing themselves if they even thought of starting trouble, but I seemed an odd choice to be the doorman. Last year's class had frequently placed one of their Titans in the role.

"Shouldn't the Viking play doorman?" asked Muse, echoing my thoughts.

"He pissed off Evelyn." Tessa shrugged. "Now he gets to pay the price."

As impossible as it seemed, someone had actually replaced me at the top of Evie's hate list.

"She wanted Walker for bathroom duty too, but one of the two needed to be female."

○○○

Roughly ten hours later, I woke to banging on my bedroom door. I reflexively reached for the steak knife under my pillow—stolen from the cafeteria to replace last year's weapon—but the banging was quickly followed by a voice I recognized as Winter's.

I yanked open the door to find the white-haired Weather Witch now hammering Poltergeist's door, across the hall from mine.

"What do you want, Penelope?"

She spun and recoiled from whatever she saw in my face. Then her eyes drifted down and widened.

"Oh my god! Put on some clothes!"

It wasn't like I slept in the nude or anything… I had boxers on, even if I hadn't bothered to pull on a fresh pair of sweats. But Winter was reacting like I'd come to the door with my dick out and swinging in the breeze.

"I'm going right back to sleep," I warned her, "unless you tell me why you're banging on everyone's door at too-fucking-early-for-this o'clock."

Behind Penelope, the door opened, and Tessa peered out, her hair sticking up in every possible direction.

"We need a team meeting," hissed Winter, "and then whoever was responsible needs to take care of their disgusting mess."

I was pretty sure Poltergeist's bedhead wasn't the mess Penelope was referring to.

"Can't it wait?" The Telekinetic in question yawned. She was in pajamas; a cropped camisole and wide-legged, comfortable looking pants. If she noticed my lack of clothing she was a lot less obnoxiously taken aback by it than the other woman.

"No!" The ends of Winter's long white hair were actually twisting of their own accord, stirred by the wind stream she'd unconsciously summoned. I was pretty sure we didn't have to worry about lightning or changing weather patterns when indoors, but it was a reminder that she was also a Wind Dancer, and that particular power set was viable anywhere there was air.

"Fine. One of you wake up Freddy," I decided. "I'm going to put on some pants."

As I closed the door, I heard Penelope's muttered reply.

"Thank God."

"Eh," said Tessa, not bothering to lower her voice. "At least he was wearing underwear."

○○○

Five minutes later, we were all in the common room. Freddy looked as miserable as I felt, Tessa could've done with about seventeen more hours of beauty sleep, and Winter… well, she was still raging.

"We're all here," said Tessa. "What was so important?"

"The bathroom," answered the other woman.

"What?" My thoughts turned back to the steak knife under my pillow. I was pretty sure stabbing a teammate was frowned upon at the Academy, but these were extenuating circumstances.

"You woke us up to…" Poltergeist's voice trailed off and she wrinkled her nose. "Wait. Is *that* what that smell is?"

"It's disgusting," confirmed Winter, "and it's everywhere. And whoever is responsible needs to clean it up. Now."

Now that I was paying attention, the noxious fumes wafting down the hall from the bathroom were quickly becoming impossible to ignore.

"It wasn't me." I let the emptiness fill me until the stench was a distant thing. "I didn't even drink last night."

"Yeah, right."

I glared at Poltergeist. "What's that supposed to mean?"

"You punched a third-year in the throat! Are you really telling me alcohol wasn't involved?"

"You wanted me to be a bouncer. That's what bouncers do."

"Chad hadn't even made it into the bar yet!"

"He was being an asshole." With my power a cold quiet in my veins, her irritation barely registered. "Besides, he started it. I don't even know why. I've never seen him before."

"You broke his arm in the brawl last year!"

"I… did?" That whole night remained a great big blank spot in my memory, but I was pretty sure I'd stayed out of the action. "Are you sure?"

"Un-fucking-believable."

"Whatever. Like I said, I didn't drink a drop last night. Alcohol's not really my thing."

There was a pause and then the three of us all turned to look at Freddy. The little Switch shrugged and then winced, as if it hurt to even do that much.

"Yeah," he finally managed. "It was probably me."

"Fix it," demanded Winter. "I'm sure the janitor's office has industrial-grade bleach."

"Seriously, Freddy," chimed in Poltergeist. "That is so foul. Once we're Capes, teams will have cleaning services for this sort of thing, but right now, everyone needs to clean up the messes they make."

"While we're on the subject of bathrooms," said Winter, who'd apparently been up for hours thinking up shit to berate us about, "you guys need to stop monopolizing ours at night." She pointed her finger at Freddy and me like it was a Legion tech gun.

"What?"

"I know guys have… needs… but I'm tired of the bathroom being unavailable for like an hour at a time."

"Needs?"

She went red, like a tomato with hair. "I'm not going to say it!"

Fucking hell. "Penelope, I'm not masturbating in the bathroom." I looked over to Muse. "Are you?"

He shook his head and winced again.

"There's barely even room to breathe in there," I added, "thanks to all your hair, skin, and makeup crap. Besides, we all have our own bedrooms. Why would we need to do it in the bathroom?"

"Don't be gross, Damian."

"Gross? You're the one imagining Freddy and me choking the chicken. I sure as hell don't randomly think about you or Tessa masturbating!"

Except, of course, that now I was. As if my Sunday morning wasn't already awful enough.

"Then what are you doing in there every night?!"

"I'm not—"

"It's me," said Tessa, finally rejoining the conversation. For some reason, she was almost as red-faced as Winter.

"Too much information," said Muse.

"Way too much," I agreed.

"Oh for fuck's sake." The Telekinetic rolled her eyes. "Get your minds out of the gutter. I've been taking baths."

It wasn't a euphemism I was familiar with.

"After a month away from the Academy, I hurt all the damn time," she continued. "Pardon me if I want to throw some Epsom salts in the water and give myself a soak."

Okay... *that* sounded like a euphemism.

"You could've just knocked," she told Winter.

"I have! Several times!"

"I must have been listening to music on my Glass then." Tessa shrugged. "If you want, I can take my baths earlier in the day, I guess."

"Yes. Please. There's one bathroom and four of us. You all need to be more considerate if this is going to work."

"*We* need to be more considerate?"

She shot me a glare. "What's that supposed to mean?"

"We all have early classes. And yet every morning, you take your sweet time showering, playing with your hair, and doing whatever the hell it is that leaves Muse and I with like ten minutes to get ready. I get that it takes a lot of work to make you presentable, but—"

"You did *not* just say that to me."

"All I'm asking for is some of that consideration you're demanding from the rest of us."

"How much time do you even need to pull on yet another pair of Academy sweats and forget to run a comb through your hair?"

"Guys," said Poltergeist, getting between the Weather Witch and me, "this is new to all of us. There's going to be an adjustment period, and we're all going to have to compromise. That's part of being a team. But for now, I think the first thing we should do—"

"I'm going to go use the showers at the pool," decided Winter, her voice still every bit as frosty as her name. "When I get back, that bathroom had better be spotless, Freddy, or I'm going to flash freeze your whole damn bedroom."

Muse looked up at the departing woman's back, glanced over at Poltergeist and I, and suddenly twitched. Eyes bulging, and with one hand over his mouth, he sprinted for the bathroom.

"I hate this team so, so much," muttered Tessa.

CHAPTER 13

I lasted exactly three shifts as the doorman at the Liquid Hero, which was how long it took for another of Chad's third-year buddies to start something. This one was a Stalwart and it was all I could do to make sure he at least ended up in the med ward with me. Then, instead of giving me a medal for not trying to death-touch the asshole, Tessa demoted me to toilet cleaning.

Other than the puke, shit, and piss of a few hundred filthy students a night—Powers and normals both—bathroom duty wasn't all that bad. With the emptiness flooding me, the stench and resulting nausea felt like someone else's concern. I swept the men's bathroom once an hour, dragged out the mop for emergencies, and didn't have to talk with anyone.

Also, Poltergeist gave me a lot less grief about working in my Academy greys when I was tucked out of sight by the bathroom.

Because I got picked for that duty every shift week, it meant whatever team we were paired with ended up having to clean the women's bathroom. After the first few weeks, that started to ruffle some feathers. Makara didn't seem to mind bathroom duty—maybe because she could accomplish all her cleaning from the doorway—but none of the other teams had a Hydromancer. Even worse, each team only had two women... and one was the team leader, who certainly wasn't going to assign *herself* toilet duty. That left Ember, Spectra, and Cyclone sharing in my punishment. Can't say they appreciated that—or me, for that matter—but like good little team members, they kept their peace.

Until the night of half-priced Tequila shots.

Forty minutes into the worst shift of our lives, London threatened to set the whole damn building on fire. She was a long way from the departed Ishmae's power level, but the white-hot flames flickering around her hands were still more than enough to get everyone's attention.

Before you knew it, our five team leaders had created an actual shift chart, ensuring that we all rotated through the available positions equally. Truth be told, it probably hurt the business' bottom line on the nights when Winter, me, or Freddy tended bar, but fair was fair. I didn't know where the money was going anyway, so I couldn't find it in myself to care.

By the end of April, our class was running the Liquid Hero like almost-professionals. If I ended up getting expelled again, I was relieved to know I'd have a bright future as a poorly paid club worker ahead of me.

That's not sarcasm. Honest. It was the first time I'd felt employable in almost nineteen years. I'd have to hide who and what I was to even get an interview, of course, but it would sure as hell beat living on the streets.

Between nights at the Liquid Hero and days spent with my tutors or first-years, my weekends were kind of a blur. Alexa still wasn't back, but all that meant was I had an hour more to sleep in on Sundays before meditation, laundry and lunch, and another long night working at the bar.

Weekdays were less hectic. I went to class, did homework for the remaining academic courses, pursued my own research into both Sally Cemetery and Tyrant—research that went absolutely nowhere because I sucked at it—and spent endless hours looking out at the Pacific, doing what I could to feed that seed of emptiness at my core. It was almost peaceful.

Whatever flaws Tessa had—and if you showed up late to this little party, worry not; I'll be happy to enumerate them again at some point—the Telekinetic did her best to turn our team around. Every

Tuesday, the four of us trained together, trying to adapt what we'd learned in Group Tactics to a squad that was as non-standard as they came.

By the time our next sim-battle rolled around, we'd all read through the manual for the Training Grounds. Turned out every team got to put together a list of gear to be loaded into the sim with them; one weapon and one other piece of equipment per second-year. Like the comm units Vibe's team had been wearing and the crossbow Paladin had shot Tessa in the face with, for example. We spent more than a few hours deciding what would be on that list, but most of our free time was focused on the tactics that would serve us best against our next opponents, Silt's Team Three.

We were as ready as a month of hardcore preparation— organized by the ultimate in type-A personalities—could make us. A Low-Four Telekinetic, a High Three Weather Witch and Wind Dancer, a Crow who could possibly kill with a touch, and a Switch that would make two of us even deadlier. It wasn't your usual Titan/Stalwart/blasters formation, but we were ready to make it work.

Instead, we got our asses kicked.

Again.

ooo

When the Training Grounds loaded up, we found ourselves in a city straight out of the Badlands… a mix of decrepit skyscrapers and storefronts. Here and there, a few honest-to-God civilians in full face masks picked over the rubble.

Simulated civilians, naturally, but I was pretty sure any incidental casualties would have an all-too-real impact on our performance grades.

Muse boosted Poltergeist and Winter and then shouldered the comically oversized flamethrower he'd insisted be added to our equipment list. He and Tessa were once again defending our flag, while Penelope and I handled reconnaissance.

This time, the Weather Witch and I split up. She took to the air and I made my way through alleyways and abandoned buildings. One of the many things we'd worked out in our training sessions was a search grid, designed to help us find the enemy base as quickly as possible. It took a bit to adapt it to a city full of buildings instead of an open forest, but soon enough, we were on our way.

Thanks to our comm units—loosely based off the proprietary tech every professional Cape team used in the field—we all stayed in contact.

That's how, seven minutes into the mission, Winter and I could both hear Tessa's startled gasp, quickly drowned out by a low snarl and the breathy fwoosh of Freddy's flamethrower.

And then? Nothing but silence.

I glanced above me. Winter was a speck in the cloud-filled sky. "Penelope..."

"I can get there faster. You keep going."

As she made her turn, something plummeted out of the clouds above her, twice the size of the Weather Witch, and moving at a velocity far beyond terminal.

"Look ou—"

I couldn't even get the words out before the object plowed right through Winter, hitting her with bone-snapping force. The only good news is I think she was dead long before she crashed into the buildings below.

And just like that, I was our team's lone survivor.

I wasn't sure what had hit Winter, but whatever it was, Cyclone was the only person on the other team who could have dropped it. So much for Penelope's dismissal of the near-ginger Wind Dancer. That one growl over the comm units told me Alan-fucking-Jackson had been at our base, and given that the Shifter should never have been able to sneak up on Tessa, I was willing to bet Oscuro had been with him. How they'd found us so quickly remained an open question, but with most of Team Three's members accounted for, it meant Silt was guarding her team's flag all by herself.

If I could reach her and get that flag, maybe I could force a stalemate.

It wasn't much of a plan, but our actual plan had gotten the team wiped out in less than ten minutes. Improvisation was all I had left.

Finding a base by myself in an arena the size of multiple city blocks seemed impossible, but that worry was an extraneous thought, flitting about like a dying butterfly somewhere beyond my bubble of emptiness. I slid through building after building, continuing my search, senses wide open as I let the details of my surroundings filter through me. I was pretty sure their flag would be at street level, just like ours. I'd already covered a fair bit of my portion of the grid and had yet to find an intact stairway or fire escape.

Plus… you kind of had to figure an Earthshaker would want to keep her feet on the ground.

I crept through the entryway of yet another abandoned tower, sticking to the shadows the way Macy Johnson had taught us in my one semester of Mobility class. What had once been some sort of receptionist desk had been reduced to rubble, and garbage now dotted the expansive lobby. Cracked tile floors and exposed pillars completed the post-apocalyptic picture.

Whatever city this sim had been based on, it was a shithole that made even Bakersfield look good. I was pretty damn sure our sim was set somewhere in the Badlands. Which was one more reason why nobody with a brain went into the Badlands.

I was twenty feet from the shattered back door when I heard something. Fuck if I know what it was, but the emptiness inside me responded, quicker than thought, and I spun to the left. Past the shells of offices in my building, past the partially-collapsed exterior wall, across the empty street, and just inside the window of an abandoned storefront, I saw her. Sofia. At that distance, I couldn't see her face, but I could sense her surprise, and then her powerful arms swept up, fingers spread wide and pointing in my direction.

And the building around me began to tremble.

I was already in motion, my 9mm firing as I sprinted across floors that buckled and tore, drywall falling away from internal pillars that were vibrating like strings on an old school instrument. Clouds of brick dust appeared around Silt as my bullets pinged off the wall of the storefront she'd situated herself in. I saw her stagger as one round took her in the shoulder. She grimaced and clenched both of her hands into fists.

And then the whole goddamn skyscraper fell on my head.

Pain. Silence. The absence of sight and sound, so different from the death I'd tasted out there in the desert, in the middle of an ocean that wasn't ocean.

No peace.

No transition.

Just an endless pause.

And then light searing my eyes as I found myself back in my real body, the pod's lid retracting to reveal our staging room.

Even after the techs released me from the restraints, I stayed there, staring up at the ceiling, trying to convince my body that it hadn't just had its organs liquefied and every one of its bones crushed into powder by a twenty-story building.

There were voices arguing—Penelope's voice spiking in anger as Tessa fired back—but the words flowed over me like one of Makara's waves. I forced myself upright with arms that should have been jelly and swung my legs to the floor where—despite everything my mind was screaming at me—they managed to hold me up without issue. Next to the two arguing women, Muse was clutching his belly as if to make sure that his guts were still in their proper place. The little Switch looked seconds away from losing his breakfast.

I ignored all three of them, and slipped into the hall, following the retreating techs. The door to Team Three's room was just starting to open, but I ignored that too. Straight to the elevator and up however many floors to the exit—past biometric security focused only on keeping unauthorized individuals from getting in—and then, *finally*, out into Los Angeles' sunshine.

And just like that, my power came flooding back into me. I let the emptiness chase imaginary pain and its ever-present memory from my body.

CHAPTER 14

It was starting to feel like a cliché; me heading off to brood on the hilltop overlooking the ocean. Problem was, there weren't a lot of other places I could go on campus. My sub-dorm was out, considering I'd spent all the time I cared to with my team that day. The rest of campus wasn't much better. My Academy greys branded me as a Power, which made it impossible to blend in with the normal students.

Now that I'd made second-year, there were probably a few normals happy to hang out if it would net them a job on my staff once I graduated, but fuck that. If I did make it to graduation, I would need support workers, but I didn't want people blowing smoke up my ass just for the opportunity.

And frankly, given the way our team had been performing, graduation was a long way from a certainty.

So instead I was out in the clearing. On the bench. Alone. Again.

When most people think 'orphan', they think 'loner'. And there's something to be said for that. Those of us who grow up in the system can be short on trust and long on 'stay the fuck away from me.' But there's a difference between self-reliance and actually wanting to be alone all the time.

Truth is, most orphanages in the Free States are barely making ends meet, even with the per-head government stipends. That means they're understaffed and overpopulated. As a first-year at the Academy, it had taken me months to get used to having only a single roommate instead of a half-dozen. Having my own room as a second-year was even weirder. And outside of class, I was spending almost all of my free time out here, with only the ocean for company.

Another thing you learn real quick in the system is that everyone is temporary. From one week to the next, you never knew who'd be shipped out to another foster family. Any bonds we made were ephemeral, strings that didn't so much snap as dissolve with distance and time.

But I wasn't at Mama Rawlins' anymore.

I missed Unicorn.

I missed the orphans I'd left behind, from John all the way down to little Nyah.

Most of all, I missed Vibe. I'd spent months with the Empath always underfoot, using me as an emotional nullifier, and even if I'd never quite felt the same way about her as she did me, she'd been a friend. One of a very few.

I didn't begrudge her spending all her free time with Paladin—even if I really, really wanted to—but between her new relationship and Silt's team leader duties, I was spending a lot of time by myself. And as anyone who's dealt with possible mental issues will tell you, that's not a particularly great thing.

That wasn't the only problem, of course, as nice as it would be to pretend otherwise. There was Alexa's ongoing absence. There was Team Five's second colossal failure in as many tries, despite all our preparations. And then there were the two unsolved mysteries in my life; what role Sally Cemetery had played in my Mom's murder and why one of the country's worst Black Hats had sent me to Cape school.

I hadn't heard a word on the first one from the second-years who'd chosen to help. And as for Tyrant? The Net had barely more than a name and the single picture that featured on the Security Council's Most Wanted board. Hell, it felt like I knew the copper-eyed bastard better than those who were supposed to be hunting him.

I was lonely. I was frustrated. I was hurting from phantom pain that my mind still wanted to make real. Most of all, I was angry. Damned if I was going to be anybody's puppet, Sally or Tyrant or even

Bard, but my life hadn't been mine since long before the world knew I was a Crow… since Mom's murder and Dad's incarceration.

I looked at their ghosts, pacing the clearing, silent and blind, unaware of each other even as they orbited about me. My knuckles popped and I released the fists I hadn't been aware I was making. Another long breath out and the emptiness billowed forth to fill me again, pushing away the pain, stilling the bubbling cauldron of *feeling*.

Even though meditation had been the key to unlocking my power, the two states couldn't have been further apart. One was about acknowledging feelings and energy without dwelling on or giving power to them, while the other was about washing those feelings away. Wrapping them in cotton and tossing them aside.

Can't say if my power was the healthier of the two options, but there was no denying its effectiveness. I took the day's irritation, the imaginary pain, and that unexpected burst of loneliness, and I buried them all five feet deep in the dry earth below my bench.

Out of sight, out of mind, and out of my fucking life.

Or so I wanted to think anyway.

That's the problem with all that stuff.

Shit has a way of coming back.

ooo

"Before we graduate, I'm gonna build a statue of you, sitting on that bench," said Silt, as she entered the clearing. "'There sits Skeletor', future students will say. 'Academy graduate and legendary Crow, he spent three years at college and almost all of it was here, cold stone chilling his buttocks.'"

"*Chilling his buttocks?*"

"I'm going to make the statue nude from the waist down. Obviously." She flopped heavily onto the bench next to me and gave me the side-eye. "Don't worry; I'll do the rest of you justice."

"Considering you've never seen me naked, I'm almost scared to ask how."

"Scared? Tough Crow like you? Nah." She grinned. "Anyway, I'll figure something out."

"I'm not going to say no to a statue," I decided, "but shouldn't you be celebrating with Team Three? Extra slices of cake at the cafeteria for everyone?"

"It's cookies today, but yeah. I'll be there in a bit. Just wanted to come check on you, and something told me I wouldn't find you in your sub-dorm." She cleared her throat. "Sorry about... you know... dropping a building on you."

"If you hadn't, I'd have shot you in the face."

"You think? It took you five shots just to wing me."

"I was running. On uneven terrain. Through a collapsing building." I scowled. "Not that I'd have had much chance of holding on to your flag even if I did put you down. Did *anyone* on my team do any damage?"

"Muse did, believe it or not, with that flamethrower of his. And I can't believe the faculty allowed that particular gear request to go through. What's next? A missile?"

A missile sounded pretty good, to be honest. Or maybe a tank. A few feet of armor and a cannon would go a long way to shoring up my team's many issues.

Some of them anyway.

"Poltergeist didn't do anything? Again?" I don't know what I'd expected from a Low-Four, but so far Tessa was sailing comfortably under those expectations.

"She didn't have much of a chance. Orson had himself and Alan cloaked. By the time she even saw Alan, it was too late."

"And Freddy's flamethrower?"

"Cooked Orson. *Through* his shadow. Kind of like how you said that Shadecaster prisoner died down at the Hole."

"I may have told Muse the same story when we found out we were facing your team."

"Well, Orson swears he can still smell his own burning flesh, so I'd say your advice paid off."

"Just not with a victory." I shrugged. "Glad you guys managed one though. I was pretty surprised to hear you'd lost to Orca's team."

"Yeah. Not the way I wanted to start off my glorious career. But weirdly enough, that's what I wanted to talk to you about."

"I thought you came out to check on me."

"I can do multiple things at once, Boneboy. It's called multi-tasking." She grinned again and pivoted on the bench to regard me directly. "I took a peek at the schedule for May, and you're facing Team Two next."

"And?"

"And I thought it was time for a little meeting of the minds. You tell me how Vibe's team beat you, I'll do the same for Orca. My team's got next month off, but I'd like to start prepping for when we face Team One."

"Is that allowed?"

"Gathering intelligence? Yeah. It's a big part of running a real team, even if it's our staff who's normally responsible. It's not cheating to research your enemy." She shot me a funny look. "Besides, since when do you care about what's allowed?"

"I..." I frowned. "I have no idea. I think this school is messing with my brain."

"All those Ethics classes are finally bearing fruit. Isabel Ferra will be thrilled to hear it."

"The only thing that would thrill her is my expulsion. What do you want to know about Team One?"

"How'd they beat you guys?"

"Pretty damn easily." I shrugged at the look she sent me. "We went into the sim blind. No gear. No idea what to expect. Muse powered up Winter and Tessa—"

"Not you?"

"I think the consensus was that I could only kill someone so dead. Boosting my power further didn't make much sense. Anyway, Tessa and Freddy guarded the flag, while Winter took me up above the tree line to search for the other team's base."

"And then?"

"And then Supersonic came in like a bat out of hell and Winter dropped me. I hit every branch on my way down, and found Spectra waiting at the bottom. After she took me out, she helped Supersonic with Winter. Meanwhile Matthew assassinated Tessa with a fucking crossbow, then broke Muse's arms and legs and took the flag."

"Damn."

"Yeah. It was a clusterfuck."

"How did they even find you guys?"

"How did *you* find us?"

"As soon as we entered the sim, I sent Cyclone up into the sky. When Winter flew up, a minute or so later, Erin gave us the general area Penelope had come from. Alan's nose did the rest."

"He smelled us out?"

"Yeah. After more than a year, he knows everyone's scent. It'd have been tough to track you guys from across the city, but with a smaller footprint to search? It was easy."

"Fucking Beast Shifters." I didn't love the idea of Alan Jackson knowing my scent. In fact, it was disturbing as all hell knowing he could find me anywhere on campus. "I guess that makes sense. That's how Team One found us too."

"With Alan's nose?"

"Kayleigh's an Empath."

I watched the realization dawn on Sofia's broad face. "She tracked everyone by their emotions?"

"Yeah. And used the comm units to give updates on our positions. With that first sim being an otherwise empty forest, it must have been easy, but I'm pretty sure she can pull off the same thing in a city these days."

"But I thought her power didn't work on you? Part of that whole dead-man-walking thing."

I really didn't love that particular phrasing.

"I was with Winter until she dropped me. If we'd split up at the start like we did against your team, maybe I'd have been a ghost, but as it was…"

"Shit. So either my team needs to take out Vibe as fast as possible, or we need to sit back and play defense. Splitting up will just make it easy for them."

"Paladin's no match for Alan," I pointed out. "And Orson—creepy bastard that he is—should give you guys first strike if you know they're coming. Olympia might be a problem though."

"Oscuro against Spectra," she mused. "That ought to be a show."

"My money's on Spectra. Lightbringers are nasty."

"Considering you fought Fallout, the biggest, baddest Shadecaster I know of, that says something."

"I didn't so much fight him as stab him in the back. For all the good it did me."

"Even so." She frowned. "This is going to take some serious strategizing. Glad I have two months to figure it out."

"How did your team lose to Orca? She and Stonewall make a pretty good combination, but even so…"

"It wasn't their fighters that were the problem. It wasn't even Ember, who tried to burn down the whole forest."

I racked my brain to try to remember the team's fourth member. "You're saying *Prince* is the reason you lost? What, did he just sing you to sleep?"

"Pretty much."

"Are you serious?" I'd been joking.

"As a Siren-induced breakdown." Silt shook her head. "I sent Alan on the offensive, while the rest of us guarded the flag. Figured he had a pretty good shot at taking out their whole team."

"Not Orca."

She gave me a look I couldn't quite decipher. "Nadia's skilled, Boneboy. Nobody's denying that. But Alan has the edge in power *and* he regenerates. Outside of a sparring pit, that means everything."

"I've seen them fight," I reminded her. "Yeah, she's only a High-Three, but still…"

"Well, we'll have to wait to settle that debate, because Alan made it to the base without encountering any opposition. And the only one left to guard the flag was Johannes, who was already singing."

"And?"

"Alan made it to within about twenty feet and started crying."

"He did what?"

"Cried his eyes out. Even with earplugs in. Collapsed to the ground, curled up in a ball, and then…" She swallowed. "Tore his own throat out."

"Because of a *song*."

"There's no such thing as mind control, but emotion control is pretty damn close."

"Fucking hell."

"Yeah. Once he went down, it was only a matter of time for the rest of us. After Orca took out Orson, I raised walls to keep her and your old roommate out, but they just walked Prince over and he sang me right down."

"You killed yourself too?"

"If I was going to do that, I'd have done it a long time ago." She scowled. "No... but it's hard to keep walls up when you're on the ground laughing your ass off for no identifiable reason. Then Orca came in and the rest was history. As the only flyer on the field, Erin stayed alive, but she couldn't keep them from taking our flag back to their base."

"Sounds awful." I shook my head. "I know this is supposed to be teaching us tactics, but it's a fucking nightmare."

"You having bad dreams, Boneboy?"

"You don't want to know about my dreams, Sofia."

That wiped the grin right off her face.

"Sorry," I said. "Sore subject."

"Because of the Hole?"

"I've had bad dreams as long as I can remember. Even before... you know." I shook off the mood, as best I could. "But I'm going to sleep well tonight."

"Because I dropped a building on your head?"

"Because I think I know how to take down Prince."

CHAPTER 15

I went straight from meeting with Silt to listening to my little flock of first-years complain about the Academy and all of its so-called sadistic practices. As usual, Paco stayed in the background, blending in with his fellow students in a way I'd never managed. And also as usual, neither Lynn nor Lucy said a word unless I dragged it out of them.

Figuratively speaking, obviously. Pretty sure Bard would have frowned on anything else. I didn't particularly like any of my charges, chatty or otherwise, but that wasn't their fault, really. I didn't like most people, and dealing with my imaginary pain didn't help.

All the noise was actually pretty nice though, if I'm being honest.

When our time was up, and I'd given what little advice I had—*don't complain about early mornings because they just get worse* and *never laugh at Amos' jokes* being two of the high points—I finally headed back to the sub-dorm.

Tessa was, yet again, on the couch in the common room. Down the hall, Freddy's door was shut. And from the kitchen…

More noise. And the smell of something baking.

I had words to say to Poltergeist, but she was watching some vid show so intently that even I could pick up on her 'don't talk to me' signals. So instead, I skirted the couch and ducked into the kitchen.

Winter had an apron on over her greys and quilted gloves on her hands. Her long hair was pulled back, twisted up, and tied off, so secure that it didn't budge even when she bent down to pull a pan out of the oven.

That pan was the source of the smell. And that smell was unmistakably chocolate.

The Academy cafeteria was the single greatest part of being a student; a broad, rotating menu with real meat, freshly made everything, and a different dessert every night. But by smell alone, I'd have put the brownies Winter had just pulled out of the oven up against anything the cafeteria could provide.

"What are you doing?"

She moved the pan to a cooling rack and then spun on me with a glare.

"What does it look like I'm doing?"

"Baking?"

"Then why did you feel the need to ask?"

"I was just surprised. They smell amazing."

"Oh." She twitched her narrow shoulders in what could almost pass for a shrug. "When I get stressed, I bake."

"I meditate."

"Nobody asked."

I let my power take the edge off my irritation. "I'm just saying that I get it. We all have ways of coping. I'm guessing Freddy's already drunk?"

"I don't know and I don't care."

As conversations went, this one was even less productive than usual. I nodded agreeably, hoping it would either confuse Penelope or piss her off, and then turned back to the common room.

In the doorway, I stopped. "You baked after our last defeat too, didn't you?"

"Those Perception classes are really paying off." Her sarcasm was as thick as the jar of icing in the bowl on the counter. "So?"

"So where did it go? You didn't eat a whole cake, or cookies, or... whatever... did you?"

"Of course not. I gave it all to the cafeteria."

"What? Why?"

"It's the baking that de-stresses me. Not eating the results. When it comes to eating a few cookies or *not* having to run an extra mile, I'll take the not-running thing every time."

"What about the rest of us? You don't think we might have wanted that choice too?"

"Why would I bake sweets for any of you?" Penelope seemed half-confused and half-incensed. "You all are the reason I'm stuck at the bottom of the class rankings!"

A part of me really, really wanted to tell her what Silt had said—that *she* was the reason they'd found us all so quickly—but I swallowed the words.

Don't know if that was a sign of maturity, the emptiness muffling my emotions, or if I was just too damn tired to deal with the drama.

Whatever the reason, I held my peace and left her with the brownies she wouldn't even eat.

Tessa still didn't make eye contact as I re-entered the common room, but when I dropped into one of the two easy chairs, she sighed, and muted the vid with a wave of her hand.

"If you're here to tell me I'm a shitty leader and it's my fault our team is winless, don't bother. I've already heard it."

"I'm sure you have. And I know who said it. But I'm going to have to disappoint you."

"Meaning what?"

"Meaning I don't think today was your fault. Any more than it was mine or Muse's or even Winter's."

"I'm the leader. I get the responsibility and the blame."

"If you say so. We went into today's sim prepared, with gear and an actual strategy. Everything that happens after that is on all of us. And our opponents."

For the first time, she looked over at me, something undefinable in her eyes.

"What?" I shifted nervously. "Do I have blood on my face or something?"

"Why would you have blood on your face?"

I paused, blinked, and shook my head. "Sorry, my brain is having a hard time separating sim from reality. But why are you looking at me like that then?"

"You're different. Than you were last year, I mean."

"I don't think so."

"No, you are." She frowned. "Still an asshole, most of the time, but different. It's weird."

"Damn. We didn't expect you to figure it out this fast."

"What?"

"Truth is, the real Damian died out at the Hole. I'm just a Body Shifter Bard convinced to come back and enroll in his place."

"Funny." Tessa smirked. "Although it would explain why you've been getting your ass kicked."

"Please. That's one thing that *definitely* hasn't changed."

That won a second smile, which was some kind of personal record. "Winter said she died shortly after Alan and Orson took me and Freddy down. What happened to you? And any idea how they found us?"

"I found their base."

"And?"

"Silt dropped a building on me. Turns out Earthshakers are scary."

"Still beats being eviscerated by the Manimal."

"Agree to disagree." Alan had sent me to the med ward as often as anyone in Combat, but the memory of being crushed by tons of concrete and rebar and whatever else made up a building was too fresh. "As for how they found us… turns out Cyclone saw where Winter took off from."

"Are you serious?! So this was *Penelope's* fault?" Her eyes darted to the kitchen, from which the sound of banging pots and pans could still be heard. Apparently, the Weather Witch was making a second batch of brownies to not give us.

"Sort of. If she had walked the streets a bit before taking off, Orson and Alan might have been sent to a different location to start. Then again, if Winter hadn't had to wait for Freddy to boost her, she might have been in the sky before Erin, and we'd have known their base location instead. As it was, between Cyclone acting as a spotter and Alan knowing what we all smell like—"

"That's fucking creepy."

"Tell me about it. But that's how they found you guys so fast."

"Are you sure?"

"I got it straight from the Earthshaker's mouth."

"I forgot you and Sofia were friendly." She frowned. "We can tweak some things for our next sim. We don't have to worry about flyers though. I managed to get a look at May's matchups when Bard wasn't paying attention, and it looks like we—"

"Are facing Team Two," I finished for her. "Orca, Stonewall, Ember, and Prince. Silt looked too. Apparently, Bard's not doing a great job keeping the schedule secure." Knowing the dean, that was probably on purpose. There was nothing fair about a Cape's job in the real world; maybe he wanted to teach the leaders to seize whatever advantage they could get.

And speaking of advantages…

"Silt also told me how her team lost to Team Two," I added, "and I think I know how to pick up our first win."

When I was done explaining, Poltergeist frowned. "There's a lot riding on your shoulders."

"I don't see any other choice. Besides, the rest of you will be dealing with trying to stop their attack. With Orca involved, that's not going to be fun. Or easy."

"I can handle Orca. I think."

"You think?"

"You're not the only one who's been getting their ass kicked. It's been…"

"Humbling?"

"Irritating." She shot me a scowl. "Anyway, let's work on your idea this week. I can fill in the others—" She paused as another crash and loud clatter came from the kitchen. "—once Muse is sober and Penelope is less… well, Penelope." Tessa waved a hand and the vid started back up again. "Oh. Remember, this is our team's free night. No shifts at the Liquid Hero."

"Good. I've got a mountain of homework."

"From your tutors?"

"Yeah. Not sure why they're bothering, but at least our school schedules have been lighter this year."

"Don't get used to it."

I stopped with one foot in the hallway and turned back. "Why not?"

"Check your Glass. You'll see."

I sure as hell didn't like the sound of that.

ooo

I'd left my Glass in my room, as usual, which my tutors had already given me shit about once that day. I swiped it on and found two notifications. The first must have been what Poltergeist had been referring to... a special assembly with Image Consulting, Incorporated, followed by an eight week course on how to present yourself as a Cape.

Media and community relations. Public speaking. Crisis management. Self-marketing. It was the first class in three semesters at the Academy that threatened to rival Ethics of Superpowers for sheer and complete suck.

On a normal day, I'd have probably dwelled on that feeling of certain and impending doom, but it was just the first of two notifications, and the second was something I'd been waiting on for months.

Tomorrow. Usual time and place. Don't be late, Damian. — A.

There was no return net address or even a header at all, but I was pretty damn sure the A in this case wasn't Alan-fucking-Jackson.

Alexa. Midnight. Shrink Spooky, as Silt liked to say.

The former Cape and current psychiatrist was back.

Finally.

CHAPTER 16

Alexa shared an office with Dr. Gibbings, one of the official counselors for the school. For a long time, I'd thought she *was* Dr. Gibbings, and the former Cape had been more than happy to let me believe that. That had just been the beginning of our trust issues. I'd lied about so much in the second half of the year… meeting with Her Majesty, the Legion tech gun, and most of all, my plan to assassinate my dad in the Hole. I didn't see how I'd had much choice in the matter, but it had turned our appointments into exercises in futility.

When I'd showed up for my first appointment as a second-year, only to find her missing, part of me really thought I'd been the reason for it.

Turns out I was, just not in the way I'd been thinking, but we'll get to that later.

The office was the same as I remembered it; diplomas along one wall, pastel landscape on another, and a comfortable couch in the center of the room, facing the wooden desk. Behind that desk was the woman herself, her pale skin the only thing about her that wasn't black, from her hair to her eyes to her wardrobe. I'd never really noticed how out-of-place the Cape formerly known as Midnight looked there, a monochromatic woman exhibiting iron-clad control in an office designed to be soft and welcoming.

She raised an eyebrow but waited for me to finish my inspection.

"Hello again, Damian." Her voice was slow and smooth, like caramelized sugar.

"Alexa." It felt weirdly good to sit down on the couch across from her. She was the one person qualified to judge my sanity, empowered at my own request to keep me from hurting anyone when I did finally crack. "I missed you."

She cocked her head, looking for a moment like one of the seagulls that dotted campus. "Did you?"

"Yeah. I wasn't entirely sure you were coming back."

"My other job required my focus for the past few months, but my return was never in question, Damian. I have patients here. I will not abandon them."

"I'm actually really glad to hear it."

"What we must discuss is whether you will continue to be one of them."

Shit.

I'd known going in that this would be a tough conversation—in some ways, I'd worried about it more than talking to Kayleigh—but we hadn't even gotten to the part I'd been worried about yet.

"In one of our sessions last year, we talked about the importance of trust," she continued, "and yet that trust seems to have disappeared completely."

"I do trust you," I told her. "Really."

"Recent history suggests otherwise, but I wasn't speaking solely of you."

"Oh." Okay. Maybe we *had* gotten to that part. "Because I left?"

"In part." She studied me for a moment, then shook her head. "Something happened last year, beyond your removal from Nikolai's Combat class. I don't know what it was—because you elected not to share that information with me—but you withdrew. You ignored offers of assistance, from both myself and Professor Farshad—"

"Who?"

"Amos."

"Oh. Right."

"And then, before the school year ended—"

"I left."

"Yes."

"I know that broke one of Bard's rules, but the expulsion board voted to give me a second chance."

"Yes, which is why you are here now." After more than a year, I was almost used to the fact that Alexa never blinked. "Jonathan's school and its rules are for him to manage. My concern is you. I cannot do my job unless you are open and honest with me, and at this point, I'm not sure that is possible."

"Worse," she continued, as I opened my mouth to try to defend myself, despite her being entirely right, "both your departure and my inability to predict it suggest I may already be compromised as an objective observer."

"How so?"

"The Damian I believed I knew, that I'd been working with for over a year, would fight until his last breath for the things that mattered to him. He wouldn't just run away from his problems."

That stung. "I didn't run away! I had to go see my dad."

"The day before school ended?"

"It was the first time the Hole was being opened for visitors. Ever!"

"I am aware. And we both know that it was intended to be a yearly occurrence. Such plans have, of course, been impacted by the prison break, but unless you had prior knowledge of that break...?" She nodded as I shook my head. "Then my question stands. Why leave, putting your future here in doubt, when you knew I was working to find a solution to keep you enrolled at the Academy?"

My hands were clenched in my lap, scar tissue prominent. "I didn't have any money. I didn't have any job skills. If your solution didn't materialize, I was fucked. I didn't run away. I was focusing on what *I* could do."

"And that was going to the Hole, and in doing so, abandoning all hope you had of a future here. These questions were that important?"

"Yeah." I stopped there, and felt the silence build between us, like a wall or a widening chasm. There was no such thing as prophecy in the post-Break world. Like mind control, it was a power Dr. Nowhere had managed to avoid dreaming into existence. But sitting there on Alexa's borrowed couch, I could almost see the future, coming into form. Whatever relationship I had with the former Cape was hanging by a thread. All it would take to disintegrate entirely was for me to do nothing. And then? A new therapist, one who might be unable or unwilling to end me if I did finally go insane. More days alone. More secrets, chasing me to my own grave. And the second mystery, the one I hadn't even told Silt, left permanently unsolved.

Fuck that. Fuck Tyrant. Fuck being a puppet in some Black Hat's unknowable plan.

So I opened my mouth and changed that future with twelve simple words.

"I didn't just go for answers. I went to kill my dad."

ooo

I started with the vision Mom had given me on Christmas, jumped forward to getting Wormhole to take me out to Ludlow, and then the meeting with my dad down in the Hole. Alexa must have been briefed on the prison break itself—either by Bard or by the nameless government agency she moonlighted for—but I gave her the rundown of those events from my perspective. Jaws and his wife. The maniacal Pyromancer known as Red. Firewall, the Technomancer I'd shot. And then Fallout and his buddies from the Legion of Blood. Dad's murder. The pitched battle that took place on the surface, under the hot desert sun. And, of course, Carnage. I told her everything.

"You're withholding something," said Alexa.

Okay. Maybe I hadn't told her *everything*. Her Majesty bringing me the Legion tech gun, and my smuggling that gun into the Hole with me, were secrets I was taking to my grave. And beyond. As far as the world knew, the bad guys had smuggled the gun down into the Hole, along with the device that nullified the dampeners, and I'd just picked it up and used it in the confusion.

"You're right," I admitted, "but it's not my secret to share. I promise I'm telling you everything I can. Everything that matters."

Those black eyes examined me for a long minute, as if I was a book still waiting to be read, and then she nodded.

"Fair enough. So you left school for answers and revenge, and found yourself in the middle of one of the worst disasters that has impacted the Free States in over thirty years?"

"Yeah."

"And managed to not only survive it, but emerge as one of the heroes who kept it from turning into an outright catastrophe?"

"It's not like I planned it that way."

She laughed softly, eyes sparkling. "That is very clear."

"So you believe me?"

"I do. Your story explains a lot. The fact that it actually fits the profile I'd developed doesn't hurt either."

"Your profile says I'd go try to murder my dad and help stop a prison break instead?"

"Not in so many words, but… yes."

"Damn." I wasn't sure how I felt about that. "So what now? Are you going to tell Bard? I can't imagine this is the sort of thing they want in future Capes."

"If anger and a desire for revenge disqualified someone from being a Cape, there would be very few Capes, Damian."

"Yeah, but I actually planned out a murder."

"Yes. And when the moment came, you chose instead to defend and protect."

"I was just trying to survive."

"Are you trying to convince me of that or yourself?"

That question stumped me for a bit. Before I could come up with an answer, she was continuing.

"The post-Break world is cruel and unfair, and the life of a Cape is, in some ways, even worse. It puts us in difficult situations. All we can control is how we respond to those situations. Do I approve of your plan to murder your father? Of course not. If you had carried through with that plan, we would be having a very different discussion."

"Or I'd be dead."

"True." She leaned back in her desk chair, still studying me. "I *would* like to discuss ways in which you can train yourself to react through something other than violence, or at least learn when it is truly necessary, but that is a discussion best saved for another session."

"Another session? So we're... okay?"

"This is our last chance, Damian. No more lies. No more evasions. This office is a space for us to work together, but if we cannot do that, I will recuse myself, for your own good and safety." Her smile came and went. "But yes, I would like to continue our sessions."

"Good." I felt the tension leave me and I sank deeper into the couch. "Because there's something I need your help with."

One dark eyebrow went up, but Alexa said nothing.

"Have you ever heard of Tyrant?"

By the time I'd finished my latest round of explanations, I was pretty sure we'd exceeded our usual session time, but Alexa didn't show any interest in stopping. She leaned forward on her desk, long fingers steepled in front of her.

"The Finder who brought you to the Academy—"

"Not to the Academy. To the testing facilities north of Los Angeles. Mr. Grey left after I was tested, and his mercenary took me the rest of the way."

"Of course. But you're confident that he and Tyrant are the same man?"

"I've only seen the one picture of Tyrant on the Most Wanted board, but..." I nodded. "Almost impossibly average white guy in a grey suit with eyes like copper pennies? If they aren't the same person, then they're twins. I've been trying to find more information, but there's basically nothing in public record. I thought maybe with your side job, you might have better resources."

"Actually, *this* is my side job. That said, I will investigate Mr. Grey and see what I can find. One does not get to be a Finder without leaving behind a paper trail. My handlers should be able to dig up something." Her professional mask slipped for just a second. "Damian, if the two men are one and the same, it raises questions."

"Why one of the worst Black Hats in the country would want me at the Academy? And how he even found me in the first place, since apparently the Free States had no clue I existed? Yeah. I've been asking those questions ever since I found out."

"You may not like the answers."

"I *know* I won't like them. But ignorance is a shitty defense. I need to know why this man is fucking with my life."

"And then?"

"Then I'll put a stop to it." I coughed. "Legally, of course."

"Of course." That smile flashed again. "I might know a few people who could help."

CHAPTER 17

When people talk about being a Cape, they focus mostly on the positives. Being able to fly or shoot bolts of condensed light out of your hands. Having your own toy line or vid series. The battles you win and the lives you save. Elaborately constructed team bases and dedicated staff to deal with all of the non-heroic aspects of being a hero. Even the standard celebrity stuff... the restaurant openings, the autographs, and the adoring public, the kids that look up to you, and the women or men or both who want to show you just what kind of a star they think you are.

Occasionally, you'll run into someone who reminds you of the downside of the job... that nobody survives being a Cape. It's a topic that doesn't get much airplay, but instead shows up in conversations between Capes, in quiet, late night discussions, or, yes, even in orientation speeches at the fucking Academy.

Thanks for that one, Bard.

But on the comparatively short list of the negatives of being a Cape, there's one that nobody ever seems to mention.

Public Relations.

We all got our first taste of that shit at the hands of Image Consulting in May.

I stared across the table at a man in a suit so shiny it would've blinded a crowd at twenty paces if we'd been outside. In the confines of the small office, it instead sort of *shimmered*. I was pretty sure that suit cost more than the car Tyrant had driven to Bakersfield. Maybe even more than the electric motorcycle Her Majesty was so proud of. The jacket was high-collared and buttoned all the way up until it gave just a hint of the shirt and tie underneath. Below the table, it extended past the slim hips of a man who measured every calorie consumed against some sort of master nutrition plan.

In a lot of ways, he was a lesser copy of his boss, Edmund Kisten, the CEO and founder of Image Consulting, who'd given us a slicker-than-shit speech in the same auditorium where Orientation had been held. Where Edmund could have charmed the skin off a snake, my assigned consultant was still a work in progress. The name he'd given when I walked into the office for my consultation was 'Ricky', as calculatingly casual as the megawatt smile he beamed my way.

That smile lasted about five sentences into our conversation.

I'm kind of surprised it was that long, to be honest. Especially given that he'd very consciously avoided offering me his hand.

"Mr. Banach," Ricky tried again, his long-forgotten smile now replaced by a frown and a vertical line between his brows that would no doubt give him a heart attack if he could see it, "I hold a doctorate in Cape relations, and more than seven years of experience in the field, and in my expert opinion—"

"I'm not changing my name," I told him for the fifth time in less than twenty minutes.

"Capes need names that inspire others… or at least lend themselves to merchandising efforts. A Cape name that scares children is antithetical to our whole purpose!"

"I'm a Crow." I kind of liked how he paled every time I said that, so I'd been doing it as much as possible. This time, I actually had a point to go with it. "A different Cape name isn't going to change that."

"Of course not," he argued, "but our goal with your name should be to rebrand you as a protector, not some sort of—"

"Shambling undead beast?"

He swallowed again. "Exactly."

"And how would you do that?" I wasn't changing my name from Walker. Not for anyone or anything. But I was kind of curious.

His smile made a comeback, and he puffed out his chest like he'd just been given the key to the city.

For those of you less versed in pre-Break history, that's something people actually used to do. I can only assume there was some sort of enormous door that key was meant to unlock. Seems weird though.

"The trick is to look to adjacent, but less morally perverse, roles for inspiration."

"Excuse me?"

"What other kinds of people in history and pre-history were known to work with the dead?"

"Morticians."

"Not quite what I—"

"Gravediggers. Pathologists. Embalmers."

"I meant metaphysically."

"Oh." I gave it some thought. The research I'd done on Crows as a first-year was actually coming in handy. "Witch doctors. Mediums." I smirked. "Priests."

"Or shamans." His smile was still in full force.

"Shamans?"

"Speaking with the ancestral spirits? I'd say that qualifies."

"Are they known to raise rotting corpses that eat their victims?"

"Of course not. But as I understand it, you don't do that either. Which is precisely the point."

Ricky had come a little better prepared than I'd expected. For all the good it was going to do him.

"There's already a Cape named Shaman. He's a Weather Witch."

"Well, yes. But I took the liberty of checking the registry and finding some suitable alternatives." He removed a sheet of paper— white and almost as glossy as his suit—and slid it across the table to me.

Maybe Tessa was right and my time at the Hole had changed me. Or maybe I was just curious to see what he'd come up with. Either way, I actually did him the courtesy of reading the list.

"*Captain Kahuna?*"

"Kahuna was a term used for Hawaiian wise men, before the Break and Pele's return." He beamed. "I think it would work. And alliteration always sells."

Things went downhill from there.

○○○

"She wanted me to change my freaking name! Apparently, Poltergeist doesn't meet their family-friendly criteria. Can you even believe that shit?"

The sub-dorm common room was actually almost full when I came in. Muse was in his usual spot in one of the easy chairs, Winter was braiding her hair in the other, and on the couch, next to the currently rioting Tessa, was London, dark-haired, single, and as lovely as ever, even in Academy greys.

"They kind of have a point though, don't they?" asked the Pyromancer. "Aren't poltergeists ghosts that haunt people?"

"By invisibly picking up objects and throwing them! It's perfect! I'm not even the first Telekinetic to use the name, but none of that matters to Sheila and her thousand-dollar glow-up."

I wasn't sure what a glow-up was, unless Tessa's consultant was also a Lightbringer, but it sounded like her initial consultation had gone as well as mine.

"My guy wanted to call me Captain Kahuna," I announced, moving into the room.

London stiffened, as if only now realizing I was there, but Poltergeist just frowned. "Isn't that like… something from the pre-Break surfer days?"

"Ricky says it means wise man."

"He didn't do any research at all on you, did he?"

It was my turn to frown. I was pretty sure I'd just been insulted.

"So?" Tessa continued. "Are you now Captain Kahuna?"

"Fuck that. I'm Walker, you're Poltergeist, and Image Consulting can blow it out their collective asses."

"My guy thought Muse was pretty good," said Freddy. "Although I think he was assuming I'd be a woman, for some reason.

Still, the whole meeting took like five minutes. It may have been the least awful thing I've had to do since coming to the Academy."

"This stuff matters," said Winter. "And Cape names do too."

"You would say that." I rolled my eyes. "How long did you stalk the registry before Winter became available?"

"I'd been keeping tabs on it since I was six." She scowled when we all stared at her. "What?"

"How did you even know you were a Power at six?" For most of the country, powers testing was part of their academic career, but it usually happened years later, around puberty. My power showing up when I was nine actually made me a bit of an outlier.

"I didn't. I just assumed I would be one. And Winter is an awesome name, so I wanted to make sure I got it, once—"

"Once the previous owner croaked."

"Don't be crude, Damian." She finally finished her braid and tossed it over one shoulder. "Anyway, my consultant was a gentleman and he loved my name. Obviously."

"You got assigned a guy?" London sounded jealous. So much for swearing off men after the whole Santiago near-disaster.

"Yeah. And he was seriously h-o-t hot." For some reason, she darted a look in my direction. "Sorry."

"I hope the two of you are very happy together and have lots of terrifying children," I told her. "What about you, London?"

For some reason, the Pyromancer went corpse-white. She climbed to her feet, and left without a word.

"What the hell?" Tessa's eyes flashed in that way that told me I was just a second or two away from a telekinetic beating. "You *know* she just got over a pregnancy scare. Why would you ask her that?"

"What?"

"Every time I think you've maybe, just maybe turned a corner, you have to go piss in everyone's pool." Because in Poltergeist's world, everyone had swimming pools.

"I was asking how her fucking consultation went! Not whether she wanted children!"

"Oh." The fire went out of her green eyes just as quickly. It probably said something that she actually believed me, but I wasn't sure what. "Well, that's not how it came across."

"You could really do with thinking more before you speak," agreed Winter, in yet another moment of colossal obliviousness.

"Fine. Whatever." I leaned against the arm of the couch on the opposite end from Tessa and looked over at the Telekinetic. "Can you explain things to London? It's not like she talks to me."

"I guess I could. We're taking a shuttle into the city tonight for dinner anyway. Not that I'm inviting you to come along."

"I couldn't even if you did invite me. I'm not allowed off campus."

"*The Hole* doesn't count as off-campus?"

"Welcome to part of the reason I was almost expelled."

"As if," muttered Muse. I waited for clarification, but the little Switch stayed silent.

Tessa shook out her dark curls and rolled her eyes. "I'll take care of it. That's what team leaders are for, right? It's better than sitting and arguing with Sheila about my name."

Winter beamed. "Our next consult won't be about names."

"Thank God," Poltergeist and I both said at the same time.

"We're going to be designing our costumes!"

It'd be a miracle if I made it through the next eight weeks without killing Ricky or getting expelled.

Again.

CHAPTER 18

"Is it true you see ghosts?" Paco was sprawled in the grass next to the bench where I met my first-years every week. I'd gotten there a bit early for once and was surprised to find him already waiting.

"It's part of the ongoing thrill ride of being a Crow."

"All ghosts?" The Summoner's voice was studiously bland.

"Pretty much." I spared a glance for the handful of mute spirits visible around us, Mom, Dad, and Unicorn among them. "But unless they've got some sort of personal connection to me, they tend to stay where they died."

"Good."

"Is there something you want to talk to me about?" I asked, doing my best Alexa impression.

"Shit no," he replied, in a perfect Damian impression.

"Fair enough. Just saying—"

"Because it's total bullshit, Shawn!" said Jacinda. She switched her glare from her brother to me as the two came marching over. "Did they even talk to you first?"

"About... what?"

"About the damn movie!"

After two months of meetings, my first-years' language had collectively gone to hell. I just knew Bard was going to find a way to blame me for that.

I looked to Shawn for an explanation.

"They're doing a full-length vid on the battle at the Hole."

"Another one?"

"Not a news documentary," said Jacinda. "A real movie! And you're not in it!"

"As a character, she means. They're swapping in the Scarlet Dynamo instead."

"It's total bullshit," repeated Jacinda. "Dynamo wasn't even there!" She frowned at me. "Why aren't you as pissed off about it as me?"

"I didn't know it was happening until thirty seconds ago," I reminded her. "Besides, there's nothing I can do about it. And it's not like they had much choice in the matter."

"Much choice about what?" asked Reid, looking up from his Glass as he ambled down the walkway.

"Walker got cut out of the movie they're making on the battle at the Hole," said Paco.

"That sucks. Who'd they swap in instead?"

"The Scarlet Dynamo."

"Nice!" The Stalwart sent me an apologetic shrug. "That guy's awesome. You all saw him in *Street Vengeance 5*, right? Guts everywhere!"

Apparently, I was the only one who'd missed that movie. Most likely, it'd been released while I was busy trying not to flunk out as a first-year.

"Why'd you say they don't have a choice in the matter?" pressed Jacinda.

"I'm not a Cape. Not yet. They don't have licensing rights to use my name or likeness. And until I graduate and become official, I don't either."

"But they did the movie on Aspen!"

"Major Disaster's Very Bad Day?" I'd actually seen that one. "Yeah, but it was filmed years after the actual event. She'd already graduated by then. And gotten acting lessons, I guess."

"It's *still* bullshit," insisted Jacinda.

"So is life," mused Paco from the grass.

Everyone finally settled down as Lynn arrived. I took a look around. We were still missing someone. "Where's Lucy?"

"She wasn't feeling well," said Lynn, hard eyes drilling into me.

"Let her know to go to the clinic if she needs to," I said. "Better that than missing one of Nikolai's classes."

The Technomancer didn't grace me with a reply.

Pretty sure she wasn't crying any tears over my being written out of my own movie.

ooo

The next day, the subject of mentorship came up during my session with Alexa. Truth was, it was really fucking nice having her back on campus. I'm sure there's some sort of rule against being friends with your therapist, but having a dedicated hour every week to vent or ask questions was kind of priceless.

It didn't occur to me until much later that I was giving my first-years that very same thing.

"I'm not sure what Bard was expecting me to do with them," I concluded. "Mostly, I just listen. It's not like I have a fucking instruction guide on how to get along at the Academy."

"I suspect that's all they need. Being able to talk to someone who just survived what they're going through has its own value."

A thought struck me. "Is Paco one of your other patients? Francisco, I mean."

"If he was, that would be between him and me."

Which, to me, meant yes.

"Well, good. If he is, I mean. He seems way better adjusted than me, but something tells me he's seen some shit."

"It sounds almost like you care, Damian," she teased me gently.

"He hasn't caused me any grief. And I get what he's going through. First Summoner at the Academy? Can't help but kind of want him to succeed."

"And the others?"

"They're alright, I guess. Really young, but… yeah. I'm not a teacher or anything—and thank fuck for that—but I think they've all got a good shot. You know Jacinda and Shawn will always watch each other's backs. Reid's got it made as a High-Three Stalwart. Lucy…" I shrugged. "Hard to say."

"Lucy David?"

"Yeah. She's more timid than I expected. Maybe Erik and Nikolai being the only Titans I know has skewed my perspective."

"Not all Titans are alike, it's true."

"And then there's freaking Lynn." I shook my head. "Weird enough to have a Technomancer choose to attend the Academy, but she really doesn't seem to like me."

"Lynn Ostovich is in your mentorship group?" For some reason, her voice had sharpened.

"Yeah. She's not at all happy about it either. Maybe a Crow killed her family, like Olympia's?"

"Actually, her grandfather gave his life to protect one." Alexa's black eyes met mine from across the room. "In February. Out at the Hole."

I put two and two together and didn't at all like what I came up with. "She's the White Knight's granddaughter? Seriously? Why wouldn't Bard tell me that?"

"Maybe he thought you already knew?"

"Or maybe this is another of his bullshit missions."

"Missions?"

"Like with Olympia last year. Suddenly, it was my job to help her get over her fear of Crows."

"And how did that work out?"

"She realized she could melt the flesh off my bones before I even twitched," I retorted. "And then proceeded to do just that in our team battle back in March."

"That sounds like success to me."

"Tell that to our team ranking," I muttered. "It's not the same thing anyway. Lynn actually has a reason to hate me. Her grandfather's dead because of me."

"Her grandfather is dead because Carnage killed him. Don't diminish his sacrifice by taking responsibility for it."

"Did anyone ever get killed protecting you? When you were a Cape?"

"I lasted four years as Midnight, Damian, and I had three teammates die during that time."

"And were those deaths your fault?"

"No. No more than the White Knight's death was yours." She shook her head, dark eyes never leaving mine. "People talk about battles in terms of victory or defeat, as if the winners emerged unscathed. You know as well as I do that it's not how these things go. All survivors have scars."

"So what should I do with Lynn?"

"What do you want to do?"

Which was no help at all. In some ways, all therapists were the same, even ex-Cape and current government assassin Shadecaster therapists.

"I'm going to talk to her," I decided, "and hope she doesn't invent a giant murderbot to make me pay for it."

"As a first-year, I suspect murderbots might be beyond her reach."

"There's only one way to find out."

○○○

After my last near-debacle in the first-year dorm's common room, I'd resolved to never, ever go in there again. That's how I found myself lurking outside the building like some sort of deranged stalker. Wish I could say I blended in and didn't cause a stir, but a second-year in his Academy greys, waiting just a few feet away from the dormitory's front door?

Yeah, I got noticed.

"If you're here to ask out Sherry, you're too late," said the loudmouth asshole Titan who'd challenged me on my previous visit. "Go creep on the women in your own class."

"I don't know who Sherry is, and I don't care," I told him. "I get that you have some weird chip on your shoulder about me, but truth is, I don't remember your name either. I'm not here for her and I'm definitely not here for you."

"What if I'm here for you?" He cracked his neck, looking down on me like a bug that needed squashing.

"Carnage was two feet taller than you, two-hundred pounds heavier, and moved faster than I could even see," I told him in a tone as mild as the Los Angeles weather, "and they needed a dustpan to collect what was left of him when I was done. I don't have a problem with you, beyond you being the stereotypical loudmouthed motherfucker, but if you'd like to start something, that's your decision. You wouldn't be the first Academy student to die on campus."

If Unicorn's ghost could actually hear me, I'd have felt a bit bad about that last line, but the spectral ginger was wandering the quad, as mute and mindless as ever.

I'm sure the first-year had some kind of retort planned—his kind always do—but before he could get to it, I spotted Lynn, making her way down one of the campus walkways.

"Study hard. Stop drinking too much. Don't be an asshole." Having done my duty as a second-year mentor, I left the Titan behind and went to intercept the woman I'd come to see.

Lynn spotted me right off and I watched her visibly grapple with the idea of taking a hard right and heading in the opposite direction. Instead, she set her shoulders and marched in my direction.

"If you want to say something to Lucy, she's still in her dorm room," she said, biting off the words.

"I was looking for you, actually."

"Why?" She went white as some stray thought occurred to her. "I'm seriously not interested."

"What?"

"At all."

I was starting to think I had some sort of a reputation. Which made no sense since I hadn't even kissed a girl since enrolling at the Academy. I shook my head. "That's not what I meant. I just wanted to talk."

"About what?"

I ushered her over to a bench and sat down. I don't do gentle well—Silt says my bedside manner is better suited for the things lurking under that bed—but I made an effort. "About your grandfather."

"Oh *now* you want to talk about him? Two months after I introduce myself? Why? What makes today so special?"

"I just found out who you were."

"What?"

"You don't have the same last name. I had no fucking clue."

"He was my mom's dad. Obviously." Her voice trailed off. "I thought you knew."

"I'm an asshole, but I'm not that kind of asshole." I paused and reconsidered. "Depending on who you ask, I guess."

"Oh. So what did you want to say?"

Her eyes were a watery blue. I don't think I'd ever noticed that all the times they'd been trying to burn a hole right through my chest.

"Just… that I'm sorry for your loss," I told her. "He was a brave man and an amazing fighter and I'd be dead if it wasn't for him."

She held my gaze, not looking away, even as watery blue became water-filled blue.

"I know it's a shitty trade. A hero for a Crow. A grandfather for some stranger you probably hoped you'd never meet."

"At least you avenged him." Her voice had gone thin and reedy.

"Yeah."

"It doesn't make it feel any better though."

"I watched my mom get murdered fourteen years ago," I told her, "and still dream of it. I don't think it's supposed to ever feel better. It's just a thing we carry."

"They sent me his sword. What was left of it." She scowled. "I'm a Technomancer. What am I supposed to do with a broken sword?"

"I used it to stab Fallout in the back."

"You did *what?*"

I guess they'd left that bit out of the vids. I nodded. "Didn't put him down, unfortunately, but I bet he had a hard time walking it off. If I find him after I graduate, I'll finish the job."

"Good." Her smile was sharp and fierce and faded as fast as it had appeared. "Saving people is why my grandpa got in the Cape business. Before there even was an Academy. He wouldn't have seen it as a shitty trade, you know." She swallowed, and tears streamed down her cheeks. "But I still miss him."

If you'd told me two months earlier that I'd be giving Lynn Ostovich a hug as she bawled her eyes out into my chest, I'd have thought you'd bought a bad batch of stim-weed. But that's the thing about the future. Shit's not set. We all burn our crazy, winding paths into the darkness and then take our rest with the voiceless dead.

CHAPTER 19

For the third time in as many months, the pod's lid slid shut, blocking out the light. I closed my eyes, then re-opened them to find myself on my feet in another forest, its trees smaller than they'd been in the first sim, but far more dense.

I know what you're thinking. Fighting a Pyromancer in a forest? That's some serious fucking bullshit.

Luckily, we had plans for that.

As soon as she appeared, Winter looked to the sky, eyes glowing. Clouds gathered above the treetops and within moments, a steady drizzle had started.

It was going to make running miserable, but at least we wouldn't have to worry about Ember starting a forest fire.

The Weather Witch was all in white, from a high-collared, hip-length tunic to leggings and knee-high leather boots that only someone with flight powers would dare wear into combat. Her waist-length hair was braided, and a white domino mask did the bare minimum to hide her identity.

Next to her, Tessa wore a full-length bodysuit in a green so dark it was almost black below a hooded cloak that actually was. The liner of that cloak was green just like the bodysuit, dozens of looped, folded, and loosely pinned ribbons that the Telekinetic could use as weapons of last resort should the five swords planted in the forest earth around her prove insufficient.

Muse's costume was something straight out of a period vid; brown vest over a button-up shirt with wide pants tucked into worn leather boots. He'd topped off the ensemble with a bowler hat and goggles, like he was some sort of ancient aeronaut. I wasn't sure what any of it had to do with his power, but he seemed comfortable. In place of the flamethrower, he held an assault rifle.

I couldn't see how it would do him any good against Stonewall or Orca, but so far, Freddy was the only one on our team to take out an opponent. I wasn't going to question his choices.

Tessa looked my way, visibly started, and then rolled her eyes. "I have no idea how you got your consultant to agree to that costume."

"It's our new marketing strategy. Appeal to the disaffected youth of the Free States." I wore a bodysuit like Poltergeist's, although black instead of green, with combat boots on my feet. I'd added composite plating across my chest and arms, and a 9mm was holstered at my waist.

That wasn't what Tessa was talking about though. In place of a domino mask or goggles, I'd gone with a full mask. Most of it was the same black as my bodysuit, but across the face was a skull in white. My eyes were the only part exposed, tombstone grey almost lost in the empty sockets of the mask's motif.

I'd stolen the idea from Her Majesty and that creepy smiley face decal on her motorcycle helmet. Unlike a helmet, my mask didn't restrict my field of view at all. More importantly, it looked badass.

Our first sim in costume. It felt momentous.

"You two kind of match," said Winter, pointing to Tessa's green bodysuit and black cape and my black bodysuit and green armor plating.

I hadn't realized it until she pointed it out, but she was right.

"Ricky suggested the green," I grumbled.

"Sheila added the black." Poltergeist shook her head. "Whatever. You know the plan. Good luck."

"You too. You know they'll be coming."

I reached under my mask, slid the single monocle we'd added to our equipment list over my right eye, and vanished into the woods.

Knowing what we did about Team Two and their past strategies, we'd made some changes. Winter was staying behind with Poltergeist and Muse, to help them withstand the attack that was no doubt coming from Orca, Ember, and my old roommate, Stonewall. That left me as our sole attacker, which meant I not only had to find and defeat Prince on my own, I couldn't afford to encounter any of his teammates on the way.

Finding him was actually the easy part. Once I'd covered some distance from our base, I tossed the palm-sized drone I'd been holding in my other hand up into the air. It ascended to just above the tree height, and then sped forward. I watched the camera footage that was being piped to my monocle for just a bit before closing that eye and focusing instead on making my way through the forest.

Cameras were a nice touch, but we'd known going into the sim that, regardless of environment, it would be hard to find Prince visually. If this had been an urban environment, he'd have found some place to hide—under a desk or inside a closet, maybe, where nobody could reach him from outside his song's range. In the forest, such hiding places took the form of tightly-packed trees or even the occasional shrub. It didn't take much to defeat the drone's limited image recognition software.

That's why the drone wasn't actually looking for Prince. It was listening for him. The only way for him to defend his flag was to sing, and the only way to ensure that nobody took him out before he was ready was to start singing as soon as he made it into the sim, and to keep singing until we were all dead and gone.

And nothing carries in a forest empty of wildlife like the voice of a Siren.

It wasn't long before the drone had located him. When it did, it ascended even higher into the sky. I blinked as the footage shifted to a top-down view of the forest, with a blinking icon identifying my location, and a red X signifying my target.

It took me more time than I want to admit to figure out my heading, but once I had, I let the emptiness fill me. I slid through the trees, doing what I could to stick to the shadows, and made my way forward.

Twice, I thought I heard someone else, rushing in the opposite direction. Each time, I froze and held my breath. Eventually the sounds faded, leaving me free to work my way forward again.

By the time I was able to hear the faintest sounds of Prince's song, I was wet and cold and miserable. Joining those sensations on the very fringe of my consciousness, exiled by my own power, was an emotion: fear.

Fuck if I wanted to end up in the dirt like Alan Jackson, tearing my own throat out. I'd rather deal with another fucking building.

It was time to see if my bet paid off.

I squared my shoulders and walked into the song.

The sound grew as I closed in, and with it the emotions Prince was pushing. Deep-seated, soul-crushing self-loathing. *You're nothing*, it told me. *Worse than nothing. A blight on the planet. A danger to all that you love. Better to end it now while you can. Feed the earth. Let something good come of your miserable existence.*

Funny thing is, none of those thoughts were new. Not for me. Not for almost ten years, since the Jacobsens, since Mom's return. Can't say for sure if that familiarity would've helped me stand up to Prince's song or if it would have made it that much more devastating. There was no way to know, because my emotions were cold and distant stars, barely even visible in the vacuum of space that I had become.

My power was controlling my body, and I was controlling my power, and the wordless tune of my opponent was just another piece of stimuli, identified, cataloged, and discarded as meaningless data.

I rounded the last tree and found Prince leaning back against its trunk, eyes closed, mouth open wide as the song poured forth. His costume was one of those tuxedos you still see in older vids, complete with bow tie and a red sash around his midsection. His arms were at his side, hands clenched, but there was a gun in his lap. Next to him was their team's flag, red as blood.

Not sure how he heard me under his song, but his eyes shot open, wide with shock. He reached for the weapon in his lap, but he was a long way from Orca's speed, or even Paladin's. I had my own 9mm out and leveled long before he could bring his gun to bear.

I didn't have anything against Johannes, even after he and Orca had gone to the Remembrance Day dance together. The Siren did his thing and I did mine and that's how most days went.

Still felt good to pull the trigger though.

ooo

I'd never seen what happened to us in the sim after we 'died', mostly because I was the one always getting killed. Got to be honest, it was a bit fucked up reaching around Prince's body to take their team's flag. Death and killing were both unfortunate parts of being a Cape, and everyone knew it, but the Academy was really putting that shit front and center early.

Guess maybe they wanted to see how we'd handle it before actual lives were on the line, but it seemed a bit much.

I tucked the flag behind one of the armor plates on my chest and headed back for the base, slipping and sliding through the increasingly wet forest. The drone had roughly a quarter of a charge left, so I'd have to hurry or be stuck trying to find my teammates on my own.

The storm still raging told me that Winter remained active, but that was as much information as I had. Thanks to the gear restrictions, I'd had to swap out my comm unit for the drone. I didn't like being out of the loop, but there hadn't been much choice in the matter. And it had gotten me to Prince. Now, I just needed to get Team Two's flag to our base.

The drone ran out of charge just before we made it back, swooping in out of the sky to return to my open palm. By then, I could hear more than just the storm, and didn't need the little bot's help. I tossed it and the monocle aside.

What had been another stretch of forest when we first loaded into the sim was now a clearing, full-grown trees shattered and tossed aside like toys. On the far side of that clearing was a very dead Muse, half his body blackened and smoking, and some sort of metal shards embedded in his chest and head. It looked like he'd gone down firing though; two-dozen feet away was London's own corpse, riddled by bullets. Winter was darting about in the air like a drunken hummingbird, raining down lightning when there was space and opportunity, and below her, Poltergeist was fighting both Orca and Stonewall.

My former roommate was fully shifted into his massive stone form, but he spun helplessly in the air, held by one of those telekinetic hands Tessa delighted in using to slap me around. Two of the five swords Poltergeist had brought were in pieces on the ground, but the remaining three wove through the air between her and Orca, a storm of steel to match what Winter was creating with wind and lightning.

So far, Orca was untouched. She flowed aside from Tessa's latest strike, dodged under the two swords that had been waiting for just that move, and sent another of those metal stars flickering through the air at the Telekinetic. Without a shield to hide behind, I was pretty sure Poltergeist was about to die.

Instead, one of the ribbons in her cloak unfurled and slapped the projectile out of the sky.

Three swords and a two-thousand-pound stone man, and Tessa *still* had power left over to defend herself with. If that didn't show the difference between a Four and the rest of us, I wasn't sure what would.

And then, as if my thought had been a challenge, she waved a hand. A loose mass of fallen branches swept from the forest for Orca's back, and the shattered remnants of Poltergeist's other two swords leapt up from the opposite direction.

The Stalwart danced through the maelstrom of swords and branches, moving like water, finding impossible openings to squeeze through, but even Nadia was human. As she ducked under one sword, spun away from another, and flipped over the third, one of the broken sword pieces pierced her calf.

She still managed to throw herself to the side, avoiding the follow-up projectiles, but the easy flow of her dance had, for just a moment, been shattered. Fifteen feet away and directly behind her, I would never have a better shot.

I raised my 9mm, started to squeeze the trigger...

And couldn't do it.

If you've been here since the beginning, if you're one of the ghosts that came along at the start of my story, you know I'd had a crush on Nadia since our very first combat class. The blonde Stalwart didn't return my feelings—had never even seemed to consider returning them—but something in me balked at the thought of shooting her in the back. Even in a sim. Even when she was the enemy.

Pretty sure I was going to hear about it from Nikolai when he reviewed the vid. Probably Jessica, too. Our professors had stressed, over and over again, that hesitation in the field would get us killed, yet here I was, doing just that, even with the emptiness of my power filling me. Hardass Crow who'd just executed a Siren now making the one mistake every Cape gets warned about.

Thankfully, Winter didn't have that problem.

The clearing went white, light so bright that even after it was over, I found myself blinking away tears and after-images. I heard Tessa grunt in effort, saw a large shape that must have been Jeremiah get lifted higher into the air, and then more light, a half-dozen times in as many seconds, followed by a massive impact as my former roommate's scorched and smoking corpse hit the ground.

Penelope was a pain in the ass, but I was happier than ever that she was our pain in the ass.

Still struggling to see, I yanked out the other team's flag with one hand and stumbled into the clearing.

Team Five had won a match.

Finally.

CHAPTER 20

To say the mood in our sub-dorm improved after that was a massive understatement. By the time I came back from meeting with my first-years, even Freddy was almost happy, having shaken off his own death enough to appreciate that our team was no longer winless. Penelope and Tessa were on the couch, chatting instead of sniping at each other, and nobody met me with a scowl as I took Winter's usual seat.

I didn't even make a show of brushing away any of the long white hairs that dotted the chair's backrest and arms.

Winning really does cure all ills.

They were busy recounting their experiences in the Training Grounds, compliments flying left and right, but Tessa turned to me after a bit. "Done with your mentorship and your tutors? I'm dying to hear how everything went down with Prince!"

I hadn't realized that Winter or Muse knew about my tutors or the first-year program until I saw their faces just then, but I couldn't find it in myself to care. Like everyone else, I was floating high.

"It went exactly as planned."

"His song didn't affect you at all?"

"Nah. Good thing too, because it was pretty nasty. Not the sort of thing I'd expect from a guy whose costume is a tuxedo. Anyway, the drone helped me track him down, my power shielded me from his, and—"

"Boom. Death-touch," murmured Muse.

"Actually, I shot him." I shrugged at the looks I was getting. "A bullet's faster than I am. Seemed easier. I made it back in time to see you two take out Orca and Stonewall. I can't believe you managed to pick Jeremiah up, Tessa. What does he weigh in stone form? Two thousand pounds?"

"At least." She tossed back her dark curls. "I tried to do the same with Nadia, but she's fast. And slippery."

"Lightning's faster," smirked Winter.

"Hell yeah, it is!" beamed Tessa. "That's teamwork for you."

"And you took out Ember?" I asked Muse.

"Yup." He managed a grin, toasting me with the drink in his hand. "Right before Nadia wiped me off of the board. Next sim, I want to swap my comm unit out for something that helps keep me alive. It's not like I ever leave base."

"That's a good point." Poltergeist nodded from the couch. "We'll think of something."

"Bringing the drone was smart," said Winter.

"That was all Damian's idea," said the Telekinetic.

"It sucked not being able to hear what was going on with you all, but…" I shrugged. "It was worth it to be able to find Prince. I got the idea from one of my first-years, believe it or not. She's a Technomancer—"

"Oh! I know her!" Winter sat up straight. "Lynn, right?"

"You've met?"

"Only in passing. When I saw there was a Technomancer among the first-years, I was curious. It's nice to finally see one of them choose civic duty over grotesque amounts of wealth. So far, she hasn't even come close to my GPA as a first-year."

Normally, someone would've made a comment about Penelope's obsession with grades, but this time, we all just let it slide.

Victory was sweet. Life was good.

○○○

That night, by sheer coincidence, we shared a shift at the Liquid Hero with Team Two. Orca's team took the defeat a hell of a lot better than we'd been taking ours and the mood was festive. The bar was packed, but that was normal. It wasn't until I spotted some of my first-years in the crowd that I realized this was the annual night when their class got free admission.

The previous year, Jeremiah had used the opportunity to pump me for information on my family and childhood. Now, he was out front, working the door, while London and I carried drinks from the bar to booths and tables. Nadia and Tessa were behind the bar in matching little black dresses that should've been illegal. Winter was our nominal inside bouncer, but spent most of her time talking to a table of third-year men. With the third-years just a few weeks away from starting their internships or joining the Mission for a multi-month sojourn into the Badlands, it seemed like a wasted effort, but Penelope was going to Penelope.

That left Prince and Muse splitting bathroom duty. It broke the whole 'one guy, one girl' rule, but the team leaders had finally realized it was easy enough to just close a given bathroom for cleaning and avoid the issue entirely. I'd expected that realization to be accompanied by my own permanent shift back to toilet duty, but so far, the standard rotation of duties had continued. And that didn't suck at all, even if I did stand out in the crowd in my Academy greys.

I carried another tray of screwdrivers over to the booth of normal women in the corner. They were all freshmen or sophomores, I was guessing, dressed up like they were going to a vid premiere, and loud enough for any three booths. They quieted down as I arrived, more than a few faces going beet red for some reason, but I was in way too good a mood to be bothered by it. As I passed out glasses, I winked at the last woman, a blushing blonde in a green tank top that did amazing things for her tan and cleavage.

One of her friends smacked me on the ass as I left.

Don't know if they knew who or what I was. Maybe they didn't care. Vodka can have that kind of effect, I'm told.

This job was sweet. Life was good.

○○○

The rest of the night went like that. I got more smiles than I'd seen in the previous month, as if our team's cheer had infected the entire bar. I'd have thought Prince was influencing things, but that sort of manipulation would get him expelled, and the Siren spent most of the night around the corner anyway, chatting with Muse.

On most nights at the Liquid Hero, there were a few students who drank too much and got sick, others for whom alcohol was an excuse to get aggressive, and still others who would need help getting home. This night was different. Peaceful. Celebratory. I kept a wary eye on my first-years, sitting on the second floor with others from their class, but everyone seemed to be having a great time. Lucy was nowhere to be found, but the rest were sticking to beer and spending more of their time laughing than drinking.

As the night continued, I started bringing out glasses of water with the alcohol orders. Nadia was mobbed at the bar, almost entirely by male students, but handled the rush of orders with a Stalwart's usual grace. Part of me was surprised to find a similar crowd at Tessa's end of the bar, but when the Telekinetic wasn't throwing people and threats around, she was plenty attractive in her own way. That hair with those eyes and tonight's dress?

Like it or not, there was a reason they were working the bar. I still didn't know where the money we made went, but it was going to be a profitable night.

I dropped off a tray of water glasses, got a second smack on the ass—the closest I'd come to sex in well over a year—and headed back for one more round. Behind the bar, Tessa had poured out a row of shots and was handing them out to the members of our team and Team Two as we each came by.

It had been a long day, and my feet were hurting, but life was good. After fifteen months at the Academy, I finally belonged. I had a team. We didn't entirely suck. Life as a Cape had never felt more attainable.

If any of you ever make it back to the land of the living, watch out for hope. It's one hell of a drug. It tells you exactly what you want to hear, and only time and experience will prove if those words were lies.

That night, I had the dream for the first time.

○○○

I opened my eyes on a monochromatic sky; layers of clouds in black, grey, and white hanging low, blotting out any hint of blue. My sub-dorm was gone, my bed swapped out for a rectangle of padded foam, laid out in the grey dirt. The occasional pile of rubble was the only sign that there had ever been walls here, dust thick on fragments of stone. Exposed to the elements, dust shouldn't have been able to accumulate like that, but the air was deathly still. The clouds above me refused to shift, as if the world were a painting, or this was a single moment, unmoored from the passage of time.

I climbed to my feet, free of the usual aches and pains from life at the Academy, and picked my way through the rubble. There wasn't a soul in sight. No birds. Not even the occasional insect. I knelt for a second, dug my hand into the earth, but found nothing but fine grey dirt. No worms. No beetles. Not even any roots or weeds.

I kept walking.

It wasn't until I reached the forest, gnarled limbs stretched outward to that cloud-filled sky, that I realized where I was. Even the pine trees were bare, and the once-familiar woods looked like nothing so much as a cemetery, stretching across the western side of what had once been a campus. I touched the bark and found it cold and hard, like stone.

A voice in my head told me I was dreaming, but its jabbering was a distant thing, the sense of wrongness and panic muffled and easily ignored. I made my way through the petrified forest to the clearing I knew so well. The bench, at least, was as I remembered it, if covered in that same scattering of fine dust. I stepped past it to look on the Pacific.

And that was when I saw them.

At the bottom of the hill, past the shattered remnants of what had been the Academy's exterior wall, they waited in silence; row after row of the dead, encircling the campus. A city's worth of Walkers, shoulder to rotting shoulder, packed in so tightly that they moved as one, swaying back and forth below me Their ranks stretched to the distant shoreline, and behind them, the ocean had been replaced by a sea of flickering light. Thousands upon thousands of ghosts, shapes bleeding into one another, forms shifting despite the absent wind.

The voice in my head spoke up again, but its words were indistinct. Something snapped under my feet. Looking away from the legion of dead, I crouched to brush away that same strange grey dirt, to dig up whatever it was I had stood upon.

It was a bone, big enough to be human, cracked in half by my weight. As I lifted it from the dust, I spotted more of them, scattered about me. Halfway down the hill, a shattered skull lay sideways in the dirt, staring in my direction. Its jaw was partially detached, hanging open in a way that anatomy had never intended.

As I looked to the ranks of the dead, energy began to beat against me, noise that was not noise, sound that was felt instead of heard. The silent world shuddered with its beat. I'd felt this once before, on the night Sally Cemetery came to visit, but the timbre of that sensation had been different. What had once felt like an accusation or a question I couldn't answer now had a rhythm to it, in and out, rushing forward to lap against the emptiness of my spirit like waves from the absent ocean.

It didn't feel like hatred or fear or even voiceless rage.

It felt like adulation.

CHAPTER 21

I woke to emptiness, to that void of power filling every inch of my body. For a moment, I was frozen, trapped in the unanswered question of where I was. Who I was. What I was doing and why.

Then the hum of the overhead air conditioning filtered into my brain, followed by snores heard through the interior wall I shared with Muse. My eyes pieced together the darker shadows that were my room's furniture. My nose picked up the smell of alcohol and stim-weed that had followed me home after a night working at the Liquid Hero.

All those minor details trickled in, one by one, each a brick of concrete data that I used to build a wall around my sense of self. Finally, the emptiness of my power drained away, and the sensations it had been muffling poured in. Sweat on my skin. Heartbeat like a rabbit. Fear as I remembered my dream; an Academy empty of all but me, legions of dead waiting on my word.

I lay there and shook for a bit. Maybe that sort of reaction doesn't stack up with your image of who I'm supposed to be? That's your problem, not mine. I'd had bad dreams as long as I could remember, every night I could remember, and not a one of them had been like this one, like something sidestepping my consciousness, whispering dread invitations directly to my soul.

Another few minutes passed before I'd finally had enough wallowing. I was Damian-fucking-Banach. Walker. Crow. Killer of

Carnage. And no matter how they felt, dreams were just dreams. They had no authority over me.

Fuck if I was going to lie there any longer, shaking in fear.

Fuck if I was going to try to go back to sleep either though. I wasn't sure what time it was, but I was up for good. I pulled the curtains on my window. The sky was just beginning to turn the deep grey of pre-dawn. 4:30 maybe. 5:00 at the latest.

Way too early to be up on a Sunday, but it's not like I'd had a choice in the matter. Maybe I could get some homework done. Nothing banished fear—or excitement, in general—faster than another damn chapter of Ethics.

I pulled on clean sweats, grabbed my Glass from the dresser, and headed out into the common room.

Tessa was already there, in her usual spot on the couch, a mug of sweet-smelling coffee in one hand, and her own Glass in the other. She gave me a nod and returned to her reading.

"What are you doing up this early?" I debated between the remaining free spot on the couch and the chair Winter usually took, but finally chose the couch. Until I did laundry, these were my last pair of Academy greys. The last thing I needed was to get hair on them.

Muse's chair never even entered my mind as an option.

"I'm almost always up by now," she told me, curling her legs under her to make more room on the couch. "It's easier to get ready in the morning before the bathroom logjam."

"But today's Sunday." I frowned, as I rubbed my eyes, finally waking up enough to take notice of my surroundings. "And what are you wearing?"

She lowered her Glass just enough to give me a look, green eyes hard. "Didn't we have a talk about you making that sort of comment last year?"

Normally, that would've been enough to piss me off, and the conversation would've taken its usual exit on Argument Lane, but the dream was still fresh in my mind, and my anger was a distant thing. "That's not what I meant. Trust me; the last thing I want right now is to get threatened again. I'm just used to seeing everyone in greys or… bar clothing."

"Which for you are one and the same."

I shrugged. Maybe when I was a real Cape, I'd have enough money to go clothes shopping. Until then, I was going to make do as best I could, and the hell with anyone who tried to make something of it.

Tessa, on the other hand, was wearing long black leggings and a bright green sports top that left her arms and stomach bare. It covered way more than a swimsuit—or even her bartending dress—but it was a shock to see her in something different. As good as she'd looked in the previous night's outfit, she looked even better now. Strong. Formidable. Like an athlete.

"When I finish this chapter," she finally explained, eyes still narrowed, "assuming I'm ever allowed to finish it, I'm going for a run."

"Why? Isn't it enough that Nikolai already makes us run three times a week?"

"If it were up to me? Yeah."

That didn't make any sense at all, so I stayed silent.

"Doing the bare minimum might be enough to graduate," she finally continued, "but the stakes will be a lot higher once we're Capes. I want to hit the ground running as a professional. Figuratively. And literally, I guess. That probably sounds dumb—"

"Not at all. But…" I paused, trying to think of the best way to ask the question without getting my pubes plucked. "It's a bit of a reversal from the girl who didn't even brief us for our first mission in the Training Grounds."

"Are you going to rub that in my face this whole year?"

"Probably?" Silt says my smile is perfectly suited for scaring children, but Poltergeist didn't even blink when I sent one her way. Maybe I was losing my touch. "Seriously though, what changed? You can tell me if it was my killer pep talk."

That won an eye roll from the Telekinetic. "That may have been part of it. A small part. Getting taken out by a Mid-Three with a medieval weapon was the real kicker though. Once Ishmae dropped out, Alan and I were the only Fours left. I just sort of assumed that would be enough to get me through anything. Dying twice in sims that are way less complex than anything we'll see in the field told me how wrong I was. I need every advantage I can get if I want to survive. We all do." She cleared her throat and gave an uncomfortable laugh, as if she'd said more than she'd expected to. "Anyway, why are *you* up so early? And… are you feeling okay?"

"I'm always okay," I said, then paused. "Why?"

"You haven't sworn once since coming out here."

"I haven't?" I mentally paged back through our conversation. "Shit, you're right. I'm going soft."

"That'll be the day." She gave me another long look. "You're okay?"

"Yes, Madame Team Leader." I sketched a salute like I'd seen the soldiers do out at the Hole. "You don't have to worry about me. I always survive. Somehow."

Tessa was a lot of things, but she wasn't dumb. Looking back at that morning, I'm guessing she'd noticed I was paler than normal. Maybe more withdrawn too. Pretty sure her concern had very little to do with my lack of cussing.

Probably should've answered her honestly. We weren't friends, exactly, but I could count the number of people who'd ask a question like hers and actually care about my response on a single damn hand.

Instead, I stayed quiet.

Nineteen years old. Still going my own way, whatever the cost. Some lessons take for-fucking-ever to learn.

◦◦◦

"I understand congratulations are in order."

It took me a moment to figure out what Alexa was talking about. Saturday's team victory already felt like ancient history.

"Yeah. We're still at the bottom of the rankings, but a win is a win, I guess."

"You don't seem happy about it."

"I was. You should have seen me yesterday."

"What changed?"

At the last moment, I decided not to mention the dream. As much as it had freaked me out, it was already starting to fade back into my subconsciousness. Truth was, a therapist could spend their career trying to analyze my dreams and still not get anywhere. And there were other things to talk about.

"I don't know. It feels weird in hindsight. Prince tried to sing me to suicide, so I shot him in the face. I don't know what I'm supposed to learn from that."

"That's a good question. Outside of battlefield tactics, I think the Training Grounds are more about preparing you for what you might face or even have to do as a Cape." She steepled her long fingers in front of her. "How did pulling the trigger make you feel?"

"Good." I didn't even have to think about that one. "Strong."

"And yet you didn't take your shot at Ms. Kahale when you had your chance."

"You've seen the vid?" It had been a long time since I heard Nadia's last name. "I didn't know the whole faculty had access."

"They don't. I am, in some ways, a special case."

"Because seeing me in combat will tell you how close to the edge I might be?"

"Not as much as simply talking to you, like we're doing now, but it does help paint a picture." Black eyes met mine. "Would you prefer I not watch the vids?"

"No. I can't ask you to monitor my sanity and then complain about it. Whatever works. As for not shooting Orca…" I shrugged. "I don't know what that was about. Honest."

"Fair enough. May I ask another question?"

"Go for it." This wasn't the way our sessions usually went. Normally, I'd come in with something to talk about and Alexa would just listen, offering thoughts or reactions upon request. But after the night I'd had, I was okay with someone else bearing the conversational load.

"As I understand it, you used your power to ignore Mr. Callum's song, correct?"

"Yeah. When I go full-walker, it's like my body pilots itself, emotions and thoughts pushed to the side. I thought maybe that would shield me from someone trying to control those same feelings. And it worked. I walked right through his song."

"And then shot him."

"Yeah."

"Why?"

"Because he would've shot me if I didn't?" I wasn't sure what Alexa was getting at. She was too smart not to realize it had been a life-or-death situation.

"Why use a gun, when you were standing right over him, your power already active?"

Oh.

"Were you saving your strength in case you would need to use it on someone else in the mission?"

"I wasn't sure it would even work," I admitted. "I killed Carnage on a battlefield littered with the dead, and I was busy dying myself at the time. I don't know how much of what I did to him came from me or just *through* me."

"You think that if you had touched Prince, nothing would've happened?"

"I don't know. I don't even really understand how the Training Grounds work. How does a machine device know exactly how our powers function?"

"That's something only a Technomancer can answer. And one with significantly more experience than your first-year, Ms. Ostovich." Alexa shook her head. "I assume you haven't tried to test your power in the real world?"

"On what? Or who?" I shrugged. "When I came back from the Hole, I felt like I'd been bled dry. Not even a drop of power in me. There was no point in even trying."

"And now?"

"It's different. Feels like it filled back up way faster this time around. Maybe there's even more of it than when I was a first-year. I don't really know if I can actually death-touch people or not, but I'd say the power is there to try. Except that I don't want to just run around seeing if I can kill things."

"Then perhaps the Training Grounds are your best option to experiment."

"Yeah, but… what if someone I kill doesn't come back? There was nothing left of Carnage but ash. What if that fucks up the sim's algorithm or something? What if they die for real?"

"I've seen the tapes, Damian. If full body obliteration had any impact on a participant's corporeal existence, you'd already know."

"Because Silt dropped a building on me?"

"I was thinking more of Ms. Kennedy. Olympia," she clarified. "There was very little but dust left of you when her blast faded."

Hearing that actually made me feel better. How fucked up is that?

"Huh. June is our team's month off, but when July rolls around, I guess I can give it a shot. Assuming I get a chance. I was the perfect antidote to Prince. I'm going to be a lot less useful against Wormhole's team. Or most Black Hats, if we're being honest."

Alexa cocked her head in silent question.

"It's a shitty power," I told her. "Yeah, I killed Carnage, but only because he decided to watch me die instead of just stomping me into paste. And being able to kill with a touch—assuming I even can—doesn't count for much when people can atomize me from thirty feet away." I shook my head again. "It's an improvement over not being able to do anything last year, but it's still pretty lame."

Silence fell as Alexa digested my words. It was one of the things I liked most about her. She didn't just listen… she actually thought about what I was saying.

Finally, she stirred. "Have I ever told you why I retired as a Cape?"

"You didn't even tell me you were one," I pointed out. "I had to guess that on my own."

"True enough, and wasn't that a surprise." Her half-smile came and went. "I served as Midnight for roughly four years. That's greater than the average, actually, but only because of those killed-in-action. If you discount early casualties, my career was far shorter than most."

Math wasn't my strong point, and statistics just seemed like a religious offshoot of math, but something told me the numbers she'd just hinted at should scare me about my chosen career.

"I retired early," she told me, "because I was a terrible Cape."

"What? But Midnight was a Low-Four Shadecaster."

"And I still am," she agreed, correcting the tense. "But every power is different. Every test confirmed that I was a Four, but I lacked the ability to do any of the usual Shadecaster things. Projectile barrages. Additional limbs. Even cloaking my team in shadows. I was hopeless at all of it."

"What could you do then?"

"This." She pointed to her desk, where a small ball of shadow formed, floating above her desk. It couldn't have measured more than an inch in diameter.

"That's it?" There were Twos that could make larger shadows, and they weren't even eligible to be Capes.

"Indeed. The hope was that time in the field would teach me how to use my power, but it never did. I worked as hard as I could to assist my team, but neither they nor I was ever able to devise an effective tactic utilizing such a limited gift. So we went our separate ways and Midnight the Cape ceased to exist." Her dark eyes glittered. "And then I met a group of people who helped show me that what I thought was useless was anything but."

"I don't understand."

"Every Shadecaster manipulates shadow, which means imbuing that shadow with our power. My flaw was that, no matter what I was classified as, I could never make anything larger than the single sphere you see before you. But what I learned was that, within those established limits, I have control over every aspect of that sphere. Its size." As I watched, the sphere shrank until it was almost invisible, a miniscule dot, virtually lost against the black of her suit. "Its position," she continued, making the sphere dart about in a complicated pattern I could barely track. "Most of all, I have control over its density. If I were a Full-Five, I might be able to give this small speck the mass of a black hole. Even as a Low-Four, I've found little that it cannot penetrate."

Which sounded pretty cool. And yet... "But you stayed retired."

"It's not a power that lends itself to teamwork, let alone the world of Capes and Black Hats. Capes need to be visible symbols, actively doing good in the public eye. I was ill-suited for the role."

"But your power is useful on behalf of some nameless government agency?"

"Yes. I'm sure you can figure out exactly how." She shrugged, and the sphere disappeared, the room brightening in response. Even that had seemed to weaken her, just a little bit. "My point is that it can sometimes take years to figure out how best to utilize our powers. Don't diminish what you have already done, and don't give up hope on what you might still become."

Words to live by. Not that what I eventually became would have anything at all to do with hope. Dreams, maybe. But definitely not hope.

Truth is, if Alexa had known what the future held for me, what I'd end up doing, she'd have formed one of those superhumanly dense spheres right in my brain, and saved the Free States a whole lot of pain.

CHAPTER 22

"Damn, Skeletor." Silt stomped out of the woods and dropped onto the bench next to me. "You're actually early. Again."

"You guys are spending your free time helping research my past. Seems like the least I can do is make sure I'm here for the meetings."

"You were out here meditating anyway, weren't you?"

"Maybe."

"Figured. That part of the bench is molding itself to your ass."

"If that were true, I think we know who'd be responsible."

"Nah. I work in dirt, not stone. More's the pity." She yawned and stretched, the muscles in her bare arms rippling. "I hope one of the others has some new information, because so far, I've been coming up empty. Records are a little spotty after your dad finished his education, but he seemed pretty damn normal before the murder."

"He moved his whole family to fucking Bakersfield."

"Other than that, I mean." Her grin faded. "I'm happy to keep digging—I'm sure everyone is—but it's mid-June now. It's starting to look like there's nothing to find, or that whatever is out there is hidden so well we won't find it. Are you going to be okay with that?"

The short answer was no. The long answer was still no. But the world had never cared what I was okay with. Why would it start now?

"There's only so much you guys can do," I said instead. "Maybe I'll find out the truth some other way. Hell, maybe my dad's ghost is waiting to give me a vision of his own or something?"

"You could check with Amos. See if he has any more of that whisky of his."

"Fuck that." I shuddered, remembering how drunk I'd gotten, and how sick I'd been after the vision of my mom's murder. And yet... "I guess I could try." I met Silt's warm brown eyes. "I have to know."

"I hear you." She squared her broad shoulders. "And I volunteer to go down that whisky hole with you."

"You won't see a vision... or even any of my ghosts... no matter how much whisky you drink," I reminded her.

"Nah, but I'll still get good and drunk off of priceless alcohol." She adopted a heroic pose. "I think I'm woman enough for the task."

Whatever I was going to say in response was interrupted by the arrival of Vibe and Paladin, still hand-in-hand more than four months later.

"Hey guys," said Matthew.

Kayleigh met my hopeful look with a frown and a shake of her head. "Sorry, Damian. We're coming up empty. There's plenty of data out there on your mom, especially since she lived here in the city until she met your dad, but..."

"But it's all totally normal," I finished for her.

"Yeah. I'm sorry. I don't know where else to look."

"Silt and I ran into the same issue with my dad." I shook my head. "This month's meeting may be even shorter than last month's. And maybe we'll make it our last."

"Poltergeist and Stonewall might still find something on Sally."

After several months of futility, we'd finally decided to divvy up the potential research topics, with Silt and I focusing on my Dad, Paladin and Vibe focusing on my Mom, and Tessa and Jeremiah tasked with researching the Crow who was somehow intertwined with my parents' respective fates.

"You never know." I hadn't seen a ton of Poltergeist over the last couple of weeks. With June being our team's month off from competition, we'd even taken a vacation from the usual Tuesday night training.

Kayleigh cocked her head, listening to something none of the rest of us could hear. "I guess we'll find out. They just entered the woods." Then her eyes widened and she snuck a glance at Silt.

"Yep. Definitely heard that," said the Earthshaker. "But don't worry; it wasn't a secret. A little birdy told me you could use your Empathy to track us. And my team's already taken it into account for next month's battle."

The look Vibe turned on me was all injured innocence, as if her team hadn't murdered the shit out of mine back in March.

"Intelligence acquisition is part of being a Cape," I told her.

"Couldn't have said it better myself," agreed Silt.

"I wish I'd thought of it," admitted the Empath. "Thankfully, there's still time. Evelyn might not be willing to spill the beans on her former roommate's strategy, but something tells me Nadia will sing like a canary."

I wasn't sure what was going on with all the bird references. I shot a look at Paladin, but he just shrugged.

"Given how Team Two walked right through us, I'm not sure they'll have much to tell you," grinned Silt. "And I've sworn Boneboy here to secrecy."

"You have?"

"By which I mean, I will be bribing him shortly after this meeting," Sofia finished smoothly.

Ah. I shrugged at Vibe and Paladin. "Sorry, my lips are sealed by whatever spectacular gifts are soon to come my way."

For the second time, conversation stopped as someone entered the clearing. Tessa and Jeremiah, as Kayleigh had correctly identified. My current housemate had a big smile on her face, and my former roommate was waving his Glass about like it was a trophy.

"You're never going to believe this," he told me, white teeth bright against his dark skin and even darker beard. "You're dead!"

"It was bound to happen sooner or later," quipped Silt.

"What are you talking about?"

Rather than answer me, Jeremiah handed over his Glass. On its screen was an obituary for… I paused, reread the text, and reread it again.

"It's only been four months since we were roommates. That's way too short a time for you to have picked up a drug habit," I told the big man.

"What?"

I handed the Glass back to him. "That obituary is for a little girl named Barbara out of Fresno. What the hell does she have to do with me?"

"You're doing this all wrong." Tessa nudged Stonewall. "I told you we should just start at the beginning."

"When was I ever going to get another chance to tell Walker he's dead and have it sort of be true?"

The Telekinetic rolled her eyes. "Gather 'round, children, and listen up." She paused and looked around the clearing. "You know, we should start bringing chairs or something, so everyone can have a seat."

"I'm fine on the grass," I decided, freeing up a spot on the bench that she quickly filled. I'd done laundry that morning, and had plenty of sets of sweats for the coming week. Besides, grass stains were a small price to pay if it meant they'd actually tell me what the hell was going on.

Tessa rearranged her skirts as she sat on one side of Silt. Kayleigh sat on the other, with Matthew behind her, and Jeremiah joined me in the grass, lowering himself down with that special brand of care unique to enormous people.

"Before I start," said Poltergeist, "did you guys find anything of note about Damian's parents?"

"Not a thing," replied Silt. "I take it you had more luck with Sally Cemetery?"

"Not really. Everything we found was common knowledge. She started out as Sally Jenkins, killed her whole family at seventeen, and then paraded up and down the coastline for almost five years, killing people at random. Mostly men. And then, the killing suddenly stopped. Almost six months later, a hiker found a body in the foothills of the Sierra Nevadas. Dental records identified that body as hers."

Like she said, that was all pretty much common knowledge, as was the nursery rhyme children had been telling of the long-dead Crow ever since.

"So… you didn't find anything?" Vibe asked for all of us, her confusion evident.

"Not about Sally. But that's how research works. Sometimes, you have to ignore the principal characters and come at things from an angle." Tessa paused, her smile widening as she let the anticipation build.

"I think I preferred Jeremiah's way of telling this," I decided.

"Thank you!" rumbled the Shifter.

"Neither of you has a post-Cape future in entertainment," she retorted, smile still as wide as ever. "We decided to broaden our search. If Sally really did induce Damian's father to commit murder—despite herself being dead for more than five years at that point—who's to say she hadn't done it before?"

"I'm pretty sure it would have made the news," said Paladin.

"Only if her involvement was known. Damian only found out Sally was part of what happened to him because he decided to interview his dad in the middle of a prison break."

Which wasn't *quite* how it had gone down, but I wasn't going to correct her.

Next to the Telekinetic, Silt was pinching the bridge of her nose. "But if Sally's involvement wasn't cited, then how could you possibly identify other occurrences?"

"We looked for cases of parents killing their children in the years since Sally died." She swallowed. "Turns out there were a bunch of those, so we narrowed the date range to within five years of, well—"

"My dad going nuts?"

"Yeah. That. Show him what we found, Jeremiah."

The Shifter handed me back the glass and I swiped through fourteen obituaries. Most were young kids, but three or four were adolescents. I still didn't see what linked them all together, but the articles on two of the older ones caught my eye.

"Wait, this can't be right."

"And now you see what we saw." Tessa's tone was smug.

"But that goes against everything we're taught—"

"Share with the class, Skeletor, before I take that tablet away from you and beat you over the head with it."

I looked up at Sofia from across the clearing. "Two of the dead kids were Crows."

"Three Crows, including you? That can't be a coincidence."

"It shouldn't even be possible. We're supposed to be rarer than Healers. Three is more than you'd expect from an entire generation." I tapped the Glass. "And they were both Threes, just like me."

"That's not the only thing you have in common," said Jeremiah. "The ages at time of death vary pretty dramatically, but check out the birthdates given."

Both of the other Crows had been born in the late winter or early spring of 55. In fact, we'd all been born within three weeks of each other. The young girl at the top of the list actually shared my birthday.

"Okay, that is seriously fucked up," I decided, after relaying that information to Silt, Vibe, and Paladin. "What does it mean that there were three Crows born around the same time, and our parents tried to kill all of us? And why did you include these other obituaries?"

"Because they were all also born around the same time."

That was just weird enough to give me pause, but I still didn't get her point. "I see that, but... people get killed. Even kids. Even in the Free States. And none of them are shown as being Crows."

"According to Bard, your testing was the first actual record of you being a Crow," pointed out Stonewall, "and that was like two days before you arrived at the Academy."

Which still didn't make sense, given I'd been dumped back at Mama Rawlins when I was nine *because* my mom's ghost had made her first appearance. It was yet another mystery that needed to be solved at some point, but it was way the hell down the list from Sally and Tyrant.

"Fourteen children, all born around the same time, all killed by parents that seemingly snapped for no reason. And we *know* that three of them were Crows, which already contradicts what the statistics tell us to expect." Tessa shook her head, sending her dark curls bouncing. "We think more of the dead children were Crows. Maybe all of them. Or maybe Sally just thought they were. Either way, this is bigger than just you. Show him the other folder, Jeremiah. Those are records we found when we widened our search parameters along a specific vector."

My former roommate obliged, toggling to a separate and smaller group of documents, and handing the Glass back over.

Most were obituaries, but there were one or two missing person reports. The one thing they had in common was that they had all been teenagers, seventeen or eighteen at the time of their deaths or disappearances.

Wait. That wasn't the only thing.

The reports were all from February, March, and April of the previous year. The dead had all been murder victims. Every person listed had been born around the same time as me.

And one of the missing teenagers was a Crow. A Low-Four, no less.

There was a long moment of silence when I finished sharing that information, handing the Glass over so the others could check the data.

"This is insane," said Paladin, finally breaking the silence. "Twenty-five people born in a month's span, all of them except you dead or missing, and *four* of them were Crows?"

"Probably more," said Jeremiah.

"I don't get it. Has the government been lying about how rare necromancers are?"

"As far as I can tell, the statistics we were taught are backed up by real data," said Tessa. "Looking over the history of the Free States, four Crows is an absolute anomaly. Let alone whatever the actual number may have been."

"None of the teenagers were killed by their parents," said Kayleigh, looking up from the Glass. "And the cause of death varies. Three were shot, one had their neck broken, and this one died in a fire. That doesn't fit the same pattern as the other murders. What does that mean?"

"We couldn't figure that part out," said Jeremiah. "And if some or all of those teenagers are Crows, how did they stay safe from Sally all those years?"

"I don't know what I was expecting to find, but a bunch of dead people born around the same time as me was not it." I shivered as a breeze came in off the ocean.

"There's a reason they called her Sally Cemetery." Silt finished her own perusal of the files on Jeremiah's Glass and handed it back. "So what now?"

"We should turn this over to the police," said Matthew.

"What would they even do with it?" asked Tessa. "It's all circumstantial."

"And how would you prosecute someone who's been dead for almost twenty years anyway?" added Silt.

"They could at least assign someone to dig into the matter with official resources," argued the Stalwart. "Maybe keep a few more people from ending up on Sally's kill list?"

"I'm still not sure that the teenagers were killed by Sally," said Vibe. "The change in methods doesn't make sense."

"Maybe she was changing things up to hide her trail?" Silt paused. "The trail of a mass murderer ghost. That sounds weird even to me."

The five of them kept debating the issue, but I had stopped paying attention, my mind returning to the most recent murders and missing persons reports. Every one of them had happened within a few weeks, give or take, of my admission into the Academy.

I remembered Tyrant's words on the car ride out of Bakersfield, back when I'd thought him just a copper-eyed Finder.

We have soldiers, he'd told me. *What I am looking for is an army.*

I still didn't know why Tyrant had wanted me at the Academy, but he'd come all the way out to Bakersfield to get me, so it had clearly been important to get a Crow into Cape school.

You are not the only individual on my list, he'd said, just before he left me with Her Majesty.

I was struck then by a thought, the sort of intuitive leap my teachers would swear I was incapable of making, and my next shiver had nothing at all to do with the breeze.

There was no way to prove it, no evidence at all beyond the cold feel of truth, coiling in my gut next to the emptiness of my power, but there wasn't a doubt in my mind.

If I hadn't tested as a Three, I'd have been one more name in Jeremiah's obituaries.

CHAPTER 23

You'd think finding out that my ruined childhood had been part of a larger, still-unexplained sequence of attempted murders would've dramatically altered the course of my life at the Academy, kind of like how Mom's vision had back when I was a first-year. Suddenly, I wasn't just dealing with a mystery, I was dealing with a country-wide conspiracy. That's the sort of shit that changes things, right?

Not so much, it turns out.

"The first lesson in public relations is that everything is a story." Edmund Kisten, the CEO of Image Consulting, had a voice that could give Dean Bard's a run for its money; smooth and polished and slick as 100 SPF sunscreen. Even without a microphone, that voice carried to the highest rows in the auditorium. "Even the truth is just another story. I know," he said, his smile wry, "that sounds wrong. How can the truth be a story? Truth is just truth, right?"

Edmund was alone on the auditorium's stage, expensive suit hanging perfectly on a lean frame. His posture was perfect—upright but not too stiff, refined but still approachable—and his silver hair and matching goatee lent him an aura of polished wisdom.

"The fact is," he continued, "truth is relative. Your truth might not be your classmate's truth, which might not be the truth of a housewife in Phoenix. Even worse, truth doesn't have any intrinsic power in and of itself. Speaking it doesn't mean anyone will listen, and listening doesn't mean they'll actually hear it."

"That's what these past five weeks have been about," he continued. "How to create a story around each of you as individuals that will make the public more receptive to your truth. A name that is easy to remember. A costume that distinguishes you from the citizens you are training to protect. It's not just about revenue and promotional opportunities. It's about creating a single cohesive image for the public; who you are and what you can do. The more someone thinks they know you at a fundamental level, the more likely they will be to accept your story and your truth."

"Why does that matter?" Sharp eyes scanned the auditorium, as if seeking out those of us who might have agreed with his rhetorical question. "It matters because people without powers, people like me, naturally want to fear those who do have them, whether those people are Capes, Black Hats, or even blue-collar Sparks working eight hour shifts at a power plant."

"But we're protecting them," protested Supersonic. "Dying for them, even."

"Yes. And yet some of you could obliterate this entire campus in the time it takes me to shave. Power inherently scares the people who lack it. And the truth, as I am sure your teachers have told you, is being a Cape is not easy. People will die under your watch. In truly unfortunate circumstances, they might die *because* of your actions. And when that happens, your future as a Cape will rely on the public accepting your truth. There is a reason Evan Earthquake was forced to retire. The Free States needs its Capes—needs all of you—too much to let that sort of outcome become the norm."

Silence fell across the auditorium. I'm not sure if my classmates were imagining their actions resulting in the deaths of people depending on them or if they were realizing how quickly and easily the positions we were working our asses off for might be taken away.

"Is that true?" asked Winter. "About Evan Earthquake, I mean."

"It is. Rupert Evans—that was his real name, for those of you who were unaware—lost more than just his vid deals and sponsorships. His team cut him loose, his license was terminated, and a class action lawsuit took the poor man for every penny. He left for the Badlands almost a decade ago and that was the unfortunate end of his story. It was one of the reasons I sold my previous company and created Image Consulting. Had Rupert been our client, I'd like to believe he'd still be an active Cape today, putting his power to productive use."

"How many of you already knew that story?" In the entire auditorium, only Paladin and I raised our hands. "That's the other reason Cape relations matters. No story—no matter how perfectly crafted—matters unless people actually hear it and buy into the truth being given them. And that's what we're here to talk about today, and what your individual consultants will be working with you on for the next few weeks. Communication. Public speaking. How to comport yourself on camera." He flashed a polished smile as his employees marched in to line up in front of the stage. "We at Image Consulting are excited to see the fruits of our collaborations."

From across the auditorium, Ricky met my eyes. His smile was an odd fusion of his boss' charm and Nikolai's professional sadism. I'd won the argument about my Cape name, and mostly won when picking my costume, but it was July now, and something told me the bastard was ready to take his revenge.

Public speaking. Debate. Press conferences.

All I'd wanted from the Academy was to not go insane.

ooo

"…which brings us back to the question of personal responsibility," concluded Isabel Ferra, eyes sharp behind the glasses I was ninety-nine percent sure she wore just to seem professorial. "What does personal responsibility mean to you in the field of Ethics of Superpowers?"

As usual for Ethics class, both Supersonic and El Bosque were in a competition to see who could raise their hand the fastest and, also as usual, Supersonic won. Four and a half months into our second year at the Academy, and the two still thought brown-nosing would somehow win them the teacher's affection.

Winter had her hand up in the air too, but Winter always had her hand up in the air. It was one of the many reasons she'd wrecked the curve for most of the class.

"Why don't you give us your answer, Caleb," said Isabel, calling on Supersonic.

"Personal responsibility means that each Cape needs to be aware of the law and ensure that the actions they take are legal and defensible."

"That's what the book says," agreed the professor, leaning back on her desk, long legs extended in front of her. "But what does it mean to you?"

"It means it's not enough to stop the bad guys and look badass doing it," he decided, running one hand through his spiky black hair. "How you do it is just as important."

Which didn't make a whole lot of sense to me. If I had a choice between stopping a Black Hat illegally and letting them go, I'd stop them every damn time.

"Excellent answer," said Isabel. Because of course she would. "There is an ongoing debate and discussion regarding our current Power-related laws, but as a licensed Cape, you are sworn to uphold those laws and behave in a manner according with them. We'll focus more on the specifics of those laws when you are third-years, but this chapter's point of emphasis is why those laws matter, and how you can navigate the ethical challenges they might present. Yes, Penelope?"

Winter had dropped her hand when Caleb first started her answer, but it had gone right back up in the middle of Isabel's speech. She frowned. "What laws are being debated?"

"There are a number of different public movements, each with their own supporters and critics," replied Isabel, "but one discussion that has seen a rise to prominence in recent years has to do with the rights of criminal Powers."

"Say what now?" Silt rarely participated in class, but that had gotten her attention.

"Any Power who commits a crime that results in a loss of life is permanently consigned to the Hole. There is a growing segment of the population that believes the current laws lack nuance. Without the possibility of parole, there is no hope for rehabilitation, and that costs the country significantly, in both expense and potential resources."

"Resources meaning the criminal Powers."

"Of course."

"What does any of this have to do with ethics?" I asked.

"Ethics are the codes of behavior we adhere to as a society. If there is discussion about altering those codes, it is germane to my class, Mr. Banach." Other students got a smile. I got a baring of the teeth. "You ignored regulations last year and left school early so you could go to the Hole."

"Probably wanted to see where he'd end up," muttered Caleb.

"What was your impression of the prison?" The professor continued sweetly. "Did it seem fair that the inmates you encountered had been banished from society for life?"

"Most of the inmates I saw orchestrated a prison breakout and went on to kill a fuckton of people above ground," I reminded her with a growl, "and Fallout's still out there somewhere. As far as I'm concerned, people like him should have just been executed."

"And a different segment of the population would agree with you. But what of the inmates who were not involved in the prison break? I was at your expulsion hearing, Mr. Banach." She loved referencing that hearing. Given how eager she was to see me expelled, it had probably been the highlight of her decade... right up until they decided to keep me. "I believe you mentioned a Stalwart who tried to help?"

"He was defending his dad." I frowned. "But yeah, he seemed like he was trying to do the right thing. And died for it."

"How much better would it be for the country if individuals like that man could be rehabilitated and reformed instead of simply discarded?"

I was pretty sure there was a gaping hole in her argument, but I was struggling to find it.

"Are you saying we shouldn't send murderers to the Hole, Ms. Ferra?" asked Spectra, silver eyes shining.

"I'm not offering an opinion on the matter, Olympia. I am simply making you aware of the complex nature of the subject. As a Cape, it is your responsibility to find a way to ethically perform your duties. But a hero does more than simply obey the law. She understands those laws, and, if necessary, lends her voice to the call to change them.”

“Is that why President Weatherly tried to create Reconciliation Day?”

“The president did not *try* to create anything, Santiago,” she told the Druid. “He *did* create it. But yes, I believe so. A politician needs to be aware of the desires of their population and make earnest efforts to meet those desires if he or she wishes to be re-elected.”

“But if it hadn’t been for that, the prison break would never have happened!”

“Correct. A lot of people are dead, including some of our brightest Capes, and the president is unlikely to win a second term as a result. Actions can have unforeseen consequences, and in this case, those consequences were disastrous. Does that mean what the President did was wrong?”

Before El Bosque could reply, the classroom door opened behind us, and a teenager with brown hair, glasses, and a ‘Student Worker’ badge on his chest stuck his head inside.

“Sorry to interrupt, Ms. Ferra.”

“Not at all, dear.” I’d always found it remarkable that Isabel could be so sugar-sweet with every student but me. “Is there something you need?”

“Yes, ma’am. I was sent for Damian Banach. The Dean wants to see him in his office immediately.”

“Perhaps the Hole wasn’t your only brush with ethical quandaries, Damian?” Her smile was sharp enough to shave with. “I cannot wait to hear what this is about. You are excused.”

Which is how I found myself hurrying across campus, desperately trying to figure out what I’d done wrong.

○○○

When I reached Bard’s office, his assistant, Agnes, waved me right on through. If anything, that made me more paranoid. I’d spent more than a few hours, all told, sitting in that waiting room’s uncomfortable chairs, wondering how my life was about to change. The lack of a delay told me things were serious.

And then I walked in to find both Bard and Alexa waiting for me, and knew things were even worse than that.

"Damian, please have a seat." When the Academy wasn't in session, Bard took casual clothing to an extreme—to the point that I'd mistaken him for a scruffy graduate student the first time we met—but today, he was in his usual suit. He looked tired and old.

Alexa looked the same as ever, although I wasn't used to seeing her out from behind a desk. She was taller than I'd expected, her form strangely elongated.

"What's going on?" I wasn't sure which of them I was asking, but it was Alexa who answered.

"There's been a fire, Damian."

"I didn't do it." I didn't know what was going on, but denial had long since been ingrained as a reflex action.

"We know."

"Then why am I—" I paused, frowning. Ishmae's eruption the previous year had forced the dean to ask student Weather Witches to push the smoke out to sea just to make our air breathable again. If the fire had been on campus, I'd have smelled it on the way over.

But if the fire hadn't been at the Academy, why would they tell me about it? Especially when they knew I hadn't been off campus and therefore couldn't be responsible?

If I wasn't responsible for the fire, then I had to be connected to it, or where it happened. There were only two places I'd lived in the past ten years. And since there was no fire on campus, it meant it must have happened in Bakersfield. And that meant...

"Mama Rawlins?" My voice was a whisper.

"I'm sorry, Mr. Banach," said Bard. "The Bakersfield Home for Lost Children burned to the ground this morning. There were no survivors."

CHAPTER 24

"How? Why?" I reached for my power to numb the shock and mute the emotions bubbling up inside of me, but nothing came.

"There are responders on the scene trying to find that out," said Alexa, her words measured, "but they suspect arson. I'm heading there shortly to assist in the investigation."

"I'm going with you." The words were out before I'd even thought them.

"I told Jonathan you would want to."

"And I thought it sounded like a terrible idea," said Bard. "However, Alexa has convinced me otherwise." He rose and came around his desk, to pat me awkwardly on the shoulder. "I am deeply sorry for your loss, Damian. If there is anything my faculty or I can do to assist in this matter, just ask. I'll be informing your teachers of the situation, and you'll be excused from classes until you feel ready to attend again."

"Okay." I wasn't sure what to say, but short answers seemed to be all I was capable of.

"If it is okay with you," he continued, "I would like to hold a memorial service when you return. Invitation-only, of course. Our community is a small one. When tragedy befalls one of us, we grieve together."

"Okay," I said again, but the truth was, grief was the furthest damn thing from my mind. Mama Rawlins was dead, along with whichever orphans had still been there more than a year after my

departure. One cranky old woman who'd done her best to raise me…
and a dozen or more kids whose only crime had been having shitty
parents or no parents at all.

And if the investigators were right, they hadn't just died.

They'd been murdered.

I wasn't sad.

I was fucking angry.

ooo

Alexa led me to one of the recovery rooms, down the hall from
where I normally met her for sessions. Thank fuck it wasn't the one
Ishmae had stayed in before leaving campus for good… I'm not sure I
could have dealt with that memory just then.

"I thought we were going to Bakersfield?"

"We are. Our ride will be here shortly, but I wanted to speak
with you first."

"Why?" I frowned, as a thought occurred to me. "What don't
you want Bard to know?"

"Yesterday, one of my *coworkers* was found dead in his
townhouse in San Francisco."

"Okay…? I mean, I'm sorry, but—"

"Yin had been digging into the matter we discussed
previously." Her black eyes were bottomless, devouring the light
between us.

"You think Tyrant killed him?"

"Someone did. Maybe it was just a random attack or the past
catching up with him, but my gut tells me otherwise."

I shook my head. Coming right after the news about Mama
Rawlins, this was too much to take. I couldn't understand why she was
telling me now of all times, unless—

"Are his murder and the fire related?"

"I don't know. They might be, so I thought you should know.
There are investigators from my agency at the murder scene. I hope to
know more by the time we're back from Bakersfield."

"Why did you convince Bard to let me go?"

"What would you have done if we said no?" Her half-smile flickered as she read the answer in my face. "Better to give permission and protection than to deal with another unsanctioned excursion."

"You could've just waited to tell me until after the fire was dealt with."

"Trust is a two way street, Damian. I have to walk it too." A knock came at the door, but before she answered, she added, in a voice that barely carried. "The dead spoke to you once. If they do so again, they might give us insight into what truly happened at the orphanage. The more information we have, the better."

Which was something I hadn't even thought of. Mom had held onto the memory of her own murder for thirteen years, only giving it to me as a vision that Christmas. What were the chances of the orphanage dead being able to interact with me at all? And if they did, did I really want to experience their deaths, like I had Mom's?

I had an answer before the door had even fully opened.

If it would help avenge them? Fuck yes.

Alexa wanted justice, and more power to her for that.

I just wanted to make someone pay.

ooo

The man waiting for us was as wide as Silt but almost my height, wrapped in a black trenchcoat despite the June warmth. A fedora sat low on his head, casting the face beneath into shadow, as if in search of an anonymity that was forever out of reach. Identifying Alexa as Midnight had been tough, but there weren't many people in the Free States who wouldn't recognize Door.

Any other day, and I'd have been excited to meet the Defenders' Teleporter. Instead, he was just a means to an end, the method by which I would travel the one-hundred-plus miles between Los Angeles and Bakersfield.

Door gave Alexa a nod, hard eyes flicking over to me and back, and then stepped into our room. A stubby-fingered hand—made even stubbier by the fact that his pinky ended at the first knuckle—closed the hallway door, turning the knob with a gentleness that seemed as out of place as it was unexpected.

For a few breaths, it was just the three of us, standing in one of the Academy's recovery rooms; Alexa as still as a brush painting, Door's steady breath loud in the silence, and me, wrapped in emptiness and anger. Then, Door pulled open the door he'd just closed.

The sun hit me like a hammer. Dry waves of heat radiated off of long-cracked asphalt and worn, drooping buildings. Above the distant skyline, a faded billboard proclaimed the city's rebirth.

That rebirth had never happened. Never would happen, as far as I could tell. Cities take a lot longer to die than people, but Bakersfield was well on its way.

I fucking hated this place.

We stepped into the street. When I looked back, the door had reverted to being the boarded-up entryway to a long-abandoned storefront, its windows broken, its façade a mix of peeled paint and caked-on dirt. A painted sign above the entrance read *Mason's Cleaners & Alterations.*

When I'd still been at Mama Rawlins', I'd walked past that boarded-up storefront twice a day for almost five months, palms sweaty with excitement and anticipation on the way up the block, stride slow and satisfied on my return. I let my eyes drift left, down the street, to the place that had been my destination all those days.

The convenience store was still open, one of the few businesses on this particular street that could say that, and the same old neon light flickered in the window—*Slushies. Strawberry. Orange. Lemonade.* For just a second, I could picture myself pushing open that door, hearing the tinny jingle of its damn bell, could see Alicia looking up from the homework her parents made her do at work, the smile spreading slowly across her round face.

But that was crazy. Alicia was gone and dead. Gone to Palo Alto. Dead in Scarlet's attack. All of that had happened long before I left Bakersfield. The store had become just another building.

I turned instead to the right.

One fire engine remained, the hum of its electric motor barely audible. Here and there, people in windbreakers and hard hats milled about. One had a Glass, another a camera with an intrusively long lens.

And beyond them was rubble. In a city like Bakersfield, you'd
think it would have fit right in, but it didn't. Destruction instead of
decay. Ruin instead of retreat. The walls of the buildings on either side
were scorched and blackened, evidence that the fire had tried to spread
and been stopped by the city's response team, but there was nothing
left of the two-story house I'd shared with more than a dozen other
orphans. Just ash, broken beams, and brick walls that had tumbled
inward, like dirt atop a coffin.

"Jesus," muttered Door.

Alexa said something to him in reply, but I was moving, feet
not feeling the asphalt below them, drifting almost like I was a ghost
myself, pulled into the destroyed orphanage's orbit. The man with the
Glass came to ward me away, but something Alexa said or did behind
me ended his obstruction before it could even begin.

The fire was out, as far as I could see, but from this close, the
heat was tangible, the air thick with smoke. A change in the wind
brought a small scattering of ash with it, grey flakes falling like snow.
The remaining fire crew still had their hose out, watering down
portions of the rubble as if to wash away what had happened.

"Be careful, Damian," said Alexa, her voice a murmur.

I didn't feel like being careful. I felt like raging, but beneath that
anger and that grief and ugly feelings I couldn't name was cool
emptiness, the peace of the death I carried. I let it expand, swallowing
those useless emotions until it filled me, until the open and aching
space that had once been an orphanage was just another landmark to
entropy in a city full of them. I left behind Alexa and the still-
protesting man, took a stance directly in front of the walkway that now
ended just a few feet off the road, and squeezed my eyes shut.

When I looked again, they were there.

Eighteen ghosts, scattered across the desolation, from the bulk
of Mama Rawlins herself to the shrunken frame of the even older man
who'd so often visited her for tea and sex. In what would have been
the common room, John wobbled back and forth the way he always
had, one leg shorter than the other, giving the impression he might
topple at any moment. With me gone, he'd been the oldest orphan left,
given the thankless task of maintaining order in my absence. Behind

him, the others played or stood or danced in their own mindless way. I recognized most, if not all.

Come. I didn't speak the word so much as will it, drawing upon what I'd learned from Sally Cemetery the year before. Instead of trying to force my command, I let it drift out on invisible tides of emptiness, on the unseen waves of my power. *Come.*

And they came, gathering before me in uneven ranks, Mama Rawlins up front with her afternoon lover. When they were alive, the children would've found lining up like this almost impossible. Someone would have stepped on someone else's toes, leading to an elbow in the ribs or a shove and before you knew it, the whole thing would've devolved back into loud chaos. As ghosts, they moved with each other and through each other, each the sole inhabitant of their afterlife. Eighteen ghosts, but even as my power corralled them, not a one looked in my direction. Not a one saw me.

"I need to know what happened," I told them, their presence enough to make me forget myself and speak aloud. "I need to see what you saw."

"We're still trying to—" began the man behind me, before Alexa cut him off.

"He's not speaking to you, Chief Wilming."

"Then who is he speaking to?"

"Why don't we discuss it over there and leave him to it."

Their retreating footsteps registered dimly, but I had my eyes on the ghosts in front of me still. They'd answered my call, but I needed more. So much more.

This was always going to be the hard part. I didn't understand how Mom's ghost had shown me the vision of her death, what had triggered it, or why she'd waited all those years, yet here I was, trying to make something similar happen on command.

I looked to Mama Rawlins, but her face was blank, mouth twisted as if chewing on one of the cigarettes she'd always favored over stim-weed.

I looked to John, but the boy I'd left in charge, now forever two years away from being able to leave the orphanage, stared right through me, still wobbling, dark hair a mess of tangles.

"Please," I told the gathered ghosts, "I have to know."

They shifted back and forth, the smoke-filled breeze coming almost as a sigh, but nobody came forward. I took a seat on the broken sidewalk, hands folded in front of me, and felt the power well up inside of me.

Tell me.

John shifted a second time, dancing to the side, but his movement didn't bring him any closer. Still a good five feet away, an invisible boundary between us. It was only when I looked back at the others that I realized his movement had created an open space, a sightline to the wreckage behind them.

A small form floated up from the ruins of the orphanage.

There weren't eighteen ghosts after all. There were nineteen.

And the nineteenth was Nyah.

CHAPTER 25

I stared at the ghost of the young girl, trying to make sense of a world gone mad.

Nyah was the one person at Mama Rawlins' that I'd never worried about at the Academy. When I'd left, she was five and cute as a button. We'd known her time at Mama Rawlins' was temporary. Only thing that goes faster than a darling little girl like her is a baby, and we'd never had one of those.

Nyah should've been snapped up by a foster family and on the fast road to adoption, not here in the smoke-filled rubble. Six years old now. Six years old forever. Dead with every other one of Mama Rawlins' final projects.

She drifted toward me, walking but not walking, shoes untied because, even though I'd taught her how to tie them myself, she liked it best when other people tied them for her. Nyah had grown a little since I'd last seen her, graduating from her overalls to a hand-me-down dress from Jasmine that had been a hand-me-down from El and so on, all the way back to when it began its orphanage journey in a donation box. Black hair still a cloud around her face, she passed through the other ghosts to take a spot near me, eyes gazing at whatever she saw in place of the empty buildings across the street.

"Nyah." I breathed her name as much as spoke it. "I don't understand. Why are you still here?"

She didn't give a sign that she'd heard me. Ghosts never did. Except for Sally. And my mom, that one solitary time. Still in her own world, Nyah balanced on one leg, kicking the other back and forth, sending her shoelaces swinging.

Don't know what I was thinking. Not sure I was thinking much, if I'm being honest, but I rose to a knee and reached out to tie her shoes, like I'd done so many times before.

My hand passed right through her foot. No surprise there. I've never been able to touch a ghost. Not even Mom. No matter how much I wanted to.

But as I fumbled at laces that weren't really there, her small hand swept up and traced a line of ice across my forehead.

For the second time in a year, the world fell away.

ooo

Fridays are my favorite.

Mama's in her room having tea with Mr. Stellman, John's up making sure the boys get their showers, and I've got the vid screen and *the couch all to myself to watch Captain Cosmo save the day.*

I'm not supposed to have my shoes on the cushion, but nobody's here to see it, and they're tucked under my fancy dress anyway.

John calls me princess. I'm going to miss him when he's gone, like I missed Damian after the grey man took him away, like I missed Sarah when she left with her new family. She said she'd come back and play but that was months ago. I'm going to show her my dress when she does.

Captain Cosmo is fighting the evil Black Hats when the knock at the door comes. I look to it, then back at the screen. I'm not supposed to answer the door. Mama says so. John too. But the knocking keeps coming. There's something like a loud sigh from Mama's room, then the squeal of springs.

I make sure my shoes are off the couch before Mama comes rushing out, fixing her clothes like she's always doing when we have guests. The knocking's continuing and she hurries to the door and throws it wide open.

"What?!?"

It's a man. Not much older than Damian was, and not nearly as tall, I think, he's all in black; coat, shirt, pants. He's not wearing shoes, and his feet are gross. There's no way Mama's going to let him track all that dirt into the house, but he doesn't even ask, pushing past her like she's just there to hold the door. He sees me on the couch and smiles.

I don't like it. I don't like him.

"Now hold on here," says Mama, moving to intercept the smiling man. "Who are you and what are you doing?"

Mr. Stellman is at the door from Mama's room now, straightening his tie. The smiling man doesn't look at either adult, but keeps staring at me like I've got synth-rations on my face. His eyes drop to my swinging shoes and their untied laces.

"I'm here to tie things up," he finally says, voice as greasy as his smile. "No loose ends, no sir. Not for me for me. Or he or he."

"We're going to have to ask you to leave," decides Mr. Stellman, closing in on the man.

"Leave?" His smile widens, but he turns back to the door, hand on the old brass knob. "How could we have a party then?"

"The place you're looking for is about five blocks thataway," says Mama gruffly, "If you want, I can have the police come and take you there."

"Do I have the wrong address? Do I do I do I?" For a moment, I think he is really confused, but that smile never wavers. "But I already sent out invitations!"

"That's just about enough of you—" says Mr. Stellman, voice hard for once instead of trembly.

"And look," continues the man, pulling wide the door, "our guests are starting to arrive."

There's a car parked at the curb. It's not shiny like the ones you see on the vids, but on any other day, it would still be the neatest thing I'd seen. But the view is quickly blocked as people start to file into the house.

No. Not people.

Things.

Dead like Mommy and Daddy. Rotting like their clothes. Jagged fingers like the talons of Screech, Captain Cosmo's bird friend.

Mama screams. I scream. Mr. Stellman goes white. The smiling man spreads his arms wide.

"And now the party party party can begin."

I try to run and hide even as John rushes downstairs. Something lunges at him. He falls. I fall too. Dead things come for us.

I wanted to show Sarah my new dress.

ooo

This time, I didn't throw up.

Not sure why that sticks in my mind still, all these months later, other than that it was something different from when Mom showed me her vision. Everything else was the same. Horror. Grief. Disgust and anger. And yes, even that faint undercurrent of surprise.

Not just because someone had killed everyone at Mama Rawlins' house, before the fire. Not even because that killer had been a Crow. Yet *another* fucking Crow in a country suddenly filled with them.

Surprise because I'd recognized the car parked at the curb.

A rattling, wheezing, primer grey death trap. Spring no doubt still poking out of the passenger seat. Windows that stuck halfway when you tried to roll them down.

"Damian?" Alexa was at my side, though I'd never heard her approach. The ghosts were gone, the emptiness inside of me gone with them, and my face felt like it was being squeezed by a giant invisible hand.

I don't know how long I'd been sitting there, but sweat was trickling down my back and my legs had fallen asleep, numb and unresponsive. I used my hands to straighten them, rub feeling back into them, the sharp pinpricks of nerve endings telling me I was alive.

Even if nobody else was.

I tried to rise to my feet, but my legs weren't there yet. A meaty hand caught me by the elbow, kept me from falling, and I heard Door's voice for the first time.

"Cold. Like touching ice."

It was a damn good thing for him and for me that I'd lost the grip on my power before he touched me. Can't say for sure what might have happened otherwise. The Defenders might have needed a new Teleporter, just because nobody thought to warn him.

"Damian?" Alexa asked again, real concern intruding on her clinical calm. "Did you find something?"

"They were dead before the fire," I told her, in a voice I recognized from the bad moments of my life. "A stranger came to the orphanage. A Crow."

Door sucked in a breath. "How does he know that?"

"This is Mr. Banach, Door. Perhaps better known as Walker."

"The student who killed Carnage."

"Yes."

"Well, shit." Despite his words, that hand stayed put as I tried to get my legs under me.

"He knocked on the door," I continued. "Nyah didn't answer because she's not old enough. Mama Rawlins came out. The other Crow came in. Something about loose ends, but I don't know if he was talking about Nyah's shoelaces."

"Shoelaces?" Door seemed confused.

"Haven't you heard?" I favored him with a smile that had him stepping back and away. "We're all crazy. Birds of a fucking feather."

"Damian." Alexa's voice was mild. I held onto it like it was a life preserver and I some doomed bastard out in the Pacific. "Is it possible that this was an isolated incident? A random act of horrific violence?"

"No."

"How can he know that for sure?" Door asked her behind my back.

"Because," I told them both, eyes fixed on the rubble and smoke that had been an orphanage and nineteen people, "Tyrant's car was parked at the curb."

ooo

That wasn't the end of it, of course. Alexa had to share more words with the fire chief, whose investigation was going to continue, regardless of what I'd seen. Apparently, ghost visions don't count for much when it comes to filling out paperwork, even in the Free States.

I pointed out where the dead had fallen, but most bodies were buried under unstable wreckage and recovery would have to wait until they were sure all hot spots had been thoroughly extinguished.

A few people wandered by on the street, pausing briefly to glance at the remnants of the city's lone orphanage, before hurrying on their way. Bakersfield was like that, full of curious people who couldn't bring themselves to really care.

Finally, Alexa came back over to me. "Are you ready to go back, Damian?"

"Yeah."

"I'm sorry. I know this was hard."

I made a show of shrugging it off and she made a show of buying it. "Better to know than not, right?"

"Yeah." She stood next to me, the silence between us drowned out by the bustle of people doing presumably important things. "If you'd like, before we head back, Door can take you to the cemetery. Give you some time at your mom's grave."

"She's not there." I shook my head. "It's just a box of bones. Besides, I see Mom everyday."

Alexa nodded. "Fair enough. Let's get back to the Academy."

We crossed the street, where Door pulled open the empty storefront's ramshackle door, revealing the room we'd left from, hours before. I started across the threshold then paused. "Do you know what happened to my dad's body?"

"Tremor's exit meant more than a few tons of stone and building collapsed in on top of that part of the Hole. They had to get another Earthshaker in just to clear it all. What was left was unidentifiable."

It wasn't really an answer, so I just waited.

"All of the recovered remains were cremated," she finally finished.

"Good."

I took the long step back to the Academy.

ooo

When we returned, I told Bard I didn't want a memorial service. He canceled it without question, but I could tell he didn't understand why.

Truth was, I didn't see the point. Who would I be remembering them to? And why? Nobody else had even known them. No words I gave would tell their story.

And as for the dead themselves? The body in my mom's coffin wasn't her anymore, and the bodies at Mama Rawlins' weren't Nyah or John or anyone else. They were just meat and bone. And their ghosts… well, that was a bit harder to answer, I guess. Sally had told me ghosts were just fragments of the people they represented, broken shards left behind. I didn't believe a lot of what Sally had said anymore, but I hoped to fuck that part was true.

Valhalla. The karmic wheel. Heaven. Whatever you wanted to call it, whatever might come after, I wanted to believe it existed. Wanted to believe that the lion's share of a little girl's soul was out there having adventures, watching cheesy hero vids, and laughing her way through the day.

Someone else would have to tie her shoes.

CHAPTER 26

I didn't go to the clearing on the west side of campus. As much as it had become my space, what I needed right then was isolation, and I was pretty sure Sofia or Kayleigh would be looking for me as soon as they heard I was back. Any other day, any other time, and I might have appreciated that—the strange sense of security that comes with having people care—but I wasn't fit for company and I didn't have the energy to hide it.

I also had just over an hour until my team's shift at the Liquid Hero. I needed to get a grip on things fast or the first customer who spilled a drink was going right out the window, taking my hopes of graduation with them.

So instead, I found myself sitting somewhere south of the clearing, my back against a tree, the bark rough through my sweatshirt. Since returning to campus, I'd been trying to call on the emptiness inside of me, but nothing was happening. Maybe part of that was the sheer depth of anger and grief running riot through my system, but the bigger issue was that the emptiness itself felt different. Normally, it was calm and still. Mere hours after finding the bodies of everyone I'd known in Bakersfield, it was closer to one of those terrifying storms Tempest had taken her name from. It made me think of Sally Cemetery and what she'd told me almost a year earlier:

Sally's eyes, mud-brown and torn, met mine, and she cupped her hands together in front of her to form a bowl. "This is the power you were born with. Each death fills the vessel a little more, turning potential into ability. Sometimes, that progression is small, almost unnoticeable. Other times," she nodded at the ghosts surrounding us, "it is less small."

The battle at the Hole had changed me. That much was undeniable. Shane's death had changed me too. Maybe even the bandits Her Majesty had massacred on the way to the Academy. Every death making the bucket of my power fill a little more, a little faster. I hadn't been in Bakersfield when Mama Rawlins, Nyah, and the others were murdered, but it felt like I'd taken their deaths into me anyway. Felt like the reason the emptiness inside of me was churning was because it was starting to overflow, lapping at the edges of my soul.

Maybe I should've been horrified by that, that the death of people I knew and maybe even cared for was serving as fuel, like I was some kind of vampire getting strong off misery. But there was a Crow out there with a greasy smile and nineteen reasons to die, and something told me he was a hell of a lot more powerful than a Low-Three like me. I needed all the strength I could get if I was going to have my revenge.

First the Crow. Then Tyrant.

As for Sally? Well, she and I would have ourselves a chat.

And with that thought, the emptiness went still. Not calm, like it usually was, but almost... pleased. Pliable. Expectant. I relaxed and let it sweep over my emotions, muting and muffling them. And then, because I still felt overstuffed, I let some of the emptiness drain out of me into the dirt below my feet. Just enough to make sure I'd be safe in public.

Odd thing was, I felt that emptiness even after I'd poured it out. Felt it pool in the earth, three or four feet down, curled up on itself like a well-fed cat. Weird as fuck, but that described my life, didn't it? The sensation faded as I left the woods, and by the time I'd gotten to the sub-dorm, I'd already forgotten it.

Sometimes, even the sighted are blind.

I entered to the smell of cookies. Which was damn weird, because our match with Wormhole and Team Four was still two weeks away. Unless Winter had failed a test for the first time in her life, she shouldn't have had any stress or unhappiness to bake away.

As if just thinking her name had summoned her, Penelope poked her head around the corner from the kitchen. "Oh good. You're back."

I wasn't sure what was stranger... her being happy I was back or the fact that she'd pulled her hair back into four ponytails and two looping braids. Just figuring out what to do with her hair had to be a full-time job.

"How do you keep all that hair out of the way when baking?"

"I'm part Wind Dancer." She shrugged, and a stiff breeze circled her, pulling loose hair back and away from her face. "It's not hard. Anyway," she continued, holding up a paper plate with three chocolate chip cookies on it, "these are for you."

"Really?"

"It doesn't mean what you think it means," she hurriedly added. "What we talked about at the beginning of the year still stands."

"What we talked about?" I clearly should have spent more time getting my shit together in the woods, because I had no idea what was going on.

"That I wasn't interested. In you. That's still true. More true than ever, frankly." She waved the plate of cookies. "These are... sympathy cookies. Not a proposal."

"Oh." Winter probably thought I was disappointed to find my apparently undying love still unrequited, but truthfully, I just hadn't expected the news to spread quite so fast. "You heard?"

"Just that there'd been a death." Winter straightened up, as if remembering her manners, and offered me the plate. "I'm sorry for your loss, Damian. One platonic teammate to the other."

"Thank you. And thanks for the cookies." I grabbed the plate. The cookies smelled like heaven. Chocolate heaven.

A minute later, safe in my room away from Penelope's sighs and sympathetic glances, I took a bite of the first baked goods the Weather Witch had actually shared with our team.

And... damn.

It was a good thing that the unrequited love she was so convinced of didn't actually exist. Otherwise, those cookies might have sealed the deal.

Twenty minutes later, there was a knock at my door. I was halfway through pulling on a fresh pair of Academy greys, but the important bits were covered, so I pulled open the door.

"What is it with you not wearing shirts?" asked Poltergeist.

"What is it with you and Winter trying to come in when I'm half-naked?" I shot back, pulling the sweatshirt on. "I was just getting ready."

"For what?"

"Tonight's shift?"

"Oh." For some reason, that hadn't been the answer she was expecting. She'd turned things around as team leader—better than I'd expected she would, to be honest—but maybe the responsibility was starting to wear on her. "Actually, that's what I came to tell you. You don't have to work tonight. Or this weekend, actually."

"But you guys will be short staffed."

"We'll manage." She chewed on her lower lip. "I'm sorry. You know, for your loss."

"Did Bard tell everyone?" I'd only been gone three or so hours. This was ridiculous.

"He told me because I'm your team leader. I told Sofia and Kayleigh because they're your friends… and Freddy and Penelope, since they're on our team." She winced. "It's possible they then told other people."

"Oh."

"I know we haven't always had the best relationship," said the woman who'd pinned me to a wall, choked me, and threatened to tear out my pubic hair, "but if there's anything I can do…"

"I'm fine," I lied, "but thanks."

Thanks. I was already getting tired of the word. And starting to regret coming to the sub-dorm, cookies notwithstanding. Even with my power active, it was hard to keep my grief and anger packed away with everyone poking at the wound.

"Okay. Just keep it in mind." After a moment's hesitation, she patted me on the shoulder. Then she was gone.

Maybe a real Cape would've known what to say in response. Maybe a real Cape would've risen to the challenge and done a shift at the Liquid Hero anyway.

But it had been a long fucking day and having a night off and to myself was an unexpected gift I had no intention of refusing. When my team headed to the bar a few minutes later, I stayed behind.

And then, when I heard the exterior door finally close, I went down the hall and threw up the cookies I'd just eaten.

○○○

I was in the common room, sprawled on the couch, when Silt came calling. Somehow, I knew who it was even before I opened the door. No idea what tipped me off, but sure enough, there she was, in the nice pair of pants and the button-up shirt she wore when working at the Liquid Hero. There was none of the overt sympathy I'd seen in Winter and Poltergeist's faces, but her brown eyes were warm, her smile just a bit wider than normal. She waved two bottles of beer in the air. "Figured you could use one of these right about now, Skeletor."

"I'm not sure me drinking is a good idea."

"Drinking's never a good idea." She scooted past me and plopped down onto the couch, kicking off her shoes and putting her feet up on the coffee table. "That's why we do it."

It was actually kind of hard to argue with that logic. I sat down next to her and accepted the offered beer. It wasn't the stuff we served on tap at the Liquid Hero, which meant it had a chance of actually being good. I glanced over at Silt's bare feet. If Winter were there, she'd be having a conniption.

"Aw damn," said Sofia, catching my gaze. "Another one."

"Another one?"

"Sad fool ensnared by the sight of my pretty feet." She mock-scowled. "I had to leave Arizona because so many people wanted to worship them."

Which was just weird enough to sound almost true, despite her feet being… well… completely average, in my estimation. Except for the iridescent nail polish, which didn't feel like Silt's usual style.

In fact… I gave my friend a more careful once-over.

"Damn, Boneboy. Beer goggles are only supposed to happen *after* you start drinking."

Her fingernails were painted too, albeit in a different color than her toes. There was product in her thick brown hair. And the button-up shirt she had on looked like it had actually been ironed.

"When were you going to introduce your new girlfriend, Sofia?"

I didn't get to see Silt floored very often, so even in the face of all that had occurred that day, I had to enjoy it.

"How does someone," she finally managed, "who went six months without realizing Kayleigh was into him put that sort of shit together so fast?"

"Maybe I just know you better than I do her."

"Or maybe you're only an idiot when it comes to yourself," she decided. "As for Colleen… I'm giving her a few more weeks before introductions."

"Don't want to scare her off?"

"I want to make sure she's worth introducing." Her grin fell away. "I know you probably don't want to talk about anything, but Tessa—"

"Yeah. She told me she'd spread the news." I sighed.

"Not to be blunt about it, but… I didn't know you had any family left."

"I don't. Didn't. Whatever." I met Silt's eyes and found only compassion. For some reason, it was easier to take from her than from Tessa or Penelope. "It was the orphanage back in Bakersfield."

"Mama Rogers?"

"Rawlins, but yeah. A Crow showed up on the doorstep this morning, murdered her and everyone else in the building, and burned the whole place down."

"The children?"

"No survivors." I shook my head. "There were a few new faces, but… most of them were there when I was."

"Fuck." Somehow, she gave the word multiple syllables. "Does this walking shit-stain of a soon-to-be corpse have a name?"

"Not yet. But I know his face. Both of their faces."

"Both?"

I didn't answer, and was relieved when Silt let the matter drop. I'd only involved her and the others in the research into Sally Cemetery because the Black Hat was long dead and shouldn't be able to reach them. Tyrant was another matter entirely.

Sofia popped off the cap of her beer with a thumb, and raised the bottle. "To Mama Rawlins and her many children, and the unholy hell we're going to unleash on their behalf."

I'd already tapped bottles with her and taken a sip when what she'd said sank in.

"We?"

"Your family's dead," she told me, swallowing her beer with a grimace. "Mine might as well be. Far as I'm concerned, this right here is family. You and me. Fuck if I'm going to sit around and let my brother carry the load by himself."

If I'd been able to cry… if tears hadn't deserted me in that long year after my mom's murder, maybe that would've been the moment. Instead, I just tapped her bottle again with mine.

"Thank you."

"Don't get soft on me now, Skeletor." Her grin was shaky. "I'm gonna need you to keep being the hardass for a few years at least."

"We'll take care of things here in the Free States, and then it's on to Brownsville," I predicted, "and fuck anyone who stands in the way of our family of two."

"Damn straight. Only—"

She coughed as another knock came at the front door, this one quieter than the Earthshaker's had been. I opened it to find Vibe, for once without Paladin in tow. Behind her was Stonewall, carrying an armful of beers.

"—it might be more than just a family of two," finished Silt.

CHAPTER 27

"Next question, please."

It was weird being on stage, staring out into an auditorium of people I couldn't see. I knew the audience was small—just enough to simulate the real thing—but with the spotlights leaving me half-blind, my mind kept conjuring images of a crowded room, dozens or even hundreds of people just waiting to tear me apart.

This whole public speaking thing was going every bit as poorly as expected. Almost made me regret returning to classes after only a few days of excused absence, but truth was, doing nothing had seemed like the quickest route to Crazytown. School busywork helped keep my mind off the shit it didn't want to deal with.

Most of the time, anyway.

Maybe the weirdest part of this practice press conference was that I was in costume. Wearing it in the Training Grounds had been awesome, but I felt pretty silly standing up on a stage in a bodysuit and armor. After twenty minutes of answering questions, I was also sweating my balls off. I was even starting to question the brilliance of wearing a full mask with a skull on it.

Apparently, I wasn't the only one.

"Walker, are you concerned that your costume—and indeed your chosen Cape name—might scare the very people you are sworn to protect?"

I couldn't see who'd asked the question, but her voice was pretty, even if her words were not.

"I think the post-Break world is scary," I replied carefully, speaking past the microphone so that it picked up my voice without the feedback I'd gotten on my first two answers. "Sometimes, it's good to have the bogeyman on your side."

Next to me, Ricky stiffened. Apparently, I'd said something wrong. Again.

"The only people who should be scared of me," I tried again, "are the people who misuse their powers."

"Next question," said Ricky, his smile almost as blindingly bright as the spotlight.

"The country has never had a Crow Cape before," said someone else, this one male but every bit as polished as the last speaker. "What made you want to be the first?"

I swallowed. Open-ended questions were mine fields. I'd learned that much from Ricky. The more specific the question, the better my chances of not saying something that would destroy my Q rating. Whatever that was.

Even worse, I wasn't sure I had an answer. As a child, I'd wanted to be a Cape because having powers sounded awesome and punching evildoers in the face did too. As a first-year, I'd mostly just wanted to avoid going insane. After the revelations at the Hole and the battle that came after, that didn't seem enough of a reason anymore.

Why *did* I want to be a Cape? To protect smug, slick civilians like the consultants currently peppering me with questions? Hell no. To get rich off of endorsement deals? Nah. I'd already been told by these same people how unlikely those would be for me.

What about to protect the people I cared for?

I gave that a moment's thought, aware that Ricky was getting more and more tense the longer I went without responding. Most of the people I cared for were dead. But the handful who remained? Of course I wanted to protect them. But was that enough reason for me to be a Cape? Given that my friends would end up in different cities and on totally different teams, it didn't feel like it.

Finally, I gave up and went with one of the generic answers Ricky had drilled into me.

"The only thing necessary for the triumph of evil is for good people to do nothing," I quoted, feeling like a dumbass. "My abilities give me the opportunity to defend this country in ways the non-powered will never have. It's my duty as a citizen to give back, and I'm proud to do so as a Cape."

It was a shitty fucking answer that had absolutely nothing to do with who I was or how I actually felt, but Ricky was nodding his fool head off, and that megawatt smile of his had made a return.

"Those are all the questions Walker has time for today, ladies and gentlemen of the press," he said smoothly. "We thank you for this opportunity."

As he ushered me off stage, the auditorium lights came back on, and the so-called members of the press were revealed as Ricky's fellow consultants. El Bosque was being escorted up onto the stage, his own handler in tow. Santiago's costume was a sleeveless bodysuit in different shades of green, with some sort of leaf pattern circling his legs. Neither the half mask nor the hooded cloak could hide his wide grin. He was way more excited about the whole thing than I'd been.

"That was almost passable," enthused Ricky, once we'd exited the auditorium, "except for the pause before you answered the last question. What happened there?"

"I wanted to be truthful with my answer."

"Nobody cares about the truth. As long as it sounds good and *seems* authentic, everyone's happy. Hesitation makes it seem like you've got something to hide."

"So we're not supposed to give our answers any thought?"

"Of course you are. Just don't do it on stage. That's why we've been doing all of this prep work. You need to know your answers before the questions are even asked."

"What if it's a question I've never heard before?"

"Fall back on platitudes. They exist for a reason. Or quote someone famous, like Paladin or Dominion. People love that. But it won't happen as much as you might think. Press conferences are rarely open to the public. Both your team's press officer and your individual image consultant will have vetted the attendees and their questions."

"So it's all just a show."

"Didn't you hear Mr. Kisten's speech? *Life's* a show, Damian. The country needs Powers, and Powers need the goodwill of the public to operate. That's how this business works."

If I knew Ricky—and after all these weeks, I was sad to say I kind of did—this was the part where he'd start back in on changing my name from Walker.

"And as you're finding out, it's not as easy as it looks on vid. It's even harder when you start with a handicap. Which is why we should really think about your name again."

Totally called it.

ooo

Even two months after our last trip to the Training Grounds, my pod still smelled like me; that weird blend of sweat and fear and odor my physical body dumped while my mind was off getting murdered in the simulation. I rolled my eyes as the restraints were tightened and the pod lid slid shut. Maybe Tessa would give me access after-hours to come down and give the damn thing a better cleaning.

And then I was in the virtual reality construct, still wrinkling my nose, even though the mask now covering my face smelled new and synthetic.

"Well, this is different." Muse was looking around, bulky flamethrower in hands. We were in another city sim, much like we'd seen against Silt's team, but this city wasn't in ruins. It could have been San Francisco, if it weren't for the snow falling from thick white clouds above us, and the foot-deep snowdrifts that had accumulated on the streets.

"Ugh." Poltergeist scowled. "Five seconds in and I'm already regretting having just a domino mask. Thank God our costumes are insulated. Any chance you can make this all go away, Penelope?"

"For an entire city?" The Weather Witch seemed the most comfortable of all of us, but she shook her head. "Heck no."

"Figures. Well, it'll probably bother Team Four even more than it does us. They don't have any flyers, and El Bosque's going to have a tough time attacking us with plants if everything's dormant because of the cold."

"As long as none of the snow melts and gives Makara all the water in the world to work with," I added.

Freddy looked at his flamethrower. "Shit."

"Wait for us to take Patty down," decided Tessa. "Then you can barbecue away."

"Cool." The Switch boosted Tessa and Penelope's powers, as usual, and Winter took to the sky. For once, I was staying behind. With air superiority, it made sense to let Winter do the scouting. Until she found the other team's base, I'd be on defense with everyone else.

Ten minutes later, I was starting to realize just how boring playing defense can be. I stomped around a bit, trying to stay loose and active. The synthetic material used in our costumes was rated for both desert and arctic conditions, but it was still all too easy to stiffen up, or even worse, let your limbs fall asleep.

Finally, we heard Winter's voice on our comm units. "Spotted the Viking and El Bosque, coming your direction on foot. Erik's got an axe as big as he is."

"No sign of Wormhole or Makara?" asked Tessa.

"None. They must be guarding their base."

Muse's shivering had very little to do with the cold, but we'd gotten used to the little guy's nerves over the past few months of simulations. At least he wasn't throwing up every damn time anymore. The smile as he shouldered the flamethrower was full of anticipation. "That's what I like to hear."

"Weird that Evelyn would stay behind though," I said, leaning on the staff I'd added to my gear list for this mission. The metal alloy it was made of was supposed to be nearly unbreakable, and I was hopeful it would provide the edge I needed against the Viking.

I doubted it would penetrate the Titan's armored skin, but it would give me a lever I could use to unbalance him. Putting his oversized ass on the ground was half the battle. I'd let Poltergeist or Winter handle the rest.

A little voice in my mind reminded me of my conversation with Alexa about using death-touch in the sim, but I pushed it away. There'd be time enough to experiment with that shit later.

"You said it yourself… she can only teleport to places she's been. That makes her kind of useless in fights like this." Tessa's swords rose into the air, circling her like a storm of steel. "Winter, why don't you lure Erik and Santi over here. I'm freezing my ass off waiting for them to find us."

"On my way," said Penelope.

Looking skyward, I had to wonder if the other team would even spot Winter in all that white. The snow was coming down even harder than when we'd first entered, and between her costume and her hair, she might as well have just been one more part of the storm.

Unlike the drone that was hovering silently in the air behind us.

I pointed it out to the others with a shout, but it was too late. Snow crunched behind me, and someone grabbed me by the shoulder.

And then Wormhole and I teleported into darkness.

I'd traveled once before with Wormhole, back when she'd taken me to Ludlow on the first leg of my journey to the Hole. This felt just the same; a transition into a world without light or life or heat, where the only sensation was the hand on my shoulder. It was a place where time had no meaning. On our previous teleport, I'd felt like I was there for anywhere between a second and an hour, unable to move or breathe as we tunneled through the boundaries of space.

This time, my power was already active. I couldn't see, couldn't hear, couldn't even feel, but my body was a puppet to my power, and I remembered where Evelyn's hand had been gripping my shoulder. Quick as thought, slow as age, I ordered my right hand up until it made contact with hers.

And then I pushed that emptiness out and into her body.

It wasn't like when I'd killed Carnage. Some of that was probably us being in mid-teleport. More of it was that Evelyn was a small woman instead of a nine foot tall colossus. Either way, I didn't get any energy back from her at all. Just fingers crumbling to dust beneath my own. Then she was gone.

Apparently, this whole death-touch thing *hadn't* been a one-time event, after all.

If I'd had a mouth to smile with, I'd have been grinning from ear to ear, but I'd dumped all of my power into the other woman, and there was nothing left to manipulate my own body.

Which was when I realized I was still in that weird interim dimension, caught between breaths, in vacuum and bitter cold that had nothing to do with weather.

I'd killed the Teleporter in mid-jump, and now I was stuck.

Ice in the lungs I couldn't feel.

Darkness so absolute I thought I'd gone blind.

A desperate need for oxygen yet no way to breathe it in.

Space without substance. Time without end.

Every millisecond in that place was an hour.

Every hour was a week.

I floated alone in the void, paralyzed and powerless, for decades.

ooo

The dim illumination of the room hit me like a hammer as my pod slid open. After so long without light, it felt more like an assault than escape. I forced myself to suck in the oxygen I desperately needed to live. It burned all the way down into my chest.

As soon as my restraints were released, I was out of the pod, pushing past the other techs still releasing my teammates. Everything felt surreal, the lights still painfully bright, the hallway unfamiliar, the Roman numerals on each door swimming slowly into shape.

Luckily, I knew Team Four's room was right next to ours.

I kicked open the door, not even paying attention to the tech who dived out of the way. Evelyn was being helped out of her pod at the far side of the room.

"Sir, you're not supposed to enter a rival team's pod room," said another tech.

I ignored him, and started for Wormhole.

The Teleporter was on her feet now, eyes wide as she saw me coming. Her shoulder-length brown hair was a mess of damp tangles around her face.

"Get out of my team room, Damian!"

"What the fuck, Evelyn?!" I asked her.

"Calm down, man," said Santiago, leaning back against his own pod without a care in the world. "By now, you guys should be used to losing."

"Easiest match we've had yet," agreed the Viking, massive arms folded across his chest. "But if you think you can do better in the real world, let's go."

"Erik…" Patty was the last of Team Four to exit their Pod.

"He's in our territory, Makara," argued the Titan. "That makes him fair game."

I ignored them all, eyes locked on Wormhole. "Years," I told her. "I spent fucking years trapped in whatever the hell you dig through to teleport. No oxygen. No food. No light. Just cold emptiness, endlessly on repeat until the sim ended."

She blanched, for just a moment, then shrugged. "Serves you right."

The world went still. I found myself taking note of the positions of everyone in the room. The techs were little more than potential tripping hazards. The youngest had to be pushing thirty, with a potbelly and the muscle tone of… well, someone who hadn't been subjected to Nikolai's insane training regimen. Even if they were willing to put themselves in harm's way, they'd be far too slow to matter.

That left Team Four. With the dampeners active, Santiago was their best fighter, but Erik's size made him the more immediate threat. Still, a punch to the throat would bring the big man down, and if I timed it just right, I could even use his body as a screen between me and El Bosque. By then I'd only be steps from Evelyn, with nobody close enough to stop me. And then…

I mentally blinked, and the world snapped back into motion. And then *what*? What was I doing?

"I was just planning to bring you up into the sky and drop you," continued Wormhole, voice hard enough to hammer nails. "You're the one who killed me mid-transit. You're the one who trapped himself. Hell, you're the one who broke his word and came back to the Academy! You're not even supposed to be here anymore!"

It was hard to believe Evelyn had been part of that original group with Unicorn, Silt, Vibe, and me. One was dead, two had become my friends, but Wormhole… somehow, all those hours together had only made her hate me.

Maybe it was time to return the favor.

I took a step toward Erik.

"Walker!" Poltergeist's voice cracked like a whip behind me.

"Control your little minion, Tessa." The Viking sneered. "Before we do it for you."

"Seriously, Erik. Just shut up already." My team leader's voice was tired. It softened somewhat as she spoke to my back. "Damian. Let's go."

I almost ignored her. One more step and everything would be in motion, and whatever happened would happen. There'd be consequences, sure, but I'd get the payback I deserved, the payback I needed.

Except this wasn't *really* the payback I wanted, was it? Team Four was just a convenient stand-in, Wormhole an easy target. She'd trapped me in an alternate dimension, but so what? Olympia had liquefied my damn body. Silt had dropped a building on me. Welcome to the Academy.

Evelyn's voice was hard, yeah, but her face was drawn and pale. I recognized fear when I saw it. Fear of me. Fear of whatever she'd seen in my face. The fear of a small woman facing down a larger, stronger man.

Fuck.

I was many things, few of them good, but I never, ever wanted to be a bully.

"I'm sorry." Not sure if I was saying it to Tessa or Evelyn. Maybe both. Maybe I was talking to myself even, to that part that so badly wanted someone to pay for what I'd seen in Bakersfield. I swallowed, pushing that part down, missing the distance my power gave me, and then turned and followed Poltergeist into the hall.

○○○

That night, I had the dream again.

CHAPTER 28

I woke just before five, chased from my bed by the images of a campus—a city, even—of the dead. It was hard to understand why the dream was so disturbing. At first glance, it was actually tamer than my usual nightmares. But there was something disquieting about it; the way it recurred, the way the silent stillness felt right, the way dream-me felt so at home being the eye of an entropic storm. It was not a normal dream, even by my abnormal standards, and it becoming a part of the fabric of my nights felt like a warning of things to come.

I shivered in the confines of my room. Pretty sure it wasn't just the air conditioning.

Tessa was on the couch when I made my way to the common room, once again dressed for a run. This time, her leggings were white and her shirt was aqua and cropped, leaving her ripped abs exposed. Slowly but surely, the Academy was molding us all into peak physical form. Truth was, Tessa could have stepped right out of a hero vid just as easily as Orca, Spectra, or Ember.

Or Paladin, Santiago, and Jeremiah, for that matter.

She looked up from her Glass, and if she didn't seem wildly happy to see me, she didn't seem too put out either. "You're up early again. Too much sleep?"

That could have been a dig about how I still hadn't returned to work at the Liquid Hero, but I didn't think it was. After all, I'd offered to return to work and it was Poltergeist who had insisted I needed more time.

Given what had almost happened with Wormhole, it's possible she had a point.

"I don't have the best dreams. Sometimes, waking up early is the better option." I waved at her outfit. "Running again?"

"Every morning. And if you're going to tell me that's crazy, save it. I get enough of that from London."

"Ember doesn't like running?"

"Or early mornings." Tessa grinned suddenly. "Or anything that involves work, if we're being honest. I've never seen someone so desperate to graduate just so she can have a support team do all her menial labor."

I could count the number of times London had spoken to me on two hands and still have fingers left over, but that did sound like the Pyromancer.

"So what happened yesterday?" she asked me, grin disappearing. "It looked like you were preparing to take on all of Team Four when I came in."

I winced. "I think I was."

"That's—"

"Please don't say crazy."

"—dumb," she finished smoothly. "And a great way to get expelled. For real, this time."

"Yeah."

"I'm serious. I know it's only been two weeks since… well… everything that happened, and I can't imagine what you're going through, but Bard's only going to give you so many chances."

"Why do you care?"

"You're Team Five. We can't afford to lose you. Especially with us getting crushed yesterday, yet again."

"Sorry about that." The more I apologized, the easier it came. Not sure what that said about me or how being a second-year was changing me. "I had no idea Wormhole had learned to teleport places she'd never been."

"Apparently, she just needs to see the place now. According to Patty, they got the idea of using a drone from our match with Nadia's team. It's just bad luck for us that they brought one with thermal imaging to a city in the dead of winter."

"So Evelyn teleported in with Makara and then removed me from the equation?"

"Yeah. And Freddy panicked and used his flamethrower and gave a Hydromancer all the water they could possibly use. Maybe if I could make shields or something, we'd have still had a chance, but water's too slippery to grab, even with Muse's boost. By the time I could get a hold of Patty, Santiago was attacking us with what must have once been a potted cactus and Erik was swinging the axe Penelope warned us about. We didn't last long after that. Apparently, they were confused that killing us all didn't end the sim."

"I was still alive. Just trapped in another dimension where time barely remembers to exist."

"Seriously?" She shivered. "That's spooky."

"It was worse to live through it. Why do you think I was so pissed?"

"You're always pissed."

Which was true more often than not, so I let it slide.

"Anyway, with Evelyn gone, they had to walk our flag back to their base, but once they did—"

"Team Five lost again," I finished.

"Yeah." She stared down at her Glass, even though its screen had gone dark. "I kind of suck at this."

"If you say so."

"Our record speaks for itself."

"You have a Crow and a Switch on your team. Freddy's useful, yeah, but also limited. I'm not even that, and it means you and Winter are on your own. Two against four is shitty strategy."

"All of my strategies are shitty."

"Tessa…" I dropped onto the couch next to her. Six months ago, that would have troubled her. Now, she just arched an eyebrow. "There's no question that first loss was your fault—"

"Wow. Tell me how you really feel, dick."

"—but since then? You've been a good team leader, whatever our record. I'm serious," I said, talking right over her protests. "You work your ass off. You listen to our suggestions. You keep us focused on what matters."

For once in her life, Tessa seemed lost for words.

"You leading us gives us our best chance to win. The fact that we're losing anyway isn't your fault. So don't take that shit to heart," I concluded. "We both know I have almost no shot at a roster spot here in the Free States, but even out in the Badlands, I'd be blessed to have a team leader like you."

"That's—"

"Just the truth."

"—very nice to hear," she said. "*That's* what I was going to say, before you interrupted me for like the third time in five minutes." Wonder of wonders, her tone was more teasing than annoyed.

"I may have picked up the habit from Kayleigh," I admitted.

"Oh god, don't remind me. The team leader meetings are complete disasters." She grinned again, tucking a stray curl behind her ear. "But seriously, that means a lot."

"Even from me?"

"Maybe especially from you." She mock-scowled. "You never hesitate in telling me when I do something wrong, so I know you're not just blowing smoke up my ass either." For some reason, that was enough to make the spots of color in her cheeks bloom again. "So to speak. To be honest, I was dreading having you on this team, but…" She shook her head. "It could be worse."

"It could be better too. You have no idea how amazing those cookies Winter made were. If we could just get her to bake for our team instead of the cafeteria, losing would almost be enjoyable."

"They taste as good as they smelled?"

"Better. If she doesn't make it as a Cape, she would absolutely kill as a baker."

We both paused for a moment, trying and failing to imagine a world where Winter somehow didn't become a Cape. Finally, Tessa shrugged.

"I'm glad she's not sharing them then. I'm already struggling to keep the calories off as it is."

Which was clearly bullshit, given the abs I'd already noticed, as well as the muscle definition in her legs, but I decided not to call her on that.

"And speaking of the struggle," she continued, putting aside her Glass with a sigh, "those miles aren't going to run themselves."

She was almost to the door when I called out.

"Do you want a partner?"

"I'm sorry?" She didn't turn around, but her shoulders went stiff like I'd just poked her in the spine.

"To run with," I elaborated. "If my power forces me to charge around death-touching people, I could really use the conditioning. And…"

"And?"

I shrugged, even though she wasn't looking. I wasn't going to tell her that the thought of being alone, dream fresh in my mind, was terrifying. I still had *some* pride. "I don't know. Just feel like getting the blood moving."

"Okay." She spun about and leaned against the door, expression almost amused. "You've got one minute to get changed and then I'm gone."

"I'm already good to go," I told her, motioning to my greys.

"Just because Nikolai makes us run in those ugly sweats doesn't mean you have to do so in your free time. Los Angeles doesn't get all that hot, but it's *still* July."

"I'll make do," I told her, not adding that they were the only clothes I had to run in.

"Alright." The smile she sent me was full of challenge. "Let's see if you can keep up."

I couldn't. Not for long anyway. Her pace more than made up for my longer stride, and she left me in the dust, but after the second mile, she moderated her speed, just a bit. And morning after morning, run after run, the gap between us narrowed.

CHAPTER 29

"So now we're 1-3," I concluded. "I thought Winter's head was going to explode when she saw us back at the bottom of the rankings."

Alexa gave that small half-smile. "How do you feel about it?"

"I don't know. I want us to do well, of course, but... it's not real, you know?" I shrugged. "We're not going to be playing capture the flag with Black Hats once we graduate."

"True. It sounds like the scenarios are being kept simple so that you can focus on basic tactics. I suspect that will change in the second semester."

"Good. Maybe we'll start winning then." I frowned. "Tessa deserves a victory or two, with all the work she's putting in."

"Interesting," said Alexa, in a voice as mild as a spring breeze. Before I could ask her what she meant, she continued. "We've talked a lot about your teammates today, but very little about you. How is Damian Banach doing?"

I sagged back into the couch. It was a subject I'd been trying to avoid, even in my own head. After a long minute of silence, I shrugged. This whole trust thing really sucked sometimes. "Angry. Still. Always, I guess. Tired. Confused."

"Confused?"

"You know we just finished our program with Image Consulting, right?" I waited for her nod, and continued. "The last few sessions were on public speaking. Interviews, sponsorship gigs, and press conferences."

"Not one of my favorite aspects of being a Cape," admitted Alexa, "but necessary. And?"

"In the press conference, one of the fake reporters asked me why I wanted to be a Cape, and I didn't have an answer. Well, I had a bunch of answers, but none of them felt right."

"Damian, you've just experienced a serious tragedy in a year already full of them. It's not unusual to experience moments of doubt."

"This isn't about Mama Rawlins. Or Nyah," I argued, glancing briefly from my monochromatic shrink to the ghosts that crowded the room. "I came to the Academy because Mr. Grey—Tyrant—told me training might keep me from going mad. The jury's still out on that, but even if it ends up being true, that's just a reason to train. It's not a reason to go on and be a Cape."

Alexa stayed silent, dark eyes intent on me from across the room.

"So why am I doing this? I've been trying to figure that out all week."

"And?"

"I was hoping you might have some ideas."

"I think it's something that everyone has to decide for themselves," she mused. "A Cape's life is not like what they show in the hero vids. You know that. The truth is, we all have our own reasons for serving. Some do it for the fame and prestige. Others because they want to do good, whatever that might mean to them. Some do it just for the thrill of the challenge."

"Why did *you* become a Cape?"

"I wanted to protect people. Much like you, I think."

"Me?" I rolled my eyes. "I don't even *like* people, Alexa."

"I think we both know you have a long list of individuals you would have protected if you were able."

That hurt. Maybe she'd meant it to. "It's a little late for that."

"So everyone you care about is gone?"

"Well, no. But the few who remain can take care of themselves. And once I graduate, I'll be deployed to some tiny team in the Badlands, and won't be anywhere near those people anyway. Yet I'll still be expected to put my life on the line defending random strangers, people who probably hate the idea of me being a Cape in the first place. Why would I want to protect them?"

"Because it is who you are. You showed that growing up in the orphanage, when you fought your way to dominance and then used your position to protect the other children. When you and Ms. Watai saved a completely random stranger from the predations of two Beast Shifters last year. When you told your Ethics professor that you'd murder the world before you let any harm come to Ms. Watai herself."

It was weird how that last bit kept coming back to haunt me.

"And yes, despite what you seem to have told yourself, when you fought and nearly died at the Hole."

I frowned, unconvinced. "That was self-preservation."

"Self-preservation would have been staying down and waiting for aid, rather than warning Tempest, attacking Fallout, and killing Carnage."

I waved my hand dismissively. "The point is, I was there already. I was involved. I didn't have much choice. Not like the Capes who flew in from the border, already tired and injured from battling Tezcatlipoca and his puppets all morning. If I'd been four hundred miles away, I wouldn't have come charging toward a massacre. That's a real hero. I don't have that in me."

"What would you do if someone attacked one of your first-years," she pressed.

"I'd kick their ass," I answered automatically. "But that's different. I know them."

"And do you like them all?"

"Some more than others, but they have their moments, I guess. More importantly, they're my responsibility."

"And when you graduate, you'll be responsible for a city."

"That's different."

"Only in scale." The bracelet of black polished stones was on her right wrist for a change. "A team of five or ten tasked with protecting the lives of hundreds of thousands. What you quickly learn is that, at the end of the day, being a Cape isn't really about the people you are protecting."

"Then what is it about?"

"It's about making the decision to protect them."

Which sounded like the same damn thing to me.

"You defend those you love," she continued. "And those you consider to be yours. Graduation or not, you'll be a Cape the moment you decide to extend that protection to everyone."

Considering my opinion of the general public, it was hard to imagine ever making that choice. I shook my head. "Maybe I'll focus on that fame angle you were talking about instead."

"So you're going to change your name and costume to something more marketable after all?" Her black eyes sparkled. "Ricky will be so pleased."

Sometimes, Alexa was too well-informed for her own good. It was time to change the subject.

"Did you find out anything about your colleague up in San Francisco?"

That wiped the merriment right off of her face. "Yes. A nosy neighbor reported seeing a man show up at Yin's door sometime in the early afternoon. He was invited inside and departed again less than fifteen minutes later. The visitor was, by all accounts, thoroughly average in appearance, except for one detail."

"He had eyes like copper pennies."

"Yes."

Shit. "Tyrant killed your co-worker? Personally?"

"So it seems. Which means, more than likely, that he somehow found out about the investigation."

"How?"

"I don't know. Besides you and me, only three other people knew, including Yin himself, and they were all in my agency."

"You don't think one of them told him, do you?"

She frowned. "If they had, I believe we'd all have been attacked. It's more likely that Yin made a mistake that caught Tyrant's eye. Some small innocuous detail that he missed when covering his tracks."

Which was kind of terrifying, to be honest, given that Alexa and her co-workers seemed to be all about covering their tracks.

"It's just one of many questions I have," she continued, "and not even the biggest."

"Why would he invite Tyrant in?"

"Exactly. That, above all, is the part that makes no sense. Yin was a cautious man, as befits people in our profession. He should have run as soon as he saw the op was blown."

An even more terrible question hit me, so awful that I almost didn't want to voice it.

"Is what happened to Mama Rawlins and the others my fault?"

"Absolutely not. It's the fault of the Crow you saw and the man who apparently sent him."

"But they were fine for a year. And then I told you about Tyrant, asked you to open an investigation, and now they're dead."

"Yes."

Her one word answer stole all the breath from my lungs.

Black eyes met mine from across the room. "If you wish to blame someone other than the creatures responsible, blame my agency. Blame me. We were the ones who somehow failed to keep an off-the-books, deep-black investigation from being discovered."

Part of me couldn't help but agree with her on that front. Someone had fucked up, and nineteen people, most of them children, were dead because of it. Maybe I wasn't the only one responsible for their death, but I sure as hell shared some of the guilt.

"It gets worse," she warned me.

Because of course it fucking did.

"How?"

"The individual who tested you. Jeremy Brown? He was found dead in his house behind the testing station four days ago."

"Tyrant's tying up loose ends, like the other Crow said," I reasoned, before my eyes went wide. "What about the Jacobsens?"

It had been ten years since Norm and Sue had sent me back to Mama Rawlins, but it still stung. And yet... I didn't want either of them dead. Not really.

"I have assigned them a protective detail, but so far, your former foster family has not been targeted."

The reason for that was obvious once I thought about it.

"They never met Mr. Grey. Tyrant, I mean."

"Yes."

Which left only one person unaccounted for, besides me. Her Majesty, the Queen of Smiles, who Tyrant had hired to escort me to the Academy. I'd been trying to remember the exact details of my conversations with the mercenary, but it had been no use. I'd spent too much of that trip off-balance, first fixated on the biker's fabulous body, and then convinced she was going to turn into a storm of shrapnel and eat me.

Even so… I'd pieced together enough to make me certain she'd known who Tyrant was. Would that give the Black Hat more reason to come after her or less?

When Her Majesty had given me the Legion tech gun, she'd said she was balancing the debt between us, but as far as I was concerned, I was the one in debt. Big time. And if she was riding around the continent with a target on her leather-clad back, I needed to warn her.

Somehow.

"What Tyrant failed to realize," Alexa added, when my silence had grown just a bit too long, "is that in his rush to tie up loose ends, he has given us new strings to tug on. How he found out about the investigation. What he did to track down Yin and convince a dedicated agent to let him inside. And of course, his connection to James Taylor."

"Who?"

In answer, she pulled a sheet of actual paper from her desk drawer and slid it over to me.

From the upper left corner of the page, the mad eyes of the Crow who had killed Nyah stared back at me.

"I ran a search on the description you provided us," said Alexa. "And this is who came up."

"That's him." I scanned the rest of the page. It looked like some sort of record or rap sheet. "That's the fucker."

"These are his records from juvenile detention."

That got my attention. "He was arrested but not sent to the Hole?"

"His crimes were petty theft and property destruction. There was no indicator at the time that he was a Crow. That came later, shortly before he ran away from home and disappeared from the police's radar."

I frowned down at the page. Something about the name was familiar, but I was sure the only time I'd seen the guy was in Nyah's vision.

"Every question we answer will lessen the veil of secrecy that protects Tyrant," continued Alexa. "That's how we're going to catch him and make sure he answers for what he's done."

I tapped the page in my hands. "Tyrant *and* James Taylor."

"Yes. But I'll be bringing the entire Defenders team with me to make the arrest." She shot me a look I couldn't interpret. "Taylor is a Low Four, Damian."

And that was when I remembered where I'd seen the name before.

'Jimmy' Taylor was a name Tessa and Jeremiah had found in their research. He'd been one of the Crows who went missing, shortly after Tyrant had come to get me.

Why had Tyrant sent a Low-Three to the Academy and kept the Low-Four for himself, to so obviously drift off into madness?

And how the fuck was I going to stop either one, when they so badly outclassed me?

CHAPTER 30

The last two weeks of the semester went by in a flash. I think our teachers were as happy as we were to reach the break. Something about the upcoming vacation had even my fellow second-years bouncing off the walls. Literally, in the case of Supersonic, who could never resist showboating.

Can't say I was looking forward to being stuck on campus by myself for all that time, especially since I'd been relying on school to distract me, but a lack of homework, tutors, and Ethics classes all sounded pretty appealing.

And maybe Sally Cemetery would stop by again to answer a question or seven.

Even on the last day before break, Tessa was up at five for her run. Wonder of wonders, I was too. After weeks of running together, I no longer struggled to keep up. Today, we'd settled on a pace that let us talk as we ran.

I know what you're thinking. Running with Tessa? Weird enough. But talking with her? Who the fuck could have seen that coming when we were both first-years?

I had a sneaking suspicion the world would have been an unpredictable mess even without Dr. Nowhere's dream.

"It still seems stupid that Dean Bard won't let you go anywhere on break," said Tessa, as we curved left past Nikolai's concrete bunker. Even a year and a half later, the building still looked to me like a giant frog squatting to take a dump. "What does he think you're going to do? Go on a summertime killing spree?"

"I think he's just happier knowing where I am and that I'm staying out of trouble."

"It's dumb."

"It's not like I have anywhere else to go." Since she'd called me on the habit, I'd been working on not interrupting her when we talked. The need to suck down oxygen as I ran made it easier than it might otherwise have been. "At least here, I have food and a roof over my head. And a bathroom all to my fucking self, for once."

"Didn't Kayleigh invite you to stay at her house in the city?"

"Yeah. Again." I still didn't see Vibe as much as I had when we were first-years, but whatever tension there was between us had finally disappeared in the aftermath of my Bakersfield trip. "But she's introducing Matthew to her parents over the break. Even if Bard was willing to relax his rules, I wouldn't want to intrude on that."

"That's weirdly thoughtful of you." Poltergeist had unconsciously lengthened her stride, but the faster pace didn't seem to interfere with *her* ability to talk.

"Is it? I just think it'll be fucking awkward. 'Hey mom and dad, here's my new boyfriend. We're going to go make out for a bit. Can you entertain the crazy necromancer I brought home? Just don't feed him after midnight.'"

"After midnight?"

I took a second to answer, still trying to match my pace to hers. "Hell if I know. It's from some pre-Break monster story, according to Silt."

"As awful as the Break was," said Tessa, "the world before it doesn't seem like it was all that much better."

"I was literally just thinking that. People are people. Dr. Nowhere's dream shattered the existing power structures, but it didn't really put anything better in their place."

"You sound like Amos."

"God help me. This is what happens when I actually stay awake during class."

We wove through a line of students carrying suitcases to the front gates. They were all normals, by the looks of them. A couple of the dumber ones whistled at Tessa as we ran past, only to find themselves tripping on invisible rocks soon after.

"Does that get old?"

"Boys being dicks or me making sure they pay the price for it?"

"The first one." I already knew she enjoyed flexing her power.

"For it to *get* old would mean it hadn't started that way." She sped up again as we turned down the path that looped along the southern wall. "Do you all think being assholes is going to win us over or something? Like 'oh, he stared at my boobs for five straight minutes. I bet he's going to be a lovely conversationalist. We should totally date!'?"

"Fuck if I know." And honestly, the one time I'd done it, it had been more like ten seconds. Tops.

"Well, it's moronic. How do you like it when the drunk women at the Liquid Hero grab your ass?"

"Depends on the day. And the woman."

"Seriously?" She missed a step, mid-stride, and would have stumbled if an invisible hand hadn't caught her and lifted her back to her feet. "You don't mind being treated like a piece of meat?

"There hasn't been a woman who wanted to touch me since Alicia," I responded. "Other than Kayleigh, I guess, and I had no idea that was true until it was over. I'll take meat over monster any day."

"Aim higher."

"Says the Low-Four Telekinetic to the Crow."

"I'm serious. You get your share of looks when you're working the bar."

"From people wondering how many breaks it took to get my nose looking like this," I joked. "I keep telling them I came by it naturally, but nobody believes me." To be fair, it *had* been broken a few times. But it had never looked great to start with. My now-dead father was proof of that much. One more reason I would never have children. "Anyway, I'm sorry that I was one of those dicks last year."

"You're still a dick." She kept her eyes on the path, but I could see her grin even in profile. "Sort of. Apology accepted though."

We ran past Amos' house on the southeastern side of campus, the small cottage with its white fence and apple trees incongruous among the larger campus buildings.

"So who is this Alicia, anyway?" Tessa asked. "An ex?"

"Someone I knew in Bakersfield." I pulled on my power just a bit to muffle the usual cocktail of anger and grief I felt when Alicia came up as a subject. "She died in the Palo Alto attack."

"Shit. I'm sorry." She managed five strides in silence before she couldn't help but press for more. "But before that, you and she were dating?"

"We didn't really put a name on it. She worked at her parents' shop down the block from the orphanage, and most afternoons, we had the store to ourselves."

"Was she pretty?"

"Kind of?" I scowled, not loving the trip down memory lane. "She was nice. She was warm. She was interested. When you're a teenager, that's huge. When you're a gods-fucked Crow, it's bigger than that."

"You're still a teenager," she pointed out helpfully.

"And a Crow. Maybe that's why I don't mind having some drunken freshman woman grab my ass?"

"Or maybe men are just dumb." She sped up yet again, putting an end to the conversation. I was pretty sure I'd just been insulted. What I couldn't figure out was why.

ooo

As ever, Poltergeist claimed first-shower rights when we got back to the sub-dorm. Thirty-four long minutes later, it was finally my turn. By the time I emerged, Winter and Muse were both awake and packing to leave. I'd never seen Freddy so happy, including after our sole victory in the Training Grounds. He was even sober, which practically made it a holy occasion or national holiday.

Silt had said her goodbyes the night before, leaving early to make the most out of her time with distant cousins in Phoenix, but Vibe was on the couch of our sub-dorm, talking with Tessa while the

Telekinetic repurposed the common room as her own personal packing area.

"You're only going to be gone for two weeks." I shook my head, momentarily debating between the chair still claimed by Winter's stray hairs and the free spot on the couch. The couch won again. As usual. "Don't you think three suitcases is overkill?"

"Says the man who lives his life in sweats." The Telekinetic sat on the largest of her suitcases to squash it down enough that she could zip it shut. "Two weeks catching up with my friends from high school? I don't know if this will be enough. Besides," she added with a grin that told me she'd forgotten whatever it was I'd done or said to annoy her, "the third bag is all dirty clothes. Might as well have someone else do my laundry for once."

"Lucky you. Then again, I have the whole laundromat to myself over the break. I'll be living like a king."

"Sure you will."

"I'm looking forward to some home cooking," said Kayleigh, jumping into the conversation. The little Empath looked almost aggressively cute in a short-sleeve blouse and a grey layered skirt that somehow set off the pink in her otherwise jet-black hair.

If I hadn't set her up with Paladin...

If I'd known she was into me...

I gave myself a mental slap. Might as well wish I was a Titan, or that Orca didn't have a fetish for chubby Sirens. Life's a river. You can swim in it or you can drown, but you sure as hell can't go back upstream.

"Are you stressed about introducing Paladin to your parents?"

She shrugged. "Matthew's way more worried about it than I am. He's even learned some Japanese to try to impress them with, although his accent is terrible."

"Wow." Tessa looked up from her suitcase. "He's taking this seriously."

"It's Paladin," I said. "He takes everything seriously—"

"When our relationship is one of those things, I can't really complain." Vibe beamed. "Given what my life was like before I got a handle on my powers, I think my parents are both thrilled I'm even *able* to date now, but even so, I know my dad will do the whole overprotective father thing."

"And your mom?"

"She's going to adore him. I just know it."

"Cool." Apparently, blonde-haired, blue-eyed, near-cyborgs were exactly what parents were looking for when it came to their daughters' potential boyfriends. Who knew?

That said, Matthew learning Japanese was a pretty killer move. I'd have to remember it if I ever got a bilingual girlfriend.

Or a girlfriend at all.

"Shouldn't you be packing?" I asked Kayleigh. Not that it wasn't nice to see her, but it was kind of weird she'd come over to hang out with Tessa of all people.

"I'm just taking some toiletries," she said, patting the oversized purse next to her. "I have plenty of clothing at home. I told John to come pick me up from your sub-dorm."

"John?"

"Her family's driver," said Tessa, tone almost professionally bland.

Before I could ask why Kayleigh's family had a driver, how someone got a job like that in a city where cars were still far from the norm, and why she'd told him to come to our team's dorm, there was a knock at the door.

"That must be him!" Vibe bounced up in a flurry of skirts, and rounded the couch to open the front door.

The older man standing there could have come directly from a pre-Break storybook, from the chauffeur's hat atop his head to the shiny black shoes on his feet. Even his nod to Kayleigh was picture-perfect; dignified and respectful.

"Ms. Watai, it is a genuine pleasure."

"John, it's great to see you again!" The Empath was all smiles. "Did you bring it?"

"But of course." The chauffeur lifted a brown paper bag up from where he'd placed it on the walkway. It was large enough that he needed both hands to carry it.

"Excellent. Just bring it in here, please." She invited her family driver into our sub-dorm, through the common room, and into the kitchen.

Tessa and I exchanged mystified glances, and followed them into the small space, where we found Kayleigh pulling tinfoil-wrapped parcels out of the bag and placing them inside our rarely used refrigerator.

"What's all this?" I finally decided to ask.

"Food from our chef, Martha." Kayleigh's eyes met mine and for a moment, she looked almost embarrassed. "Since Bard won't let you leave campus to stay with us, I asked her to make some meals you could heat up while you were here."

Rich. Cute. And ridiculously kind.

I really had fucked that up, hadn't I?

"That's…" I coughed, clearing my throat for no reason at all. "That's really thoughtful. Thank you. And Martha. And you, for bringing it over, John," I added, just to make sure all my bases were covered.

"It was my pleasure, sir," said the chauffeur, turning to his charge. "Are you ready to leave, Ms. Watai? I know your mother has prepared a welcome home celebration."

"John, how many times have I told you to call me Kayleigh? Or Vibe, if first names are too *informal*?" She turned to both Tessa and I. "See you all in a couple of weeks! Have fun!"

"You too—" I started to say.

"And if you run into trouble, or another unexpected visitor," she said, her eyes drilling into me, "I can be back on campus in twenty minutes or less. Just send me a message."

Then, just like that, she blew out of there, leaving the sub-dorm quieter and emptier for her absence.

"Why didn't you want to date her again?" asked Tessa, after a long moment of silence.

"I don't want to talk about it."

"I'm just saying…"

"She's better off with Matthew. And he genuinely seems to adore her." I felt like I was telling myself as much as I was telling her.

The odd thing was… it was totally working. "Who knows if it's a long-term thing, but she deserves someone who'd learn Japanese just to impress her parents."

"Yeah, they're both catches in their own way, I guess." Tessa scowled. "And so damn sweet together I could die. If I ever get like that, I want you to just death-touch me and put me out of my misery." She checked her Glass, and then went back into the kitchen. "My shuttle leaves soon, but I'm not going anywhere until we try one of the meals Kayleigh left."

"Don't you have two weeks of home-cooked meals ahead of you already?" Maybe it was the orphan in me, but I wasn't thrilled with the idea of someone taking my food.

"Do you think *my* family has a chef? My dad's a decent cook, but I'm not passing up the chance to eat something professionally prepared." She pulled a tinfoil packet from the refrigerator. "Let's try this one. It's even still warm."

It seemed there was a downside to Tessa no longer hating me.

CHAPTER 31

One day.

That's all I got.

One day of peace and quiet and having a sub-dorm to myself.

One day of staying up late watching vids and sleeping in until almost noon.

That's all I got, because the next afternoon, there was a knock at the door. And I opened it up to find that the oldest man in the world had come calling.

Amos Farshad had been sixty-nine when the Break happened, and all these decades later, he was still sixty-nine. He'd seen a lot of things go down and was never shy in telling the students of his History classes all about it.

Technically, Grannypocalypse was probably older than Amos, but I wasn't entirely sure she counted as being alive. Her Majesty had told me she'd seen the ancient Power with her own eyes, sitting in a rocking chair, drinking a cup of tea that never went empty, on a porch in front of the one house still standing in West Virginia, surrounded by miles and miles of irradiated wasteland from the last time someone had pissed the old woman off. Still, if there was one thing I knew as a Crow, it's that there was a whole wealth of possibilities between life and death. I had no idea where Grannypocalypse fell on that spectrum.

Amos, on the other hand... he was definitely alive. Grumpy as hell, liable to take a nap whenever he felt like it, and entirely unwilling to suffer fools... but alive.

And standing at my door in all his slumped-shoulder glory.

"Banach!" His voice snapped like a whip that had been left in the sun to dry and crack. "What are you doing here?"

"I live here, Amos."

"I'm not an idiot, boy." His scowl was all the more ferocious for the network of lines in his leathery skin. "I mean why aren't you at my house getting some work done?"

"What?" There'd been some debate—very quiet debate— among the students about what all those years might do to a man who'd already been old before the world ended in fire, but Amos was usually a lot sharper than this.

"Bard didn't tell you?" He read the answer in my face, and the scowl deepened. "That man. Entirely too much on his plate, especially with Marissa, and yet he still thinks he can do everything."

"Who's Marissa?"

"His wife. It's a shame what happened to her."

I waited for an explanation, but one never came.

"So what was Bard supposed to tell me?"

"That's Dean Bard to you, Banach! Show some respect! He was concerned that you'd have too much time on your hands over the break. Coincidentally, I have a fence that needs repair, apple trees that need trimming, and a body too damn ancient to waste itself on either." His smile was all Amos; part warmth, part joy, and part amused calculation. "I'm guessing you can do the math on your own?"

I could... and didn't love the answer I got. "I thought I was going to get to relax over break."

"Guess you're not an oracle."

Not that oracles were a thing, thank god. Like mind control and time travel, prophecy had apparently been a bridge too far even for Dr. Nowhere.

"Anyway, put on some work clothes, and come over. I've got lemonade. And a hat, if I can find it."

The cottage that Amos had lived in since long before the Academy's existence now sat in the southeastern corner of campus, past the enormous buildings that were the normal student dorms. When I'd first enrolled at the Academy, I'd been surprised to realize that Powers were a tiny fraction of the student body. For every one of us, there were a dozen normals, pursuing a variety of four-year degrees in Cape support-related fields.

Before I graduated—assuming I did actually graduate—I'd need to develop some relationships with seniors on that side of the divide, so that I at least had the nucleus of my staff in place when I became a Cape.

The bigger challenge would be finding an agent and a public relations specialist that I could stand. By mutual agreement, Ricky and I had decided that we would *not* be working together on a professional basis. He preferred clients who at least pretended to be manageable, and I preferred working with people who weren't smug, smarmy assholes.

Anyway, next to those oversized dorms, Amos' cottage seemed even smaller. A simple one bedroom, surrounded by apple trees, and encircled by a white picket fence that had seen better days. A few of the horizontal struts had actually broken off, and the whole thing was cracked and worn, paint peeling after so many years exposed to even Los Angeles' mild elements.

Amos was out front with the promised hat. I didn't see any lemonade, but I knew it would be coming eventually. Amos didn't stint when it came to food. Or drinks. I'd learned that much when we'd had Christmas dinner together the previous year.

"Glad you made it, Banach," he said, as I opened a gate that creaked badly and seemed to have come free from one of its hinges. "Was starting to think you fell asleep again."

"I wish." I frowned as I looked around. The fence was in bad enough condition, but the apple trees were also overgrown. I didn't know a damn thing about gardening—or even if orchards counted as gardening—but I was pretty sure the trees were supposed to look neater than that. "Things are kind of falling apart, Amos."

"I've had arthritis for a century," he grumbled. "I do what I can around the house, but—"

"I get it." The house itself had actually been transported intact from Santa Barbara, back before the town fell into the ocean. Amos had held onto it, despite Bard offering newer, larger, and better facilities, because it was the home he'd shared with his wife, Alicia.

Another Alicia. It was one thing Amos and I had in common. Maybe the only thing.

"If there're any house repairs you need help on, let me know." I wanted to kick myself as soon as the words slipped out. I liked Amos well enough, but why the hell would I volunteer for extra work?

"We'll see." He handed me the hat and a pair of work gloves, and pointed to the small shed that sat next to a pile of fresh lumber. "Tools are in the shed, along with a ladder." He brought out a folding chair and set it up on the shaded porch. "I'll supervise from here."

"Awesome." The hat was floppy, somewhat stained, and probably older than I was, but it at least kept the sun out of my eyes. I tugged on the gloves, and headed for the lumber.

"Don't you think you should remove the old boards from the fence first?" he called after me.

"I'm definitely going to remove *something*," I muttered under my breath.

"I heard that!"

"You were meant to!" I lied.

Amos' cackle startled a number of birds into flight. I watched them wing away, and wished I could be one of them.

ооо

It took me two days to fix the fence, another for the gate, and two more after that to repaint the damn thing. Amos wanted it white. Again. Even though it would show dirt and need regular upkeep.

The only good news, for me, was that I'd be gone from the Academy by third-year's semester break; either interning for one of the Cape teams or traipsing through the Badlands with the Mission and any other unwanted soon-to-be graduates. Amos would have to find someone new to do his landscaping for him.

When I was finally done painting, I learned who that someone was.

"You know Diaz, don't you, Banach?"

Paco and I shared a look across the table. The first-year Summoner had already been seated at Amos' dining room table when I came inside.

"Paco and I have crossed paths a time or two," I said, bringing over the platter of roast beef Amos had left on the kitchen counter, and placing it between the bowl of green beans and the basket of freshly-baked bread.

"I thought as much." There was a knowing glint to Amos' eyes. The faculty was made up of notorious gossips. "As he has also chosen to remain on campus for the break, I decided it only made sense that we all eat together."

"Bard's not letting you leave either?" I asked my first-year.

"Nowhere to go," he replied. "I got some offers from my classmates, but they live here in the city." He shrugged. "I'm trying to keep my head down for a bit."

I didn't know a thing about gangs or the people who joined them, but something told me Paco's departure—to be a Cape, no less—hadn't gone over too well.

"Well, I'll warn you now," I told him. "Amos is probably going to put you to work as soon as I'm off campus next year."

"Why wait for that?" asked the old man in question. "Cleaning up the orchard is a two-man job." He grinned again and waved his gnarled, crooked fingers. "I'd help, but... arthritis."

"Right." I looked at all the food on the table, food that he'd made for us despite the supposedly crippling effects of his arthritis, and rolled my eyes. Then, to Paco: "What is it that you summon anyway? It'd be really helpful if they were gardeners."

"Rats," he told me.

"Rats?"

"Well, *a* rat, so far." It was a rare treat to see him flustered. "But I'm working on that."

"Cool," I lied. It was hard to imagine what a Cape would be able to do with a single rat, but at least Summoners didn't all go crazy and murderous. "How does your rat feel about climbing trees and gnawing off branches while we watch from the porch, drinking lemonade?"

Paco winced.

"Yeah," I sighed, "I kind of figured."

○○○

Paco's power sucked, but he was still a hell of a lot more helpful than Amos had been. It took the two of us a little under a week to trim back all the apple trees to the old man's demanding specifications, and another day to tidy the yard after the mess we'd made. When we were done, we both had blisters on our hands, farmer's tans on whatever skin we'd left exposed, and a grudging feeling of accomplishment.

As much shit as Amos gave me, he'd also been one of those who fought for me as a first-year. I'd never admit it to the cranky old fart, but it felt good to give something back.

The chocolate cake we all split to celebrate the yard's completion didn't hurt either.

Thankfully, Amos didn't pull out any more of the whisky we'd shared over Christmas. Even the thought of that stuff was now forever tied to my mom's vision of her own murder. Instead, he brought out a dusty bottle of rum and poured us all cups.

"No long-winded story about where this bottle came from?" I asked.

"Call me long-winded again, Banach, and see where it gets you!" His rheumy eyes squinted in the dim light. "You're still a student in my class."

"That's how I know you're long-winded," I retorted, prompting another cackle from the old man.

"Don't learn from Banach here, Diaz," he said to Paco. "Boy has to do everything the hard way."

"I'm all about keeping things easy," said the first-year.

"Yeah, I could tell that much from your group presentation." Amos shook his head dismissively. "Anyway, there's no story for this bottle. Just something I've had a while and decided to share."

"I'll drink to that." Paco had the glass halfway to his lips when he saw Amos holding his own glass high.

"To Alicia," said the old man, meeting my gaze.

"To Alicia," I agreed.

"Who's Alicia?"

Amos' smile was almost lost in the contours of his weathered face. "A hell of a woman, Mr. Diaz."

"Two of them," I agreed.

I'm not sure Paco understood, but he raised his glass anyway. Smart kid.

CHAPTER 32

"Welcome back, second-years."

At the front of the classroom, Jessica Strich paced back and forth. Matthew's older sister was my favorite remaining professor, and not just because she'd taught me how to shoot. Despite the obvious familial resemblance, the two couldn't have been more different. Matthew was calm, controlled, and—with one notably fabulous exception—focused on always doing the right thing. Meanwhile, Jessica was a riot; quick with a joke, and even quicker with her fists, elbows, and knees.

Cute as hell too, not that she'd have anything to do with us students. If we had been classmates though, I'm pretty sure we'd have gotten along. As a first-year, she'd parachuted onto campus for orientation, and nearly gotten fragged by the school's air defenses for her troubles. If that didn't mark her as a kindred spirit, I wasn't sure what could.

"Last semester was all about teaching you to function as part of a team. Which," she added with a wry grin, "came easier for some of you than others. But that was the easy part. This semester is about teaching you how to actually operate as Capes."

That got some odd looks and murmurs started. Wasn't that what we'd been doing?

Predictably, Winter's hand shot up in the air.

Just as predictably, Jessica ignored it, and instead answered the question on all of our minds.

"I know, I know. You just spent the past five months blasting each other to atoms. What's more Cape-like than that?" Her dark hair was pulled back in a pony-tail that wagged when she shook her head. "Surprise! Cape life isn't like what you see in vids. Pitched battles are an exception rather than the rule. More often than not, Capes are called in to deal with individual Black Hats, and frequently, those criminals are more interested in making a quick dollar than they are in burning down the city, let alone trying to rule it."

"Street-level crime, investigations, hostage situations, bank robberies, and natural disaster relief efforts all fall under our jurisdiction if there's a Power involved or the local law enforcement officials have requested our assistance. Being a Cape is more than just matching your abilities against the enemy's and letting loose."

"That means," she continued, "that you'll need to know how to respond to those situations. Sometimes, you'll be the only Cape on scene. Other times, your team will be just one piece of a larger operation. First-year was about teaching you how to fight. Second-year is about teaching you why and when."

So far, it had mostly just taught me what getting killed in a variety of different ways felt like.

The answer, just in case any of you have forgotten your own deaths, was universally *not great*.

Unlike Winter, Supersonic rarely bothered to raise his hand. "But Cape versus Black Hat battles do happen, right? I mean, the hero vids—"

"Of course they happen, Caleb, and every one that you survive will stick with you forever. But in my years as a Cape, my team and I fought organized opposition only a half-dozen times. The truth is, criminal cabals like the Legion of Blood are rare, thank God. Black Hats tend to be loners, megalomaniacs, or just clinically insane."

It said something that only a handful of my classmates shot me a look when Jessica said *clinically insane*, and that none of them were on my team... but I'm not sure exactly what.

"Team leaders will receive their briefings from Dean Bard by Friday," announced Jessica. "Thanks to the break, that means you'll only have a week to prepare for the exercise."

"Seriously?" Since mastering her power and becoming a team leader, Vibe had lost all reticence about speaking up in class. "Isn't that like dropping us into the deep end?"

"Sooner or later, you have to learn to swim." Jessica grinned. "Hopefully, you've all been doing your reading and actually paying attention in class."

"Still…"

"It's more lead time than you'll get in the field, Kayleigh. I *can* tell you that this will be a joint, multi-team operation. One sim's taskforce will be led by Team One. The other will be led by Team Three."

Vibe's team and Silt's, respectively.

"Why are *they* in charge?" demanded Wormhole.

"Because we're the highest ranked teams, Evie," drawled Silt. "To the victors go the spoils. And the mandatory backrubs."

"Don't get too comfortable up on your throne, Sofia," Jessica said with a laugh. "After each mission, you'll all be evaluated based on your performances, but teams in a leadership role will take partial responsibility for mistakes made by the other teams in the sim."

"And then you'll be the ones giving us back rubs," snickered the Viking.

"Not if you're the team that screwed up," shot back Caleb.

The Viking scoffed. "Never going to happen, Supersonic. I get the job done. If you know what I mean."

"That's not what Melanie said," interjected London, in a voice as sweet as sugar and every bit as bad for you.

I wasn't sure who Melanie was, but just the mention of her name had the normally unflappable Titan going red in the face.

"Whatever she told you was a lie. Besides, I was drunk! That doesn't count."

"That's one thing you'll all have to learn," said Jessica, happy to join in the banter where another teacher might have tried to restore order. "When you're a Cape, it *all* counts."

ooo

Whoever had built the Academy clearly hadn't taken normal student behavior into consideration. Multiple classrooms in each building and only a couple of exits meant there was an inevitable logjam when everyone tried to rush outside after class. Silt found me while I was waiting for the traffic to clear.

"So, what do you think?" she asked.

"I think the next sim is going to be complicated. And I hope our teams get paired together," I said.

"You'd rather take orders from me than Vibe?"

"It's not Kayleigh I'm concerned with. It's Caleb. You know he's going to be a huge asshole to his so-called subordinates."

"That's our Supersonic."

The hall in front of us was flooded with students. It was funny how distinctive the second-years were, and not just because we were all in the Academy greys that served as our class uniforms. We weren't all enormous, but we were fit. More importantly, we just moved differently. Like weapons, slipping through a sea of humanity.

"Speaking of Kayleigh," I said, as the flow took us toward the exterior door, "have you talked to her since she got back? Any idea how things went with her parents and Paladin?"

"Nah, I've been busy with team stuff." Silt shrugged. "But the two of them seemed as cuddly as ever in class. Besides, this is Vibe we're talking about. Do you really think she'd have *let* things go bad?"

"Good point." I squinted against the sudden glare as we finally made it outside. "It's hard to believe the difference a year has made. Those first months at the Academy, she barely even spoke. Now, she's running a team."

"And even Supersonic thinks she walks on water," Silt agreed. By unspoken agreement, we both took the trail that would lead us to the woods on the west side of campus. "But it took a lot of time and effort for her to come so far. And you know you were a part of that."

"I didn't teach her to control her power. That was all Kayleigh."

"But who helped her manage that power while she was struggling for control? I'm pretty sure it was our resident baby Crow."

"If anything, it was Unicorn. He was the glue that brought us all together as friends."

"That's not how I remember it, but fair enough." Sofia sighed. "I miss that kid. I could have him blushing like a three-alarm fire in five words or less."

"Yeah." I eyeballed the spectral ginger, barely visible past the ghosts of my parents, Nyah, and all the others who had died because of me.

"Does it help or hurt to see his ghost?"

"I don't know. I used to think it hurt, but… the ghosts aren't them. Not really. They're just pieces. Reminders, really."

"Like a spooky photo album."

"I guess so. I can make them go away, but they always seem to come back eventually. Mostly, they're just part of the background. Except when they have something to show me."

Silt shivered. "Have I mentioned how glad I am that I'm me?"

"Every damn day, for as long as I can remember."

"Then consider it said again."

ooo

The change to our Training Grounds missions wasn't the only obvious difference between the two semesters. Our course load mostly stayed the same, but cardio and strength training sessions with Nikolai were actually reduced from three times a week to two. Not that it mattered much for me; Tessa just expanded our running schedule to include the suddenly-free morning. I wasn't getting much sleep, but there was no question I was in the best shape of my life.

My weekends didn't change much. I still met with my first-years, but the questions I could adequately answer were diminishing as they took part in advanced classes my power had made all but impenetrable for me. I also continued to meet with my tutors and Alexa, though the first seemed like cruel and unusual punishment, considering I'd actually passed my classes the previous semester. It turned out actually studying made a difference. Who would have thought?

So what *did* change?

For starters, that second semester spelled the end of our research into Sally and my parents. Everything that had gone down in Bakersfield had already put a temporary halt to our meetings, and when the semester break was over, I'd thanked the others for their help, and officially called it quits. Truth was, the only name on Tessa and Jeremiah's list that *wasn't* a complete (and mostly literal) dead-end was Jimmy Taylor, and I didn't want any of my classmates going near him. Not even Silt, who I knew would happily throw down on my behalf. A Low-Four Crow was bad news, and his link to Tyrant made him damn near poisonous. I tried doing some research on my own, but the trail stopped with Jimmy's disappearance, and that was the end of that. I could only hope that Alexa's agency would succeed where I had failed.

The bigger change came a few days into the semester. Weekday nights had always been free. Weekends were another matter entirely, thanks to the Liquid Hero, but with four shifts and five teams, one team had gotten a break on any given night. That all ended when Nikolai informed us that our duties would now include standing watch on campus. One team each night, spending four hours out on the wall that encircled the Academy.

I wasn't sure what the point of it was. The Academy had armed guards for this sort of thing. I'd had to deal with them—or at least with sneaking past them—as a first year, and they were way more enthusiastic about the task than I was ever going to be. Also, when we were professional Capes, wouldn't we have people to do that sort of thing for us?

I know what you're thinking. I was starting to sound like London. But at least I'd done everyone the courtesy of not saying that shit out loud, right?

Truth was it didn't matter why we were doing it or what I thought about the loss of more free time. Like all things at the Academy, playing pretend-guard was part of our grade, and that meant we had to do it.

Up on that wall in the dark, fully exposed to the regular wind coming in off the ocean, Los Angeles wasn't nearly as fun as it seemed during the day. Using my power let me ignore the *sensation* of being cold, but it didn't do a damn thing to keep that cold from seeping into my bones. I started wearing a sweatshirt, layered over my bodysuit. Probably looked like an asshole, but it wouldn't have been the first time.

Besides, it's not like I owned a coat.

CHAPTER 33

True to Jessica's word, the team leaders came back to their sub-dorms on Friday night with a briefing on what that next sim would have in store for us. And true to our expectations, it looked like one big fucking mess.

We'd be operating in the Training Grounds' version of Los Angeles, where, needless to say, everything was going bad. An earthquake had hit, far stronger than any local Earthshakers were prepared to handle, and Teams Three, Four, and Five were being dispatched to assist with the response. Gas explosions. Collapsing buildings. A fire right through downtown. It wasn't quite on the level of what Major Disaster had done to San Diego, but it was pretty damn close.

Worse, the briefing warned of the likelihood of looting, and the even more worrisome possibility of Black Hats taking advantage of the chaos. We'd have to listen for new events as they were called in and respond and adapt accordingly.

With all of one damn week to prepare.

The good news is that we had the right personnel for that kind of disaster. Makara, Winter, and Cyclone could all put out fires. Silt and El Bosque could shore up foundations or crumbling walls, and Poltergeist, Wormhole, Alan Jackson and the Viking were, in their own ways, each perfectly suited for rescuing trapped survivors.

That left Oscuro, Muse, and me as the three Capes whose powers didn't lend themselves to relief efforts. Silt designated us as the response team. If anything came up, it would be our job to handle it until additional second-years could be freed up to assist.

It wasn't a bad plan. Given the time constraints, and all that could go horribly awry, it was probably the best we were going to be able to come up with.

Pretty sure you can all guess how well it worked out.

ooo

The city was on fire. From the Academy walls, I should have had an expansive view of my surroundings, but all I saw was smoke and chaos, the night sky lit up in shades of crimson and yellow.

Yeah; night sky. They hadn't told us the whole thing would be going down in the dark. Guess that's one of those wrinkles they'd waited to throw at us.

Orson was happier than Winter during a math test though. Nothing a Shadecaster likes more than night.

The Academy itself was untouched, if empty of students, guards, or faculty. It gave me unpleasant reminders of the way the campus looked in my recurring dream, enough so that I actually circled around to the west side to make sure there wasn't a legion of the dead, waiting just down the hill.

There wasn't. Thank whatever God you believe in for that. There was enough shit going wrong in Los Angeles already without the addition of an undead apocalypse.

I worked my way back around to where the other two second-years were waiting. Orson was all in black from head to toe, complete with a cape and collar that made him look even more like a pre-Break vampire than usual. He gave me a glare as I came back into view.

"We're supposed to wait here so Evelyn knows where to pick us up." Even his voice was Shadecaster-standard; a weak knock-off of Fallout's far more sinister whisper.

"Yeah, I heard you the first three times." I rolled my eyes. "I was just taking a look."

"It sounds like everything's under control," said Freddy, adjusting the AK-47 he'd brought in lieu of the normal flamethrower.

"If Winter or Makara were Fours, they'd probably have all the fires out already."

"Until the next gas line ruptures." I frowned. "Why are so many places still running on natural gas in Los Angeles?"

"The city's as old as it is big," he replied. "Retrofitting everything would be a nightmare, and I don't know if there are enough Sparks to support the extra load on the grid."

I gave Muse a surprised look. That was way more information than the Switch usually had to offer.

"My mom's an engineer," he explained. "Works for the city."

"Really? How's the pay?"

"Okay, I guess. Lot of schooling involved, but at least she doesn't get shot at. It's hard to—"

There was a crackle over our comms. Moments later, we got our first alert from the city's simulated police department.

"Looting in progress on Melrose. Cape assistance requested."

The voice sounded almost human. Gage, the Technomancer who'd built the Training Grounds, had been an absolute genius.

I looked at the other two second-years. "How far is Melrose from here?"

"Too far. We have to wait for Wormhole."

Silt's voice came next. "Oscuro, you're up."

Moments later, Evelyn appeared on the wall, ten or so feet away from where we were standing. She'd been transporting people all about the city since the sim started, and the energy she'd absorbed along the way had translated into mass, leaving her almost as bloated as she'd been after taking me to Ludlow back in February.

"Let's go, Orson." She reached out a heavy hand. As soon as the Shadecaster grabbed it, they were gone.

"What are the chances that we'll get to just sit here and not do anything for the rest of the sim," Muse asked me, eyes enormous and hopeful behind his goggles.

"Robbery in progress at First Independent Bank, Long Beach," announced the dispatch. "555 East Ocean Avenue. Units on scene report Powers may be involved."

"You just had to ask."

"Walker, Muse. Your turn," said Silt over our comms, barely audible beneath the background noise. "I'll send backup as soon as—"

The wall shook like it was trying to throw us off. A sound like a giant grinding its teeth came over the comms, and Silt went silent.

"Shit. What the hell was that?" Freddy climbed to his feet. He was pale and sweaty.

"Aftershock? I don't know." I waited for Silt to come back online, but there was nothing.

Moments later, Evelyn reappeared. "Let's go."

"You can teleport to Long Beach?"

"I've actually been there with my family. And I spent the last week looking at footage of the rest of the city. If I've seen it, I can get there." She was quick to offer Muse a hand but paused when she turned to me. "You're not going to murder me in mid-transport again, are you?"

"How did you guess?" I rolled my eyes. "Can we focus on the mission and maybe deal with your issues some other time?"

"Fine." She grabbed my hand with a growl, and the world disappeared.

Maybe I was getting used to being teleported. Maybe spending what had felt like years in that lightless, airless hellhole had numbed me to the experience. Either way, I barely had time to miss my body before I was back in one piece, on a wide street dominated by tall buildings.

"I'm going to see what happened to Silt," Evelyn told us.

"How many more teleports do you have in you?" Her grey and black bodysuit was struggling to contain her increased size.

"I don't know," she growled. "We should have had Cyclone transporting people at the beginning. It's slower but I'm already almost tapped out."

With that, she disappeared, off to bring her insights and criticisms to the woman in charge.

Assuming Silt was still alive.

With all the chaos going on in the city, there was only a single squad car outside the bank, its cherry lights flashing in silence. Two cops were crouched behind it, guns out and trained on the building.

The younger cop looked our way as we came over and audibly sighed in relief. "Capes. Thank God."

I took another moment to admire the skill that had gone into the simulation. We'd seen people in the Training Grounds before, but they'd been random bystanders, more urban detail than actual active participants. These police officers looked real, right down to the scattering of acne on the nearest one's chin.

I'd never wanted to be a Technomancer—at least not until I found out I was a Crow and wished I could be literally anything else—but damn if I couldn't see the appeal all of a sudden. Some of this stuff might as well have been magic.

"What have we got?" asked Muse, making his voice as gruff as possible.

"Bank robbery in progress. One visible dead civilian in the lobby. Looks like security. We tried to make entry but there are at least four perps, and they're all armed. They've also got someone with energy powers. A Lightbringer, maybe?"

"What about hostages?"

"Hard to know. At this time of night, there shouldn't have been any customers, but *someone* hit the alarm."

"Could have been people here working late," said the other cop, his voice so deep and gravelly that Muse's own attempts just seemed kind of sad.

We'd studied how to assist the police in this sort of situation in class, but the examples had involved a lot more backup than we currently had. And a Crow and a Switch weren't the greatest of Powers for the job either.

Which meant we'd just have to make shit up as we went. As fucking usual.

"Can you bring up the building's schematics on your Glass?" I asked the first officer.

He shook his head and pointed to the dark buildings around us. "Power's out, and the Net repeaters went with them. Maybe you can still get a signal up north, but down here, all we have are comms."

"Great."

"I've been out here before on a call," said the deep-voiced cop. "Front room is tellers and service reps. Vault should be down a hallway and in the back. Can't imagine what else a Black Hat would be looking for. We'll uh—" He glanced at his partner. "—stay out here. Keep them from running."

I wanted to be pissed about that little bit of cowardice. Hell, I *was* pissed about it. But with Powers involved, it was standard procedure. They'd try to contain the situation, as impossible as that was with only one car, two cops, and a bank the size of a city block, but we were responsible for taking down the bad guys.

"Guess we're up, Freddy." I turned to the wide-eyed Switch. "I don't suppose enough time has passed since you boosted Makara and Winter?"

"Actually, it has." He paused with both hands an inch above mine. "I don't know exactly what amplifying a Crow will do."

"Wait. He's a *Crow?*" Even the cop's simulated horror seemed authentic.

I could really have done without that little bit of technological verisimilitude.

CHAPTER 34

I didn't feel any different after Muse did his thing. At all. Emptiness filled me, but it had been filling me ever since Wormhole had dropped us off, and nothing seemed to have changed. No army of undead marching at my command. No crackling nimbus of death around my hands. In fact, if it weren't for the fact that Freddy suddenly looked even more sweaty and pale, I'd have questioned if he'd used his power at all.

What a fucking disappointment.

Not sure if I was talking about Muse's power or mine. Maybe both. It said really bad things about my chances against Jimmy Taylor, assuming I ever found the bastard.

The double doors into the bank were still locked, but the glass had been melted right out of them by whatever Power had sent the cops back to the safety of their car. All we had to do was step over the warped metal frames, and we'd be inside.

I met Muse's eyes from across the way. He hefted his rifle and nodded back.

Guess that meant I was going in first.

My gun was a 9mm. Heavier and way less destructive than the Legion tech gun Her Majesty had found me, but at least it carried more than a single round. It was also metal and not some sort of weird semi-organic construct that pulsed in my damn hand. I wasn't going to complain about that either.

With the electricity out, the dead security officer was just a lump on the floor. I carefully skirted around him and the blood pool I couldn't see but knew was there. Behind me, Freddy finally left his post at the door and followed me inside, sweeping the right half of the room as I canvassed the left.

A row of cubicles along my wall were empty. Freddy's wall had doors leading to restrooms, but apparently those were empty too. We moved deeper into the room, toward the teller counter.

We were ten feet away when they attacked.

I was diving before I knew what was happening, before my mind was able to translate the sudden bursts of light and sound into the reality of assault rifles firing. Three of them, wielded by men in masks who had popped up from behind the counter and were busy filling the lobby with a firestorm of lead.

Mind empty, emotions safely locked away, I leaned out from the cubicle I'd sought refuge in and squeezed the trigger. Once, twice, three times.

Then a fourth and fifth time, when the furthest gunman didn't go down. Finally, he staggered back and fell over.

I'd gotten better with guns this semester—had, in fact, dedicated a shitload of time to shooting, following my experiences at the Hole—but apparently, I still had a long way to go.

I stayed low, creeping out of the cubicle and forward until I reached the side of the counter. Then, knowing how stupid I'd feel if someone was still alive and just waiting for my head to come into view, I peeked over the barrier.

Three dark lumps. None of them moving.

Five shots. Three kills. It wasn't up to Jessica's standards—the Stalwart would have found some way to use a single bullet and multiple ricochets to take them all out—but at least I'd gotten the job done. Hell, Muse hadn't even fired a single damn shot.

A wet cough and anguished gasp from the other side of the room told me why.

Freddy was on the floor, not far from the dead security guard. Either he'd reacted more slowly than me, or been screwed by the lack of available cover on his approach.

Most likely, it was a bit of both.

With emptiness flooding my soul, it would have been all too easy to just keep going, focusing on the mission. Especially since I knew Muse would be fine as soon as the sim ended. Instead, I forced myself back across the marble tiles to my downed teammate.

"Can you move?"

"Move?" Bubbles of air and blood formed on his lips. Our costumes were reinforced for small-arms fire, but there was only so much even modern gear could do. Apparently, multiple assault rifles was a bridge too far. "I'm shot!"

Which was both obvious and not really an answer.

"If you stay here, you're dead," I tried again, "and there's a Black Hat and at least one henchman still unaccounted for. *Can you move?*"

"I can't even feel my legs, you—" Wet, hacking coughs interrupted him, jackknifing his upper torso off the tile. His legs didn't even twitch.

"Fuck." If he had a spinal injury, I wasn't supposed to move him. But if I didn't move him, he was dead as soon as another of the Black Hat's crew came through the door.

The best way to keep that from happening was for me to keep going. I hurried to the dead security guard, pulled off the man's bloody and tattered mess of a shirt, and brought it back to Muse.

"Use this. Keep pressure on your wound. Wounds," I amended, realizing that blood was pouring out of numerous locations. "Try to stay alive."

"Sure," he hissed, voice going weird. "I'll just lie here and not die."

"Cool." Honestly, I hadn't expected it to be that easy. Maybe Freddy would make a good Cape, after all.

○○○

There were two doors at the back of the lobby, past the teller counter. The right one turned out to be a supply closet. The left led to a long hall with doors. Light was coming from a room at the end of the hall; a silvery-blue illumination that flickered.

That had to be the enemy Lightbringer.

Surprisingly, nobody was rushing down the hall to reinforce the lobby. Was it possible that they hadn't heard our gunfight?

It seemed unlikely.

I tried clearing the rooms as I went, but by myself, and without any light other than what was making it to me down the hall, it was hopeless. So I probably shouldn't have been surprised when I passed one open door and a shadow jumped out at me.

My power jerked my body out of the way in a way that pulled every muscle in my lower back. That pain barely registered as I turned to my attacker. Without surprise on his side, he was shockingly slow compared to Orca or even Paladin. I ducked inside a lazy, badly telegraphed knife thrust, and smashed the barrel of my 9mm right into his throat.

Hardened polymer frame versus human trachea. Guess who won that matchup?

I left the man to his suffocation and kept moving. I'd already fired five rounds, which meant I had twelve shots left. If the police outside were right, the Lightbringer was the only target left, but Nikolai and Jessica had lectured us at length about the dangers of expectations. And faulty intelligence, for that matter. For all I knew, I'd need every remaining round.

Up ahead, the hallway turned to the right and kept going, but the silver-blue light was coming through an open, larger doorway to the left. I peeked inside.

A tall man in a blood-red lab coat stood in front of an enormous vault door. One of his hands was flat against the metal surface. The other was curled in with its fingers pointed forward. Crackling beams of light poured from his fingertips, hissing and spattering against the metal.

That door was reinforced titanium, but he was slowly—very slowly—burning his way through.

I realized three things, very quickly. One, the Black Hat could only manipulate light with one hand, or he'd have used both to accelerate his progress. Two, that made him a lot less powerful than Spectra, who could not only shoot light from her hands, eyes, and even mouth, but did so with a force and power that would have shredded those doors in under a minute.

And three, the cops had been way off on their enemy troop estimates.

There were four more masked men in the room, all of them holding assault rifles. One was watching the Black Hat work, but the other three were looking in my direction.

They saw me even before I saw them.

I squeezed off a half-dozen shots, and I think at least a few of them landed. Then a Titan kicked me in the torso. Twice.

That's what it felt like anyway. Hard to believe that, in that entire insane battle out at the Hole, not to mention all the sims I'd run since, I'd never actually been shot. Almost as hard to believe that the impact was enough to send my 9mm flying out of my hand.

I already knew what Jessica was going to say about me dropping my weapon. Hell, I'd probably get shit from Tessa too.

I scrambled for the safety of the wall. One of the two bullets had flattened on impact with my chest armor, and it now fell to the ground with a weirdly musical tinkle. The other had torn through the meat of my abdomen, the light sufficient for me to see the blood dripping onto the floor.

In the vids, some wiseass would've explained to the audience that the bullet had somehow missed every vital organ, leaving our hero with a flesh wound that would in no way keep justice from being done.

In reality—even the pseudo-reality of the Training Grounds—I was pretty sure multiple organs had been perforated, but my power kept me going. When one of the remaining gunmen charged through the door—maybe in an attempt to surprise me, or maybe because he'd seen it in a movie—I was ready. One punch to the side of the man's head and he staggered. I kicked his legs out from under him, scooped up the assault rifle as he fell, and dove into the vault room.

Two of the other gunmen were already down from my earlier attack. I sprayed the room with my borrowed assault rifle, firing all twenty-three remaining bullets in one long, barely controlled burst.

The last masked gunman danced like a puppet and then collapsed to the floor. The Lightbringer though…

He moved in a blur, dodging behind his henchman's flailing body and then entirely out of my cone of fire. It was an impossible move, and it told me he wasn't *just* a Lightbringer.

"I'm so damn tired of Stalwarts," I told him. I reached for my 9mm, only to remember that it was still out in the hall where I'd been shot.

"I like your clown mask, Cape," he shot back.

"*Clown?* It's a—" You know what? If the fucker couldn't tell a clown from a skull, that was his problem. I rushed him, barely avoiding the crackling rays of light that scorched my side. The side I *hadn't* already been shot in, naturally.

Dodging those light blasts brought me almost into punching range. Unfortunately, that meant I was well inside kicking range, especially considering that my opponent was almost seven feet tall.

A size twenty-three boot blasted into my chest.

It was unfortunate for my ribs, but even worse for Mr. Clown Lover. Even as I started to fly back from the impact, I clamped one hand down on the man's ankle, and let my emptiness go.

I only had a second or two of contact before I soared across the room and into the far wall, but it was enough. When my eyes managed to focus again, there was nothing in the vault room but me, a bunch of dead gunmen, and an oversized pile of clothing and dust.

The good news was that I was still alive. The better news was that even after death-touching the asshole, I could feel the emptiness inside of me.

The bad news was that I hadn't held on to the fucker long enough for his life energy to heal me. Or maybe there hadn't been enough of it to matter. Either way, I was still bleeding, burned, and now dealing with at least a few broken ribs.

The worse news was that the guy I'd punched in the hallway was starting to get back up. And I could hear even more noise coming from down the hall.

Whoever had programmed this sim needed to die.

I forced myself back up to my feet. It hurt to breathe, let alone walk, but I was now an old hand at using my power to muffle pain. I checked the magazines on the remaining assault rifles, found one that still had rounds, and dragged myself back into the hall. With the Lightbringer dead, the whole place had been plunged back into near-darkness, but my eyes adjusted quickly enough. One shot ended the bank robber in the hall, but the noise I'd heard was coming from yet another room on this endless bastard of a hallway.

I waited for a masked head to peek out and blew it off.

Three more steps took me to the room, where a half-dozen shadows huddled against the wall. Four shapes loomed above them. One rushed me, but I stepped to the side, grabbed him, and let a little bit more of the emptiness go. One down, three to go.

As the pile of dust that used to be a man fell gently to the tile, I shouldered my assault rifle and squeezed the trigger.

"Don't shoo—!" One of them shouted.

"We surr—" screamed another.

It was way too late for that.

Three more bodies fell to the floor.

I coughed up some blood and went to find Muse.

CHAPTER 35

"Does anyone want to tell me what went wrong?" asked Jessica Strich, as the lights came up and the vid screen turned off.

"Everything?" Supersonic's smirk was on full display. "That was a comedy of errors."

"You might want to save the jokes until the class has watched the vid of *your* Training Grounds run, Caleb." The dark-haired professor shook her head. "It wasn't any prettier. Trust me."

"You put us in an impossible situation!" Caleb was on his feet, as fast as only a Jitterbug could be. "Don't blame us for failing an unwinnable test!"

"Unwinnable, eh?" Nikolai was leaning against the far wall, not so much standing at the front of the class as forcibly occupying the space. "Would you like to make a bet on that, Flyboy?"

Supersonic was many things—loudmouth, sucker-punching asshole among them—but we'd all gone through enough at the Academy to recognize a trap when we heard one. He frowned, and didn't reply.

"Anyone else?" pressed Jessica, to resounding silence.

It had been three days since our disastrous attempt to save Los Angeles, but we were still feeling the effects from the simulation. In addition to the earthquake, fires, and collapsing buildings, there'd been widespread looting, three attempted robberies, one assassination attempt, and an invasion by—and I shit you not—mole people from tunnels beneath Los Angeles. Of the fifteen of us, only six had survived, and in the process, there had been more than a thousand civilian casualties and millions of dollars of property damage.

Most of that wasn't our fault, as far as I was concerned, but the professors and our team leaders seemed to feel otherwise.

"Protect the city. Evacuate civilians. Keep the peace." Jessica tapped them off on her fingers as she spoke, finally filling the uncomfortable silence. For once, I didn't find her mannerisms charming. "Those were your high-level priorities. This simulation included fourteen different specific objectives. A passing grade would have meant you'd achieved at least half of them."

Which frankly said something about the sim. And maybe Cape life in general. Where else did fifty percent equate to a pass?

"And how many of those objectives were achieved?" She looked around the room. "Anyone?"

"One," said Silt, all the drawl gone from her voice.

"One. And if this were real life, the person responsible would be headed straight to the Hole." Jessica's dark eyes found me across the room, and in that moment, the slim Stalwart was far scarier than the bank-robbing Black Hat had been. "What were you thinking?"

"What?" The last thing I'd expected was to be put on the spot out of nowhere.

"Capes have discretion with Black Hats caught in action," rumbled Nikolai. "But normals have rights. Those last two bank robbers had their hands up. You should have arrested them."

"While Muse was bleeding out in the lobby?"

"He was dead by the time you made it back anyway," pointed out Caleb helpfully. "Maybe you should have gotten him out of the bank to the cops so they could help him instead of deciding to go all *Street Vengeance V* on the bad guys."

"I didn't want to risk further injuring him, asshole."

"How'd that turn out?"

"Oh for fuck's sake," said Silt. "Give it a rest, both of you."

Got to be honest. That kind of hurt.

Wait. Something Nikolai had said was wrong. "I think you meant the last *three* bank robbers, Nikolai."

"I meant what I said," the older Titan responded. "The third person you killed was a hostage."

Well, fuck.

"Everyone involved gets zero points," said Jessica. "Since Team Three was in charge, they're losing fifty."

That would cost Silt's team their leadership role in our next sim, although I'd have to check the ranking board to see which team was set to succeed them.

"What were we supposed to do differently?" asked Cyclone. Erin was pale, but she was pretty much always pale.

"That's an excellent question. It's also your assignment for Thursday. I want every team to submit a list of ten things they would do differently if given the opportunity. We'll discuss those answers next class. Now, let's move on to the lowlights of Team One and Two's performance."

The lights dimmed again, and we all settled in to watch another debacle unfold.

Kind of sucks that we were all too frustrated and annoyed to enjoy watching Supersonic screw up.

○○○

"Sofia was right. You really do live out here."

I kept my eyes on the ocean. "What do you want, Tessa?"

"I came to check on you." She dropped down onto the bench next to me. "Obviously."

"Why?"

"Because you're on my team. You and the others are my responsibility."

"So you're going to go bother Muse too?"

"Freddy is so drunk he can't even see straight. I'm going to talk to him once he sobers up. If he sobers up." Her voice sharpened. "Now, stop being an asshole. I'm trying to do my job."

She wasn't wrong. About me being an asshole, anyway. After Group Tactics, I'd muddled through my few remaining Tuesday classes, and then made a beeline for my little sanctuary in the woods. Which wasn't much of a sanctuary anymore now that everyone knew to find me there. Still, meditating hadn't been doing me much good, and for some reason, I wasn't in the mood to let my power sweep everything away.

"Fine."

"Fine? As in, you'll stop being a dick?"

I gave her a hefty dose of side eye. "I can't promise the impossible, but I'll stop giving you a hard time for trying to be a good team leader."

"Good. Between Winter's angry cupcakes and Muse's latest bender, I'm pretty close to losing it. And we're high enough up that I bet I could toss you over the wall if I had to."

"I thought you were done with the threats."

"I can't promise the impossible." She snickered. "Anyway, I wanted to see how you were doing, after—"

"Killing a hostage?"

"Getting called out by the professors."

"I'm okay."

"Meaning emotionally unavailable and primed to explode?"

"Meaning *okay*." I shook my head. "It was humiliating, yeah, but I had it coming. What if that had been real life? Jessica's right. I'd be headed straight to the Hole."

"You think casualties don't happen?"

"I think someone has to pay when they do. And when a Cape guns down a civilian—"

"And two defenseless criminals."

"—it's pretty clear who's going to end up doing the paying." I shrugged. "My dad killed my mom. One person. And it's looking like it wasn't even technically his fault, but he spent thirteen years in the Hole before he died."

"There's a difference."

"If you say so. Truth is, when I'm using my power, I'm not sure I'm entirely me. Does that make sense?"

"Not really." She turned to me on the bench, eyes glittering. "What are you saying? You're schizophrenic?"

"No, but… it's like all of my emotions, my thoughts, and my reluctance are kind of packaged away and put on a shelf for a bit. The things happening to me are almost happening to someone else, distant enough that they don't keep me from acting."

"That's how you ignore pain."

"Yeah. And push my body to its limits."

"Going full-walker."

"Whatever that means, but yeah. I'm not being controlled, but I'm letting the power move through me."

"And?"

"And in the sim, those three people were dead when I walked through the door. I was killing them before anything they might have said would have sunk in."

"Jesus."

"So how do I keep from doing that in the future? The guy who rushed me, the one I ashed? He could have been a hostage too. I sure as hell didn't stop to check before I death-touched him."

"It won't just be you next time," she pointed out. "You're not always going to be alone, facing down the enemy."

She'd end up being both right and wrong on that front. Mostly wrong.

"Besides, the whole exercise was bullshit," she continued. "A city-wide disaster and they think second-years would be prepared to deal with it?"

"Welcome to the Academy." Even I was getting tired of the oft-repeated refrain.

"Yeah. I've been trying to do our homework—"

"Already?"

"It's due in two days," she reminded me, "and tomorrow night is our time on the wall." Something invisible slapped me gently on the cheek. "Now stop interrupting."

"Right. Homework. You were saying?"

"I've come up with a few ideas. We should have kept more reserves. We could have done more to coordinate with emergency services. And Sofia should have given each team more autonomy, so it didn't all go to shit when that building fell on her." Tessa scowled. "But a million things went wrong, and would have gone wrong, no matter what. I don't think we were supposed to win."

"So you think Caleb was right? Nikolai said both scenarios were doable."

"Yeah, but by who? Second-years in the first multi-team engagement? Or full-fledged Capes?"

"Jessica did say they were going to throw us in the deep end." After some careful asking about, I'd learned the phrase was referring to swimming pools. Because those were something I'd had so much exposure to before coming to the Academy. "Sink or swim. We sank."

"Did we?"

"Given that we failed the exercise, yeah."

"That doesn't sound like the unstoppable death machine that lives across the hall from me."

"So what are you saying?"

"I'm saying they threw us in to show us just how deep it gets. Now it's time to show them we can swim." As if the universe had been listening, a breeze blew in from the ocean, tossing her curls back to frame the resolute firming of her jaw. If I could have captured that image and distributed it across the Badlands, Academy enrollment would have doubled. Tripled, even. "Are you in?"

"Have we met?" I asked her, borrowing one of Silt's favorite phrases. "I wanted to call myself Baron Boner. If I was going to let a humiliating defeat stop me, I'd never have made it to the Academy."

"Good," she said, flashing me a wide smile, "because there's one thing I've learned from our failure to save Los Angeles. A leader needs to learn to delegate."

Whatever answering smile had started to make its way to my face was gone in an instant. "Meaning?"

"Meaning I want you to talk to Freddy. His drinking's way past the point of being acceptable. It needs to stop."

"How am I supposed to do that?"

"Hell if I know." She met my gaze, green eyes clashing with tombstone grey. "Think of something, and get it done."

"And what will you be doing while I work miracles?"

"I'll be confiscating Winter's baking supplies until she agrees to share."

I'll be honest; I hadn't seen that one coming.

CHAPTER 36

Wednesday night found Team Five out on the wall for our third guard rotation of the semester. Repetition didn't make it feel any less pointless. The Academy already had security personnel, stationed at each corner tower and the main gates, so it's not like we were really adding anything to the school's defense. And it's not like the school had been attacked even once since its founding either.

Santiago had called it security theater, and he was right.

With four walls and four team members, you'd think we would each have had a wall to ourselves, but Tessa put us in pairs, and that meant we were constantly sweeping back and forth to cover our assigned walls. Pretty sure the guards thought we were crazy. For once, that had nothing to do with me being a Crow.

Two guesses who I got assigned as my partner that night.

If you didn't think *Muse*, you don't really know Tessa. And you haven't been paying nearly enough attention.

If we second-years were useless in general as watchmen—or watch-people... or watch-Capes...or whatever you wanted to call us—Freddy was one step below that. He wasn't drunk, but I'm not sure he was entirely sober either. Mostly, he just shuffled along, eyes on his own feet.

Two hours into our shift, I still hadn't raised the topic of his drinking. This may come as a surprise to all of you, who came to listen to me out here in the desert simply because you love the melodious tones of my voice, but truth is, I've never been much of a people person. Or a 'let's talk things out' kind of person, for that matter. Even at Mama Rawlins', I kept peace more through threat of violence than anything else. Kids are like pets. They like rules. Make sure those rules are fair, be prepared for them to test you once or twice, and things stay sane more often than not.

I thought about threatening to throw Freddy off the wall if he kept drinking, but that probably wasn't the sort of solution the Academy would be happy with.

Finally, I just waved him to a stop and slid down to take a seat, the raised battlements cool against my back.

"My feet hurt," I lied. "Let's take a break."

He shrugged and followed suit. Legs extended in front of him, his toes remained his focus.

I sat there as the silence built. Finally, I gave up on strategy and adopted my usual *charge-them-and-hope-you-don't-die* approach. "What's going on with you lately, Freddy?"

That took his eyes off his toes for a brief few seconds. "What do you mean?"

"Ever since the sim, you've been off."

"I was *shot*!"

"And I killed a hostage."

"And two defenseless bank robbers."

I shrugged. "Why does getting shot matter? You've had your limbs broken, been assassinated by throwing stars, and were even drowned alive by Makara. So what?"

"You wouldn't get it. Your power lets you just waltz through all that shit."

"I feel every damn thing that happens to me," I said, shading the truth just a bit, "and half the time, it's my own power doing the damage."

"Whatever."

Maybe tossing his ass off the wall *was* the better solution.

"Seriously, Freddy. What is going on?" When he didn't answer, I pushed. "Talk to me now, or I get someone I know to send rats into your bed while you sleep."

"Rats?"

"Yeah." One rat, really. It had only been a few weeks and I was pretty sure Paco hadn't had a breakthrough yet. "Or maybe I'll just toss a lit match through the door. I'll bet you five dollars the whole room goes up before that match hits the floor."

"Do you even have five dollars?"

"Fuck off."

Muse snickered, and then shrugged, letting his head fall back against the reinforced concrete battlement.

"It took me almost five minutes to die. On my back, legs unresponsive, bleeding out right through the bandage you'd given me—a bandage that had started out as a shirt on yet another dead guy—and you know what I kept thinking the whole time?"

"I should have ducked?" I guessed.

"You're an asshole." He shook his head. "No. I was thinking 'why am I here?'"

"In the bank?"

"At the Academy. Doing any of this. Did you grow up wanting to be a Cape?"

"Sure. Then I found out I was a monster instead. Decided to give the whole Cape thing a try anyway. Maybe I can be both."

"I wanted to be an accountant."

"What?" I was only vaguely familiar with what accountants even did, but it hadn't seemed exciting.

"Something boring," he added, as if reading my mind. "Something predictable. I'd make some money, get married, have some kids, and then die in my sixties, watching vids and eating popcorn. And then I took the Test."

I kept quiet.

"Fucking Powers," he finally continued. "If it weren't for all of you, my being an Amplifier wouldn't have changed anything. But Switches are rare, and every damn team wants one. Soon as my results came back, I knew I was screwed."

"Why are you at the Academy if you don't want to be a Cape?"

"That's the question, isn't it?" He adjusted the goggles that were currently protecting his forehead instead of his eyes. "I failed the first round of entry tests. Just guessed A on every single multiple choice question. A month later, they sent me a whole new batch of tests, and I intentionally failed those too. Guess what arrived in the mail a month later?"

"More tests."

"More tests. I should have kept failing them."

"Why didn't you?"

"I have a little brother. Hercules. He's seven now. Thinks Capes are the coolest things ever. When he got old enough to understand what a Power was, and that I was one, he smiled for days."

"You're here because of him," I reasoned.

"Sort of." He swallowed. "There's not a lot of good in Herc's life. He's been in and out of the hospital since he was born. He could use something to be happy about, and my parents could use the money that comes with me being a Cape. But…"

"But what?"

"You wouldn't get it."

"Because I'm a Crow? Or because I'm an orphan and don't have any family?"

"Because nothing stops you! You break your own damn arm just so you can grab Paladin by the balls. You end up three hundred feet underground during a prison break with almost the entire Legion of Blood, and you not only survive, you kill one of them and stab another in the back. That's not normal."

"We're Powers. What does normal have to do with us?"

"I'm not talking normals versus Powers."

"Then I don't know where you're going with this."

"Forget it. Let's just say I don't have whatever you or the other second-years have. This isn't fun for me. It's not some sort of spirited competition. I'm doing it because I have to, but I hate every minute of it. I'm tired of lying down in that pod knowing that as soon as I open my eyes, I'll be getting burned or blasted or stabbed or just plain shot. It's awful, and it's terrifying, and I'm sick of it."

He was right. I didn't get it. Did life at the Academy suck? Yeah. But so did life outside the Academy. At least here, we were being given the tools to maybe do something about it.

"So your whole extracurricular alcoholism thing?"

He groaned. "I'm just trying to keep from going insane."

That much, I did understand.

"I'm sober for missions, and most classes," he continued. "Why can't we just leave it there?"

"Because our team leader has a fatal flaw."

"What's that?"

"She apparently gives a shit about her team members." I sighed. "You and I aren't friends, but we all live together, and nobody wants to see you drink yourself to death."

"Oh yeah?"

"Yeah. Especially if it leaves our bathroom unusable. I've had enough of Winter waking me up to last me a lifetime."

He gave me the courtesy of a chuckle.

"Seriously though. We lost Shane. Ishmae left. Jason and Becky dropped out. If you want to drop out, you can too—"

"If they'd even let me," he muttered.

"Otherwise, you need to cut back on the drinking. Find some other way to cope."

"Like what?"

"Fuck if I know. I'm the one who's actually going crazy, remember?" I shrugged. "Tessa and I run in the mornings. Maybe you should start coming along?"

The look he gave me made it clear he thought I'd already gone insane.

○○○

Freddy didn't stop drinking after our talk, but he *did* scale it back some. Wish I could say that lasted. Wish I could say a lot of things, really, but that's not how life works.

Maybe Tessa should have delegated the task to someone other than a nineteen-year-old Crow with anger issues.

CHAPTER 37

Poltergeist was right. That first Training Grounds mission, while *technically* possible, had been designed as a worst case scenario. We weren't supposed to win it. We were supposed to commit every mistake in the book so we'd learn what not to do.

Mission successful, I guess.

Unfortunately, we all still paid a price for our performances in the destruction of Los Angeles. Silt's team had lost their place at the top of the rankings, but Team One had taken a lesser hit, due to the smaller number of teams under their command. And that meant Teams One and Four were now ranked at the top. Which gifted us another month of Supersonic swaggering around campus like he owned it.

Finishing the first semester matchups with one win and three losses was coming back to bite my team in ways we could never have anticipated.

As we moved deeper into September, the new schedule became almost routine. One or two nights a week were spent on the wall, and at least two nights were spent at the Liquid Hero, but that still gave us a minimum of three nights of free time.

And then the team leaders decided our entire class should run its own multi-team training. Even though our September mission was going to involve single-team patrols. Even though we had no idea what the group compositions would be in October.

Three hours a night.

Two times a week.

Every damn one of them was a sadist. Or a masochist. Or both. And with the possible exception of Wormhole, every damn one of them was also going to make a hell of a leader for a professional team someday.

Assuming their eventual teams didn't mutiny.

Assuming *we* didn't mutiny first.

Got to be honest. It was a close thing.

Truth was, I was tired and I was stressed, but I didn't want to disappoint Kayleigh or Sofia, and some part of me *still* didn't want to look bad in front of Nadia.

And Tessa? Well, she was Team Five. That meant something. As much as we all still bickered among ourselves in private—and holy shit, did we ever!—we had her back.

Anyway, free time became a stim-weed dream during the month of September, and that had some seriously unanticipated effects. I didn't make it out to the bench clearing more than once a week. Meditation became almost wholly restricted to Control class. And without my careful regulation and release of energy, the emptiness that was my power grew and grew.

Bad time for a one-night stand?

Fuck that. I was nineteen and hadn't had a date with anything but my hand in almost two years.

As far as I was concerned, it was a *great* time for a one-night stand. Or a dozen of them.

In September, someone finally agreed with me.

ooo

It was my night to tend bar at the Liquid Hero, and for once, I wasn't paired with one of the too-damn-many second-year men who were prettier than I was. No Santiago. No Erik. No Matthew. No Orson, who had demonstrated an inexplicable ability to attract female attention while I was stuck mixing drinks that would have been illegal pre-Break.

That night, I was teamed up with Erin Pearson, the near-ginger Wind Dancer also known as Cyclone. Even after two years of school, we barely knew each other, but she worked hard and that was a damn sight better than what I could expect from London or Prince. And even though she was *also* prettier than I was, Erin being a woman meant I had at least a scattering of women at my side of the bar, chatting me up.

And that didn't suck.

As the night wore on, those numbers dwindled, of course. It was a Sunday, and even the normals at the Academy had class the next morning. Last shift at the Liquid Hero was way too late for most people. By quarter to two, the handful of increasingly drunken women who'd been hanging out near me had found other places to be or other people to do.

That's when she made her appearance.

Long black hair. Heart-shaped face. Smoky eyes that locked onto me from the moment she left her booth. I watched her sway across the dance floor as I polished the glass in my hands.

That's… not a euphemism. I promise. The Viking may be infamous for his public displays, but I'm sure as hell not him.

She was shorter than me, even without the raised floor behind the bar, but the heels she had on made her legs look a mile long under that sinfully short black dress. She leaned forward, letting her arms and the wooden bar frame her cleavage.

I dragged my eyes up from the mouth-watering sight to catch a small, satisfied smile on her face.

"You're him, aren't you?" With less than fifteen minutes until closing time, the music and crowd noise were both quieter than usual. She didn't have to shout to be heard, and I loved the deep purr in her low voice. "The man who killed Carnage?"

I liked even more that she'd called me a man and not a Crow. Not that the two were mutually exclusive or anything. It was just all too rare that anyone considered the former due to the latter.

"Yeah. I'm Damian," I told her.

"I think that glass is already plenty clean, Damian," she said, throwing in a smile that warmed me down to my toes. "Surely, there are better things you could be doing with your hands?"

I barely managed to set the glass aside without dropping it.

"What's your name?"

"Emma." She laid her hand on top of mine, fingers cool and unbelievably soft. "Sagittarius. Fire sign. Perfectly sober. And horny as all hell."

I kind of doubted the sober part, but the way she was touching my arm meant the blood had long since left my brain.

"So when do you get off, Damian?"

I glanced again at the clock on the wall. Somehow, only two minutes had passed. "About thirteen minutes or so—"

"No." She shook her head, sending a ripple through hair that shimmered like dark silk. "That's when you finish your shift. Let's make sure you get off soon after."

Holy fucking shit.

"But not *too* soon," she continued. "After all, the hero of the Hole has a reputation to uphold."

○○○

Emma's jacket—a cropped bit of vinyl that looked great and probably provided no warmth at all—was off before we even reached my bedroom, and my sweatshirt was quick to follow. We stumbled through the door, attached at the lips, chest, and groin, and I don't know whose hands were busier. The coolness of her fingers had faded, and now every touch left fire across my skin, but I was drowning in the feel of her; the silk of her hair, the satin of her back, the tight curve of her ass under a dress that needed to be gone.

Thank fuck I didn't have any possessions to clutter up the room. I wasn't worried about a mess scaring her off, not with her tongue busy battling mine into submission, but it's damn sure we'd have tripped on something, and with my luck, probably died in a freak accident.

Don't believe the vids, kids. Blunt force trauma is a killer.

Instead, it was smooth sailing back to my small bed. She pushed me down and I went with it, flopping back until she was standing next to me. Faint light from the street lamps outside filtered through my room's only window to paint her form, the peaks and valleys of a body barely constrained by that little black dress.

"What was it like?" she whispered, toying with a hem that barely reached mid-thigh.

"What?"

"Killing a Black Hat." Her voice was breathy. I watched that hem rise up a fraction of an inch, bringing even more of her into view. "Stopping a murderer."

As bedroom talk went, it was kind of weird, but who the fuck was I to judge? Or complain, for that matter?

"It wasn't just one Black Hat," I told her. "I also shot a Technomancer named Firewall. That's how the guards up on the surface found out about the prison break."

The tongue I'd just been tasting slipped out and wet already glistening lips. "And then you drained the life out of Carnage with a touch." In a bit of magic as impressive as anything I'd ever seen in a Cape vid, she reached up, kind of rolled her hips, and her dress was a pool of fabric on the floor of my bedroom. No bra, not that she needed one. No panties either, but I sure as hell didn't mind. "Now it's my turn to return the favor."

If she hadn't been naked, I might have worried that that was some sort of a threat.

Instead, it was a promise.

There's something to be said about kissing. Alicia had taught me to enjoy it, taught me how to do more than just gnaw at her lips like a moron, and we'd spent more than a few hours making out in her parents' store, waiting for the moment we could slip into the back room for a hurried, half-clothed quickie.

Kissing in the privacy of my own room, the woman on top of me fully naked and smoldering to the touch, was better by orders of magnitude. Despite the depressing regularity of my masturbation, I almost popped off in those first few minutes.

Wouldn't that have been a story for her to tell?

Instead, I gave her something even better. Or worse.

She had rolled to her back, hair spread across my pillow. Those legs I'd admired so much were wrapped around my waist as I thrust in and out, and her moans and the sounds of our shared breath filled the space. She felt incredible, inside and out, and I was desperately trying to hold off long enough to make her peak first. Once I blew, I was going to be good to absolutely nobody.

When I felt the emptiness swell up inside of me, it was a relief at first. My pace quickened. Exhaustion fell away. She groaned beneath me as my thrusts pushed her closer and closer to her own edge.

And then, as my orgasm began to rise, like a wave I couldn't stop but could only ride, I felt the emptiness rise with it, flowing outward to the hands that gripped Emma, the hips squeezed between her thighs, and even the cock buried deep inside.

I'd felt that sensation before. Three times in the Training Grounds. Once in the Mojave, under a burning sun, dead soldiers and Capes littering the earth around me.

I pulled out in a blind panic, breaking the hold her legs had on me without even thinking, and staggered back.

"Don't stop!" Emma's hips twitched for a few seconds after I'd left, and a look of confused annoyance crossed her face. "I'm *this* close!"

She reached out for me, but I shrank back against the wall, the emptiness filling every inch of my vibrating body.

"Go."

"What?"

"You need to go," I told her, voice hoarse.

"Are you fucking *kidding* me?"

"Leave! Now!" I roared. It was all I could do to keep myself from reaching out and touching her, my arms wanting to move on their own, the emptiness inside me looking for an exit.

Whatever Emma had been going to say in reply—and given the look on her face, it wouldn't have been pretty—was lost beneath the sound of Poltergeist charging into my room. Before I'd even turned her way, bands of telekinetic force pinned my naked ass to the wall.

"What is going on?" she demanded.

"Your dorm mate is an asshole," answered Emma. Whatever magic she'd used to get her dress off apparently didn't work in reverse. She picked it up off the carpet, along with her heels, and stalked out into the hall. "I should have just gone for a damn Stalwart, like everyone else."

The front door slammed, but Tessa was already focused on me, green eyes cold. "What did you do to her?"

"Nothing!"

"Bullshit." She shook her head with a scowl. "I'd remind you that we're supposed to be Capes, but even civilians should know that no means no."

"Wait… what?"

"It's a woman's right to change her mind," she continued, voice hard enough to hammer nails. "I don't give a damn how far along things were."

"That's not what happened!"

"Then tell me what did, or I'm going to drag your naked ass all the way to Bard's office. Or the Hole." Something sad crept into her expression. "This shit is *not* okay, Damian."

"I was the one who stopped," I managed. With my orgasm no longer imminent, the emptiness was slowly receding to its usual levels.

"What?"

"That's why she was pissed. *I* stopped. Not her."

"You can't expect me to believe—"

"How does your power work, Tessa?"

"What does that have to do—?"

"Please. Just answer me."

Maybe something in my voice got to her. She shrugged. "I focus my mind on points of space and use them like they were extra hands. Why?"

"My power doesn't work like that. Instead, I step aside, and let it rise up and take over."

"So you've told me. So what?"

"So what does that sound like to you? A fucking uncontrollable tide that rises up and spills out."

Almost against her will, her eyes glanced down to where my dick was, in the sort of willful optimism unique to my gender and age, still rock hard.

"Exactly," I answered, voice tired as I sagged in her telekinetic grasp. "The closer I came, the more my power took over."

"And?"

"And what do you think happens when I'm touching someone and that emptiness runs free?"

Her eyes widened a second later. "Oh shit."

"Yeah. I think I was three seconds away from killing her."

"That's—" She stopped and tried again. "You can't—" Another head shake. "What the hell? Crows can't have sex?"

"If that were true, I wouldn't have been born," I pointed out. "But most Crows raise walkers or sacrifice school children." Or both. "Have you read about anyone other than me that killed with a touch?"

We both knew the answer to that.

There was a long moment of silence as we considered the new heights of bullshit my life had just managed to attain.

"So you're a virgin?"

"What? No! Alicia had no complaints. But all I could do back then was see ghosts. Now, my power's halfway useful and it's completely ruining my life."

"Maybe you just have to get better at control?"

"Who's going to risk being the monkey in that experiment?" I sighed. "'Hey you! Come have sex with me. It might not be fatal!'"

"*Hey you?*" Tessa wrinkled her nose. "Please tell me that's not how you picked up whatever-her-name was."

"Emma. And she picked *me* up." I rolled my eyes. "And now regrets it, although not even half as much as I do. So… are we done here, or do you still think I should be expelled or arrested?"

"What? No. Yeah. We're done. Sorry, I just thought…" Her cheeks went red as her eyes wandered down again. "Could you please put some damn clothes on?"

"You're pinning me to the wall," I reminded her.

"Oh. Right."

The bonds holding me released, and I locked my knees to keep from sliding to the floor. I grabbed my boxers from where Emma had thrown them. And then pulled on my greys for good measure.

I think we both felt a bit better when I had pants on, even if I was still, in an almost literal middle finger to common sense and rational thought, completely erect.

"Frankly, we're both lucky I didn't accidentally kill you," I decided.

"What do you mean?" For some reason, that made her blush even harder. I had no idea what was going on with Tessa sometimes.

"You were touching me with your power."

"So?"

"So I saw a Shadecaster get burned alive when a Pyro torched the shadow he was using to pin someone down. And hell, I stabbed Fallout's shadow when it was holding me. That's the only reason I got free to stab the asshole himself."

"Telekinesis isn't like that."

"It's not?"

She shook her head. "There's no route back to me through my power. That's how I knew I was going to end up with you on my team."

"What?"

"You're a Crow. Even though they let you back into the Academy, they have to still be worried you might go crazy. There was no way they were going to put you on a team that didn't have at least one person who could take you down." Her voice was matter-of-fact. "With Ishmae gone, there are two Fours left in our class, and I'm the only one who doesn't have to touch you to stop you."

I wasn't sure what was worse... that what she was saying made perfect sense or that it hadn't occurred to me even once. Either way, I finally, finally lost my erection.

"I'm tired," I decided.

"You know I wouldn't... unless it was the only..." She swallowed and scowled. "It's just a contingency plan. I didn't ask for it."

"Tessa." I met her eyes and shook my head. "It's fine. I'm just tired. I'm going to bed."

"Okay." She paused in my doorway, voice quiet. "Run tomorrow?"

"Might as well," I told her from the darkness of a bedroom that smelled like sweat and sex.

It's not like I had much else to fucking look forward to.

CHAPTER 38

Things stayed awkward for a bit after that, and not just because of the ugly looks I started getting from random women in the Liquid Hero. I hadn't seen Emma since that night, and I didn't know what she was telling people, but the story was apparently spreading.

I was embarrassed, yeah, and maybe a little angry, as always, but for the most part, I was just depressed.

Which just goes to show you how a teenager's mind works. Survive a battle larger than anything seen in the Free States in decades? No problem. Deal with losing your mother, father, and everyone else you grew up with? Sure thing. Uncover dueling conspiracies involving a long-dead Crow and a copper-eyed bastard? Weird, but okay. But learn that you can't have sex without possibly killing your partner?

That was what sent me spiraling.

Tessa knowing everything sort of helped and sort of didn't. I caught her eying me a few times, as if she was waiting for me to explode or something, but as far as I could determine, she hadn't told a soul. We kept running in the mornings, life moved on, and I made damn sure I didn't take anyone else home from the bar.

Not that there were any offers to turn down. Whatever Emma had told people, it sure as hell wasn't flattering.

By the end of September, I was ready for a little violence. Thankfully, the Training Grounds were there to provide.

ooo

I wasn't sure what city this was supposed to be, but it didn't look like Los Angeles. Skyscrapers crowded out the skyline, neon lights painting the wet streets below in a flood of garish colors. I pulled my mask more securely over my face and decided, yet again, that my costume really needed some sort of coat, no matter how much it might restrict my movements.

It was raining. Because *of course* it would be raining. The day we had a Training Grounds mission in perfect weather conditions was the day I'd know the teachers had programmed a blood match with Tezcatlipoca, Legion, or the Weaver. Might as well have a little sunshine to go with all that carnage, right?

Since today's mission was a supposedly routine city patrol, there was no sun in sight. Just rain and cold wind and that neon that made the city streets look like some sort of art project gone wrong.

"This sucks," announced Muse, twenty feet to my left across a stretch of cracked asphalt. His costume *did* have a jacket, but he looked as miserable as I felt.

"Keep the chatter off our comms," said Tessa. "Let's at least try to maintain radio discipline."

She was out of sight, taking a different patrol route, but didn't sound much happier than we did.

"Movement at your nine, Poltergeist," warned Winter. Then, a few seconds later. "Never mind. Looks like a civilian heading home."

Penelope was the only one of us who seemed to be enjoying herself. Part of that was because she was high above the city, but a bigger part had to be because she was using her powers to keep herself dry.

We'd asked her to do the same for the rest of us, but got back some sort of nonsense about the size of our patrol area and the need to conserve her power.

If I slipped in all this rain, and we lost because of it, I was damn well going to eat some of her inevitable baking.

The streets were mostly empty, probably because of that same rain, so I guess it wasn't all bad. Patrol duty was a real responsibility for professional Cape teams. There being only four of us—and a single flyer—made the task more obnoxious than it might have otherwise been, but I felt almost like a real Cape; stalking the streets, looking for criminals, and keeping the peace.

We'd covered a lot of ground already though, and the most we'd encountered was a single wannabe mugger, who was dumb enough to think a man in a skull mask made a good target. Unless Jessica was trying to bore us to death, there had to be more to this mission than that.

Our first instinct on patrol had been to creep around each building, sticking to the shadows, and guarding each other's blind spots. Turned out that was great for infiltrating a small space, but way too slow when your area of responsibility was fifteen to twenty city blocks. Mostly, we were supposed to serve as a visual deterrent, and to make sure we were available to lend support to local law enforcement.

As if thinking their name was enough to trigger the next stage of the sim, there was a crackle over my comms. Today's police dispatcher had a voice like smooth chocolate. If she hadn't been completely simulated, I'd have been dying to meet her.

"Shots fired at 3rd and Main. Backup requested."

"Team Five, 10-4," replied Poltergeist, for once using the radio calls we'd been taught. Switching to our team's channel, she added, "That's only a few blocks away from me. I'm headed over. Winter, provide overwatch."

"Need an extra hand?" I asked. We had just passed 10th street, but I was pretty sure I could reach Tessa in a few minutes.

"Negative. Maintain your current patrol route."

"Roger that."

We almost sounded like professionals. Hopefully, the teachers were taking notice.

"Walker." Freddy's voice was pitched low as he called across the street to me. For once, he managed to avoid triggering his comms when talking. "Just saw a bunch of pedestrians heading down 10th."

"And?"

"I think they were armed."

I crossed to his side of the street and took a look. By now, the people Muse had spotted were more than a block away, but one of them had a bat, and another looked like he might be holding a pistol.

More importantly, all four had red bandanas tied around their left arms.

My first-year Summoner, Paco, didn't talk a lot about his life on the streets, but one thing he had told me was how the gangs of Los Angeles used colors to show their allegiance. We weren't in Los Angeles—and I didn't know enough to identify gangs by their colors even if we had been—but I was willing to bet the gangs of this city did the same thing.

Visible weapons? Possible gang colors?

"Let's check it out," I decided.

"You first." Freddy hefted his assault rifle. "I'm better from a distance anyway."

It wasn't the real reason he wanted me to go first, and we both knew it, but I didn't argue.

"Just don't shoot me in the ass."

"No promises."

ooo

"Poltergeist, we have a situation here," I whispered over the comms. We were three blocks off our assigned route, and the four gang members we'd been following had multiplied with every block. There were now more than a dozen of them, spread across the street, and we were close enough to see that every single one was armed.

That wasn't the situation I was referring to though.

No, that would be the twenty gang members coming down the street from the opposite direction. They too were armed, but their bandanas were blue and worn across their faces, in a crude approximation of a Cape's mask.

"Little busy here, Walker," said Poltergeist, and if the sharpness of her tone wasn't enough to tell me things were still pear-shaped on her end, the chatter of gunfire across comms did. "Call it in to the police if you think normal backup will help."

I was pretty sure the police had better things to do than get killed, but so did the rest of us. I shrugged and switched to the general channel. "Team Five here, designation Walker. Possible gang conflict about to go down at 10th and Broadway. Over."

"Walker, be advised all units are already deployed. Dispatching a car from the 7th precinct now. ETA fifteen minutes."

"Roger that." I looked over my shoulder at Freddy. Fifteen minutes was an eternity in a fight, even before you added guns to the mix. "Guess it's up to us."

"Try not to kill anyone after they surrender this time."

"No promises," I parroted.

The best way to keep a battle from turning into a slaughter is to keep the battle from happening in the first place. That's why I sprinted through an alley, turned down 11th street, and then sprinted back up Broadway. By the time the leaders of each gang were stepping forward to confront each other, I was there waiting.

"Gentlemen. And ladies," I amended smoothly, realizing that two of the lieutenants were women, "it's cold and rainy out. Don't you think we'd all be more comfortable in our respective homes?"

Thank god I'd been doing all that running lately. Pretty sure huffing and puffing my way through the speech would have hampered the aura of total badass I was trying to project.

"Who the fuck is this guy?" asked one of the other lieutenants, a hulking man who looked half-Titan. He'd torn the sleeves from his shirt, and the red bandana was wrapped snugly around a bicep as big as Freddy's head. "Maybe we should—"

The smaller man in front of him raised a hand, cutting off Big Arms' words in mid-speech. "Mr. Cape," he said, voice soft and pleasant in a way I didn't buy for even a second, "I'm sure you know that there are times when the weather must be considered to be of secondary importance."

He talked like Fallout, if without the creepy damn whisper. I disliked him already.

"My family and I," he continued, words so oily even the rain couldn't wash them off, "were merely out for our evening constitutional and who should we encounter but the Skyborn. A group of petty criminals and loud mouth braggarts in our territory? Surely, you understand such things cannot stand."

"These have been our streets, Sirus, ever since Jackson and the rest of you Bloods turned tail in 70," rumbled the man I assumed was the leader of the so-called Skyborn. "Apparently, you and your *family* need to be reminded of that fact."

"You're not treating with Jackson anymore, Egg. Our esteemed friend and mentor had an unfortunate accident with a bad batch of stim weed, eleven bullets, and a second smile below the chin," Sirus responded smoothly, spreading his hands. Of the six people out in front, he was the only one without a weapon in hand, but I spotted a bandolier of knives under his coat. "I'm here to show you halfwits who you're dealing with." His eyes flickered lazily in my direction. "For the good and safety of our fair city, of course."

This was not going the way I'd hoped.

"This is your only warning," I said, keeping my voice hard even as I let the emptiness swell inside of me. "Go home. Figure out a better way to handle this dispute. Beer pong, maybe. The police are on their way."

"Let them come," said Egg. "Could do with some pork to go with one dead Cape and a street full of Bloods."

"You see what I'm dealing with, Mr. Cape?" asked Sirus, tone slow and lazy. "Morons. And yet—" He shrugged, and knives appeared in both his hands like magic. "—you know what they say about broken clocks."

In my experience, a broken clock was one that didn't show any numbers on its screen. But something told me that wasn't what Sirus had been talking about.

Not that it mattered, because Big Arms was already coming to tear my head off.

I really sucked at this, didn't I?

There were a lot of laws about what Powers could do to normals, but most of those laws went out the window when the Power was a Cape, and the normal was attacking them. That made the enormous henchman fair game.

I stepped forward and inside the big man's overhand right, one hand chopping at the inside of that elbow, while my other hand snaked forward and caught the bastard by the throat.

I'll give you two guesses what happened next.

I stepped past the pile of clothing and the cloud of dust and dried skin that had been a man and found both Sirus and Egg staring at me, weapons only half-raised.

I let my voice go flat, let that emptiness fill my eyes. "Who's next?"

"He's just one Cape," shouted someone safely in the crowd of Skyborn, fifteen feet away. "You can take him!"

A spray of bullets chewed up the empty space between Egg and his troops, and I worked hard not to sigh in relief. Freddy had finally made it up the building's fire escape and into position.

"We have numbers, and a Weather Witch itching to fill this street with lightning," I lied, pointing up at a sky I was betting they wouldn't be able to see was empty. "You can keep pushing things and die, you can stand here and wait for the police, or you can go someplace dry and forget all of this ever happened. Maybe spend the night watching Cape vids? I hear they're entertaining."

"Another time, Sirus," rumbled Egg, gesturing to his troops as he turned to leave.

"Count on it, Egg." Sirus turned to me and his smile curdled. "As for you, Mr. Cape—"

"Walker," I corrected him.

He shrugged. Apparently, he'd never heard of me. Even though this was just a sim, that kind of hurt.

"We are departing, as instructed. I can only hope and pray that you don't have an accident like what happened to dear departed Jackson."

"Death comes for all of us," I told him, "but I'm not going to worry too much about it. Especially since you don't even exist."

ooo

Believe it or not, we aced the simulation. Even better, Team One dropped two places in the rankings because Supersonic slipped while chasing down a fleeing robber and ended up taking out a boutique dress shop on the corner.

He sat through the entire video replay with a face like a tomato and teeth grinding so hard I could hear them from two rows away.

Not a bad way to end a shitty month.

CHAPTER 39

"Maybe spend the night watching Cape vids?"

"Too much?"

"Nah. It was perfect." Silt dropped down onto the bench and looked out to the ocean. "Nice job stopping that gang war from going down. And without killing any bystanders this time."

I shrugged. "I guess maybe our lessons are starting to sink in. Did your team face something similar?"

"They played our vid in class not long after yours," she reminded me.

"Yeah, but..." I rubbed my face. Even the brilliant sight of the sun on the waves was struggling to hold my attention. "I may have had my eyes closed for some of the class. These last few months have been rough."

"Rub some dirt on it and keep going," she told me, a phrase that made very little sense at all. "You'll have plenty of time for beauty sleep when you're a Cape."

"If I sleepwalk off the wall one night during guard duty, I'm going to come back and haunt you and the Academy both."

"Ha! That'll be the day." Silt's grin turned into a yawn of her own. "Anyway, we had a riot, not a gang war, but we cleared that up damn quick."

"How?"

"Alan Jackson."

Alan-fucking-Jackson. Of course.

"Civilians took one look at that thing he shifts into and scattered," she continued. "Nobody ever even threw a punch."

"Damn. You should probably ask *him* to go to Brownsville with you after graduation."

"Already did." She shook her head. "He said he's not going back to the Badlands. Ever."

"Really? *Alan* said that?"

"Not in so many words, but yeah. He's got a bit of a history, you know. You two are more alike than you might think."

I was pretty sure I'd just been insulted.

"Although he's prettier, of course." She grinned.

Given that Alan Jackson was a hulking slab of meat who turned into an even more terrifying blend of animal and man, I now *knew* I was being insulted.

"So," Silt said, after a few moments of silence to enjoy her own joke, "there are rumors going around campus about you and a freshman woman?"

"I don't want to talk about it."

"So they're true?"

I sighed. "Do they say that she and I went back to my dorm room, got it on, and then I had to kick her out to keep from killing her when I came?"

"Uhm. No."

"Then they're not true."

"So sex is a trigger?" She whistled. "Was that a one-time thing, you think, or...?"

"I don't want to talk about it," I said again. "Why do you think I'm out here again?"

"I've never been clear on why you came out here in the first place, other than the view."

"Meditation," I told her. "Dealing with my power away from everyone."

The fact that she didn't scoot further away from me on the bench said all you needed to know about Sofia Black.

"And how is that—" She paused. "Wait. Did you hear that?"

"Hear what?"

"Sounded like something in the woods."

"Bard and Alexa both swear the forest is jaguar free."

She looked at me weirdly for a second, then shook her head. "Jaguars live in jungles, Damian."

That wasn't what I'd heard, but I let it go. "Can't you track it with your power? Like Vibe does with her empathy?"

"You mean try and sense things moving across the earth? That's not how—" An odd look crossed Silt's broad face. "Honestly, I never even thought of that. Let me try."

Not sure if it was because I'd just suggested it to Silt, or if I just didn't want her feeling weird trying new things on her own, but as she closed her eyes and tried to extend her senses through the earth, I did the same.

It was an exercise in futility, of course. I wasn't an Earthshaker. I couldn't manipulate the earth, let alone sense things moving across it.

Except... I just had.

Not the earth part. The dirt beneath my feet was as inert as ever, and totally impenetrable. But out there in the forest, maybe ten yards to our south, I felt... something.

Even weirder? It felt *familiar*. Like a piece of me. A small bubble of emptiness that had taken seed and was only now coming home.

Maybe that would have seemed cool if I'd been another Power—Hydromancers probably had some sort of dopey saying about water returning to the ocean—but I was a Crow, and given my recent experiences, it scared the crap out of me.

I opened my mouth to warn Silt, but just that quickly, the bubble was gone.

Sofia frowned. "I thought I sensed—" Her head snapped around in a different direction, and she pointed to the east edge of the clearing. "There. It's small but it's coming."

This time, I didn't sense anything at all, but twenty seconds later, an oversized rat waddled its way into the clearing.

Silt jumped to her feet—*away* from the rat, I couldn't help but notice—and clenched one fist. Earth shot up to form a two-foot diameter wall around the rat.

"When the hell did our campus get rats?" she demanded, face pale and eyes wide.

I could count the number of times I'd seen Silt so off-balance on one hand and still have fingers left over. A woman who would blithely befriend a Crow… who didn't seem at all concerned about Alan-fucking-Jackson sleeping two rooms over… was scared of *rats?*

Weird.

"Not rats, plural," I told her. "As far as I know, this is the only one." And it wasn't the first time I'd seen him either.

"What?"

"One of my first-years, Paco—"

"The Summoner?"

"Yeah. Welcome to what he summons."

"That's disgusting," she decided.

"Careful," said the first-year himself, stepping into the clearing. "You'll hurt Woodrow's feelings. He's surprisingly sensitive about these things." Paco nodded in my direction, face a mask. "Sorry for intruding, Walker."

"It's fine," I said, "but how did you find me?"

"The whole first-year class knows this is your place," he said easily, gesturing at the clearing, "and stays the hell away because of it. But I needed to talk to you. I sent Woodrow ahead to make sure I wasn't interrupting."

We both ignored Silt's muttered imprecations and the death glare she had fixed on the dirt prison she'd built around Woodrow.

"What's going on?" I asked. "Something you needed to say before the whole group meets up this weekend?"

Paco's eyes flickered over to Silt and then back to me.

"It's okay," I told him. "Silt is—"

"Heading back to my dorm for some much needed me-time," declared my friend in a loud, no-nonsense voice. "You boys have fun. We'll catch up later, Damian."

"Tessa's invited some people over tonight to watch vids," I told her. "You're welcome to come."

"Who's *people?*"

"London, Olympia, and Patty, I think."

"Well, hell. How could I say no to that?" She flashed a grin, and marched out of the clearing, taking a circuitous path that kept her at least fifteen feet from Woodrow the entire time. It was only after she'd disappeared into the forest that the earth prison finally crumbled.

The rat, upon his eventual reveal, didn't seem particularly troubled.

Paco, on the other hand…

"What's going on, Paco?"

"I need to show you something." The Summoner always played things close to his chest, but this was extreme even for him. Still, of all my first-years, he and Lynn were the two whose judgment I trusted most. I could press for more information, there and then, or I could do my job as a mentor and go see what he wanted to show me.

I spared a glance to the south, where that bubble of emptiness had disappeared, then followed Paco back through the woods towards campus.

Once we were out, Paco made a beeline for a building I knew all too well.

"Why are we going to the med ward, Francisco?" I didn't use Paco's real name very often, but this seemed like the time and place.

"It's Lucy."

"Lucy?" I didn't have much of a relationship with my first-year Titan, to be honest. She regularly skipped our mentorship meetings, and when she did show up, she barely ever spoke. I didn't know a lot about people, but I recognized crippling shyness when I saw it. After my attempts to draw her out had seemed to only make things worse, I'd decided to give her space instead.

Maybe that had been a fuck-up on my part.

"How do you even know Lucy's here?" I asked him, as we neared the medical building's front door.

He stopped, cocked his head, and shrugged. "I've been keeping an eye on things with Woodrow."

"Spying?"

That was enough to crack his street face. "No! Just keeping aware. I don't have steel skin or any sort of regeneration. I need to know if and where an attack is coming from."

Paco was possibly the only person on campus more paranoid than me.

Unless you counted Alan-fucking-Jackson.

Or Midnight.

We Capes were a neurotic bunch.

"And Lucy?"

"She fainted while walking back from Weapons class this morning. Her roommate, Malia—" He paused and shot me a look. "Do you know Malia?"

I shook my head.

"Kind of stuck-up," he informed me, "even for a Wind Dancer. Anyway, Woodrow saw her helping Lucy to the med ward."

I frowned. Fainting was unusual, especially for a Titan, but the first year at the Academy was brutal, and it wore everyone down. I wasn't seeing the emergency here.

"I talked to Malia," the Summoner continued, dark eyes reading my face. "This is the third time in a week."

Okay. *That* was unusual.

He shrugged. "Anyway, I figured you'd want to know."

Shit. Unless Lucy was secretly an Empath who needed a break from the emotions of everyone around her, I wasn't sure what help I could be. But there was only one way to find out.

I pulled open the door to the med ward and Paco and I slipped inside.

CHAPTER 40

As a first-year, the med ward had been my second home. Ironically, given the number of times I'd been severely injured or even killed in the past few months, this was only the third time I'd been there as a second-year... and one of those visits had been to steal more Academy greys.

Simulation training had some benefits, I guess.

It hadn't changed. Five steel gurneys occupying the center of the room, with a sink along one wall, and shelves with supplies and clothes along another. Lucy was on the third gurney, instantly identifiable due to her size. Above her stood Gladys, one of the school Healers and a no-nonsense old woman whose sharp tongue was the stuff of legend. She eyed us both as we came inside.

I gave her a noncommittal nod in reply. I was pretty sure Gladys had a thing for baby Crows, but this wasn't the time for that. And, given what had happened with Emma, there'd probably never be a time for that.

Not to mention, the Healer had to be at least sixty.

"Damian. Francisco." Her voice was rough and grumpy. Lucy didn't react at all, suggesting she was asleep. "Neither of you seems injured. For once."

Paco stayed silent. Looked like I was the designated speaker.

"Hey Gladys," I said, trying for some of El Bosque's effortless smoothness, "it's been a while."

"Has it?" She shrugged bony shoulders. "I guess so. What do you want?"

Apparently, my Santiago impression sucked. Or Gladys was immune. Maybe it was a Healer thing.

"We came to check on Lucy," I told her, voice quiet. "Is she okay?"

Something in the old Healer's face softened, just a bit. "Tired. Dehydrated. Malnourished, somehow."

Now *that* was weird. Vibe was an outlier in that the food she got at home put the Academy's to shame. For the rest of us, even those who hadn't grown up eating synth-rations, we had never eaten better than since arriving on campus.

"Malnourished? How is that possible?"

Gladys shrugged again, looking pensive. "It means she's not eating as much as a girl her size should. But I think those are all symptoms."

"Of what?"

"Depression." She scowled, adding more lines to a face already full of them. "She lost her first fight in Nikolai's bloody pits, but was still cheerful while I healed her; smiling and chatting up a storm. Each time I've healed her since, there's been less and less of that girl visible. I put her to sleep and told her teachers she'd be out for the day, but I think there's more going on than just too much partying."

Paco spoke up for the first time. "I've never seen Lucy out. Not since summer break anyway."

"Huh." Gladys peered at me. "How do you know her anyway?"

"I'm her second-year mentor. Paco's too."

"You're a mentor?" She paused, looking like she was choosing her words carefully. Which was weird. Gladys never chose her words carefully. "That's an interesting choice."

"It wasn't mine." I frowned, looking at the sleeping Titan. "She's been skipping our mentorship meetings. I figured she needed space."

"She needs something." The old Healer shook her head. "When Dean Bard gets back, I'm going to tell him Lucy should start attending counseling with Dr. Gibbings. Maybe you can make sure she actually goes?"

"I can try," I said absently, thoughts still racing. "Wait. Where's Bard?"

"Away." Eyes that had seen tens of thousands of injuries met mine, hard as stone. "And if he'd wanted you to know more than that, he'd have told you himself."

I was starting to think Gladys didn't like me anymore. Maybe she'd heard Emma's story too.

"He'll be back in a week," she continued. "If you want to help, make sure Lucy gets the food and sleep that she needs. I'm going to keep her overnight, but after that, she's all yours. Nine sharp, Mr. Banach."

I recognized a dismissal when I heard one. Less than a minute later, Paco and I were back outside the med ward. "Nine o'clock," I mused, doing the math. "That gives us just over sixteen hours."

"To do what?"

"Find out what the fuck is going on." I spared the Summoner a glance. "What class are you supposed to be in now?"

"History of Powers." He winced. "I'm going to hear about it from Amos."

"Let's go then."

"To class?" It was his turn to scowl. "I said I was going to hear about it. I didn't say I was looking forward to the lecture! I'll just wait until Thursday. Maybe he'll have forgotten by then."

"Amos might forget the time, the subject, and how to use basic technology," I said, "but someone missing his class? I don't think so. Besides, we're not going there for you."

"We're not?"

"No. We're going there to talk to Malia."

○○○

For most of our first year at the Academy, I had been anything but friends with my roommate, Jeremiah. In fact, we'd barely spent any time together at all until he'd asked for my help training to fight. If

Malia and Lucy were anything like we had been, our trip to find Malia was going to be a waste of time.

From what I understood though, that was far from the norm. Maybe it wasn't always friendship, but most first-years had *some* sort of relationship with their roommates. And I was pretty sure Malia knew something about what was going on with Lucy.

By the time we reached the History auditorium, class was already almost over. A minute or so later, students started flooding out into the hall.

"That's her," said Paco, nodding to a young woman in Academy greys. "Malia!"

The woman in question turned when he called her name, frowned, and slowly made her way over. Malia had golden skin, shoulder-length black hair, and eyes as grey as mine. "Paco," she said finally, "what do you want now?"

Apparently, she hadn't seen me. I stepped forward. "I have some questions for you."

Her eyes went wide, but she stopped herself from physically shrinking away. It was a close thing, but I appreciated the effort.

"What is this about?" She swallowed and shook her head, answering her own question. "Lucy."

The hallway was full of students, but there was a small bubble of space about us that I ascribed more to normals seeing three students in Academy greys than to people recognizing who I was.

Although, thanks to Emma, I couldn't be sure.

"I'm trying to find out what's going on," I told her.

"I'm sorry," she managed. "I don't know anything."

She spun away to head down the hall, but I was already in front of her.

"Malia," I said, trying to keep my voice from going cold, "why don't you let me be the judge of that? Or we can go straight to Bard."

She flinched, but that could have been just to keep from running into me. "Fine. Lucy swore me to silence, but I'll tell her you threatened me."

Which wasn't exactly how things had just gone down, but... life with Winter had taught me there was a time to argue and a time to let someone have their so-called victory. What mattered here was finding out what was going on with my first-year Titan.

We followed her down the hall and into a smaller classroom. Malia closed the door and leaned against it, arms folded across her chest. She was almost the physical opposite of Silt; tall, slender, and delicate where my friend was a tree stump with limbs and a punch that could drop a rhino in its tracks.

If you don't know what rhinos are, think cows, but grey, armored, and with horns like unicorns. Apparently, they were everywhere pre-Break.

"Maybe I should have said something sooner," she decided, chewing on her bottom lip, "but like I said, Lucy swore me to silence."

"Is it drugs?" I asked. "Something harder than stim-weed? Or drinking?" I'd never smelled alcohol on Lucy, but you never knew, and Muse's own issues were still fresh in my mind.

"What? No." She sighed, hands fluttering in the air like bird wings. "It's about a boy."

"Oh."

"Not like that." She colored a bit. "Anymore anyway. His name is Todd Evans."

I turned to Paco, but he shrugged. "Not a first-year."

"He's a sophomore," she said. Which also made him a normal. I wasn't entirely sure why the Academy used different names for years for Powers and normals, but it probably had something to do with their degrees taking four years instead of three.

"So Lucy and Todd dated?" I was starting to think Malia had been right and that I really shouldn't have pried. The last thing I wanted was to get involved in first-year romance. London and Santiago had been bad enough.

"No. Not really. She had a crush on him at the beginning of school, and he was a huge dick to her when she finally approached him back in May."

"How so?"

"Just… he was mean. He's hot and popular, and he made a big spectacle of shooting her down. Like it was the comedy event of the decade or something."

That was enough, in my opinion, to merit a random—and totally untraceable, hopefully—beating, but it didn't explain why Lucy was still a wreck all these months later.

"Since then, it seems like it's almost become a hobby or something for Todd and his friends to taunt her. About her size or her weight or her hair or a million other things. It's all so petty and stupid, but Lucy never wanted to be a Titan. It's like they know exactly what to say or do to hurt her."

"And you've known this was going on for *how* long?" Whatever Malia saw in my eyes had her going pale and shrinking back against the door.

"Since before the semester break. But… she made me swear I wouldn't tell anyone!"

"And now she's barely sleeping and just fainted three times in a fucking week." My voice was flat, my power filling me.

"I'm sorry! I thought I was being a good friend!"

That didn't make a damn bit of sense to me, but Paco was nodding. "Secrets are secrets," he told me. "Loose lips get people dead."

"This isn't the streets, Paco." I shot both first-years a look. "Sometimes, you have to do the right thing, and fuck the consequences."

If anything, Malia went even paler. "Are you going to Bard?"

"Not yet. Bard's off campus," I admitted.

"Then what are you going to do?"

"It's probably better you don't know." I looked her dead in the eye. "Gladys is keeping Lucy asleep until tomorrow. You're going to pick her up at the med ward, get her back to the dorm, and keep her company."

"But my classes—"

"Are you her friend or not?" snapped Paco.

Malia's jaw firmed as she looked over at the Summoner. "Screw you, Paco. I'm her *only* friend."

"Then watch her damn back!"

"It'll only be a few days," I told her. "And we'll go to Bard when he gets back. There are just a few conversations I need to have first."

"I was trying to help her, you know."

Malia was probably telling the truth. It's not like there was policy for how to handle a Power being bullied by normals. This was the first time I'd even heard about it happening at the Academy.

All the same, I looked at her and felt absolutely nothing.

"Help her tomorrow. Tell Gladys I sent you."

We waited for her to scurry back into the now-empty hall. I turned to Paco.

"Thoughts?"

"Lucy is crew," he said simply. "We can't let this shit stand."

"Exactly."

"Back home, they'd find him dead in his bed, and that would be that." He glanced up at me, face emotionless. "But I hear this isn't the streets."

"Killing one guy won't stop anything anyway, unless his friends know why he died. And it would mean a life in the Hole for the Power responsible."

That rocked Paco back on his heels. I could see the gears turn as he tried to step out of the thought patterns forged by his time in a gang.

"So what do we do?"

"We convince Todd to put an end to things himself. That his health is directly linked to her happiness."

"You mean give him a beating?"

"No." I smiled that smile Silt hated. "Pain's temporary. Fear is forever."

I watched several emotions battling in Paco's eyes. Anger. Worry. Maybe his own slice of fear. And then, they all faded away, replaced by determination.

"How do we start?"

"With something Jessica Strich harps on in every Group Tactics class," I told him. "Reconnaissance."

CHAPTER 41

It took three days to get ready. Three days, a fair bit of observation, and far more convincing than I'd have expected, but it was all totally worth it for the look on Todd Evans' face when he woke in his dorm room bed to find me staring down at him.

"What the—" was all he got out before I drove a knee into his gut, forced a sock into his mouth and duct taped the whole thing shut.

I know what you're thinking, and no, the sock wasn't mine. I wasn't sure whose it was, actually. I'd found it out on one of the campus paths, all by itself, and it wasn't particularly clean, but so far Todd hadn't said a word of complaint about it.

None that I could understand, anyway.

Behind me, there was thrashing as the same scenario repeated with Todd's roommate, Anton. I hadn't wanted to involve any innocent bystanders and luckily, I hadn't had to; Anton was another of the crowd who'd been making Lucy's life hell.

This was as much about him as it was Todd.

Both Jessica and Nikolai harped a lot on efficiency; of movement and action, tactically and strategically. My getting a two-for-one on a Saturday night in the sophomore dorms had to qualify. It was almost a pity I'd never get to tell my professors about it.

Beneath me, Todd started to thrash about, making noise that might be heard if their dorm's walls were as paper-thin as ours. I reached one hand behind me and another pair of gloved hands passed me a small, square, and crudely designed device. I brought it around in front of me and hit the thumb-sized switch on top.

Crimson fire shot forth. The tongue of flame was only five inches high or so, but right in front of Todd's eyes, it must have looked like a bonfire. He went still, the whites of his eyes visible.

Which meant it was time to begin.

"I know what you're thinking," I murmured, voice quiet and empty. "What? Who? Why?" I patted his cheek with my free hand. "We'll get to those answers in a second. Let's start with you instead."

His eyes went even wider. Apparently, he didn't like the sound of that.

"Todd Evans," I said softly. "Sophomore at the Academy. Major in Marketing. Minor in being an asshole. Member of the campus swim team and captain of the hacky sack club." I hadn't known the Academy had either, to be honest. Normals had too much time on their hands. "Only child of Maurice and Amanda. Maybe that's why you're such a dick."

I thumbed off the device in my hand, and the room plunged back into darkness.

"Your blindfolded roommate is Anton Nils, but we're going to focus on you, Todd, because here's the thing. There aren't a lot of rules on campus that matter to me. Don't eat people? That's a good one, I guess. Don't cheat? Whatever. Don't drink so much that you make a fool of yourself? Hell, one of my own roommates struggles with that one. There's only one rule that you need to worry about tonight: don't ever fuck with me or mine."

The flame roared back to life, all the brighter for the brief moment of darkness.

"Do you know who I am, Todd?"

I waited for him to frantically shake his head back and forth. My smile didn't seem to comfort him at all for some reason.

"My name is Walker," I told him. "I'm the only Crow at the Academy. Only Crow that's ever been a student here. See, a lot of people are worried that I'm going to go insane, like every other necromancer. That I'll just—" I waved the flame in front of his eyes.

"—up and start murdering people for no reason. The fact that I can kill with a touch probably hasn't helped calm those fears."

Todd shrank away from my bare hand. He was trying to say something through the sock, but I wasn't in the mood to translate.

"Can you and your boy Anton over there keep a secret? I have dreams, Todd. Dreams where this entire campus is destroyed. Where it's just me and the dead, ghosts and walkers as far as the eye can see. Could be all of Los Angeles, for all I know. And you know what? It just feels *right*. It feels like that's the way things should be. Maybe I'm already crazy. Maybe the Academy just doesn't know it yet."

"That's the what and the who," I finished. "Now that we're acquainted, we should talk the why. Would you like that?" I didn't wait for the panicked nod. "With the third-years gone on their internships, there are thirty-eight student Capes left on campus. Thirty-seven if you don't want to count me." My smile widened. "And after our discussion tonight, I can understand why you might not. Thirty-seven teenagers, and every one of them is training their asses off so that they can risk their lives protecting petty motherfuckers like you."

"So when I hear that you're making the life of one of those students a living hell, it doesn't make me angry," I lied. "It makes me want to make an example out of you and all your fragile little friends."

I'd never seen so much sweat pour out of a man before, and that was saying something, considering I'd known the Viking for almost two years. He was trying to speak again, trying to mouth words that I couldn't read through the duct tape over his lips. Beneath the smell of stale beer, there was now another one, sharp and acrid. Someone was going to have to wash their sheets when this was over.

"But cooler heads have prevailed, for the moment." I jerked my head at the masked figures in black behind me, their details impossible to make out in the darkness, especially with a flame right in front of his face. "They reminded me that this is a place of learning. They think you should get a chance to grow from this, to make up for your transgressions. Do you want to do that, Todd?"

This time, his frantic nod wasn't enough. "I want to hear you say the words, Todd. Say them quietly, here and now." I ripped the tape back off, pulled out the sock, and tossed it aside.

"You can't do this!" he hissed, voice thin and reedy. "You can't just—"

"Fuck can't," I told him. "Right now, *can't* doesn't even enter into the equation."

"Please don't kill me," he whispered.

"I'm not going to kill you. How would you learn from that? I've seen a few walkers raised and they're great for slaughtering civilians, but learning's not really their thing."

My mind flashed to Nyah's vision of the walkers that had stormed into the Bakersfield orphanage, and I struggled to keep my tone steady.

"All I want is for the harassment to stop. Can you do that?"

"Yes! Yes!"

"That's good to hear." I thumbed off the flame again and passed back the cube to the person behind me, receiving an unlit Glass in return. "Because I'm holding you responsible for more than just your actions."

"What?"

"When you and Anton wake up tomorrow, you will be new men. You will do everything in your collective power to make sure that Lucy David is shown the respect she deserves, as a woman, as a Titan, and as a Cape." He started to say something, but I spoke over his words. "Fuck the hacky sack club. You're the new president of the Lucy David fan club."

"Did she set you up to this?"

"No," I answered truthfully. "She never even said a word to me or anyone else. In fact, I'm pretty sure she'd be horrified if she heard this conversation, because she's a good person. Not like you or me, Todd, but an actual, genuinely nice soul. Do you know how I know that?"

I thumbed the Glass to life and held it in front of Todd's tear-streaked face. It took his eyes a moment to adjust enough to see the video. The sound was set to low, but the dull booms of powerful impacts could be heard.

"This is first-year Combat class," I told him, having watched the video a half-dozen times since I'd acquired it. "In the back corner, you'll see where all that noise is coming from." I waited for his eyes to track, and continued. "Most heavy bags are leather filled with sand. That one is solid titanium. Look at the dents Lucy is putting in it."

He seemed transfixed.

"If Lucy were a dickhead like you or me, she'd have broken your dumb ass in half months ago," I continued, "or ripped your arm off and beaten you and your friends to death with it. Instead, she's tried to take the high road, tried to focus on training for a career that inevitably ends in death. That's a good person. That's the sort of Cape this country needs. How do we treat people like that, Todd?"

"Nicely?"

I rolled my eyes in the darkness. "Right. Nicely. That's all that's needed. Leave her alone, make sure she's treated with respect, and everything will be good. If you can't do that... if you feel compelled to get some sort of revenge, or even just want to share the details of tonight's conversation, then we will have ourselves a problem."

I turned his head, directing his attention to the room's sole window. Something small crouched on the exterior sill, shreds of black fur on white bone, gaping sockets where there would once have been eyes, and a tail of pale vertebrae thrashing about.

I barely got my hand over his mouth to muffle the scream.

Apparently, undead cats weren't to his liking.

ooo

Yeah. I should probably explain the zombie cat. That three-day delay wasn't entirely about reconnaissance. Part of it was getting the video of Lucy. Part of it was gathering the people I needed to break into the sophomore dorms. Part of it was giving a certain Technomancer enough time to create the flame cube.

And part of it was me going out into the forest and hunting down that spark of emptiness I'd felt, back before Paco started this whole thing in motion.

Turned out, it was a cat. Sort of.

Some teacher had buried their beloved pet out on the west side of campus years earlier, and when I came back from Bakersfield, when

I forced my overflowing emptiness down into the dirt, that answering spark I'd felt must have been the cat's body, reacting to my power.

First walker I ever raised, and it ran around on four legs.

Took it over a month to dig itself out and weeks more to come looking for me. That much was my fault. Pretty sure a Crow is supposed to be controlling their walkers, not just leaving them to figure shit out on their own. But now that I knew what I'd done, I could feel the link between us, feel a small but steady trickle of emptiness out of me and into the cat's corpse, powering its form.

Most interesting thing about any of that, aside from the whole zombie cat thing in general, was that the dampeners on campus—in Control, Nikolai's pits, and the Training Grounds—didn't sever the link. I couldn't sense the cat while the dampeners were on, let alone control it, but as soon as I re-emerged, it was out there, ready to do my bidding.

Can't say I hated having a pet. Or a minion, for that matter. Even if it was fifteen inches long, from tail to nose, and weighed less than five pounds.

It was a long fucking way from the brain-eating horde that Jimmy Taylor had unleashed in Bakersfield, but it was a start.

ooo

Getting out of the sophomore dorms was a lot easier than getting in had been. I left my feline walker behind to make sure we weren't followed, and we all retreated into the woods. Masks and gloves were removed and then we all looked at each other in silence.

I'd involved three of my first-years in my plan. Paco was a given, both because he knew how to pick locks, and because he'd been the one who brought the shit-storm to my attention in the first place.

Lynn had been almost as easy a choice. A Technomancer could access the exterior dorm cameras and make sure we never showed up. And when she heard what was going on, she'd been plenty eager to put the fear of the dead into those responsible.

And the last first-year? None other than Lucy herself.

I hadn't quite been truthful with asshole Todd. In fact, the biggest reason it had taken us three days to implement my little late night visit was because Lynn had insisted I get buy-in from Lucy. And then, when Lucy had finally agreed to let us move ahead with our plan, *she'd* insisted on coming along.

That had been part of the reason for the fire box Lynn cooked up for me. Masks are great for anonymity, but the only way to keep someone from noticing the hulking figure at the door is to give them something else to focus on.

Turns out fire works great for that sort of thing.

Now, the young Titan was looking at me with eyes like small plates. Next to her, Lynn was tiny, but equally nonplussed.

Even Paco looked a little taken aback. "That was a bit…"

"Over the top?"

"Yeah." He swallowed.

"Sometimes it has to be. Assholes don't speak subtle."

"Still. It's different than just stabbing someone and moving on." He coughed and looked over at the two women. "Or so I've heard."

"This way, we didn't do any harm at all, but he still got the message." I shrugged. "He better have, anyway."

"But why didn't you wear a mask?" asked Lynn.

"It's like your fire cube. Give him something else to focus on. Or in this case, someone. Crows have a reputation. It might as well work for me for once."

"What if one of them goes to Bard?"

"Then Todd, Anton and I will have a problem. I'll deal with that when and if it happens. Wouldn't be the first time I got in trouble. Honestly, I care more about whether or not it worked." I turned to the Titan in our midst. "Lucy?"

"He peed his bed," she told me, that soft voice such a strange match for her oversized form.

"Yeah. And cried until snot ran down his face. Pretty sure he swallowed some of it. Still think he's dreamy?"

Paco made a face, but Lucy just shook her head. "Not for a while, and now…" She frowned. "He seems kind of pathetic, doesn't he?"

And that had been the second objective of the whole exercise, once Lynn insisted Lucy be involved. Yeah, my threats would hopefully have the desired effect, but it was just as important that Lucy see Todd for who and what he was.

The only power he had was what she gave him.

"He's a loser," confirmed Lynn. "An egomaniac who had no idea just who he'd been messing with."

"A Titan," said Lucy, dropping her head, as if just saying the word was a burden.

"A Cape," corrected the Technomancer. "And we Capes stand together. The next time someone starts something, tell me. I'll kick them right in the balls. I'd let you do it, but—"

Lucy giggled unexpectedly. "I have super strength. They'd probably fly out of his mouth."

Which seemed both anatomically impossible and way more over the top than anything I'd done back in the dorms.

I did my best to push aside the mental image and nodded. "I know you can defend yourself if it comes to it, Lucy, and it's okay that you tried to take the high road instead. Hell, it's more than okay; it says good things about you. But Lynn's right. One thing I'm learning is that none of us are alone in this profession. Someone will always have your back."

I still believe that, oddly enough.

Even now.

Even after all that's happened.

Even knowing I'll never be a Cape.

Fuck if I don't envy that sense of unity.

CHAPTER 42

"Is there anything you'd like to tell me about?"

I'd only known Alexa for a year and a half, but I recognized a leading question when I heard it. And considering that it had only been eight days since my field trip to Todd's dorm room, I was pretty sure I knew what she was asking about.

Her follow-up removed any doubt.

"Specifically, in regards to you, several first-years, and the sophomore dormitory."

"I don't know what you're talking about," I replied blandly. I'd decided to be honest this year with Alexa, but it wasn't *really* dishonesty when she knew I was lying and I knew that she knew. Right?

"Of course you don't." The quirk of lips that was her smile came and went. "Incidentally, when infiltrating a facility, even one as lightly secured as a college dorm, it is preferable to loop the camera vids rather than just blacking them out."

Damn it, Lynn.

Black eyes fixed on me from across the room. "That same strange camera disturbance charted a path directly from the dorm in question to the woods on the west side of campus. And then, ten to fifteen minutes later, who should emerge from those woods?"

"Who?" I asked, as if I didn't already know the answer.

"Damian…"

"He was fucking with Lucy," I told her, anger washing away my intention of playing dumb, "and I didn't even break a single bone. I should be getting a medal for self restraint."

"He who?"

That gave me pause. "You don't know?"

"Despite what you might think, I am neither all-seeing nor all-knowing. I focus my attention on my patients."

"So Lucy's not one of them." I picked up a spark of something—irritation?—in Alexa's dark eyes, and moved on. "Okay. Then I guess you wouldn't have known."

More silence. I cleared my throat. "Lucy had a crush on a sophomore named Todd Evans. He shot her down and ever since then, he and his friends have made her life a living hell. For some reason, she's got issues with being big and strong as hell, and like all bullying assholes, they sensed weakness and went for blood."

"And last weekend's excursion?"

"Put a stop to it."

"You broke into this Todd's room and… threatened him?"

"Maybe?"

In one of her rare displays of utter humanity, the Cape formerly known as Midnight put down her Glass, pinched the bridge of her nose, and sighed. "Did you at least maintain a disguise? Mask? Gloves?"

"The others did." I shrugged. "I figured my threats would carry a little bit more weight if Todd knew who they were coming from."

"And that if you made yourself a target, it would shield the others."

I shrugged again. "Better me than them, right?"

She shook her head and muttered something under her breath.

"Damian, to the best of my knowledge, there have been seven Powers who faced expulsion and were able to remain at the Academy." She drummed long fingers on the wooden surface of her borrowed desk. Today, the black beaded bracelet was back on her left wrist, whatever that meant. "Nobody has ever survived two such hearings."

"What use strength, if not to defend those who have none?"

"I'm well aware of your propensity for quoting Dominion to get out of trouble." Alexa's voice was bone dry.

"You think I shouldn't have done anything?"

"I think you could have been more judicious with your actions." She read my expression and explained. "Making yourself a target to protect your first-years was noble, in a way, but nobility gets you dead. Better to find an option that protects all of you."

"Like what?"

"Wage a campaign of suppression and aggression. Enlist all of Ms. Davis' classmates instead of just two. Work slowly and subtly rather than committing everything to a single strike that might easily blow up in your face."

"I didn't have time for any of that."

"Didn't you? This Todd character was not going anywhere."

"No, but Lucy might have." I squeezed the cushions of the couch in my hands, leaving fingermarks on the fabric. "She was in the med ward last week. Even Gladys was concerned. Fuck subtlety."

The silence between us snapped and crackled with tension, like a live wire or a Spark's conjuration. Finally, she nodded.

"Fair enough. What's done is done."

"Is this the part where you drag me to go see Bard?"

"I think Jonathan has enough on his plate. There's a reason he asked me to come to the Academy, after all." Again, she read something in my expression. "Why does that disappoint you? Did you *want* to force his hand?"

"What? No. I'm just wondering why the hell nobody saw what was going on. There are only eighteen first-years. It shouldn't be that hard to keep track of things. Why didn't anyone know?"

"Bard is concerned with the university as a whole. In addition to the fifty-three first-years, second-years, and third-years, there are several thousand undergraduate and graduate students, and he is responsible for all of them."

"And our instructors?"

"Are focused on instruction. The school provides counseling, of course, but it is strictly voluntary. In most cases."

"So nobody has time to see that a Cape student is spiraling," I growled. "That's bullshit. Vibe, last year. Lucy, this year. Hell, even Ishmae. Someone should step the fuck up and—" The words I was saying finally sank in. "Shit. *Someone* was supposed to be me, wasn't it?"

"It is why Jonathan created the mentorship positions, yes. And between this and the other situation, I would say it is working, if not in quite the fashion he might have hoped."

"Other situation?"

She waved a hand, dismissing the matter entirely. "Irrelevant. The point is that this *is* how a mentorship role works. You will see some issues long before they make it to the faculty, and be in a position to address them. Knowing Jonathan as I do, I doubt he expected those duties to include breaking and entering, let alone threats of bodily harm, but as you said, there are times for subtlety and there are times to send in a hammer."

"I'm the hammer in this equation, I'm guessing?"

"That does seem to be your role so far, yes." Again, her lips quirked, and whatever tension had built between us disappeared. "My hope is that by the time you graduate, you will have learned to be a scalpel. Power is all well and good, but precision and control offer so many additional options."

Another silence fell, but this one was comfortable. Patient. I thought through what she'd said and pivoted to a different topic.

"If I graduate, I'm going to be defending people like that, won't I?"

"Like Ms. David? I suspect she will be more than capable of defending herself."

"I mean Todd Evans. Assholes who might be Black Hats if they had any shred of actual power."

"Yes."

"Why? How?"

"We've talked about this before," she reminded me.

"It was easier when it was all abstract." I looked over at the diplomas on the wall. "If Todd got run over tomorrow, I wouldn't give a damn. Hell, I think I'd probably be happy."

"Serving as a Cape is not necessarily about liking people, Damian. Some of the most antisocial, emotionless bastards I've known were Capes. But they did the job anyway."

"Why?"

"The reasons vary, just like the people. Some simply identify with the concept of order. Others operate on a desire for vengeance or to inflict punishment or even to atone for something in their own past. As for you…" She trailed off. "As I said, we've talked about this."

"I want to protect people."

"Those you claim, yes. Like Ms. David, for example."

"How does that help with someone like Todd?"

"It might not." She shrugged. "But people are living, growing organisms, and we are all connected. Even you. Maybe you're not defending some small-dicked egotist on his own behalf. Maybe you're doing it for the mother who loves him, or the children he will one day have, or even the marketing work he will one day do to keep a small Cape team financially solvent."

I stared. "How did you know he was majoring in marketing?"

She raised her Glass. "This does more than just take notes."

"Oh. Right." I chewed on her words. Like she'd said, it wasn't the first time we'd had this discussion. "What if I can't make that choice? To protect even the assholes?"

"Then you might be better suited seeking employment elsewhere."

"Like your agency?"

"Indeed. Although we have no need for hammers."

I winced.

"On that front, however, I do have some news."

At first, I thought she was still talking about hammers. Once I realized she meant her agency, my eyes widened. There was only one reason she'd be bringing them up.

"Did you find them? Tyrant and Jimmy Taylor?"

"Yes. And no." It was her turn to frown. "On Friday, my colleagues located the car you saw in your vision—the same one that transported you to your testing—outside an abandoned factory in

Fresno. Individuals were spotted on premises, including two that matched the descriptions of Tyrant and James Taylor."

I was already out of my seat. "What are we waiting for? Call for Door. We can be there in no time."

Alexa didn't move. "With two high value targets spotted, the agency elected to forego the usual observation period. I didn't even hear about the discovery until yesterday morning, long after the assault was carried out."

"And?"

"Nobody was there when they kicked down the doors."

Which could only mean one thing. "They have their own Teleporter."

She nodded. "Wysteria Appleton. Mid-Three. They didn't identify her from the photos taken until after the assault."

"Even with a Teleporter, how could they all get away so cleanly? Wouldn't some of them have been asleep or in different rooms or *something*?"

"You may be better suited for this type of work than it seems." As usual, Alexa seemed disinterested in blinking. "That is the central question. It is possible the entire group was staying in a single space, all were aware, and they were able to enact their escape within seconds of our assault, but the greater likelihood—"

"Is that they somehow knew you were coming. Again."

"Precisely. Between this, Yin's murder, and Fallout's disappearance, the evidence has become impossible to ignore."

"Fallout?" Just the mention of that long-haired, whispering bastard had me on edge. "What does he have to do with anything?"

"We were tasked with hunting him down after his escape from the Hole. I chased him up and down the coast for more than a month, finally cornered him outside of Seattle, and then he vanished."

"Another Teleporter." Which was starting to get absurd. Teleporters were not nearly as rare as Crows or Healers, but they didn't grow on trees either.

"Or the same one." Alexa's eyes were dark voids in the symmetry of her face. "Three instances where a target of my agency knew things they could not, and either escaped or committed murder because of it. Twice might be a coincidence. Three times makes it an inevitability."

"Makes what an inevitability?"

"That there is a traitor in my agency or the presidential cabinet that funds us."

"Fuck." Like any rational person, I didn't particularly like the government, but that was a long way from thinking it was literally out to get you. "So Fallout and Tyrant are connected?"

"It would appear so."

"And the prison break? Fallout mentioned a benefactor."

"Tyrant would seem to fit that bill, yes. And Wysteria Appleton would explain how Carnage and the others managed to sneak up on the Hole's defenses."

"Fuck," I said again. This time, it didn't feel sufficient for the scope of the shithole I'd found myself in. "What the hell is going on and what are we going to do?"

"My colleagues share my suspicion, and the few I know personally have gone to ground. They will do what they can, but they are isolated, and their primary identities may be blown."

"I'm sorry."

"It is the job. We all know the risks. But as for you and I, there is little that we can do. If my colleagues turn up any leads, I will hear about them, and so will you."

"Fallout. And a Low-Four Crow. And a Teleporter. And whatever the hell Tyrant is." I swallowed. "I don't think this is something you and I can handle on our own."

"Even if it was, you're a second-year, Damian. My job is not to throw you into danger."

"Then what are you thinking?"

"Stormwatch. The Defenders. Some or all of the Red Guard."

"And Dominion?"

"If we can secure his time, yes."

"Fallout killed Tempest," I reminded her. "Dominion will be there."

"Then all we have to do is find them."

Which ended up being a hell of a lot easier said than done.

CHAPTER 43

A few weeks later, after yet another night of restless sleep, I pulled on my greys, laced up my shoes, and headed to the common room to find Tessa.

If the still-lingering smell of fresh baked cookies wasn't enough of an indicator that we'd lost yet another sim, the look on Poltergeist's face sure as hell was.

For the first morning in months, Tessa wasn't dressed for a run. She had on an Academy sweatshirt, like me, but had paired it with pink and white striped pajama bottoms.

And as a further sign that she had no interest in our usual morning exercise, she had on fuzzy slippers instead of shoes.

"No run today?" I dropped into my now-customary spot on the couch next to her.

She shrugged and said nothing, green eyes fixed on the far wall.

"Still pissed about yesterday, I take it?" I cracked my neck, trying to rid myself of the phantom pains another disaster in the Training Grounds had left me with. "You know Freddy didn't mean to fuck things up, right?"

Our sim had been straight-forward enough. Defend a position against overwhelming numbers. Those numbers mounted the longer things went on, and no team was expected to last forever, but our time had been the lowest of every second-year team.

And even if he hadn't meant to fuck up, it had definitely been Muse's fault.

One building of fortified concrete and steel. Three ways in, two at ground floor, and one on the roof. Tessa had wanted to collapse two of those entrances, but the rules of the sim precluded us from doing so, so we were stuck guarding all three entrances. Winter was up on the roof where her versatility could come into play. I was on the front door and Muse was around the corner at the back, allowing Tessa to rotate to support us as need be.

That was the plan anyway.

Problem was, the attackers overran Freddy's position so fast they were on Tessa and crawling up my ass before we even knew they were there.

Not a word of warning from Muse over the comms.

Not a sound from the shotgun he'd chosen for the mission.

Just chaos and blood and disappointment.

"I'm not mad at Muse," Tessa finally said.

"Well, good—"

"I'm mad at you."

Wait, what?

"I thought you said you'd fixed things with him? Isn't that the one task I gave you?"

"You told me to talk to him. And I did! And he hasn't gone on a bender since!"

"Until last night." She threw a green-eyed glare in my direction.

"That's not…" For the safety of my own pubic hair, I gritted my teeth, and counted to ten. "I can't change who someone is, anymore than you can. Maybe you should have made him the rover and taken the back door yourself?"

It was her turn to bite back an angry retort, though fuck if I know why she bothered. It wasn't like there was much I could do to threaten her. "Maybe I should have," she finally said.

"Did he say what happened?" When we'd woken up in our pods, Freddy had made a beeline for the elevator, leaving us all behind.

"Apparently, he panicked. Just froze up and died." Tessa waved her hands around a lot when she was angry. I watched them flutter through the air like birds. "At least I think that's what he said. He was two bottles in by the time he came back to the sub-dorm." She glanced over at me through a wave of dark curls. "You know he's a liability, right?"

"Yeah."

"So what are we going to do?"

Apparently, she'd stopped being mad at me long enough for Muse to once again be *our* problem.

"I don't know," I said helpfully.

"In a real Cape environment, they'd just leave him at the base or in the battle van or somewhere out of the action. Freddy's power means he doesn't have to be front and center. But these stupid missions are designed to be hard for *four* of us. We can't afford to try them with only three."

"We could always let him go into the mission drunk."

That actually got her to turn and face me, just so I could see her rolling her big green eyes. "Even if that wasn't the dumbest suggestion ever, only his physical body would be drunk. In the sim, he'd still be cold sober."

"Then I don't know what to say. All we can do is put him in a position where he can be helpful but won't get us all killed when he drops the ball."

I wasn't sure where that phrase had come from. *Drops the ball.* It almost had to be a pre-Break sports thing, right? Or maybe it was a weird reference to puberty, when a boy became a man?

Fuck if I knew. Pre-Break history had never been my favorite subject.

Don't tell Amos that, if you see him.

"Have you checked the standings?" she asked.

"Fuck no. If I did that, I'd have to accept that Supersonic is still ranked higher than me."

"We're at the bottom," she said. "My team is at the bottom."

"It's not your fault."

"I don't care about fault," she said angrily, ignoring that she'd cared very much about it just a few minutes earlier. "Did you know we don't have sims in November or December? Instead, we have one last mission scheduled for January that all five teams are going to work together on."

"That's... good, isn't it?" I was just as tired of losing as she was. Two months of peace sounded fantastic.

"It means our rankings aren't going to change for two months."

"So what?" When she didn't immediately answer, it was my turn to shoot her a look. "It sucks being the lowest-ranked team in the class, but if the January sim is such a big thing, I'm sure the points will be weighted accordingly. I'm not saying we'll catch the top-ranked teams, but we could still end up somewhere other than the bottom."

"That's in *January.*"

I'd literally just said that, so I wasn't sure what she was getting at.

She sighed and explained. "Nobody but the team leaders has been told this yet, but the high team gets an extra day of Christmas break."

"And the low team?"

"We get guard duty. On Christmas Eve. And Christmas."

It honestly didn't matter that much to me—I had nowhere to go anyway, and no permission to go there—but I could tell it bothered Tessa.

"I'm sorry. That must suck for you."

"For me? For all of—" Halfway through the sentence, she realized who she was talking to, and went bright red. "Shit. I'm sorry, Damian. I wasn't thinking."

"Do you guys at least get to leave for time with your families?"

"We get the rest of Christmas break off, like everyone else." Her smile was bleak. "Sad thing is, my parents will be thrilled to celebrate Christmas on December 23rd this year. All I have to do is tell them it's a Cape thing."

"I hated Christmas at the orphanage. Mama Rawlings did what she could to make things nice, and the older kids did too, but..." I shook my head. "Whether it's the 23rd or the 5th or the actual day, you're lucky to spend it with parents who love you."

"Yeah. I guess I am." She had a look in her eye just then—the same one she normally had when a last-minute tactical development meant she was about to send us into hell—but kept her thoughts to herself. Instead, she bounced to her feet. "So are we running or what?"

"I'm up for it. Anything to clear my head."

"Bad dreams again?"

That caught my attention. "What do you mean?"

"Nothing. Just…" She blushed again. "Sometimes, you yell out in your sleep. We're not eavesdropping. I promise."

"We?"

"Penelope and me. Freddy's usually dead to the world."

"And snoring like a buzz saw." I scraped the last vestiges of sleep from my eyes. "He's half the size of Jeremiah. How can his snoring be every bit as loud?"

If she noticed my careful change of subject, she didn't call me on it. It was hard to tell with Tessa these days. She had a way of shocking me with the occasional kindness.

"So… run?" She reminded me. "Shall we?"

"You're still wearing pajamas. And slippers."

She looked down and visibly started, as if surprised to find that it was true. "Right. I'll be right back."

"I'll be waiting."

CHAPTER 44

It was an uncommonly cool day for Los Angeles. Even for November. Not cold, exactly, but the wind blowing in from the ocean was harsh enough to make me glad I had my greys on. Not all of the people in the clearing with me were so fortunate.

Wormhole, in particular, looked miserable, shivering like the temperature was sub-zero instead of somewhere in the low sixties. The fact that she'd worn a skirt and blouse probably didn't help. The stone bench she was sitting on didn't either. Even in the summer, that bench was cool to the touch. I had to assume it was even worse now.

I wasn't sure why the four team leaders (and Paladin) had wanted to meet with me out in my clearing, but here I was, like a good little soldier. Hopefully, answers would be coming soon.

"Should we get started?" asked Kayleigh. She wore a skirt too, albeit one that made it down past her knees, paired with a long-sleeved, off-the-shoulder top that looked like it had come straight out of a romance vid. She'd been shivering too, until Paladin offered her the jacket he'd seemingly carried for just that purpose.

"Please," said Wormhole. "I've got things to do."

"He's not going to say no, Evie. Be cool." That was Silt, the only person other than me to be wearing her greys. Like me, she was sitting in the dirt, ceding bench space to the other team leaders. Unlike me, she didn't seem to mind. "Just bat your pretty eyes and make him beg."

"Sofia!" For whatever reason, Wormhole went white, spots of color appearing in her cheeks.

"The dance is less than three months away," the Earthshaker reminded her former roommate. "And you and Marcus have been hanging out a lot. It's not like he doesn't know it's coming."

Which explained, I guess, why Evelyn was dressed up. I didn't know who Marcus was, but he had to be a normal, if Wormhole was asking *him* to be her date. Once again, the damn Remembrance Day dance was on the minds of every woman in the class. Probably the men too, although at least some of them resisted the urge to talk about it at every possible opportunity.

As second-years, it turned out we were responsible for hosting the festivities. In fact, that was where most of the proceeds from our year of running the Liquid Hero would be going. Even after working a bar for eight months, the logistics of putting on a dance for hundreds of people—Cape students, graduates, and their dates—seemed like a nightmare, but nobody seemed to care about that part. All anyone could talk about was who was going with who and what they would be wearing.

Kayleigh and Matthew going together was a given. The same was true for Orca and Prince, which remained a source of personal disappointment for me... one made worse just then by the sight of the curvy Stalwart in leggings and a thin knit sweater. Silt was planning to go with her newest girlfriend, a normal named Cynthia, but I only gave the relationship fifty-fifty odds of lasting that long.

As for everyone else? Hell if I knew. I'd learned as a first-year what a mistake it was to get involved, and I was doing my very best to stay out of the whole thing.

Which made my summons out to the clearing all the more concerning.

"Please don't tell me that we're out here to talk about the dance," I said. "I have other things to do with my life, you know."

Next to me, Tessa snorted... probably because I'd been lying in bed, staring at the ceiling, when she'd come to get me.

I pretended I hadn't heard her.

"No," said Orca, voice almost as smooth as her movements. "We wanted to start the planning for our final Training Grounds mission."

"Okay?" I frowned. "Then why am I here? Isn't this a team leader thing? You ladies come up with new and inventive ways for us all to die?"

Paladin's cough sounded suspiciously like a poorly-disguised laugh. Maybe his latest firmware update had included a sense of humor. I didn't question why *he* was here... he and Kayleigh were practically attached at the hip. Even more so since he'd met her parents.

Silt drove an elbow into my side. "Be nice, Skeletor, or we'll give you the *really* shitty work."

"How would that be any different from usual?"

"Fair point." She grinned.

"The final mission is worth forty percent of our grade in Group Tactics," announced Vibe. For some reason, she seemed to be avoiding looking in my direction. "And enough points to completely upend the team rankings."

"In other words, we can't screw it up," said Wormhole.

"Great. But that still doesn't answer—"

"We just found out what it's going to involve," murmured Poltergeist, almost apologetically.

"It's a re-enactment of the Battle at the Hole," said Vibe.

"What?"

"We've all seen the vids," added Evelyn, "but you were the only one who was actually there for it. We need your help working on our strategy."

"You mean you want me to talk about the day I nearly died. The day two dozen Capes, almost a hundred soldiers, and my father were all murdered."

There was a moment of embarrassed silence.

"It's... for our grade," said Wormhole, as if that explained everything. Hell, maybe it did, for her.

"Sorry, Boneboy," muttered Silt. "I didn't think this one through at all."

"Whatever." I unclenched my jaw, letting the emptiness inside me sweep away all emotion. "What do you guys want to know?"

"No. Sofia's right," said Tessa. "This is dumb and unfair. We should make Jessica and Nikolai change the sim."

"Because Nikolai is so famous for his flexibility?" I rolled my eyes. "Just ask your questions. It's fine."

ooo

It was not fine.

Not to me, and not to someone else either.

In the twenty months we'd known each other, Alexa had been something of a constant in my life. Dependable and unchanging, controlled and analytical, sympathetic but unflappable.

And then I told her about the Training Grounds mission and got to see her well and truly angry.

The door from her office hit the wall so hard that several of Stephanie Gibbings' framed diplomas fell off their hooks, glass shattering. By the time the door had rebounded and shut, Alexa was already gone, leaving me alone to clean up the mess.

Twenty minutes later, she was back, anger radiating off of her like waves of heat from a Pyromancer. She stepped right through the area of carpet covered in glass, and I heard fragments crunch under her booted heels.

"This is bullshit," she told me, words clipped and hard. "Worse than bullshit. It's unacceptable."

"I take it you talked to Bard?" Oddly, seeing Alexa angry on my behalf caused some of my own anger and hurt to drain away. For the first time in more than a day, I let go of the emptiness. I was still pissed, yeah. It seemed like a shitty thing to do, and I was tired of being the one who was always the recipient of shitty things, but it meant something to have her defend me.

"And Nikolai and Jessica. They acknowledged my *concerns*, but are going to proceed with the simulation anyway. The battle at the Hole was the largest scale battle involving Powers in multiple decades. The faculty felt that merely studying it in class would be a disservice to the other second-years. And Jonathan agrees with them." Alexa shook her head. "At least, you've been excused from participation."

"I have?"

"It was either that or I was going to sue the Academy for gross misconduct toward a student and trauma survivor."

"Oh."

She caught something in my tone. "What is it?"

I swallowed and shifted on the couch. "What if I wanted to participate?"

"I'm sorry?"

"My whole team is going to be there," I said, trying to figure out why I had just suddenly changed my mind. "We're the worst ranked team in the class. This is their only opportunity to improve their shots at getting internships next year. And I think I can help."

"Damian, what happened to you at the Hole was traumatic. I know you believe you can just lock that pain away, but that's not how the human mind works. Revisiting the Hole has a strong chance of triggering a disastrous reaction."

"Better to have that happen in a sim than in reality," I decided. "If I break in the Training Grounds, it just costs me points. If I break in the real world, people will die."

"And yeah… the Hole sucked." Except for the part where I'd killed Carnage. And Firewall. "But so did Mom's murder. So did my foster-family failures. So did what went down in Bakersfield. All of it shit, all of it trauma, but I'm still here. Fuck if I'm going to back down from a challenge. Not now. Not ever."

Alexa's hands were motionless on her desk, black eyes somehow bright as she stared at me from across the room. After a long moment, her head inclined, halfway between a nod and a bow. She sighed, and the anger I'd been sensing finally dissipated entirely. "You know you don't have to make the decision now, right?"

"I don't think there's a decision to make." I coughed, suddenly embarrassed. "Guess I should have thought this all through before today's session. Sorry."

"As your therapist, it's my job to defend you, Damian. Not the other way around. I may owe Jonathan a new teapot, and some minor paint touch-up, but he knows my patients come first. That's why he asked me here, after all."

She ran a hand through her dark hair and sighed again. "Doing this *will* stir up emotions and stresses that you may think you've already dealt with. When that happens, I need you to be honest about it. With yourself and with me."

"Okay." Despite everything we'd gone through, our many, many ups and downs, I found it easy to trust her.

Or maybe it was *because* of what we'd gone through.

"*Their* opportunity?" she asked.

"I'm sorry, what?"

"You said if your team did well in the sim, it would improve their chances for getting internships."

"Yeah." I nodded. "I mean, it's hard to go anywhere but up, right?"

"Very true. But wouldn't a good performance improve your chances as well?" I gave her a flat look, and she shook her head. "You don't think you'll be offered an internship."

"Last year, less than half the class got one. Those positions are reserved for the golden boys and girls. I'll go on the Mission with the others who are left behind." I shrugged. "I'm okay with that. I'm more concerned about whether I'll get offered a position at all after graduation. If I learned one thing from Ricky, it's that Crows are a hard fucking sell."

"Whatever it is you end up doing, whichever team you end up working with, I believe you have the potential to be great," she told me, voice quiet. "Those who only know of you might think you're a monster, but that couldn't be further from the truth."

I really wish she'd been right.

CHAPTER 45

After more than four months of running together, I could finally match Tessa stride for stride. We must have been an odd sight at five in the morning; an attractive woman in skintight running clothes and a matching jacket, paced by a pale-faced, crooked-nosed lunatic in grey sweats.

Frankly, I'm shocked nobody tried calling campus security. Guess it was enough that people knew what my Academy greys meant.

"I think we're the only two people left in class who don't have dates to the Remembrance Day dance," she said, as we curved past the boundary of the woods on the west side of campus.

"Actually, Silt and Cynthia just broke up this past week," I replied absently. Within the woods, I could feel the pull of my zombie cat. I'd tried to think of a way to sneak him into the sub-dorm, but until decomposition ran its course, the little guy stank like one of Fat Joey's infamous farts.

"Then they must have gotten back together. They were making out in the Liquid Hero last night."

"Seriously? Where was I?"

"Toilet duty."

"Oh yeah." It had not been one of my more pleasant shifts. The partying had ramped up as we got closer and closer to December and Christmas vacation. "Wait... how the hell do *you* not have a date?"

"I'm waiting for the guy to ask."

I scoffed. "What an idiot. I know we've had our issues, and I never would have thought this last year, let alone said it, but..."

"But?"

"You're hot, you're smart, and you're strong. Guy should be throwing flowers at you. If he hasn't asked you by next week, let me know. I'm happy to go give him an anonymous ass kicking."

She stumbled, barely avoiding a fall that would have been the stuff of legends. When she caught back up with me, the look she sent my way was impossible for me to decipher.

"I'll do that," she said.

"Cool." I wasn't going to the dance—not unless someone could promise it would have as much drama as last year's—but I knew it meant a lot to most of my classmates. And they all deserved a bit of downtime and fun.

Even Winter, who was importing her date from off campus. Because of course she was. If I heard one more time about how he was twenty-three and already successful, I'd go to the dance just to ash the guy.

"Thanks for helping with the Training Grounds planning," Tessa said, after about a minute of silent running. "I hope it hasn't been too hard."

"Honestly, looking at it as a puzzle to solve kind of helps. Not that I have much of a head for strategy."

"I don't know," she teased. "*Let's just murder them all* technically *is* a strategy."

"Kill Lucien to keep him from making whatever signal he sent to bring in Carnage. Shoot Fallout and the others as they emerge from the Hole." It wasn't easy to shrug as we ran, but I gave it my best shot. "Kill them all and kill them fast. Who needs a strategy after that?"

"You're right," she said, that teasing tone still in her voice. "You really *don't* have a head for strategy. But seriously, your input has been super helpful. For our team. All the teams. So... I was trying to think of a way to thank you for that."

"I think you just did."

A telekinetic hand gave me a smack on the cheek, but it was a light smack.

"I talked to Dean Bard," she continued.

I waited for more but there was nothing but the sound of our shoes on the asphalt path.

"About?"

"About him relaxing the rule regarding you not leaving campus. For Christmas break, at least."

"That's..." My mouth worked for a minute, but nothing emerged. It was only through a minor miracle that I didn't swallow a bug in the meantime. "That's incredibly kind of you, Tessa. But there's not really anywhere for me to go."

"Kayleigh's family is having a party a few days before Christmas. My parents are already having to drive me over. They'd be happy to swing by the Academy to get you too."

A night away from campus? Eating food prepared by the Watai family chef? It sounded kind of like a dream.

Or a trap.

"Or," she continued, words coming so fast I thought she was a Jitterbug, "you could stay at my house for that week and we could just go directly to the party instead of swinging by the Academy."

"What?"

"My parents have an extra room and they've already said you're welcome. Maybe you could have a real Christmas for once, even if it's not actually on Christmas?"

If I'd been speechless before, I now felt like I'd just been hit by one of Orca's hard right crosses. Was I concussed, or was this really happening?

We kept running and Tessa kept talking. "It's just an idea. You don't have to say yes. I just thought you might want to get away from campus, and it seemed like an easy way to make it happen. We wouldn't have to break our running schedule. And it would let me pay you back for all you've done. For our team, I mean."

Another few strides of running in silence, and I heard irritation enter her voice. "So... what do you think?"

I almost said no. Just out of habit. Maybe it was my experience as an orphan, or as a short-lived foster kid, but I didn't like the idea of being a stranger in someone else's house, full of people and history and rules I didn't know or understand.

I almost said no. But it sounded like she was genuinely nervous about the whole thing. And not in a *hope you don't kill my family and raise them as walkers* sort of way either. Nervous that I would decline.

I couldn't figure out why it mattered so much to her. I hadn't done anything special for our team. No more than Winter, really. Muse… well, he was a different story, but he was also a very, very low bar.

I didn't understand why she'd made the offer. I didn't know why her parents had agreed. And I damn sure didn't want to find myself in a situation where anything I said or did might inadvertently fuck things up for everyone.

But to my own surprise, I said yes anyway.

Turns out that even with all the stuff I didn't understand and didn't like about the situation, I was even more worried about the idea of making Tessa unhappy.

What the fuck was that about?

ooo

It took just under a week for the whole thing to blow up in my face. More accurately, it took a single comment from Tessa as I passed her, heading to the bathroom.

"Everything's set for Christmas week," she told me excitedly.

That wasn't the problematic part.

"Kayleigh let me know that dress for the party will be casual-nice. No ties necessary, but a jacket wouldn't be out of place."

That was it.

The problem, of course, for those of you who just wandered into this little storytelling session, is that I didn't own a jacket. Or a tie. Or any fucking clothes at all besides socks, a number of increasingly worn boxers, one Paladin-branded t-shirt that was far too tight given the muscle I'd added, and two weeks' worth of Academy greys.

I'd had a suit, briefly. It had been a hand-me-down from Jeremiah's *little* brother, received in exchange for fight lessons, and it hadn't survived the Battle of the Hole.

Where was I supposed to get new clothes, and how was I supposed to afford them? And for that matter, what the fuck did casual-nice even mean? *Casual* felt like something I could manage. But *nice?*

And then, stuck on the toilet, pants and boxers down around my ankles, I heard the words that really brought things to a head.

"Hey Damian, I'm going to take a look through your closet. Might as well make sure our outfits don't clash."

CHAPTER 46

"So."

It had been just under five minutes since Silt dropped down next to me on the bench where I'd been pretending to meditate. Apparently, she'd gotten tired of waiting for me to say something.

"Yeah?"

"Want to talk about it?"

I finally cracked an eye and looked over and down at her. "How does everyone in our class know whenever something happens? Is there some sort of daily newsletter?"

"Winter told Patty, who told London, who told Erin, who told me, if you must know. But from all accounts, even people in Team Four's sub-dorm could hear you and Tessa fighting, so the news was making the rounds already. Penelope just provided context."

"Fucking wonderful." I shook my head. After an hour out in my clearing, I'd come to one really unhappy conclusion. "I overreacted."

"Do you really not have any other clothes?"

Somehow, Silt asking didn't trigger the same reaction that Tessa finding out had.

"There aren't a lot of clothing donations that are suited for eighteen-year-olds. I had a pair of jeans and a second t-shirt, but we got attacked on the way from Bakersfield to Los Angeles, and that kind of put an end to those."

"But you were wearing a suit when you left for the Hole."

"Jeremiah gave it to me in exchange for teaching him how to fight. It didn't survive the trip. Why do you think I wear greys all the time?"

"Why does the Viking seem allergic to shirts?" Silt shook her head. "Men are weird. I just figured sweats were your thing."

"I have no clothes and I have no money. If room, board, and laundry weren't free for Cape students here at the Academy, I'd be fucked."

"I would be too. Have you seen how much the normals pay for tuition? Even back in Brownsville, we didn't have that much cash just lying around. So? Why did that start the fight to end all fights with Poltergeist?"

"She was in my space. She had no right to invade my privacy. And..."

"And?"

"The look on her face when I came out. I'm sick of that look. I don't need pity. I don't want it either. Once I'm a Cape, I'll have money, even if I'm stationed out on the fringe with the Mission or the Hammers of God. Until then, greys are fine."

"Unless you want to go to a party. Or a dance." She cut me off before I could respond. "Yeah, I know. *Fuck dances!* You know I love you like a brother, right? A deadly, mopey, possibly insane little brother?" She waited for my nod, then continued. "Then please understand that I have only your best interests in mind when I tell you to grow the fuck up."

"Excuse me?"

"You can't do it all on your own. Learn to rely on your friends. And for fuck's sake, learn the difference between sympathy and pity."

"I know what I saw—"

"Even if you're right, so what? It means someone gives a shit! Do you want to be proud and totally alone or do you want to get off your damn pedestal and let people help you?"

"How? By giving me hand-me-downs? I don't want charity. If that makes me an asshole, then I'm an asshole."

"Oh please." Silt's grin came out of nowhere, somehow undercutting the tension in an instant. "The asshole ship sailed a long time ago, and you're its captain. Charity isn't going to change that."

"Funny." I blew out a long breath, trying to send my annoyance with it.

"Anyway, nobody's offering you charity in the first place."

"Really? I guess you didn't hear that Tessa invited me to stay at her family's house for the week before Christmas then."

Sofia's eyes widened, and then drifted shut, like she was trying to block out my face. She shook her head, as if in denial.

"Exactly—" I started to say.

"After last year, I should have realized..." she said, speaking right over my words, "but the problem is you have these occasional moments of insight and even wisdom—"

I wasn't entirely sure where she was going with this, but I was betting nowhere good.

"—and it somehow keeps fooling me into thinking you're not a total idiot."

Totally nailed it.

"Tessa didn't invite you home for Christmas out of a feeling of charity! Anymore than Kayleigh asked you to the dance last year because she just wanted someone to hold her hand! How did you not learn from that whole experience?"

"Learn what?" I frowned. "Wait. Are you saying that Tessa likes me? But she has a guy!"

"She does?"

"Yeah! She's waiting on him to ask her to the—" I let my voice trail off, as a few things suddenly made sense. "Fuck. It's me, isn't it? I'm the guy."

"Eureka! Maybe you *can* lead a horse to water and make him drink. You just have to dunk his whole head in first."

"But how do *you* know any of this?"

"You guys sit together in most classes now."

"We're teammates."

"And run together every damn morning, which is itself some sort of sign of mental illness, mind you."

"We're training partners."

"And she talked her parents into letting you come home with her for the whole Christmas break."

"It'll save them a trip to the Academy to pick me up for Kayleigh's party." I paused. "Okay, that one's a bit of a stretch."

"You think?"

"But why?"

"Why what?"

"Why would she be interested in me?"

"Hell if I know. You've got the wrong equipment for me to be able to answer that one for sure."

Which of course brought to mind a subject I'd worked hard to keep out of my brain. Emma and the revelations from our not-quite-a-one-night-stand.

"She knows I can't... you know."

"Give her the old one-two?"

"That saying's about fighting, not sex."

"From what I hear about men, it might as well be both." Her grin made a comeback and she took a moment to appreciate her latest zinger. "I don't have any insights into what goes on in that girl's head. Doubt we'd be friends at all if it weren't for you. If you want to ask someone, ask her. Just please... ask her to the dance first or the rest of the second-year women might decide to string you up and put us all out of our misery."

I couldn't say exactly why, but the space inside me normally reserved for the emptiness of my power felt lighter just then. Almost bubbly even. Then a new thought occurred to me and my face fell.

"If I'm going to the dance and Kayleigh's party, I really will need something to wear, won't I?" I ran my hand through hair shaggy enough to warrant another haircut. "Maybe it's dumb, or just empty pride like you said, but... I really don't like charity, Sofia."

"Then don't ask for it. What did Bard tell you when you survived your expulsion hearing?"

"That it was the only second chance I was going to get?"

"After that."

"That all his rules were staying in place for second-year."

"Oh for the love of God… at the end, Damian!"

I had to think. "That even though they'd decided not to expel me, they were still going to punish me."

"By?"

"Giving me a job."

"Exactly." Silt's smile right then was beatific, pure enough to qualify her for sainthood on its own merit.

"So?"

"So there's one major difference between volunteer work and an actual job. With a job, there's supposed to be pay."

○○○

When Silt was done with me, we walked over to Bard's office. The dean wasn't there, but his secretary, the ancient and terrifying Agnes, confirmed that yes, I was getting a small salary for my work as a mentor to the first-years, and yes, it had been accruing in the account set up on my behalf, and oh by the way, all of this information had been in the forms sent to my Glass back in March.

She seemed kind of put out that I didn't know. As if anyone actually read through all the forms they had to sign.

It wasn't a lot of money. Eight months of meeting with my first-years added up to $640, or roughly $20 a meeting. But that was $633.61 more than I'd finished the last year with, and a hell of a lot more money than I'd ever expected to see until after graduation. I wasn't complaining.

As for Tessa? She was waiting in our sub-dorm when I got back, flanked on the small couch by both London *and* Olympia. I'm not sure which of the three was most unhappy with me, but Alan Jackson could've shaved with the difference. When I asked the other two women if I could speak to my team leader alone, I got back a sniff from London and a slow shake of the head from Olympia.

Probably should've just waited for a better time, for Tessa to be alone and maybe not quite so pissed off, but I didn't like letting things fester. So instead, I faced down the triumvirate of angry, smoking-hot women.

"I left Bakersfield with less than ten dollars and little more than the clothes on my back. That's not my fault, but it's still pretty fucking humiliating when people find out."

"Were you just planning to wear greys until graduation?" That was London, who apparently felt like she was a part of this conversation.

"Yeah, I guess." I shrugged and turned back to Tessa. "I've been mostly focused on other stuff."

Having been part of the first-semester research project into Sally Cemetery, Tessa knew what I was talking about. The set of her jaw softened.

Slightly.

"Regardless," I said, "I'm sorry for losing my temper and…" I coughed. "…anything I might have said in the process."

This was turning into the school year of apologies. I'd rather have still been fighting at the Hole, to be honest.

When it was clear that was all I had to say, London and Olympia looked from me to Tessa and then back again. After way too many uncomfortable seconds had passed, the Telekinetic finally spoke.

"And I'm sorry for invading your privacy, even if I was just trying to be helpful." She blushed and looked away. "And for what I did to your bedroom after you stormed off."

"Wait. What?"

Instead of waiting for an answer, I ran down the hall to my room.

When I'd left, my room had contained two largely empty dressers, one bed, and a closet.

It still had the bed and the closet—although there was a crack as long as my forearm in one of its doors—but the two wooden dressers had been demolished, leaving a dent in the opposite wall and wooden fragments literally everywhere.

I spun back to the common room to find that Tessa had followed me down the hall. The look on her face was half regret, half stubborn belief that the destruction was all my fault. In the common room behind her, London and Olympia were both on their feet, although the silver-eyed Lightbringer seemed like she wanted to be pretty much anywhere else.

"I may have overreacted," Tessa admitted. "Slightly."

I shook my head, leaned back against the hallway wall, and studied the woman who was my team leader, friend, and maybe something more. Her cheeks were flaming red, her hair was a mass of dark curls around her face, and she still had one hand curled into a fist as if she wanted to punch me.

She'd never looked better.

"Do you want to go to the Remembrance Day dance?" I asked.

"What?"

"With me, I mean."

"Is this some sort of fact-finding mission, or are you asking me out?"

I couldn't tell if she was being dense or I was. "I'm asking if you'll go to the dance with me. I promise I'll wear something other than greys. Once I get something other than greys."

"You're asking me now? In front of everyone, after this morning, and..." she carefully avoided looking at the damage she'd caused, "...everything else?"

"...yes?"

I was starting to think Silt had set me up to look like an idiot. Then a smile broke out on the Telekinetic's face.

"Yes, I'll go to the dance with you, you idiot."

"You two are really weird," said London.

"But kind of sweet too," added Olympia.

Not that anybody had asked either of them.

CHAPTER 47

Of course, it wasn't that easy.

Turned out that asking someone to the dance wasn't the same as asking them to be your girlfriend, so I ended up having to do that too, and only at a time and place of Tessa's choosing, as if anyone was there to take a picture of her in the dress she'd picked for the occasion.

Not that I was complaining about the dress. At all.

And then she'd wanted to establish the boundaries for our new relationship. Which mostly seemed to involve stating what I was allowed to do with her... when I would, at some point, be allowed to do anything. It all seemed like way too much oversight, considering we hadn't so much as kissed yet and were most likely *never* going to be able to have sex.

It had been easier with Alicia. Not that I was going to compare the two or anything. Certainly not where anyone could hear.

Besides, Tessa spent those next two weeks smiling, and somehow, that made up for a lot. There was hand holding and cuddling on the couch too, which was strange but not unwelcome.

Getting me new clothes ended up being the biggest problem. Bard was allowing me off campus for Christmas break, but no sooner, and according to Tessa... and London... and Olympia... and even Silt, in a stunning betrayal... that wouldn't give us anywhere near enough time to make sure we were a matched set or whatever the fuck boyfriends and girlfriends showed up to rich-person parties as.

Which was how I ended up in my boxers in my bedroom, having a man I'd just met measure my inseam, waist, neck, and chest.

Kayleigh's family knew a tailor, and while I certainly couldn't afford his prices, he'd agreed to come get my measurements so that Kayleigh and Tessa could go shopping on my behalf.

Given that I was neither a doll to be dressed nor an automaton to be ordered about, I wasn't wild about the idea, but the two came back with four dress shirts in varying jewel-like colors and a charcoal grey suit that fit better than Jeremiah's hand-me-down ever had. They'd even gotten a belt and a pair of dress shoes that weren't half as uncomfortable as they looked.

No idea how they managed all that, given my budget constraints, but when I checked my account, I still had a bit of credit left over. And putting on that suit was a lot like when I'd tried on my costume for the first time.

I felt like a new man.

For a moment, I could forget about what I was, about the mysteries I still hadn't solved, and the murderers seemingly trapped in my orbit. I was just a guy, wearing nice clothes for the first time in my adult life, enjoying those first few days of a new relationship.

Nicest December I could remember.

Not that that was saying much, but still.

oOo

Los Angeles was a strange city. Better than Bakersfield, obviously, but still strange. I'd seen more of its chaotic sprawl in the past week than I had at any time since arriving at the Academy as a snot-nosed first-year. I'd walked the streets of Tessa's neighborhood, visited her old high school, even taken a bike ride down the remnants of a freeway that had been destroyed during the Break and was now an improbable miles-long stretch of flowers, thanks to the local Druid. Our day trips had given me a better appreciation for the size and scope of the city the Defenders and the Society were responsible for.

But I'd never seen the city quite like this.

Kayleigh's house was three stories tall, inside a gated community that was itself at the top of a winding drive. The building was at least four times the size of the orphanage I'd grown up in, and in place of a front or back yard, it had what everyone referred to as estate grounds… a space large enough to warrant an entire team of landscapers.

Vibe and her family weren't just rich. They were filthy rich.

An enormous balcony ran the length of the back wall, facing west toward the ocean I could sense but not quite see, and the lights of the city spread out below me like a carpet of stars. The Academy was somewhere down there and to the southwest, but I'd given up searching for it, content to feel the cool winter breeze on my face and relax in the stillness that was so different from what was going on inside.

"There you are." Her dress a murmur of silk, Tessa joined me at the balcony rail. "Sofia was right. You really do head for the ocean whenever you can."

"I grew up in Bakersfield. Figured I'd die there too. The ocean was something I only got to see in vids." I nodded out to where it spread, a ribbon of darkness past the city lights. "Not that I can see it tonight anyway."

"The view here is incredible."

I turned to her, and to my own embarrassment, couldn't hold back a sigh of appreciation. "It really is."

In heels, Poltergeist wasn't that much shorter than I was, and the dress she wore was the furthest thing from our Academy greys. Deep burgundy silk clung to the curves of her torso, emphasizing the narrowness of her waist and the still-surprising-to-me quantity of cleavage up above. Unlike the dress she'd worn when I asked her out, this one went all the way to the floor, but the skirts reminded me of the ribbons of her Cape costume; a hundred vertical strips of fabric ranging from that same burgundy to black. The dark curls that normally brushed her shoulders had been pulled back into some sort of complicated up-do that left her long neck bare except for a simple golden chain with a heart shaped pendant. Other than that pendant and two thin shoulder straps that reached down to her neckline in front and crossed once on their way to an even deeper dip in back, there was nothing but spectacular skin on display.

"Have I mentioned how good you look in that dress?"

"Only about a dozen times." Given our nights at the Liquid Hero, I was used to seeing her in makeup, but she'd done something different for the party, and her always-pretty eyes now seemed enormous. "And you've only said it to my boobs half of those times."

"Sorry," I said, feeling my gaze inexorably drawn down as if by telekinesis. "If it helps, I spent most of our walk from the car staring at your butt."

"I know. You don't think I normally swing my hips like that, do you?" Tessa laughed. "I'm glad you like the dress. We don't get a lot of chances to go formal at the Academy, and it's fun to mix things up." She shivered suddenly, and wrapped her arms around herself. "A little colder than I thought it would be though."

Luckily, I'd spent enough time around Paladin and Vibe to know what to do. I took off my suit jacket and draped it over her shoulders, almost like a cape.

Boyfriend-of-the-year material, right there.

"I meant we should probably go inside, but…" She tucked herself against me and I let one arm drift around her. "This is nice too. They're going to do cake and toasts soon, just so you know."

"Okay."

Something in my voice caught her attention. The one thing I had learned in my short time as one half of a couple was that tone meant everything.

Tessa pulled back to look up at me. "Is this all too much? It feels like you're ready to run away."

And my new girlfriend, in particular, was a mind reader.

"It's a lot," I admitted. "A lot of people, a lot of attention, a lot of rules."

"Kayleigh had to stay isolated while she learned to control her powers. I think her parents are just proud to be able to show her off again."

"I get that. And they should be. Proud, I mean. I just keep thinking I should be elsewhere *doing* something, instead of…"

"Having a life?" She'd maintained that small space between us, green eyes intent on my face. "If we weren't here, we'd be at my parents' or at the Academy. What would you be doing in either place other than eating worse food?"

"Your dad's not that bad of a cook," I argued. "And he hasn't threatened me even once, which makes him some kind of saint."

"You've been a good guest." She poked me with an elbow sharp enough to qualify as a weapon in the Free States. "Maybe too good. Besides, he's terrified of you."

"Because I'm a Crow." My voice sounded flat even to me.

"What? No. My dad doesn't judge people like that."

If that was true, he really *was* a saint. As far as I could tell, *everyone* judged people like that. Hell, almost my whole class had done so, and they were all going to be Capes.

"He's terrified that you're going to take his little girl away from him," she explained. "My mom, on the other hand…"

"You heard about that?"

"About what?"

I winced. "Nothing."

Mrs. McShane had been… less of a saint. In fact, she'd sent her daughter out on an errand and then pulled me into her home office and interrogated me for almost half an hour.

What were my intentions toward Tessa?

Where did I plan to serve after the Academy and for how long?

How many children did I want, and why did I think anything fewer than three would be sufficient?

We'd covered every possible damn subject and I still don't think the older woman was satisfied. As much as I hated to admit it, Ricky's lessons on giving interviews might have been the only thing that got me out of that room alive.

"She gave you the talk, didn't she?" I could hear Tessa's scowl in her voice. "Did she ask about children?"

"I guess she interrogates all of your boyfriends?"

"You're the first I brought home since high school, but… yeah, it seems like it. If it makes you feel better, she gave me that same talk while you were helping Dad with the tree trimming."

That had been another instance of something I'd learned at the Academy coming in handy. All those days spent on Amos' apple orchard had made trimming the two trees in the McShane's tiny front yard child's play.

"And what did you tell her?"

The breeze strengthened for just a moment, and she snuggled back into my side, head on my shoulder. "The truth. I don't know where things are going, I don't know what city I'll end up in, and she's not getting grandchildren anytime soon, if I have anything to say about it. As crazy as our life at the Academy is, life as a Cape will be even worse. I'm just focusing on short term happiness right now."

"How's that working out for you?"

"It's still early days, but so far, so good. And having some eye candy on my arm to parade in front of Kayleigh's high society acquaintances doesn't suck either. Although if Sharon touches your arm one more time, I'm going to shotput her into the ocean."

"Which one is Sharon?" The sheer number of people at Kayleigh's party—most of them friends of the family or former classmates from her high school—had quickly overwhelmed my already shaky ability to pair faces with names.

Apparently, that had been the right response. Tessa beamed up at me. "For someone so new to this whole boyfriend thing, you don't always suck at it. A little initiative wouldn't hurt though."

"I'm sorry?"

"It's just you and me. Outside in the dark, with the stars above us and the city below. Are you going to kiss me or what?"

Her lips were soft and cool. There was hunger and passion, but none of the frantic need I'd felt from Emma. Maybe it was because Tessa and I actually knew each other. Maybe it was because we even liked each other. I don't know what the reason was, but it felt natural. Easy, even.

She leaned into me as the kiss deepened, and I let one hand slide under her borrowed jacket. Her ass fit into my hand like they'd been made for each other.

When we finally broke apart, however many minutes later, she was out of breath and I was hard as a rock.

"There we go." Tessa's smile was wide and pleased, and it did amazing things for her eyes. "What the hell took you so long?"

I leaned in for a second kiss, trying in vain to ignore my continued reaction to the feeling of her body pressed against mine. "I guess I didn't want to start something we couldn't finish."

"Under my parents' roof?" Her eyes sparkled. "Yeah, I could see that."

"You know what I mean. We can't have sex."

"I know you have even less experience with this stuff than I do, but..." She laid a feather-light kiss on my lips. "It doesn't always have to be about sex."

Which was exactly the opposite of what my body was saying right then.

"Besides, *you* can't have sex," she continued, smile going wicked. "That leaves a fair bit of stuff on the table, you know. And if it hadn't been for your discovery with Emma, we might not even be together."

"What do you mean?" It *had* been the first and only time Tessa had seen me naked, but—

"I don't want children. Not now, maybe not ever. And that makes dating difficult. Being single sucks, but being pregnant would suck even more. London almost realized that too late."

"So you're dating me *because* I can't have sex?"

"I'm dating you because you're different than I thought. Angry? Sure. Foul-mouthed? Definitely. But also thoughtful and kind and driven and not nearly as dumb as you pretend to be. You make me feel safe. And you have a really nice ass. But it doesn't hurt at all," she added after a moment's thought, "knowing that you're not going to put my career at risk."

"People had sex all the time, pre-Break," I told her. "Birth control was available on shelves in every convenience store." In fact, I was pretty sure that's why they called them convenience stores.

"Those women didn't know how good they had it," she decided, pressing her body against mine again. "Not that I'm entirely complaining."

Someone stuck their head out the open doorway leading to our spot on the balcony. I had no idea what her name was, but she was one of the moms in attendance. "Come on in for cake, kids. We'll be doing champagne toasts too."

"We're not done with this conversation," Tessa told me, giving me one last kiss. "We'll continue it tomorrow when we're back at the Academy. In the meantime, I'm keeping your jacket."

Considering how much warmer it was inside, with the heater on and at least a hundred strangers milling about, I was fine with that arrangement. I waved to the doorway. "After you."

"I don't think so." She grinned. "It's my turn for a show. And Damian?"

"Yeah?"

Tessa's hands were in sight, which meant the swat on my ass had been nothing but telekinetic force. She smirked. "Let's see you put some swing in those hips."

CHAPTER 48

"So you and Poltergeist, huh?" Freddy wrapped his coat more tightly around himself as we paced back and forth on our section of Academy wall. "When did that happen?"

"Almost a month ago, I think."

"Really? How did I miss that?"

"It's been a bit of a slow build." He'd spent most of it in his room, but I didn't see any need to point that out. Especially when he'd walked in on Tessa and me making out on the couch only a few hours earlier. "How was your week off?"

"Not bad." We passed through one of the four small towers that marked the corners of the Academy walls and nodded to the armed guards within. They looked as happy to be up there on Christmas Eve as we were, but at least they had a space heater and plastic cups of something suspiciously alcoholic. Once we were back outside, Muse continued. "It was good to see my parents. See my brother. Kind of helps put things in perspective, you know?"

My parents were walking the wall with us—well, Mom was kind of floating off to the side, and Dad was mostly turning in circles—but I nodded anyway. This was the best Freddy had looked since our disastrous October sim, and I wasn't going to fuck that up if I could help it.

Especially with the Battle at the Hole sim barely a month away.

"I would never have picked you two as a couple," decided Muse. "I mean… *Poltergeist?*"

"You have a problem with Tessa?" I wrinkled my nose as we paced the wall. There wasn't much of a breeze, but I'd somehow gotten a strong whiff of brine and sulfur from the distant ocean.

"No. I think she's a pretty good team leader, all things considered. Which I never would have guessed when we were first-years. But you're already taking orders from her out in the field. Who wants to—?"

Whatever Freddy had been going to ask was lost as a dark shadow pulled itself up onto the wall and then hurtled in our direction.

I reacted before I even knew what was going on, lashing out with my staff and catching the attacker right in his face.

Or... *its* face. Its skin shimmered in the dim light, almost like it had a film of oil on its skin. And... were those scales?

It was already climbing back to its feet—which were webbed, a part of my brain couldn't help but note—looking none the worse for my strike. And behind it, more clawed hands were appearing on the wall's rim.

I charged the first creature as it was still finding its feet, and sent it careening off the wall to the pavement below. Before I could raise an alarm, the sound of gunshots filled the night, and I saw muzzle flashes from the two nearest towers. None of the Academy's guards were shooting in our direction. Which meant they were dealing with their own invaders.

"Freddy...!" As I tried to stem the tide of climbing monsters, I risked a glance over my shoulder. My teammate was white-faced and shaking, pressed back against the battlements of the wall behind him. "Muse!"

That was enough to break his spell. His wide eyes darted in my direction.

"Give me a boost." Knowing he'd have to touch me to amplify my power, I focused on keeping the emptiness at bay, but that meant I was grappling with my own fear. There were already three other creatures on the wall. Many more and they'd just bury us under their numbers.

Thankfully, before that could happen, I felt Freddy's sweaty hand touch the back of mine. "Done," he whispered.

"Thanks. Let's work our way to one of the towers. You shoot the ones on the left, I'll take the ones on the right. Deal?" I was already moving when I realized he hadn't responded. "Freddy? Muse?"

I glanced over my shoulder and saw the little Switch sprinting in the opposite direction. He'd left his gun behind.

Fuck.

I turned to follow him, but the path he'd charted was already filling up with scaled creatures.

If there'd been a free path, I might have taken it, honestly. Hell, I even thought of trying to jump the wall. As long as I didn't break both my legs, I might get away, and the Healers would fix me up afterward.

Problem was, my team wasn't the only group of students on campus. There were at least a hundred others, mostly those attending on scholarship, who hadn't had anywhere to go or the funds to get there. And they were all normals. Hell, half of them were probably studying to be accountants. These things would tear them apart.

A claw coming out of my periphery reminded me that they'd tear *me* apart just as easily if I didn't start paying attention. I let the emptiness fill me and bent backwards, avoiding the attack, then caught a webbed foot and used it as a lever to upend the attacking fish-thing, sending it back over the wall. I dropped my staff, swept up Freddy's abandoned assault rifle, and let loose on the creatures in front of me.

Whatever these things were, they weren't immune to bullets. I mowed down four of them before the magazine went empty. It was enough to clear a path to the tower in front of me. I spun, swinging the spent rifle like a club, and caught the closest creature behind me just before it could attack. And that gave me the time and space to reclaim my staff and start rushing to the tower full of armed guards.

I was halfway there when the guns went silent. The shapes spilling out of the tower toward me were not human... had clearly never been human.

Lightning split the night, striking the Academy's west wall. Winter, at least, was still in the fight. And if she was, I had to believe Poltergeist was too.

All we had to do was hold out long enough for one of the city's real Cape teams to arrive. All I had to do was hold this wall all by my-fucking-self.

Scaled fish things ahead of me. Scaled fish things behind.

I really should have fucking jumped.

Instead, I spun the staff in my hands and went to work.

INTERLUDE

Jonathan Bard, Dean of the Academy of Heroes, was not having a very merry Christmas Eve. He'd been in his wife's long-term care room, reading *A Christmas Carol* to her comatose form, when the bulletin came in that the Academy was under assault. It had taken less than five minutes to get to the basement, to the hospital's security room and its hard line connection to the Net, but things were already in chaos by the time he logged in.

Only one of the Academy's four guard towers remained active, and both they and the gate guards were finding themselves hard pressed by what was being frantically described as 'an army of some sort of fish things with claws'. Only the west and east walls were holding steady, and the west was starting to show signs of slipping.

"Evacuate the dorms into Nikolai's bunker," he ordered over the comm unit to the retired police captain that ran the Academy's own security team. "I've sent the dorm numbers for those still on campus. ETA on the Defenders' arrival?"

"Half of them are up north for Velvet's memorial," came the answer. "The rest will be here in five. And Macy Johnson said she was on her way."

"How long ago?"

"Three minutes."

"Shit." Macy could run an entire marathon in three minutes. If she hadn't made it to the Academy yet, something had gone wrong.

"How many troops do you have with you in the security center, Captain?"

"None, sir. I just sent my squad out to handle the evacuations."

Which meant there weren't any reinforcements immediately available. Bard bit back another expletive, eyes darting from screen to screen as information was relayed to his console. "Pull some of the troops from the east wall. Use them to reinforce the other positions."

"Sir…"

"There's no point in holding the east wall if the rest of the perimeter collapses!"

"Sir, there's nobody *to* pull."

"What are you talking about? How many people do we have on that wall?"

"Just one. And it's not one of mine either. It's one of your Cape students."

Bard went still. "Who?"

"Walker."

CHAPTER 49

I was bleeding in at least three places. My knee was swollen from one of the many times I'd used my power to wrench my body aside in a way biology had never intended. Even in the dim lighting, it looked grotesque, but the pain at least was distant. My leg refused to collapse under me because I refused to let it collapse, because I had flooded it with so much emptiness that it felt like a balloon, fit to burst. My left check and eye were swollen from one of the blows that *hadn't* cut me, and the swelling was already starting to interfere with my peripheral vision.

In short, I was fighting for my goddamn life.

I felt something twinge in my hip as I let a clawed thrust slip past me, pivoted, and drove that same claw a few inches further into the belly of the creature who'd been coming from the other side. It went down in a shower of blood, taking the first creature with it, and giving me a half-second to catch my breath.

There were enough monsters on the wall to bury me outright, but the first who had tried to bring me to the ground had ended up dust in the wind, and the others seemed reluctant to repeat the attempt. Damn good thing too… even with Muse's boost, I wasn't sure how many more death touches I had in me. Better to use the threat as a deterrent.

Problem was, the creatures were starting to wear me down. Mentally and physically both. Two of my three bloody wounds had been suffered in the last minute, and while my power was still keeping me upright, I knew I was slowing.

I jabbed the end of my staff into the throat of another creature, pulled back, and spun, letting the other end crack it in the skull. One more fish man down, but it tore the staff from my hand as it went.

Where the fuck were the Defenders?

When faced with superior numbers, no defensible position, and no path for retreat, Nikolai had taught us to always attack. To be honest, I'd never needed that instruction. Years of being outsized and outnumbered at the orphanage had turned me into an aggressive little fucker.

Even so, I thought he'd be proud if he ever saw the vid footage of me charging the nearest mass of monsters.

Right up until the point where I slipped in the slime sewage the creatures used for blood, and went skidding right into the tree-trunk-sized legs of my intended target.

I was six feet tall and more muscle than bone after all the food the Academy had been feeding me, but the thing I smashed into had to weigh at least as much as the Viking. It staggered back a half-step, but I took by far the worst of the impact, bouncing off and banging my head on the hard stone of one of the battlements. For a moment, I was stunned even beyond my power's ability to keep me moving.

And that should have been it. Defenseless, injured, and barely able to even see my attacker, I was easy meat. But as the creature took its first step toward me, something streaked in from the other direction, tufts of black fur barely clinging to bone, and a smell that somehow still managed to overwhelm the stench of fish and ocean surrounding me.

Zombie-fucking-cat to the rescue.

It leapt, hitting the fish man just above the waist line, and small claws tore a line through scales as my not-so-furry minion climbed the thing like a tree.

My cat was digging a hole in the fish man's throat when a clawed hand as large as the entire cat plucked it away. A second fish-man smashed the remains of my very first walker into dust.

By then, I was back on my feet.

"Bad fucking move," I croaked, raising my fists. But before I could charge the cat-killing motherfucker, my gaze fell on the other fish man, who'd just now breathed its last.

I felt a smile spread across my face, bright and bloody.

And then I took some of the emptiness still tossing and turning inside me and pushed it down into the freshly made corpse.

○○○

Any doubts I'd ever had about Muse's power were long gone. In fact, I almost didn't even resent the bastard for leaving me to die on the wall. I'd killed *four* of the monsters now with just a touch, and the only thing keeping me from killing more was the need to have a body left over to raise afterward.

I regretted the destruction of my zombie cat—you always remember your first—but fuck if the fish-man walkers weren't spectacular upgrades. I'd only managed to raise them singly so far, but each time one went down, I was ready with another. And between my undead not-quite-a-horde and I, damned if we weren't somehow holding the wall.

Pretty sure I was laughing, but the emptiness muffled that just as much as it did everything else.

Whatever these creatures were, their numbers weren't infinite, and they were aggressive, not suicidal. The flood I'd been working to stem had slowed to a trickle of fang-faced fish-things that seemed decidedly reluctant to advance.

Which was when I heard a chuckle and a whisper from behind me, where nothing had been three seconds before.

"And so we meet again."

I recognized that whisper and was already in motion, spinning about, sending my walker charging forward, when darkness thicker than night fell over me.

"What an unexpected present," hissed the Black Hat known as Fallout, "wrapped up for me and waiting."

And then something sharp pierced my arm, and the emptiness shattered into a thousand pieces, taking my consciousness with it.

ooo

I don't know how many of you have fought for your lives against an army of fish creatures, then been drugged, moved while unconscious, and drugged a second time, but even if that *is* an experience we somehow, impossibly, have in common, I'm pretty sure you woke up to something better than what was waiting for me.

Either that or you didn't wake up at all.

Before I'd even opened my eyes, I could feel the thrum of the dampeners, every bit as overpowering as what I'd experienced down in the Hole. It was both a sound and a feeling, a warning in non-verbal form.

I reached for the emptiness anyway, because fuck it, am I right? Nothing.

Worse, as I regained consciousness, all of the stuff that emptiness so regularly blocked out was right there, screaming for attention. The physical stuff, the ache of partially healed wounds, the soreness of muscles that hadn't been used during my lengthy unconsciousness, and the torn skin at my wrists and ankles, rubbed raw by the manacles I could feel pinning me to the floor.

Then there was the mental and emotional stuff. Fear for myself and for Tessa and the rest of my team. Confusion about where I was, why I was alive, and how I'd been taken. And beneath all of that? Anger. I hadn't been able to finish the job on Fallout out by the Hole and now that long-haired, whispering motherfucker had come back for revenge.

But when I finally cracked open my eyes, the Shadecaster was nowhere to be found. Instead, a man stood over me. Average in height, build, and appearance. Easily forgotten, except for two eyes that shined like copper pennies, like cold metal gateways to the white noise and hunger I knew lurked beneath.

"Hello, Mr. Banach," said Tyrant, his voice as colorless as the man himself. "We meet again, and sooner than anticipated."

Behind him lurked another familiar figure with wide, staring eyes and bare feet striped with scar tissue and dirt. The smile on his face was greasy but overjoyed, and he was dressed all in black, just like when he'd murdered everyone I knew in Bakersfield. Jimmy Taylor. Crow. Walking dead man.

"I know you," I hissed, tugging on my chains. "I'm going to tear your heart out and make you eat it."

"I suspect it would taste like chicken." Tyrant's voice was mild as he reached down to place a basket of white plastic and copper wire onto my head, easily avoiding my attempted bite. "But we will have such conversations at a future date. For now, I have tasks to complete and you are low on my list of priorities."

"Then why are you here?"

"Because, Mr. Banach," he said absently, jabbing a needle into my right arm, an arm that already showed bruises from prior injections, "it is never too soon to begin gathering data."

"Toodleloo little bird little bird," said Jimmy.

And then I was falling back into darkness.

CHAPTER 50

I spent at least a few days floating in and out of consciousness. Always greeted with the blurry sight of a rough stone ceiling above me, always drifting back into darkness before I could do much else.

Finally, something changed. I woke and knew who I was, if not precisely where. The attack on the Academy, my capture by Fallout, and now… this. My imprisonment, leaving me at the mercy of the man who'd sent me to the Academy in the first place.

Tyrant and his pet Crow.

Why they or Fallout hadn't killed me was one more mystery to add to the pile, but escape was more important than answers just then. My wrists and ankles were still pinned to the ground—cold stone, just like the ceiling, by the feel of it—but there was nothing to keep me from moving my head. So I did, first just turning it side to side, and then, once I'd verified there were no traps waiting to decapitate me if I moved, lifting my head off the ground enough to look past my feet to where something told me the door was located. The helmet Tyrant had placed on my head weighed at least five pounds, making the whole process that much more difficult.

Thank god for all the crunches Nikolai had made us do.

The cell I was in was roughly eight by ten, crudely hacked out of stone as if some beast had simply dug it out with a massive claw. The door, on the other hand, was wood, wrapped in horizontal metal bands, and featuring a small barred opening at head height. Light poured through that opening from whatever hall or room was on the other side of the door. It was the only reason I was able to see anything at all.

Nothing about my cell was reassuring, so I turned my attention to my bonds. At some point, I'd been stripped out of my costume, left only in my underwear. Thick steel manacles wrapped my wrists, and equally thick links of chain connected those manacles to loops that had been driven into the stone floor.

While I was out, a hypodermic needle had been inserted into my left arm and taped to the skin. A clear plastic tube ran from that needle to a bag of some sort of liquid, hanging from a hook in the near wall, and a slow but steady drip resonated through my veins. I'd spent enough time in the med ward to recognize an IV drip when I saw one. Since I couldn't remember eating or drinking since my capture, I assumed it was feeding me nutrients.

Which again raised the question of why this trio of Black Hats was keeping me alive.

My right arm was now free of needles, and the yellowing of the bruises from prior injections told me it had been at least a few days since the visit by Tyrant and Jimmy. I gave that arm an experimental tug, watching to see if there was any give in the chains or floor loops.

Nothing.

My feet were just as tightly bound. That didn't leave me a lot of options. If I could break enough bones in one hand, I might be able to slip it out of its manacle, but that would still leave me with three limbs chained down. Reducing all of my extremities to boneless slop would get me out of the chains, but I'd be left crawling for freedom.

Assuming I could even break anything at all. I didn't have any leverage, and those dampeners were still in effect. Without my power, I didn't know if I'd be able to stay conscious through the pain of multiple breaks, let alone puppet my body through a no-doubt locked door and past whatever guards might be waiting in the supervillain's lair.

Which meant I was fucked.

I let my head slide back to the floor. All I could do was wait. Bide my time, look for an opening, and seize it when it came. The slow but steady dripping continued to send pulses up my left arm. I closed my eyes and tried to focus on better things.

ooo

I heard them coming long before they arrived. A loud clanging, followed by the squeal of something heavy turning on massive hinges. Beneath that were other sounds. Footsteps, wheels on stone, and the slight rattle of metal against metal.

The noises came toward me, and then stopped, still far short of my cell. There was a murmur of words I couldn't hear, and then both footsteps and wheels started up again.

Relying on my ears for information was aggravating as all hell, but I was pretty sure whoever was coming had been charting a line directly toward me. Did that make the area outside my cell a hall? If so, that stop and conversation suggested there might be other cells along this same hall.

And that meant I wasn't alone. The enemy of my enemy might not be my friend, but they were a potential ally. All I had to do was get us out of our cells.

Somehow.

The footsteps stopped at my door, and the light was briefly blocked as someone peered through the barred opening. Moments later, I could hear the sound of a key being inserted and the door swung wide open.

If the light before had been bright, this was damn near blinding. I blinked dry eyes and did my best to turn away as two figures entered the cell.

Tyrant looked the same as ever. No hairs out of place. No expression on his face. A grey suit more befitting an out-of-work lawyer than a Black Hat.

Jimmy Taylor, on the other hand, was recognizable only by his bare and badly scarred feet. He was all in black, but had a new addition to his wardrobe: a full mask with a skull in white across the face. From behind that mask, mad eyes laughed at me.

Fucker was wearing part of my costume.

Tyrant gave a nod and his pet Crow pushed a cart into the room. Little more than a steel tray on a metal frame with wheels, it looked like a miniaturized version of the gurneys in the Academy med ward. I couldn't lift my head high enough to see what was on that tray, but it sounded like it was carrying a number of implements, all of them also metal.

My blood went cold in my veins. It didn't take a fucking genius to guess what might be on that tray.

"So you kept me alive just so you could torture me?" My voice came out as a croak.

"It is not yet time for torture, Mr. Banach." Tyrant pulled a small box with dangling wires from the tray and nodded again to Jimmy Taylor.

The Crow planted a bare, unwashed, and thoroughly disgusting foot on my chest, toes digging into the hollow of my throat. Tyrant reached down and attached the wires in his hands to the helmet on my head.

"With the drugs having cleared your system, we should be able to get a good baseline, stresses of your current predicament notwithstanding," he murmured.

None of which meant a damn thing to me, even after he showed me the small screen on one side of the wired box. All I knew for sure was that it looked like some sort of Technomancer's creation, and that was bad news.

"Not as sleek as the devices you have used at the Academy, I know," he said. "Nor as singular as the weapon you used when disrupting my carefully planned prison break, but I think it will do."

"So you *were* behind the events at the Hole." My voice was a little bit stronger this time. With the dampeners active and my body chained down, words were the only weapons I had. "What a fuck-up that was. I thought you were supposed to be some sort of mastermind?"

If I'd hit a nerve, Tyrant didn't show it. "The world exists in a perpetual state of chaos, Mr. Banach. You can plan for every conceivable eventuality, only for a schoolboy with a stolen weapon to bring it all crashing down."

"I didn't need any weapons to kill Carnage."

"No, you did not. The way powers manifest in their hosts remains one of life's singular mysteries. I still have hopes that, with sufficient focus, your abilities will follow a more traditional path."

"What are you talking about?"

"As I told you when we first met, I don't need another soldier. What I'm looking for is an army." He turned to Jimmy Taylor, and in doing so, missed the look of surprise that must have flashed across my face. "Mr. Taylor, please bring in the chair. After that, you are free to depart."

The chair in question was a folding thing, all metal like the cart. Tyrant sat down, waited for the loud squeal I'd already heard once, followed by an equally loud boom, and then turned back to me.

"I will send someone down to oil the hinges," he promised, confirming my suspicion that what I'd been hearing was an enormous door, somewhere on the other end of the hall outside my cell.

I added that to the list of obstacles to overcome on my escape, but most of my mind was grappling with the realization I'd had only moments earlier.

Tyrant didn't know I could raise walkers. Either Fallout somehow hadn't seen that one of the dead fish things was fighting on my behalf—which seemed unlikely, given I'd commanded my last walker to kill him—or he hadn't told the other Black Hat.

What the fuck was going on?

"And now that it is just the two of us, I think we should have a talk."

"I have nothing to say to you."

"Nothing of value, at least." He nodded. "I agree. Despite the best efforts of higher education, you appear to remain the same foul-mouthed teenager I met almost two years ago. Thankfully, I will do the talking."

"There's not a damn thing you could say that I want to hear."

"No? Not even the fate of your classmates, your country, and indeed the known world?" The smile that spread across his face was as bland as the face itself. "I suspected that might get your attention."

"You think your threats scare me? I don't even like my classmates," I lied. "Fuck all of them. And fuck you."

Those copper coin eyes slipped aside for a bit, exposing the white noise and fury barely contained by Tyrant's drab form, but the man's mask was back in place in an instant.

"I don't need to make threats, Mr. Banach. The world already faces a danger greater than I could muster." That smile again, flavorless and quick. "Tell me, what do you know about the creature named Tezcatlipoca?"

CHAPTER 51

I shrugged. "He thinks he's some sort of pre-Break civilization's god. He claims land south of the Free States and every person crossing into his domain becomes his puppet. Permanently." I trailed off. "If you want to know more, watch a vid. I'm not here to educate you."

"If you think I need education, you are sorely mistaken." His voice remained mild. "And your choice of pronouns is ill-suited. I have met the creature, and do not believe it was ever a man. Or human."

"If you'd actually met Tezcatlipoca, you'd be a puppet too."

"Oh? Then how were the Capes able to battle him while you were serving as the fly in my prison break ointment?" The man I'd first known as Mr. Grey waved a hand dismissively. "Its greatest ability—to devour the minds of its opponents—does not extend beyond the boundaries of its domain. When it crosses those borders, it is as formidable as any Full-Five, but nothing more."

"And you talked to it."

"Know your enemies and make use of them when you can." He shrugged. "I needed a distraction to pull Capes from the Hole. Forcing a small border town's population into Mexico as sacrifices to the so-called deity was a small enough price to pay."

I shook my head, sending wires bouncing. "You murdered an entire town, and yet you want me to believe *Tezcatlipoca* is the real threat?"

"Seventy-eight lives in total, Mr. Banach. When compared to the world's daily death toll, it is a rounding error at best, and nothing at all compared to what will happen when Tezcatlipoca's domain expands to include the Free States." He paused at whatever he saw in my face, and that same humorless smile flickered across his face. "And now, at last, I have your attention."

"Tezcatlipoca's domain is fixed. Everybody knows that."

"So the government would have you believe." He took a Glass from the cart, switched it on with a flick, and turned the screen in my direction. "I assume you are familiar with the map of our country? To the west is the Pacific Ocean. To the east, the Badlands. To the north, the Weaver mostly keeps to herself, and here, in the south…"

"San Diego, and then what used to be Mexico."

"A country which is now Tezcatlipoca's kingdom, helpfully color-coded in red. Precisely." He swiped to the left, bringing up a new image. "And here is a look at just the area south of San Diego."

"That's not right," I said. "I've never heard of some of these places. San Ysidro? Otay Mesa? What is this?"

"A map of the Free States' border twenty years ago. And this," he added, swiping to yet another brightly colored map, "is thirty years before that."

The red that identified the fire god's territory was even smaller, exposing some town called Tijuana.

"You're saying Tezcatlipoca's domain is spreading?"

"Like an infection, yes. In starts and spurts, sometimes separated by months and sometimes by years. First, Tezcatlipoca pushed east, all the way to the Gulf of Mexico. In the last few years, the expansion has been northward instead. At the current rate, San Diego will be gone in little more than a decade."

"Bullshit. If this were true, the government would know."

"The government *does* know. And has been moving people out of San Diego as it can. Or do you think it was sheer misfortune that the city did not have its own professional Cape team assigned? If it had not been for Aspen's appearance, Major Disaster would have leveled the entire region, providing the government with a buffer zone and an additional decade to continue ignoring the inevitable."

"Major Disaster wasn't working for the government."

"Of course not. But much like their sainted brethren, most super-powered villains are lazy and easily led. He saw an easy target and capitalized."

I wasn't buying any of this garbage, especially given the source. Anyone could put together some maps and color them as they pleased. It didn't mean a second apocalypse was on its way.

But I *had* always wondered why Los Angeles had two Cape teams and San Diego none. The southern city had been forced to rely on a trio of amateurs and Major Disaster had made short work of them.

"How do you know any of this? Even if you really are a Finder, this isn't the sort of information someone could just find lying around."

"In a different life, before I became who I am, I was a scientist," he said smoothly. "A junior member on the research team that produced these maps. Admittedly, some of what I'm showing you is conjecture. There is no indication, visual, energetic, or otherwise, of the border between Tezcatlipoca's domain and ours. It can only be identified through test subjects and experimentation."

"You mean by sending people south—"

"And noting the point at which they become puppets, yes." He tapped the massive area of land southeast of San Diego, across the border. "That Tezcatlipoca was expanding east for the first few decades post-Break is merely a hypothesis. The era preceded the starting point of our research, and we would have had no means of reaching the areas in question, regardless."

"If any of this were true, the government would have done something."

"Politicians. Bureaucrats. Pencil pushers." For the first time in the entire conversation, emotion leaked into Tyrant's voice. Contempt. "They are weak. They look for solutions but are blinded by their own short-sightedness."

"Dominion then. He fought off Tezcatlipoca in New Mexico."

"Yes. The two are evenly matched outside of the fire god's domain. It would be a different story within Tezcatlipoca's borders.

For all our supposed savior's gifts, he is as susceptible as any other to the deity's control."

I rolled my eyes. Now I knew he was just talking bullshit.

"You may doubt me, Mr. Banach, but the man himself does not. Why else would he have allowed the infection to our south to spread and fester? There have been Capes who sought to end Tezcatlipoca's threat. One and all, they were lost when they crossed the border. Dominion knows that, just as I do. He knows this is all a matter of time. The Free States' future is now measured in mere decades. Not that the Cape himself will be here to witness that end."

"Dominion will swat you like a bug. You, Fallout, and your pet Crow." I'd watched the Full-Five clear the battlefield outside the Hole in minutes. The gulf between his power and even a High-Four was almost immeasurable.

"Thankfully, I need but sit back and wait for nature to take its course with that one," mused Tyrant, rising to his feet after checking the screen on his Technomancer-crafted device. "But we will talk about that on my next visit. I believe this session has gone on long enough."

Without Jimmy there to pin me down, he was far more careful when detaching the wires, but honestly, I was too muddled to try to bite him anyway. And when he left, taking the cart and chair with him, I almost welcomed the return to darkness.

Tezcatlipoca.

Dominion.

The Free States' own government.

I didn't know what to believe. All I knew for sure was that in Tyrant's twisted mind, I was somehow a part of the whole story. The Black Hat needed me for some reason, and that meant he would be coming back.

He could talk about whatever the fuck he wanted.

I'd be waiting for him to slip up.

ooo

Without a watch or any view of the outside world, time in my cell passed weirdly, but I was pretty sure it had only been a day when I heard the massive outer door swing open yet again.

This time, Tyrant was accompanied by a middle-aged woman in a white lab coat with a hard face and tired eyes. She replaced the nearly empty bag of fluid on the wall, hooked it back up, and departed again without a word.

Pre-Break doctors had been notorious for sleeping with their staff and killing their wives, but I wasn't sure post-Break doctors were all that much better. So much for the holographic oath.

It's a thing. Look it up.

When she was gone, Tyrant wheeled in the cart again. Given that I hadn't heard its wheels until just then, he must have parked it outside my cell. I wasn't sure how that helped me, since that still put it four chains and a locked door away, but it was one more piece of the puzzle I'd have to solve to escape.

The Black Hat connected the wires of his box to the unseen nodes on my helmet, turned some dials, checked the screen, and nodded. There was no emotion on his face—I wasn't sure he even felt emotion the way the rest of us did—but something in his body language suggested he was pleased.

"So then," he finally said, voice as empty as it was relaxed. "We were speaking of Dominion."

"And how he's going to kick your ass? And Tezcatlipoca's? Yeah."

"This is the real world, Mr. Banach. It has no patience for your wild fantasies. What do you know of our country's famed protector?"

The answer to that was *not much*. I'd only met the Cape twice. Once out at the Hole, and once when he served on my expulsion board. Both times, his appearance had shocked me. The most powerful Power in the country, maybe the world, was shorter than I was, with a bit of a paunch, and a worn face full of wrinkles.

Even so, he'd exuded power. More importantly, he'd exuded gravitas. A kind of tired nobility befitting a man who'd won the superpowers lottery and used his gifts to save a nation.

Fuck if I was going to tell Tyrant any of that though. For all I knew, the bastard was hoping I'd let something slip… some sort of weakness that he could take advantage of.

Truth is, Dominion didn't have any weaknesses.

Unless what Tyrant had said about Tezcatlipoca was true.

I kept silent, but the man I'd known as Mr. Grey seemed content to sit there all day, glancing occasionally at the display of his device, and waiting for me to speak.

"He's one of a handful of Full-Fives in the world," I finally said. "That we know of, anyway. He's a Flyboy, Titan, Stalwart, and Lightbringer."

"That is the Cape. I was speaking of the man."

Which didn't make a bit of sense to me.

"The man you know as Dominion was born Dominic Bryant, son of Charles and Candice, in the year 1961. Pre-Break," he clarified.

Given that the post-Break calendar had yet to reach triple digits, I thought that much was obvious, but nobody had asked me.

"How do you know that? Records back then were all paper. Almost none of them survived the Break."

"Some state and federal institutions were already starting to digitize their records. Tax boards. A handful of hospitals. And state prisons." His copper-penny eyes met mine from across the cell. "Mr. Bryant was an inmate, you see, at Nevada State Prison, where he was serving twenty to life for his part in an armed robbery that cost four people their lives."

"So you found someone with the same first syllable as Dominion. So what?"

"So this is a picture of the inmate in question." He pulled his Glass off the cart and showed me the screen.

The photo was grainy as hell, and the man in it looked twenty, not fifty, but otherwise, the resemblance was uncanny.

"Maybe it is him." I admitted. "But who cares what or who he was before the Break? He's literally saved hundreds of thousands of lives since."

"I agree," said Tyrant, surprising the hell out of me. "When I stumbled on this information, I saw it as no more than a footnote in the man's history. Certainly nothing worth making a fuss over. But the prison database had more than just intake forms and head shots. It also had medical records."

I couldn't make out a damn thing from the form and subsequent images he showed me and said as much.

"At the time of the Break, Dominic Bryant had been diagnosed with stage 4 pancreatic cancer. He had at most months to live."

"Then I guess he got even luckier than we knew. Is this going anywhere or are you trying to fucking bore me to death?"

"Keep a civil tongue, Mr. Banach, or I will cut it out." Those eyes flashed again. "Speech is a luxury I have chosen to allow you. Like all such luxuries, it can be taken away."

I reminded myself that I was chained to the floor, powerless, and entirely at this asshole's mercy. I had to be patient.

"As for my point, it is simple. Every Cape in the country undergoes routine medical checkups as part of the government's oversight program. In continuing my research, I acquired Dominion's. This," he continued, swiping to yet another image, "is his scan from the year 30, post-Break. And this is ten years after that."

I wasn't a doctor. I had no idea what I was looking at, other than two pictures of abstract white shapes and shadows. But even without a medical degree, I could see one substantial difference between them. "What is that?" I asked, nodding to the dark space that was almost twice as large in the second picture.

"That would be a cancerous mass. One of several. Continuing to grow and spread." He set his Glass on the cart and leaned back in his chair, copper eyes glittering. "Dominion's powers extended his life far beyond the span of a normal human, and dramatically slowed the explosive expansion of his disease, but all things must come to an end. Judging by the continued progression, the man has five years left. Maybe less."

I had an expletive-filled denial on the tip of my tongue, but something stopped me. And it wasn't fear for that tongue either. It was something Dominion had said, out there on the bloody fields surrounding the Hole.

And what happens to this country when I'm gone?

I'd thought at the time they were just the words of a man heartbroken over the death of a woman he'd loved like a daughter, but now… I wasn't so sure.

In the Free States, Capes lived and died trying to keep the peace, but Dominion had always been our country's backbone. The man who had helped found the nation and who had spent the last eight decades defending it. The reason none of the warlords in the eastern half of the continent dared invade.

What would happen to the Free States if he died?

"The day I found these charts was the day I was reborn. A twenty-five-year-old scientist faced with unavoidable truths. Dominion was dying. Tezcatlipoca was growing in power. Something had to be done, and it was clear that only I had the will to do it."

"Is this the part where you tell me about your doomsday laser, and how you're going to set the country on fire as soon as Dominion's dead and unable to stop you?"

"You misunderstand me, Mr. Banach. I am not here to destroy the country, but to save it. Even if I must do so through violence and blood."

The smart move would have been to stay quiet. To humor him and see where it led.

Unfortunately, I'd never been great at making the smart move.

"Call it what you want. Truth is, you're still just a terrorist and a criminal. And if you thought this little speech would convince me to join you, you're a fucking idiot too."

"Convince you to join me?" For the first time I could remember, that smile contained something recognizable as humor, even if none of it reached his eyes. "You are a boy, little more than a short-lived shell with limited ambition and nonexistent social mores. I don't need *you* at all, Mr. Banach."

I frowned, but before I could point out that there had to be some reason he'd kept me alive, he was talking again. One last sentence that made no sense but somehow still shook me to my core.

"All I need is your power."

CHAPTER 52

More time in the dark. More time to myself. Another day at least, drifting in and out of sleep. I still wasn't hungry or thirsty, but I felt weaker somehow.

Maybe that was just the dampeners again.

I'd spent more than a few hours hatching increasingly improbable plans of escape, but mostly I just lay there on the cold stone, feeling my body vibrate with the dampeners' thrum, thinking about what Tyrant had told me so far.

If what he'd said was true, the country was fucked. Tezcatlipoca encroaching from the south. Nothing to stop the Weaver expanding into Vancouver and Seattle. And as soon as word spread that Dominion was gone, Steel or Legion or one of the other half-dozen warlords who'd carved up the rest of the country would start moving on the Badlands.

Maybe it was all a lie, but if so, Tyrant had gone to extraordinary lengths to fake the data. Worse, he didn't seem to really care whether I believed him or not, which was, in my opinion, the hallmark of someone secure in their truth.

The bigger question was why he'd told me at all. And that led right back to the one thing I'd been doing my best *not* to think about.

All I need is your power.

What the hell did that mean? There was a reason the public referred to us as Powers; we *were* our gifts. Where my power went, I went. Yet something told me Tyrant had been honest on that front too.

And that scared me in a way that being mostly naked and chained to the floor couldn't.

When I heard the outer door boom open again, I was almost relieved. I'd had enough time in the dark. Enough time chasing my fears in a circle. It was time for some answers.

And then the cell door cracked open and Tyrant stepped inside. He was accompanied again by Jimmy Taylor, this time mask-less, and the mad smile on the other Crow's face made something shiver, deep inside me.

Fuck if I was going to let either of them see that though.

"Time for more exciting revelations? Is Grannypocalypse out there living in sin? Another Voidsinger sighting in the Badlands?"

"Not this time, Mr. Banach." Tyrant finished attaching the wires, his movements slow and unhurried, and then pulled something new off the cart. It fit in his hand, a plastic handle in a bright, playful color, topped with an inch-long, single-sided blade. "Now, it is the time for torture."

Alexa had said I was a hammer who needed to learn to be a scalpel, but I didn't think this was what she'd meant.

"Let me guess… you used to be a doctor too?" I tried not to shrink away from the blade in Tyrant's hand. I wasn't going to give either of them that satisfaction.

"Of a sort, I suppose," said the man, examining the scalpel, as if searching it for defects. "If you pursue the science of superpowers far enough, it is inevitable that you will attain a certain level of understanding of biology and the human form."

"I thought you were a researcher?"

"I am many things." Apparently satisfied with the quality of his torture implement, he held it in one hand, and leaned in over me. "Is this where I am supposed to give you my origin story, providing the hidden piece of truth that will enable you to defeat me?"

"It's tradition," I agreed. I'd much rather listen to him blather on than—

His hand moved so fast I could barely see it. Just a shimmer of steel across my bare chest, light as a feather. The pain came much more slowly; a line of fire sliced into my skin.

"Traditions are for the weak-minded," he told me, voice still mild and detached, as I twitched beneath him, reaching for the emptiness that could not come, "but we do have time to kill between tests."

With his free hand, he moved the wired box closer so that he could see its display, and then nodded at whatever it showed him.

"I had a twin, once. A sister, born three minutes before me." Those copper eyes gleamed. "Three minutes, but it might as well have been three years. She was the golden child, favored in all things. I was the unsightly creature who stumbled along in her wake."

My heart fucking bled for him… but I resisted the urge to tell him so, knowing he could make that saying literal.

"For the longest time, I thought it was my fault," he continued. "There'd always been a hole inside of me. Not like you Crows profess to experience, but a literal gaping space where something should have been. When we were twelve, I discovered what that something was, and why I was blamed for everything that my sibling did."

"She was a Power," I guessed.

"Yes. She actually told me so herself, proud that she'd slipped through testing, that the devices were not calibrated to detect a gift like hers."

That didn't make any sense. The testing machines were designed to identify every Power. Even Crows. But before I could say so, he carved another line across my chest.

"Fuck!" I couldn't hold it in that time, but the Black Hat just nodded, as if I had been continuing our conversation.

"Yes. I was understandably angry, myself. If I had been born three minutes earlier, would I have been the Power instead? Would I be the one who felt complete, and would my sister have been left with that same gnawing need?"

He shrugged, taking another glance at the box's screen. "That question haunted me as she skated through school and then university, experiencing every success despite her laziness and merely average intelligence. In some ways, I should thank her. I would never have achieved such heights without her existence serving as a continuous reminder of what I did not have."

Now he was in full supervillain monologue mode. The last thing I wanted to do was interrupt, especially with blood dripping down my chest, but there was a problem with his story.

"But I thought you were a Power?"

"It is impolite to interrupt, Mr. Banach, especially when you are the one who asked to hear my story." He shrugged again, wiping the scalpel clean against the inside skin of my arm. "The more I studied the science of superpowers, the greater the injustice seemed. Why did I have this space inside of me? Why should one twin be gifted while the other, the far more deserving other, was not? And most importantly of all, what if I could fill that space?"

Science wasn't on the Academy curriculum, so I didn't have a clue what he was talking about.

"I found some of my answers in old, abandoned case studies. I found others through careful experimentation. But the final piece came to me all the way from the other side of the continent, when I reached out and made contact with the lord of Baltimore."

I frowned. "You know Legion?"

"A brilliant man. A genius, really, and I do not award that title lightly. Yet short-sighted, for all his intellect, content to run his city-wide experiments and otherwise keep to himself. When the time comes for my conquest, he will regret his lack of ambition."

Another slice, this time down the outside of the arm. Unlike the cuts on my chest, I could actually see this one; shallow but perfectly straight. I watched blood well up to the surface and trickle down my arm.

I told myself that the blood would make me slippery, maybe even slippery enough to get out of the manacles.

It was a lie, but I tried to believe it anyway.

"You wouldn't understand even an iota of the science involved, but eventually, I became convinced that I could take my sister's power for my own. Fill the empty space inside me. Do something meaningful with a gift so rare as to make you Crows almost commonplace."

"And so I did. It was easy, once all the preparations had been made. She came to my lab—to the brother who alone knew what she was—for what I had described as a simple experiment. Her body was recovered a block away from her home. The police believed she was shot by muggers on her way back, and because she was merely a normal, that was the end of it. She was gone, and I had become something more. All the research, all the study, but that was my first overt act as Tyrant."

A fourth cut, this time on the other arm, and he glanced one last time at the display before placing the bloody scalpel back on his cart.

"If I had known then what I know now, I would never have bothered with her piddling gift. But at the time, I thought our bond as twins mattered. It wasn't until after I took her gift and found I still had space left inside me that I realized what had been a one-time process might be repeatable."

"You... steal powers?" That wasn't supposed to be possible. Not even in science fiction or terribly written vids. "How?"

"Through science, years of effort, and the one quality that makes me truly unique."

"The hole inside of you."

"I believe I was meant to be a Full-Five, but something went wrong at birth. My sister ended up with a tiny slice of power, and I ended up with all that wasted potential, like fertile soil that no seed had ever been planted in. And then the first gift I planted in that space barely even qualified as Mid-Two. What a waste. I could have had Tezcatlipoca's power instead, and none of the rest of this would've been necessary."

He glanced over at the cart, picked up a small, square-headed mallet with a rubber grip, and placed it on the ground at his side. This time, I *did* squirm, but there was nowhere for me to fucking go.

"I don't understand," I said, words spilling out of me in a rush. "Why does taking your sister's power mean you can't do the same to Tezcatlipoca?"

"I've discovered that I can take only one power of each classification, and I am stuck with the rank of the person I took it from. Trying to take another power of that same type, even one higher-ranked, merely wastes that gift. The creature's great power remains its own because I was a fool and filled that space with a lesser version."

"Your sister was a lava god?"

"There is nothing religious about Tezcatlipoca's ability, Mr. Banach. It is easy to see the process as a deity claiming its followers, but at the heart of things, wiping a lesser being's mind is no different than planting suggestions in that same mind. It is all just a question of scale."

"You're talking about mind control. There's no such thing as mind control!"

"Tell that to the teachers who gave my sister A's despite her complete disinterest in academics. Tell it to the CEO who gave her a six-figure salary to do nothing at all. Tell it to the thousand or even hundreds of thousands of former people Tezcatlipoca has turned into human puppets. Mind control is very real."

I shook my head. The one subject I knew well was History of Powers and there had *never* been a reported case of mind control.

"Is it so hard to believe?" asked Tyrant. "Sirens control emotion. Empaths read it. Why wouldn't there be similar powers dealing with the control and interpretation of thoughts themselves? In fact, I have discovered that those four powers are more closely related than I originally thought. And they all have the same weakness."

I'd spent enough time game planning for Vibe and Prince that the answer came to me without even trying. And with that, a whole lot of things fell into place.

"Crows can't be mind controlled?"

"Correct. The answer to our country's safety, and it lies in the hands of the criminally insane."

This sister-killer had no business throwing accusations of insanity around, but I swallowed that retort too. So far, I'd made it through with only four incisions. And yeah, they hurt like hell, but I'd had worse in sparring. A lot worse. But I really, really didn't like the look of that mallet.

"I don't get it then. You've already got Jimmy. Why not use him against Tezcatlipoca, if he's immune? Hell, why not send us both down there? Maybe one of us will win?"

"And exchange one opponent for something potentially even worse?" He shook his head. "I think not. Necromancy is the key to more than just Tezcatlipoca's destruction. It is my path to saving the world."

"You're going to have to run that by me one more time." Mostly, it had been the path to getting my ass kicked.

"Why is it that every great Power, every so-called Black Hat, has staked out their own small fiefdom, when an entire world lies waiting for someone to assert his dominance?"

"Lack of vision?" Now I was just pandering.

"Fear of the inevitable. Every major Power on this planet, from the Voidsinger to Grannypocalypse to Dominion himself, is constrained by a single unavoidable truth; we are grossly outnumbered. Were the world to rise up against any of us as a whole, we would eventually fall. How many High-Fours does it take to kill a Full-Five? Ten would get slaughtered, but thirty? A hundred? One such man fighting against a million might survive, but against a billion? The math is undeniable."

He paused, those penny eyes flickering as if thoughts were racing behind them at the speed of light. "In a numbers game, the world's population reigns supreme over all comers, except one."

"The dead."

"Exactly. As I've told you twice now, I don't need a soldier. I need an army. An army whose ranks swell with every passing moment, an army that already outnumbers the world's living exponentially and whose numerical advantage will only grow. A Crow's power is the key, and it will be mine."

"You already have Jimmy, and he's a Low-Fucking-Four. Why haven't you taken his power? Trust me, nobody's going to miss him."

Behind Tyrant, the Crow in question giggled and pantomimed like he was taking a bite out of me. I sent him back a silent message full of nothing but hate. Nyah and Mama Rawlins would be avenged.

Tyrant ignored my question and continued his monologue. "It's been more than two decades since I became Tyrant. Since I took my sister's gift and recognized I had the capacity for more. I have not been idle in that time, but the need for a Crow has remained foremost in my mind. Twenty-one years ago, I had a candidate, but she proved unsuitable in the end. The few others I could find were much like my sister had been; weaklings whose powers would do me no good."

"So I took my cue from Legion himself, from the experiments he'd run in the city he calls home. I gathered up those same weaklings, those Ones and Twos, and paired them with genetic matches whose family histories showed no signs of mental illness. And then, because one can never be too careful, I harvested them for seed and embryos and ensured that material made its way into the fertility clinics and sperm banks."

"*You tried to breed Crows.*" The scale of his plan was exceeded only by its monstrous nature.

"DNA plays a part. We know that much even if the full answer remains out of reach." He shook his head. "The success rate was shockingly low, even so. And there were challenges along the way. In the end, seven candidates survived to adulthood, each having been placed in their own distinct environments and situations."

"Why?"

"Necromancy is the only power that leads to insanity, and not even I know why. Would taking the power of an insane Crow curse me with that same fate? I had no interest in going down that road, which meant I needed a candidate who was both powerful enough to matter and who had not succumbed to that insanity."

Which clearly ruled out Jimmy Taylor and his disgusting feet.

"Of those seven, only four tested at Three or above, and ironically, the two greatest successes came from the same Low-Two's seed. After the testing was complete, I disposed of the useless specimens and took one back to my base. The other one, the stronger one, I sent somewhere else entirely."

I swallowed, eyes finally leaving the mallet as I realized where he had been going with all of this, and exactly how I fit in.

"The Academy."

"Yes."

Which meant two things. First, that Jimmy Taylor was my brother. Half-brother, assuming he'd been a result of one of the sperm bank swaps. I had too much of both my dad *and* my mom in me to believe I'd been born anything but naturally.

Secondly…

"I'm not a Low-Three, am I?"

"You are not, though even my sister's weak gift was sufficient to convince the tester otherwise." He finally reached for the mallet at his side. "Congratulations, Mr. Banach. Your gift will save the world."

He flattened out my right hand and lifted the mallet high.

"Wait! Why torture me then? Why do any of this, if you can just take my power?"

He paused, mid-strike. "There is a recovery period after I absorb a given power. It will be weeks, if not months, before I am ready to take yours. In fact, you were supposed to remain at the Academy until graduation, continuing to grow and learn and improve. If Mr. Taylor can raise the dead, I have little doubt that you should be similarly capable. Sadly, some minds are more slippery than others, and a particular fool chose to take his revenge upon you rather than sticking to the plan." He raised his voice and turned so that it was carried down the hall. "A fact that he now no doubt regrets."

I didn't have the vantage point to see down the hall, and was pretty sure even trying would accelerate my blood loss, but I could hear an answering clank of chains and something like a hiss of anger.

"If I had to make the decision again," said Tyrant, turning back to me, "I would have skipped the prison break entirely. Carnage for Fallout was far from an equitable swap. The only bright lining in your premature capture is that it has given me time to thoroughly map your brain. Electrical charges that light up different areas of your mind based on the appropriate stimulus. Surprise. Despair. Rage. And, of course, pain. I have studied the aberrant minds of many Crows, including Mr. Taylor himself. If you share their malady, it will be apparent through this testing." His smile came and went again, and his penny eyes sparkled. "And so far, I must say, things look good. Very good. For the world's sake, we can only pray that this continues."

And then he brought the mallet down hard on the pinky of my right hand.

Fuck putting on any sort of brave face. I howled in pain.

"Interesting," said Tyrant, checking the display on his device. "Let's try that again."

CHAPTER 53

In the darkness of my cell, I tried to focus past the pain. Tyrant had stopped at three fingers, having gotten whatever data he was looking for. He'd even had the grey-haired nurse come in to bandage my chest, so I guess the test results were still good enough that he didn't want me bleeding to death.

The nurse had taken one look at my mangled hand and just sprayed it with some sort of antiseptic. I guess there wasn't enough of those fingers left to splint.

I tried to marshal my thoughts, but the pain was everywhere. It was one thing to ignore it for a few seconds in a battle, power or no power. It was something else entirely to feel it bearing down on me, hour after hour, a fresh wave seeming to come with every pulse of the dampeners, every drip of my IV.

At some point, I passed out. It wasn't the first time either, but when I regained consciousness, I felt just a little bit more in control of myself. Not enough to block out the pain—never that—but enough to at least chain one thought to the next.

Focus on the positives.

What a thing to fucking tell myself, down three fingers and in the heart of some bastard power-vampire's lair, but I took it to heart. Focusing on the negatives would drive me every bit as crazy as Jimmy himself, and I wasn't willing to go down that route just yet.

So what was the good news? Was there any?

I knew I wasn't getting killed yet. That was something, I guess.

I knew what had happened to at least some of the Crows on Jeremiah and Tessa's list. That wasn't a good thing, but it was knowledge. And knowledge was good, right?

I knew I had a half-brother. No, that was all bad. Because fuck that insane, orphan-murdering freak.

Something else. What?

I knew I was stronger than Jimmy. Stronger than a Low-Four. If I somehow escaped, I might have the strength to end him. Nyah, John, and the others would all be avenged.

It still wasn't enough. My mind was trying to tell me there was something else, something that Tyrant had let slip in his endless monologue, exactly like the cartoon Black Hats always did in the vids.

But what was it?

Finally, it hit me.

Tyrant wanted my power. I didn't know how the process worked, but from what he said, it involved him using his own unique gift, that space he kept trying to fill. And that meant there wouldn't be any dampeners in effect at the time of the transfer.

Whenever that happened, whatever was left of me by that point, I'd have one last chance to act.

I was so fixed on that idea, on the thought of turning Tyrant into a pile of ash, that I didn't hear the outer door open and close. Didn't hear footsteps coming my way.

Didn't know I had a visitor until Jimmy's mad, staring face filled the cell door's small window.

There was no Tyrant this time, but he marched right in on his filthy feet, creeping past my mangled hand to crouch next to my head. His greasy smile showed gaps where teeth had gone missing.

"And here we are alone. Isn't this nice for me for he?"

I'd once thought Fat Joey's farts were the worst thing I would ever smell. That had changed when I walked into the bathroom after one of Muse's binges. Jimmy Taylor's breath was worse than both put together.

I tried to keep that thought off my face. Maybe I didn't have to wait for Tyrant's power-stealing procedure. Maybe I could convince my insane half-brother to let me go?

"Jimmy," I managed weakly, through a throat already hoarse from screaming. "I wish I'd known I had a brother."

"To play catch and ball and all and all and all?"

"Yeah." Whatever the fuck that meant. "I'm sorry this happened to you."

"Are you really?" Some sort of emotion swam in his mad eyes.

"Yeah."

I was too, sort of. We were all just pawns in Tyrant's decades-long scheme. That wasn't his fault.

I was still going to kill his ass as soon as I was free though.

"Big brother little brother same dad different mother."

Hell, I'd do it just to stop the rhyming.

"That's right," I said. "Our dad's dead, but we're still family. We can leave. Get out of here and go someplace better."

"Family matters." He nodded his head up and down, spittle flying everywhere.

"It does."

"And the Tyrant who makes things burn?"

"I'll protect us from him. You and me."

He rocked back on his heels, digesting that thought like it was one of the entrees made by Kayleigh's chef.

"You'll be safe," I added.

"Like the boys and girls at your orphanage home home?"

Maybe with access to my power, I could have hidden my reaction. Without it, I was suddenly nothing but naked anger and hate.

Jimmy cackled. "Thought I was stupid, didn't you? Thought you were something special special instead of one more bird of a feather!" His voice dropped to a threatening whisper. "Tyrant thinks so too but we know he's wrong. Twice as strong and twice as wrong."

I refused to shrink away. "All we have in common is a little bit of blood and this power. A power that I'm handling just fine." I let my lip curl up derisively. "Guess you're the weaker brother in a lot of ways, aren't you?"

If I couldn't play on our supposed brotherly bond to convince him to free me, maybe I could push the other way. Get him angry enough to make a mistake.

"You'll fall, little birdy bird." He smiled again, that same nasty smile he'd worn while his walkers killed Nyah and the others. "We all fall down."

"I'm not you."

"All birds are me. All birds are we." His smile turned crafty. Almost conspiratorial. "Have you started having the dream?"

Just like that, my blood went cold. There was only one dream he could be talking about.

"You've had it," he said, nodding knowingly. "It's how it starts. A dream and a dream and a dream. Where it ends, everyone knows."

I swallowed past the pit in my stomach. "Keep telling yourself that. Whatever makes you happy to be Tyrant's little pet, put aside and forgotten as soon as I came along."

"He thinks you're special," he hissed again, smile forgotten. "Thinks you're better. Thinks you matter. But you've got no song song."

He lunged back out of the cell door, spun and came right back inside. In his hands was another implement from the cart parked just outside.

Fuck if it wasn't a cleaver.

"No song," he roared, spraying spittle across the cell, "and only one wing!"

And then he brought the blade down like Dr. Nowhere's own wrath, cutting straight through the bones of my right wrist.

Maybe I passed out then. Maybe I didn't. When I blinked, he was still bent over me, and blood was spurting everywhere from the severed end of my right arm. I was screaming and so was he, and I knew, the same way I'd known out in the fields with Carnage, that death was creeping up on me. Life was leaking out of the space where my hand had once been, and cold was invading.

Only this time, I didn't have my powers to call on.

This time, I didn't even have a fucking hand.

But that also meant I now had one limb free.

I pulled the stub of my limb up, blood going everywhere. Jimmy shrank back as some sprayed in his eyes, but he was too late. I had the crook of my elbow behind his head. No leverage to speak of.

No strength either, but he was already off-balance, and that was all I needed to smash his face down into my chest. My freshly bandaged wounds started to flow again, and I kept his face crushed into my skin, trying to cut off his air flow. Trying to drown him in my own blood.

Maybe it would have worked. Maybe I'd have suffocated him before blood loss did me in. Problem is, we never got a chance to find out. Footsteps raced down the hall to my cell, and someone pulled Jimmy out of my weak grasp.

From the doorway, I heard Tyrant's voice, somehow dispassionate and filled with urgency at the same time. "Go. Get Fingers now."

Which was weird, I thought to myself, as the darkness closed in yet again. My fingers were right over there.

ooo

I opened my eyes on the confines of my cell, but something was different. The blood was gone. The people were gone. Even the noise was gone. The walls about me wavered in and out like they'd been formed from tissue paper instead of stone. Low light filled the space, but it wasn't streaming through the cell's open door. It was emanating from the door itself. Above me, the ceilings seemed impossibly far away.

I didn't see her until she moved. One shadow in a corner already full of them, slowly resolving into the slim shape of a dark-haired woman in an old-fashioned black dress, bits of lace at her throat and hands. Small, mincing steps took her out of the corner until she was standing over me, eyes mud-brown and torn like freshly dug graves.

"Hello, Damian." Her face was exactly as I remembered it, young and unlined, a doll's mouth under a button nose. It might have been pretty if not for those eyes.

I looked up at her, caught in that strange place between awe and fear.

"Hello, Sally."

CHAPTER 54

Everyone knows about Sally Cemetery.

Everyone knows the things she did.

I'd been searching for her ever since I discovered her role in my mother's death, in my father's turn to murder. Ten months, and all we'd found was evidence that I was not her only victim. With what I had since learned from Tyrant himself, I had nothing but questions. One hand and so many questions.

"How are you here?"

That wasn't supposed to be one of them.

"The man has summoned his pet Healer to keep you from dying," she said, her voice empty and quiet. "For this moment, the dampeners are silent."

"Can I wake up then?"

Sally shook her head. Her dark hair was pulled back into a tight bun that stretched the pale skin of her thin face, adding a decade to her appearance. She looked exactly like she had the last time I saw her, from the long black dress buttoned up to her throat to the emptiness in her eyes.

"Before the dampeners were turned off, they would have drugged you. You are free, but only here. In this dream that is not a dream."

"How do you know any of this?"

"It is how he operates."

Something clicked. Maybe it was because, for the first time since Tyrant's speech, there was no pain to distract me.

"You were the Crow he was talking about. The one he captured twenty-one years ago."

"I was." A chair formed out of shadow, and she sat, skirts pooling on the floor just out of my remaining hand's reach. "I had just finished my instruction of Carl and his brother Edward—" Her smile was cold and quiet and sharp as a razor. "—when I heard about a man trying to create more of our kind. I investigated, but my time teaching the humans had made me careless. I was ambushed and taken, spirited away to a cell three doors down from this one, a former laboratory in the heart of a city that was at that time still thriving, like an organism unaware of the rot at its core."

Carl and Edward. I knew those names. The Morgenstein brothers, just out of Portland. They had been the last of Sally's many, many victims when she was alive.

I shivered. It wasn't until I'd wrapped my arms around myself that I realized I wasn't chained to the floor in this place. I pulled myself to a seated position, my severed wrist giving off darkness like smoke.

"How did you get away from Tyrant?"

"I didn't." She lifted one lace-covered hand. "I waited until they were gone, tore my hands out of the manacles, and crushed the bones of my feet until they too were free, but I could not get past the cell door itself." Again, that smile that died somewhere in the cemetery of her eyes. "The man had not yet found his Healer. I bled out on the prison floor."

"I'm sorry."

"Are you?" She tilted her head, as if studying me, but her eyes were distant, fixed on the ephemeral walls behind me. "I was not. When no other options remain, death is itself a victory."

I swallowed, but kept my spine straight. It had been more than a year since I'd last seen Sally. I'd learned things. Done things. I was not going to cower in front of her.

"Is that why you're here? To kill me? Like you tried to have my dad do when I was five? Like you did to all the other Crows?"

"You and they were products of the man's breeding program. Flowers in a field waiting to be harvested." Something cold and dark crept into her expression. "I would not let his plans reach fruition."

"Then why am I still alive? Why didn't you kill me on campus last summer? Why help me at all?"

"I am twenty years dead," she told me, in a whisper that whipped around the room like something wild. "There are limits to my influence on the world. For all my efforts, too many slipped through. I sent someone else, a Crow with eyes like blood, to lay waste to this city, to destroy the man and his machines and experiments, but even that failed. The city was destroyed and abandoned, but Capes intervened too soon. The man at the heart of my misfortune survived unscathed."

An abandoned city. A Crow with blood-red eyes.

"You were behind Crimson Death's attack on Reno?"

"All it took was a nudge."

Thousands of people had died. My classmate, Olympia, had lost a sister and her parents. And all of that had just been an effort to kill Tyrant?

I shook my head. "That still doesn't answer my question. Why am I alive?"

"I am fighting a losing battle. If the man does not die, he will eventually be victorious, having taken what he desires without consent or fear of retribution. When I felt your call in Los Angeles, I knew you might be the one. Someone to succeed where I and the others had failed." She turned empty eyes on the nebulous stone walls surrounding us. "It appears I was mistaken. And so I have come."

There was no threat in her voice, but lace-covered hands twitched in her lap, fingers extending and curling as if to wrap around an unseen object. The ghosts that crept into the room then, seeping through walls gone porous and thin, were misshapen creatures that had never been human, multi-limbed monstrosities with faceted eyes or double-hinged jaws. Their green light cast Sally's eyes into shadow.

I opened myself, let the emptiness seep into my core, pushing away the shivers and the memory of pain, quieting the small voice screaming in the back of my mind. My own ghosts gathered. Mom and Dad. Shane and Nyah. The bandits Her Majesty had killed on the way from Bakersfield. More and more flooded into a cell too small to hold our shared power. Soldiers from the Hole. Tempest, Carnage, Moth, and Lucien. Even Academy guards and a slim black woman who'd been my professor for only one semester, who I hadn't even known was dead. I nodded to Macy Johnson, but the question of how and when she had died was a distant thing, a stray thought floating on the periphery.

When my ghosts had filled the cell and the space beyond the cell, the unseen sky and the earth beneath us, I let my eyes, tombstone grey like my father's, meet Sally's.

"Do you really think you can?"

She paused.

Sally Cemetery paused.

"This single moment in time can be stretched, but it is not infinite, Damian. The Healer has sealed the blood vessels in your severed wrist. Next, he will replenish the blood in your body, and after that, the dampeners will be reactivated. It is now or never. Please. Put aside your power. I will not let the man finally win."

"Tyrant already took someone's gift," I told her. "It will be weeks before he can come for mine. Give me that time."

"You are lost in the belly of the beast. You are alone and you will soon be powerless again. You have no chance of survival."

I unleashed my own smile, full of pain and sorrow and rage and the power that made them all nothing but background music in the soundtrack of my life. "Since when have I let that stop me?"

She was shaking her head, but the fact that we were even having this conversation told me something. If Sally believed she could stop me, believed her power could overwhelm mine, I would already be dead. I thought of Tyrant's revelation. I wasn't just a Low-Three. I wasn't even just a Low-Four. Whatever I was, I was a prize the Black Hat wanted and someone Sally Cemetery herself wasn't convinced she could destroy.

I looked at the spectral creatures that had surrounded her, and let the emptiness leach out of me through my voice.

"Go."

There was a moment of resistance, like I was pushing against a wall, although I couldn't tell if that wall was inside of me or out. And then it was gone, and the ghosts surrounding Sally were gone too, leaving just the woman herself, sitting primly on a chair of shadow.

Her doll's mouth twisted. "This is the strength you would let the man take."

"It's not over yet. And Tyrant will have to turn off the dampeners when it's time to steal my power. If I'm still here, you can kill me then." I swallowed and shrugged. "I won't fight. I don't want him winning any more than you do."

The room around us shivered and Sally's head whipped around to look at the quaking walls. "So be it. We are out of time."

"Wait!" The dream started to disintegrate around us, but she stopped. Close enough to hear me, but not close enough to touch. Never close enough to touch. "I need you to do one more thing."

"I am a creature of the dead, Damian. My reach into the world of the living is limited. If I could kill the man, I would have already done so."

Cracks spread through the stone floor. The door vanished in a sea of light, and I squeezed my eyes shut against the suddenly painful illumination.

"All I need," I managed, "is for you to find someone and get them a message."

She stood against the light, as slender as a single stream of smoke, her eyes dark and deep. "Give me the message and the name."

So I did. And then, because the world was a toilet and life loved to shit all over me and my plans, I gave her a second name.

ooo

When the space I'd shared with Sally collapsed, I didn't return to consciousness like I'd expected. Whatever drugs were in me kept me out, but even in my sleep, I could feel the thrum of the dampeners again.

You'd think those things, the drugs and the dampeners, would've been enough to keep away dreams, but they did just the opposite. Dream after dream, blood and absence and hollow echoes of emotions. And whenever the usual dreams had worn thin?

The dream. The one Jimmy had mentioned. The one we apparently all shared. The sign that I hadn't avoided insanity after all, that I'd maybe just somehow nudged it a little bit further down the road.

I was in my cell this time, instead of the Academy. Rotten shards of door hanging from a single hinge. Steel outer door, as massive as found in any bank sim, blown outward. In the manner of dreams, I floated through empty halls that blurred and became indistinct until I was outside on a cracked asphalt street. The buildings around me were empty shells, holes gaping in their facades like eye sockets or toothless mouths.

There was no ocean, because Reno was inland. Further inland even than Bakersfield. A dusty ghost town in the northern desert, abandoned when I was just a child. There was no ocean, but the ghosts had gathered anyway. All those I had summoned against Sally and thousands more, souls I had never met, who somehow still had come to my call in the dream.

But where were the walkers? At the Academy, they'd been lined up in ranks around the school, silent as only the dead can be. But here, in this dream-Reno, the streets were empty of anything but ghosts. The buildings were empty. The scene felt incomplete.

And then I turned to look at the building I had just somehow escaped. Three stories aboveground, nobody knew how many below. I couldn't tell if it had windows, couldn't even tell if the walls were brick or stucco, because every inch of the exterior was covered, floor to sky, by a writhing, seething mass of bodies.

The walking dead, swarming over my prison like ants on a soda can. Thousands of them, moving to the beat of my heart.

For the first time in months, since long before I'd been kidnapped from the Academy, I woke with a smile on my face.

ooo

Days passed. Nights too, not that I could tell which was which. I didn't see Jimmy again, but Tyrant came by once, took one last reading, and then removed the helmet I'd been wearing for weeks. He paused in the doorway, copper eyes glittering.

"Soon, Mr. Banach. Soon."

I guess my readings were still good, even after losing the hand. Even with the dream occurring more and more frequently. Seemed like Tyrant's little device didn't work as well as he thought it did.

If I wasn't able to escape, if Sally wasn't able to kill me when I was transported for the procedure… then I could at least take comfort in the fact that Tyrant would be signing himself up for that same insanity he was so focused on avoiding.

Wouldn't make up for my death, of course, but fuck if it wouldn't give me something to laugh about in hell.

After that visit, I counted days by the number of times the granite-faced nurse came to swap my bag of fluids and the almost-as-frequent times someone in a full hazmat suit opened the door to hose the whole cell down, washing the filth of my waste into tiny drains along the walls.

Guess it was good I'd long since gone nose-blind to my own stench. Pretty sure I really would have gone mad otherwise.

Sixteen days since Sally's visit, by my estimate, and even with the nutrients being fed into my blood stream, I was steadily getting weaker. I had my one arm free, the severed end inexpertly healed into a stump, but the rest of me was still chained down, and I could feel my muscles starting to waste away from the lack of activity.

More than two weeks gone and I hadn't made any progress on my escape. No sign of Sally. No sign of the two people I'd sent her to find. Just silence and new bags and a high-pressure hose that felt like it was scouring my skin when turned on.

And then, not even an hour after the person in the hazmat suit had left, I heard the massive outer door swing open once again. Footsteps, loud and purposeful, pausing at each of the cells in the hall, but steadily progressing in my direction.

A shape blocked the light streaming in, and then a key was inserted in the lock and the door opened.

I knew that silhouette. It wasn't Alexa, the first name I'd given Sally, in the faint hope that the sometimes-therapist's agency could mount a rescue operation. This woman was taller and all in leather, a body so perfect it seemed like it had been built and not born. And her head was hidden, as always, by a motorcycle helmet with a yellow smiley-face decal covering the visor.

"Bakersfield," said Her Majesty, known to the wider world as the Queen of Smiles, "someone told me I'd find you here."

CHAPTER 55

"Glad you were in the neighborhood, Your Majesty." My voice was hoarse and strained, my throat dry.

"I wasn't, really." Her voice, on the other hand, was a quiet snarl of metal. She crouched down and rotated through keys on her keyring until she found the one that fit my manacles. "I was in the Badlands when a past client reached out to tell me that her town's local nutjob was suddenly singing my name."

She released my ankle cuffs, and moved up to my wrists, stopping when she came to my missing right hand. For a moment she went still. Then she shook her head, the smiley-face decal on her visor more maniacal than ever, and moved to my left hand instead.

"Took a day to get there, but when I did, it turned out this Kevin person was speaking on behalf of a dead woman, and that dead woman wanted me to rescue your sweet ass. We came to terms." She paused, and fixed me with a gaze I couldn't see through the visor. "First the Hole, now this. It might be time to reevaluate your life choices, kid. Set your sights on something a little less fatal maybe."

"This wasn't something I did. I was just in the wrong place at the wrong time. Like fucking always." With my wrist free, I tried to sit up, but my muscles didn't want to cooperate. "So Sally hired you?"

"I don't work for free. Turns out she had some information I was looking for."

"Information?"

"Yeah." She slid a gloved hand under my back, the leather cool and smooth on my naked skin, and tilted me upright. "In a way, I guess I should thank you for that."

"Happy to—" I hissed as she yanked the needle out of my arm. "—help. But how did you get in here?"

"I've done jobs for Tyrant before, remember? Not just getting you to the Academy in one piece either. I'm a known face." Her laughter was harsh and grating, like a hacksaw attacking a crowbar. "So to speak, anyway. If he were here, there'd have been some questions, but he's off dealing with some sort of government strike on one of his other bases. Guards let me walk right in."

"And the keys?"

"Guy who had them decided he didn't need them anymore." The humor left her voice, leaving it flat and impersonal. "But sooner or later, someone's going to find what's left of him. We should be gone before that happens. Can you walk?"

"Get me away from these dampeners, and I'll fucking run."

"I'll take that as a yes." She grabbed my only remaining hand and pulled me to my feet... then caught me when my legs tried to sag under me. "Or not."

"Legs are just weak," I told her. "I haven't been getting much exercise lately."

"No shit. You could also use some pants. And new underwear," she decided, half-supporting and half-carrying me as we shuffled for the door.

I was just thankful she hadn't mentioned the smell. High-pressure hose or not, I was disgusting.

The space outside my cell was, as I'd guessed, a hallway, with doors to a dozen more cells. At the far end of the hallway was the steel door I'd seen in my dream.

We'd made it about a fifth of the way down the hall when that door swung slowly shut.

"Uhm..."

"Not to worry," she growled. "I have the code. How do you think I got in?"

The further we went, the better my legs functioned. By the end of the hall, I was mostly upright on my own. Problem was, when she entered the code into the keypad recessed next to the door, nothing happened.

"That's odd." She tapped in the code a second time.

Again, nothing. The light stayed red. The door stayed shut.

"Are you sure you're remembering it correctly?"

Her motorcycle helmet turned in my direction. "It's five digits, not a hundred."

Mocking laughter emerged from one of the cells we'd passed, followed by a voice I knew all too well... a voice that carried easily to us despite its whisper.

"When is a queen not a queen, oh bright lady of smiles?" A second later, the answer followed. "When she is a prisoner, just like the rest of us."

"Great," grumbled Her Majesty. "I was hoping that asshole would stay unconscious until we were gone." She dragged me back down the hall and looked in at the only other occupied cell in the hall.

Fallout looked like shit. Shackled to the floor, just like I had been, his pale, wiry body a mass of bruises and scars. Someone had shaved his head and thick bunches of his formerly waist-length black hair were scattered around him like the world's foulest nest.

I'd grown used to my smell, but this, this was awful.

"You have something to say, Shadecaster?" asked Her Majesty.

"The door that stands in your way has two codes, my leather-clad horror show. One for entry and another for egress. Without that second code, you are as trapped as we are."

That was bad. Her Majesty was a Shifter of a kind I'd never seen before, one who turned into a living storm of shrapnel, but she was presently crippled by the dampeners just like the rest of us.

"It is fortuitous indeed," continued Fallout, his words slightly slurred as he spoke through a jaw that had been broken and inexpertly healed, "that I spent much of the past ten months as one of our captor's lieutenants. And even more fortuitous that I took the liberty to memorize this facility's many, many codes, should an eventuality like this one present itself. Release me, and I will deliver us to freedom."

"Fuck that." My voice was a pale shadow of Her Majesty's snarl. "Stay here and rot."

"As short-sighted as I would expect from one of your dubious origins." Fallout's sneer was partly ruined by the teeth missing from his mouth.

"You two know each other, I take it?" asked Her Majesty.

I nodded, shifting to finally stand on my own. "We met at the Hole."

"Ah."

"*And* he's the reason I'm here in the first place," I added.

"One might say the same holds true in reverse," whispered Fallout. "You have had every part to play in my sudden and precipitous fall from grace."

Even worse than the incessant whisper was the man's tendency to talk like the bastard son of a thesaurus and a cartoon villain.

"Tyrant could return at any time," Her Majesty said to me. "We need the code if we're going to get out."

"He killed Tempest. And my father," I added after a moment.

"And you killed my friend and ally, Carnage, who was worth both of those pathetic souls put together," answered Fallout, letting his head drop back to the floor with a thud. "But I am nothing if not a man of generosity. And so I will throw in a second code for the price of one."

I could hear the frown in Her Majesty's voice. "A second code?"

"One that provides access to our jailer's secret escape tunnel." Something vicious crept into Fallout's words. "Or did you think you would be able to carry the boy out the front door? Two codes and we all walk free."

I shook my head again. "You know he's just going to betray us as soon as he gets the chance."

"You're not wrong." Her Majesty was silent for a second, then shrugged. "I can try to pry open the keypad. Maybe cross some wires. See what happens."

"And then you will smuggle Tyrant's highest value prisoner out past his very many and very merry men? Using what? A towel?"

"We'll figure something out," said Her Majesty. "Bakersfield's right. As soon as you see freedom, you'll turn on us."

"Would that it were possible." For once, the cartoonish malevolence left Fallout's whisper. "Would that our jailer had begun with this young Crow instead of me. Alas, life is not so kind. Tyrant has become a Shadecaster and I am reduced to this sorry state."

"What a load of complete and utter bullshit." Her Majesty was already walking away toward the panel. She stopped when she realized I had not followed her. That yellow smiley face turned my way. "Kid?"

"Tyrant *did* say he'd just taken someone's power," I told her. "It's the only reason I'm still around."

"It was the price I paid for taking you from the Academy," agreed the former Shadecaster. "For disobeying orders." He tried and failed to spit. "Neither of you will see me again once we have our freedom. When word spreads of what has befallen me, my enemies will come in force. My only hope is to escape into the Badlands."

I didn't trust the shady bastard, but between Her Majesty and me, we should be able to handle a depowered supervillain without much difficulty. If he really did have codes to get us out, it seemed worth the risk.

But once we were out? Fuck letting him go. I was taking him into custody. Life in a prison for normals seemed like a suitable punishment for all he'd done.

Granted, killing him sounded even better, but I was training to be a Cape. At some point, I should probably start acting like one.

I couldn't see Her Majesty's face, but she had no difficulty seeing mine. "You think this is a good idea?"

"Hell no. But I don't think we have much choice." I waited as she rotated through the keys until she found the one for Fallout's door, and then followed her inside. "Make a noise, Fallout. Signal a guard. Breathe in the wrong direction. I promise you *will* die."

His voice sounded tired. "I desire freedom just as you do, boy. I will not risk my own escape for so petty a thing as vengeance."

I didn't have much to say to that, and the smell from his cell was really starting to get to me. I backed up, letting Her Majesty undo his shackles.

Soon enough, the criminal was on his feet, looking far less intimidating than when I'd first seen him at the Hole. He staggered out into the hall, and then, using the wall as a support, started shuffling toward the steel door that stood in our path.

Neither Her Majesty nor I offered to help.

When he reached the keypad embedded into the wall next to the door, Fallout nodded. His long slender fingers appeared to have each been broken sometime recently, but that didn't stop him from tapping in the code.

For the third time in the past ten minutes, nothing happened. Red light. Locked door.

"Are you fucking kidding me?"

The man looked over at me, teeth gritted and dark eyes hard. "Just like the keys in your smiling queen's hands, each door is matched to its own specific code. I will work my way through the codes I know until the right one is found." A smug smile spread across his face as his eyes drifted to where my right arm ended in a stump. "I would ask you to lend a hand, but…"

On second thought, maybe I *would* just ash the motherfucker as soon as we were free.

It took three more attempts, but finally, the light above the panel turned green, and the massive steel door disengaged, swinging slightly open.

I was behind Fallout as we stepped into the hall, and out of the range of the dampeners. No point in giving an asshole your back if he was lying about the whole power theft thing, right? I let the emptiness flood into me, muffling my pain and carrying the weight of my body.

Part of me just wanted to dump some of that emptiness into the Black Hat… watch his body collapse in on itself. Leave one more pile of dust for Tyrant when he returned. If we hadn't needed him to get out through the so-called escape tunnel, maybe I'd have killed him right then.

So much for me behaving like a Cape.

He looked over his shoulder at me like he knew what I was thinking and just shrugged. There'd been no last-second betrayal now that he was out of the cell block. No shadows coming to life to kill Her Majesty and me both. Just a pale man with a raggedly shaved scalp.

"Up or down," asked Her Majesty.

"To reach a tunnel? Down, of course." He waved a twisted hand. "Be warned. Alarms may be triggered from every floor. Stealth is paramount."

Considering that one of us was wearing black leather and a motorcycle helmet with a day-glo decal on its visor and the other two were mostly naked, reeking, and clearly recent victims of torture, stealth seemed like a bit of a reach. Thankfully, the halls we worked our way through all seemed deserted.

"Where is everyone?" I asked, once we'd descended another floor.

"Upstairs," said Her Majesty, her voice an uncharacteristically quiet buzz. "Be thankful for it. There were more than a few names and faces I recognized. Fighting our way out would be suicide."

Even as the words left her mouth, someone rounded the corner ahead of us. His eyes widened and his mouth opened to cry out, but the Queen of Smiles was already there, keys in hand as a makeshift weapon that she drove into the man's throat and chest.

"Crude but effective, I suppose," decided Fallout, as the unknown man crumpled to the floor.

"Quieter than the storm," she shot back. "How far to the tunnel?"

"Fifteen minutes. Maybe more."

"Too far to leave the body in the open then." She looked from the emaciated Shadecaster to my one-handed self, her sigh a dull hum of agitated hornets and steel. "I'll take care of it."

The room she chose to stash the corpse in was empty. She emerged moments later with a pair of pants, only slightly spattered with blood, and threw them in my direction. They were somehow both too short and too wide, but I didn't even care. I yanked off the disgusting scrap of cloth that had begun life as a pair of boxers and pulled on the pants.

"Warn a woman before you're going to strip down," grumbled Her Majesty, tossing me a shirt that was significantly more blood-stained than the pants, but still better than nothing. "I'd have brought singles. Or a cattle prod."

I'd never seen a cattle prod before, but I had a pretty good idea what it was, and didn't know why anyone would bring it to a strip show. The woman had her own definition of fun.

It took us ten minutes and two different staircases to finally reach the storeroom that Fallout declared was our destination, and we didn't encounter another soul along the way. Either the place was oversized to match Tyrant's ego, or the Black Hat had taken some of his troops with him when he left.

A heavy shelf full of boxes swung easily aside, revealing a dark hole in the wall. Tyrant's emergency escape tunnel.

It was my turn to sigh. I was well past the point of exhaustion. If it hadn't been for my power, I wouldn't even be standing anymore. And Fallout was even worse... a shambling ruin of a man.

I really hoped it was a short tunnel.

CHAPTER 56

It was not a short tunnel. It curved back and forth through the earth like it had formed naturally instead of being bored, dimly lit by wall sconces mounted every fifty to a hundred paces.

I don't know what kept Fallout on his feet. Every few minutes, he almost went down, and each time, he just barely caught himself, clinging to the rough stone wall.

It didn't change my opinion of the asshole, let alone my plans for him, but it was hard to deny the man's willpower.

More importantly, it meant neither Her Majesty nor I had to carry him.

The last stretch of the tunnel was arguably the worst. It finally straightened out, but that small blessing was accompanied by a noticeable incline, as the tunnel brought us back up to whatever qualified as Reno's surface. Those last few hundred yards took Fallout almost as much time as the rest of the tunnel put together.

And then we were there. Just as the former Shadecaster had said, the tunnel ended in another security door with a keypad embedded in the nearby wall. This door was smaller than the one outside our cell block, but looked every bit as impenetrable.

Maybe Her Majesty could have torn through it in her other form, but it would have taken a while and been noisy as all hell.

Luckily, we didn't have to try.

Fallout leaned against the wall by the keypad, dripping in sweat and gasping for air. He swallowed a few times before pushing away from the wall.

"I can't promise that—" He coughed, a wet hack that resulted in a wad of blood and phlegm on the floor. "—our hated jailer does not have this point of egress under observation. Be prepared for the possibility of at least minor impediments."

Her Majesty made a noise somewhere between a laugh and a snort, mixed in with the rattle of metal and steel. Her helmet gleamed in the dim light. "Just get to it."

This time, it only took Fallout one try. The light above the panel turned green and the door disengaged.

"Bakersfield." The smiley-face decal turned in my direction. "Get the door. Fallout, you're out first."

The former Shadecaster didn't object to being used as a human shield, waiting as I forced the heavy door open. Fresh air rushed in, cool and sweet for the three seconds it took Fallout to step out into the night.

After that, we were mostly just smelling *him*. Somehow, that singular moment of freshness made the odor even worse.

The tunnel's entrance was hidden within the ruins of an old building, virtually invisible with all the rubble carefully strewn about it. With no signs that anyone had witnessed our escape, Her Majesty followed Fallout outside.

I started to join them, then stopped, looking at the door I was still holding open. As soon as Fallout was in custody, I was going to let Alexa know about this base, and a backdoor in would be invaluable when it came time to assault Tyrant and his forces.

Still holding the door open with my body weight, I reached down, found a piece of torn rebar in the rubble, and placed it across the threshold. When I released the door, it hit the rebar and stopped before the lock could engage.

"What are you doing, Bakersfield?" Her Majesty turned to see what was keeping me.

"Giving some friends a way in—" I started to say.

Of course, that was when Fallout finally struck.

○○○

There was no sound at all as a dozen, then a hundred, tendrils of shadow hit Her Majesty from behind, slicing through leather and flesh, and then leather again to burst out of her chest, abdomen, and pelvis. She staggered in mid-stride, and then a dozen more shadows tore through the motorcycle helmet, shattering the visor and its yellow smiley face.

Her Majesty collapsed to the floor in a half-dozen different pieces.

I was already in motion, charging Fallout, ducking under the first of his barely visible shadows, too close for him to stop, close enough to lash out in a punch he didn't have time to dodge.

I'd always been strongly right-handed, even after years of training with Nikolai and Jessica. When the time came, with my power flowing through me, making the pain distant, I instinctively lashed out with that same arm.

That's why I missed.

Missed by just under five inches. The five inches of the hand I'd lost back in my cell.

I followed my miss with a lightning-swift left cross, just trying to make contact so I could dump my power into the Shadecaster's body, but this time I was the one who was too slow. The darkness literally picked me up off my feet and threw me against the door. I cracked my head on the steel, slumped to the earth, and the world swam about me. By the time things came back into focus, the Black Hat was crouched above me like some kind of malevolent spider. My limbs were splayed to either side of me, pinned to the ground by shadows wrapped around my sleeves and pant legs.

"I think this farce has gone on long enough, don't you?" he whispered."

"You lying motherfucker."

"Ah, profanity. The last resort of the simple mind. I must thank you for my freedom. While Tyrant already possessed a Shadecaster's powers long before my escape from the Hole, I suspect I would never have seen the outside of my cell."

I'd escaped Fallout once by stabbing his shadow. I didn't have a weapon this time, but I tried sending my power into the coils of shadow that held me down.

Nothing.

Maybe it was because the shadows weren't touching my skin. Or maybe my power just didn't work like that. Either way, the emptiness inside of me churned in futility, denied a channel through which to flow.

"Good luck getting out of Reno under your own power," I spat up at the Shadecaster. "Tyrant's people will hunt you down before you even make it a half-dozen blocks. Unless…" I let my voice trail off.

"Unless what, pray tell?"

"Unless he has someone else to chase instead. Someone he wants way more than your sorry, broken ass."

"And you are volunteering to be the rabbit in this scenario, I take it?"

I had no idea what rabbits had to do with anything, but nodded. "You know I'm the real prize here."

He cocked his head, considering the matter, but the shadows pinning me down never slackened. "It is not without merit, this hastily conceived stratagem. Yet why would I leave my enemy that same prize when I could instead take it away from him forever?"

Another half-dozen tentacles of shadow reached into the rubble around us, finding more rebar, splintered wood, even one large and jagged shard of glass. Each implement came from the darkness, on shadows I could barely see, hovering above my chest like the world's most horrific chandelier.

The Black Hat sneered. "If I could, I would visit this fate on all of Tyrant's prisoners, but I will content myself with you, his greatest prize. I spent countless hours researching the boy who slew Carnage— who stabbed me in the back with the old knight's broken sword—in anticipation of this very moment. I will not let it slip it away. We have ample time before the sun rises again. I intend to make your death last."

I pulled the empty strands of my power back and sent them instead toward the unseen pieces of Her Majesty's corpse, but again, I found nothing.

Two years at the Academy, and what I'd learned of my power still wasn't anywhere enough to keep me alive.

Fallout stroked the shard of glass along my cheek and I felt the skin split open like an overripe apple from one of Amos' trees.

"Tyrant will face his own reckoning in time," he said, "but he is absent and you are here, and I have so very much anger to work my way through. I want to hear you scream, boy. Scream like you did when the other Crow took your hand."

If I hadn't been flat on my back, head pinned to the ground, I would never have heard it; the faint, barely perceptible scrape of steel against stone, the low buzz of something like wasps or hornets. I glared up at Fallout, feeling my cheek flap open with every word. "I guess that research didn't cover my trip from Bakersfield to the Academy, did it?"

He paused, his smile freezing for just a moment. "How can you be sure?"

"Because if it had," I told him, feeling my own smile grow obscenely wide, "you'd have known you can't keep a good woman down."

Fallout was on his feet in a flash, but it was too late. The low sound I'd heard went from whisper to roar, and a storm of shrapnel threw the Black Hat away from the door. He rolled like a trained acrobat, shadows dancing on the end of long, broken fingers, but there was nothing for his power to strike at, just a whirlwind of steel and metal and rusted rail spikes where a person should be.

I watched as the man's skin was flayed from his bones and my smile only grew.

If Bard had seen me right then, all the power in the world might not have kept him from expelling me.

ooo

When it was over, my father's murderer was just a tattered skeleton, scraps of meat spread across the ruins. The storm of steel came together in the middle of that carnage and was replaced by the tall shape of a woman in motorcycle helmet and leather riding gear.

There wasn't a mark on Her Majesty. The helmet that had shattered was all in one piece again. Her leather jacket and painted-on pants looked brand new. Even the dust and dirt from the tunnel was gone.

My voice was a whisper, seeming even quieter after the sounds Fallout had made while dying. "*What are you?*"

"Not something to fuck with." Her voice was all snarl, the impossibly intact decal across her visor leering like a lunatic. She pulled me to my feet with a gauntleted hand. "Let's go. I left my bike a few blocks from the front door to Tyrant's base. We need to figure out where we are so we can get it and get the hell out of here."

She was a half-dozen strides away, maybe five feet from the empty doorway that led from the shell of a house to the street, when she realized, once again, that I wasn't with her. She spun. "Bakersfield?"

"Fallout said something."

"I think that's your imagination, kid. There's not enough left of that man to fill a box."

"I mean before he died."

"Oh." She shrugged. "The storm doesn't have ears, so I didn't hear it. Why do you care?"

"Because…" I pressed my left sleeve against my cheek, trying to stop the bleeding. The fabric was dirty, but infection was something the Healers could take care of once I made it back to the Academy. "…he said there were other prisoners."

"Ah." Her Majesty was still, a tall, dark shape in the greater darkness, three steps from freedom. "It's true. Three other cell blocks on the same floor as yours, most of them full. So what?"

"That's like forty people. Helpless captives. Maybe being tortured, like I was."

"So make sure the Capes you send free them when they come. I assume that's why you kept the door open in the first place."

It had been, but… "How far is Reno from Los Angeles? Or any city with net access?"

"Los Angeles is on the far side of the country, but Sacramento is a couple of days away."

"So by the time we got word out, Tyrant would be back and my escape would be public knowledge." I shook my head. "He has a Teleporter now. He could empty the whole base, prisoners included, before any Cape team ever made it here."

"That would suck for them, but it's not our problem. This is not the time to grow a conscience."

She wasn't wrong. I'd been held captive for weeks. Maybe even a month. I'd been tortured. I'd lost a fucking hand, and a large part of me wanted nothing more to escape into the night, to ride bitch on Her Majesty's motorcycle all the way back to safety.

Now that I knew I was stronger than a Low-Four, who knew what sort of progress I could make in training? Maybe I could get strong enough to keep anything like this from happening again. Tyrant could keep. Revenge could too.

But those other prisoners couldn't. Even worse, another thought was wriggling through my brain like a maggot through a corpse. Tyrant had punished Fallout for capturing me during the attack on the Academy. Which meant I hadn't been the target.

And if I hadn't been... who was?

Was Tessa in a cell just a few hundred feet from mine? Was Winter? Or was it one of the faculty instead? I'd seen Macy Johnson's ghost. Who else had been on campus on Christmas Eve?

I didn't know. I only knew one thing for sure.

"I can't leave them. There might be someone else from my school."

"Maybe. Maybe not." Her voice went soft in that way it so rarely ever did. "Either way, nobody expects you to save them, Damian."

"I know." Oddly, a discussion I'd had with Alexa, months earlier, came back to me. I didn't know who Tyrant's other prisoners were, and I didn't need to know, any more than I needed to know the names or faces of the normals I would one day protect as a Cape. The only thing that mattered was me and the decisions I made. "I'm going to do it anyway."

Her Majesty shook her head and sighed. "Well, best of luck with that." She turned to leave.

"Where are you going?"

"To get my bike, like I already said." I couldn't see her face, but the smiley face seemed to lock eyes with me. "Job was to get you out, and that's what I did. If you go back in, that's on you."

"I can't do this by myself," I told her. "I need your help."

She took another step toward the street.

"Please?" I hated begging more than anything, even apologizing, but whatever else Her Majesty was, she seemed damn near invincible. I had a much better shot at pulling off this rescue attempt with her assistance.

"That's not how it works, Bakersfield." Her voice was still soft and honey smooth. "It's not how *I* work. Not how he made me. I wish things were different, really I do, but the job's done, and so am I."

I'd thought we were friends. Of a sort, anyway. Thought I was more than just a job, but there she went, squeezing through the fallen doorway. Leaving me behind.

Then it hit me.

"What if I hired you?"

She stopped again, and turned back in my direction, saying nothing.

"I don't have much money," I admitted. "Seventy-two dollars, last I checked, but it's all yours. And I can get more from friends." At least I hoped so. "Maybe a few hundred? Even a thousand?"

"I don't work for money. Never have, never will."

"Then what *do* you want? I'll get it for you. Somehow."

The moment of silence stretched into an eternity; mercenary rider and pleading Crow, the remnants of a man scattered across the rubble between us. Finally, she nodded.

"I'd take an IOU."

"A what?"

"A promise that when I need you, you'll put your sweet ass to work on *my* behalf. A favor for a favor. A job for a job."

"I can do that." Hell, it was so much better than bankrupting myself again.

"It won't be something small," she warned. "A balance must be maintained. For this—for what you're hiring me to do—what I ask in return will be significant."

I looked her dead in the visor and nodded, crossing through Fallout's gore to shake her outstretched hand. "I'm your man."

"Not yet you aren't." The scraping of metal leaked back into her voice, humor returning with it. "Probably not ever, not without serious quantities of alcohol in me anyway. But we'll see."

I'd had a rough time of things lately, but not even torture could make me miss that innuendo. Her Majesty would be crushed when she realized I already had a girlfriend.

As we pulled the tunnel door back open, I stopped.

"Second thoughts already, Bakersfield?"

I'm not sure what I said in reply. Maybe nothing. I was too busy focusing on sending my power into Fallout's tattered skeleton. Stripped of flesh and muscle and especially tendons, it shouldn't have been able to move, let alone stand.

It did anyway, coming to join us in a quiet clicking of bone.

I looked from the monster on my right to the mystery on my left, and nodded. "Let's go."

CHAPTER 57

The tunnel hadn't gotten any shorter during our brief absence, but soon enough, we found ourselves back in the storeroom.

"Have you thought about how we're going to even get into those other cell blocks?"

I winced. "I was hoping you'd gotten the combinations for all of the doors, not just mine."

"It never occurred to me that you'd want to free everyone. That school really has mucked with your brain, hasn't it?"

She wasn't wrong.

I was quiet as we climbed two flights of stairs, exited onto a still-empty floor, and then started to make our way across to the second stairwell that would take us to the cells.

"This used to be some sort of top-secret research facility, right?" I finally asked.

"Yeah. Co-opted by Tyrant a decade ago, I think."

Given what Tyrant had told me—not to mention the fact that Sally had been held here—it had been way longer than that, but I nodded anyway. "Don't facilities like this usually have some sort of security room, where a guard can watch the cameras, check for alarms, and remotely lock and unlock doors?"

"Hell if I know. I haven't seen any cameras. Have you?" She waved a hand at the empty hall. "Besides, why bother with a setup like that, when a Technomancer can handle it all themselves?"

"Technomancers don't grow on trees," I pointed out, "and I think Reno predated the Break anyway. In fact…"

"In fact?"

I retraced our steps back to the stairwell. I'd seen something as we exited but had ignored it, focused on our goal. Something red. But where and what?

I found it on the floor next to the stairwell door, mostly covered in a mound of trash.

An evacuation map.

In the pre-Break world, people hadn't had to worry about things like a Flyboy crashing through the 18th story window, or Titans duking it out in the lobby, shattering support posts as they went. But office life hadn't been idyllic either. There'd been someone named Karen, overdue TPS reports, and the ever-present threat of fire. And bombs.

Or maybe firebombs. I wasn't entirely sure.

The point being that when nobody can fly or teleport or survive multi-story jumps, it becomes necessary to have some sort of official strategy for leaving in case of emergency. And that's exactly what the evacuation map was; a metal sign with a crude approximation of the level we were on and a red line that showed the route the office workers should follow to get to the stairwell.

None of which was super helpful, since we were already at the stairwell, of course. What *was* helpful was the fact that the map had labeled some of the rooms.

And in the very far corner of our current floor was the room I'd been looking for.

On the map, it was the size of a closet. Reality wasn't all that much better; a small door in a corner, just before the hallway turned to make its squared loop back to the stairwell. If there'd ever been a sign on the door, it was gone now, and we might easily have walked on by if it weren't for the map in my hand.

Well… that and the loud snores coming from inside.

"Let's try to keep this one alive," I murmured, setting the sign on the tiled floor. "Even if they can't open the doors from here, maybe they'll have the passcodes."

"They're all yours. You're sneakier than I am," replied Her Majesty. Her leather creaked, as if to support that point. "I'll be right behind."

I instructed my walker to stay out in the hall and turned the door handle as slowly and quietly as I could. The door eased open, and I slipped inside.

A man lay slumped over a wooden desk, head nestled in the crook of his arms. Two vid screens had been mounted in an upright position on the desk in front of him.

I'm not sure what woke the guard. Maybe I wasn't as quiet as I'd thought. Or maybe it was my odor, which had only gotten worse over the past hour. Either way, the man surged to his feet in alarm. Before he could shout, I had him pinned to the wall, my hand wrapped around his throat.

My left hand, this time. Fuck if I was going to make *that* mistake again.

"Don't make a noise and you might—"

His eyes flared golden-white, but before they could fry the flesh from my bones or fire a laser right through my skull, I dumped emptiness into his body. I tried to limit the amount of power I used, to see if I could simply stun him or at least leave a usable corpse, but he crumbled to dust, just like all the others.

"Fuck."

"What happened to keeping him alive?"

"He was a Lightbringer. I didn't have a shit ton of choice." If nothing else, I'd gotten some small bit of energy back. A trickle compared to Carnage's flood, but it was enough to ease the pain I'd been ignoring every time I took a breath. Even better, in the pile of clothing and dust that had once been a man, I found a second keyring, identical to the one Her Majesty was carrying.

One of the two screens featured what looked like a grainy pre-Break porno vid, paused right before the handyman came inside to fix the hot and apparently bored housewife's leaky pipes. The other screen was what I'd been looking for: controls for a number of systems throughout the complex. I found the cell block level and disengaged the locks on the four giant doors.

Lynn could have done all that way faster, of course, but two years of owning a Glass had taught me a thing or two about navigating user interfaces. A few minutes later, we were back out in the hall.

So far, my prison break was going way better than Tyrant's.

○○○

I hadn't paid much attention to the cell block level my first time through, but now that I was back, the difference between it and the other floors was painfully clear. In lieu of offices, a single hallway made a circular loop around the far perimeter of the space, ceding all of the interior volume to the prison area itself. Four vault-like doors led to the cell blocks, each pointing away from the center like spokes on a bicycle wheel. I hadn't been able to find an evacuation map for the level, but I was pretty sure I knew what sat at the wheel's hub.

The room with the dampeners.

My recent and painful experience told me there was a way to turn those dampeners off, but we hadn't found it, and the effects didn't extend beyond the cells themselves anyway. So Her Majesty took her keyring in one direction and I took my keyring and walker in the other. Once everyone was free, we'd meet back at the stairwell and make a dash for the escape tunnel.

As much a dash as the prisoners' conditions allowed, anyway.

Cell Block D was the one Fallout and I had been stashed in, and it had been empty except for the two of us. That just left me Cell Block C. Twelve cells. I glanced in through the barred window in each door while I progressed to the end of the cell block's hall. Few of the prisoners had needles in their arms but everyone looked emaciated and filthy. I didn't see a single person I recognized.

Not until the very last cell.

A man, always old, now inexplicably ancient.

"Amos?"

It took me six tries to find the right key for the door, but then I was inside, scooping up a body that felt like a bundle of bones. Tyrant hadn't bothered to shackle Amos, and looking at the man now, it was easy to see why. His eyes had gone milky white. Liver spots dotted his scrawny arms, and there wasn't a strand of white hair left on his shrunken skull.

Age had finally caught up to the ageless man.

But how? Not even the dampeners should have been able to do that.

It took me longer than it should have to make the connection.

Fallout and the fish things must have been seeking Amos. And there was only one reason Tyrant would want the world's oldest man. He'd stolen Amos' power. And then left the man to the ravages of time.

The body in my arms stirred. Amos thrashed about, but whatever strength he'd had was gone. Even with only one hand, it was easy to restrain him.

"Easy, Amos. I've got you."

"Banach?" His voice was thin and querulous. "Is that you?"

"Yeah." I kept my words gentle, despite the fury welling up inside me. "I'm getting you out of here. Just hang on."

"Oh good. I do love Santa Barbara," he told me. "Knew I was going to retire there even when I was a boy."

Santa Barbara had fallen into the ocean more than a decade earlier, but I nodded anyway. "Save your energy. We'll get you to a Healer and then home."

"Home?" His smile was wide and toothless, filled with an almost manic joy. "I can't wait. You'll have to try one of Alicia's pies. Cherry's my favorite."

I was still thinking of what to say to that when he stiffened in my arms and died.

ooo

Take those feelings. Wrap them in emptiness and push them to the side. There'll be time for grief some other day. For fear, for nostalgia. There's always a better time to deal with that shit. It's like the pre-Break joke that still makes the rounds even now.

What's the most popular day to start a diet?

Tomorrow.

When I got back to the Academy, maybe that would be the right time to grieve. Or maybe once the school year was over. Maybe never. Maybe that was what death was for; an endless moment of stillness and space to address all the shit you buried and tried to forget.

I don't believe that last bit. Not really. Pretty sure death is just an end. Energy back into the closed system and a body left behind for some fuck like me to turn into a weapon.

I didn't do that to Amos' body, still in my arms even though it had made unlocking doors and shackles next to impossible. I didn't know where Amos' wife was buried, but I was going to see his body put next to hers even if I had to carry the damn thing through the desert.

The other eleven people I'd released were now clustered together in the hall beyond the cell block, some of them naked, some of them crying, all of them probably wondering who I was, what we were doing, and why I hadn't said a word yet. When Her Majesty came looking for me, she had another eighteen prisoners in tow.

"I don't know how some of these people are going to make it through the tunnel," she told me. "You can't carry everyone."

She paused, took a closer look at the body in my arms, and turned that smiley-face in my direction. "You know that one's dead, right?"

"Yes."

Something in my flat voice caught her attention, because her voice went soft again. "Someone you knew?"

"Just the oldest man in the world."

She waited for more, then shrugged. "I found a couple corpses, but left them in their cells. Two live prisoners too. I recognized them... can't say I want to leave them to Tyrant, but they'd sure as shit have stabbed us in the back as soon as we let them out." She turned to scan my group. "All of yours are above board though?"

I was going to admit I hadn't even checked, that I'd just opened doors and let people follow me out into the hall. I'm pretty sure she'd have responded by muttering something about amateurs.

Before either of those things could happen though, one of my prisoners shifted into something that looked like a bear crossed with a snake and bit off his neighbor's head.

CHAPTER 58

It was absolute pandemonium. Those prisoners able to walk under their own power scattered in every direction, screaming. Others fell to the floor, trying to crawl away from the irate Shifter. One woman was too slow, and a scaled paw turned her into a bloodstain on the wall. The Shifter threw back his head and roared.

And then my walker was on him.

Her Majesty hadn't left Fallout with both of his arms intact, but it didn't stop the skeleton from climbing the mass of fur, scales, and muscle that now blocked the hallway. The splintered end of its humerus jabbed into the Shifter's chest and throat, tearing gaping holes that sprayed blood in all directions.

Problem with Beast Shifters is that they all heal, but whoever this was, he wasn't anywhere near Alan Jackson's level, let alone Kodiak's. By the time he managed to pull Fallout off of him and throw the skeleton into the wall, he was bleeding in a dozen locations and struggling to stay on his feet.

Fallout's skeleton was shattered into a million pieces, but enough space had cleared around the Shifter for the Queen of Smiles to go to work.

Her human form fell away, like a shell giving birth to a nightmare, and the storm swept through the hallway. Maybe there was a Shifter out there whose hide was tough enough to stop that sort of onslaught, but this asshole wasn't him. A body hit the floor, and just beyond him, a leather-clad woman formed out of nothing.

"Well, this is officially a clusterfuck," she growled. "There's no way we haven't been heard."

"I know." I shook my head and passed her Amos' body. "Start herding the prisoners down to the tunnel, if you can. I'll hold Tyrant's men off in the stairway and join you below."

"With what army?"

I looked at the corpses in the hall, including the shattered remnants of my own walker.

"With this army."

Tyrant had said the dead were the world's only infinite resource. It was time to prove the asshole right.

ooo

At least I knew where the enemy would be coming from. The building had two stairways, tucked away behind metal doors, but each had been blocked by rubble at different points. It's what had forced us to cross back and forth across each level to reach the basement and its escape tunnel. Once Her Majesty and the prisoners were out of the way, I could pull back and use those stairs as chokepoints.

Unfortunately, the prisoners were all in rough shape. What had been a thirty-minute hike for Fallout, Her Majesty, and I might be an hour-long death march for them.

Maybe a literal death march.

I tried to keep that in mind as I heard hurried feet on the stairwell I was standing just outside of. I needed to hold long enough at each point of my staged retreat to give the people we'd rescued a chance at survival.

Fuck if I knew how I was going to do that.

The knob on the door from the stairwell started to turn. If that door had opened outward towards me, I'd have tried to block it. Since it opened inward instead, I'd had to come up with a different plan.

Like moving one of the dead prisoners into the stairwell.

The door shuddered with an impact, as my walker slammed into Tyrant's man from behind. I couldn't see the action, of course, but as I'd found with my dearly departed zombie cat, walkers were able to operate autonomously, once raised.

Just give them enough juice and a party was all but guaranteed.

Someone screamed and a flash of light and heat reached me even through the door. Lightbringer or Pyromancer? Hell if I knew. With my walker already on him, I wasn't sure it mattered.

One thing we'd learned from Group Tactics; the best way to fight ranged opponents was to take away their range. The stairwell was doing that just fine.

Even so, I was glad my walker was in there and not me.

Raised voices signaled the arrival of reinforcements. I was already retreating back down the hall, but the tiny bubble of emptiness that was my walker vanished almost instantly. As I'd seen with Fallout's skeleton, there was a serious limit to how much damage one of my minions could take.

Good thing I had access to more.

As the door pulled open, my second walker attacked, its lack of a head not slowing it down at all. Given how quickly the first walker had died, I knew this one would be at best a speed bump, but it had the desired effect of causing Tyrant's men to clump up in the stairwell.

And that gave me just enough time to raise the Pyromancer or Lightbringer my first walker had brought down.

Multiple walkers raised in as many minutes. I was starting to think what I'd done on the Academy wall had had nothing at all to do with Muse's boost.

Unfortunately, these two walkers were destroyed almost as fast as the first, and I didn't feel any new corpses for my power to latch onto. At least one of the Powers in the stairwell was too much for my minions.

Still, it gave me enough time to make it to the stairs on the other side of the cell block level. I sprinted through and slammed the door shut. My wheezing pants echoed in the stairwell, not quite masking the sounds of the prisoners still exiting below.

At this rate, they'd be caught long before they reached the tunnel. They needed more time.

I positioned myself a few stairs down from the doorway and looked at the lone walker I had left. Fallout's skeleton had been shattered to the point of uselessness, and it had seemed only right to replace it with the hulking form of the Shifter who'd caused this mess.

As our pursuers neared, I instructed my walker to lean its bulk against the stairwell door. Now that we were *in* the stairs, we could take advantage of the direction the doors opened.

Whoever was there didn't even bother trying to open the door normally. Instead, they started to smash their way through, enormous dents appearing in our side of the metal door as if by magic. He almost had to be a Titan. Most likely the one who'd stomped my other walkers into paste.

I crept back up the stairs to the increasingly battered door, trying to time the Titan's punches as I went. And then, right before the Titan's next blow landed, I had my walker tear the door open.

Warped as it now was, the door barely made it a few inches before getting stuck, but that was enough. As the Titan's massive hand came forward, my left hand slid through to tap it on the wrist.

I let some of the emptiness in me go.

Their eyes widened—*her* eyes, I realized, having mistakenly assumed the Titan would be a he—and she collapsed.

That was the good news.

The rush of energy pouring back into me?

That was the better news.

The bad news?

She hadn't been alone in the hall. As her body crumbled, I became a big fat target for the people standing behind her.

A flicker of metal was my only warning. Power flooding my body, I tried to spin away from a knife thrown with the precision and speed only a Stalwart can bring to the table.

If I hadn't moved at near-superhuman speed, tearing something in my back as I did, the knife would have struck me dead center. Instead it caught my left shoulder, spun me around and hurled me down the stairs I'd just climbed.

I slid to a halt at the first landing and watched fire and light tear through the space above me, obliterating both the door and the walker who'd been behind it.

Fuck.

Whatever I'd just done to my back wasn't enough to keep my power from lifting me to my feet, but I wasn't going to win any awards for grace as I hurtled down the stairs, death on my heels. I was out of walkers, I was bleeding again, and I was pretty damn sure the escaped prisoners hadn't even made it across to the other stairwell on the floor below me.

By some miracle, I reached the rubble of torn metal and stone that choked off this particular stairway's access to the basement and threw myself through the door right ahead of a beam of light that would've cut me in two. The fall knocked the knife in my shoulder loose, which gave me a weapon but also allowed that wound to bleed freely. And down the hall from me, as predicted, were the last few fleeing prisoners, easy pickings for the Powers even now coming down the stairs.

I rolled to my belly and levered myself up with my aching left arm and my handless right. I'd told Her Majesty I would give them time. Fuck if I was going to be a liar.

Knife in my only hand, I charged the stairwell.

I was three steps from the door, the pursuing Powers having just reached the bottom landing, when the rubble beneath them shifted. Rebar and scrap metal. Wire and steel. I fell back as a storm of shrapnel filled the space I'd just escaped, tearing through the Powers in its midst.

I don't know how many Black Hats died in Her Majesty's trap, but a roar of fire came down the stairs in answer, so hot that even the metal stairs began to melt beneath its onslaught. The storm pulled back to the stairwell door and became a woman in black leather and a motorcycle helmet. I caught her as she stumbled and felt the exposed skin on my arms and hand blister just from the contact.

Smoke poured out of the seams of her jacket, the cuffs of her tight leather pants, and even the motorcycle helmet itself, but Her Majesty's voice was unchanged.

"Tyrant just *had* to fucking leave Red Dragon behind." The motorcycle helmet turned in my direction, the fire having left the smiley face on its visor one-eyed and grimacing. "What are you waiting for, Bakersfield? If he catches us, we're dead."

She didn't have to tell me twice.

Before I'd killed him, Carnage had been number six on the Security Council's Most Wanted. Tyrant was now number eight, although I was pretty damn sure that would change as soon as they found out what I knew.

And Red Dragon?

He was number seven.

Fire filled the stairwell behind us, metal burning like it was oil-soaked wood, but I saw the silhouette of an intimidating figure descending through the smoke and flame. The building's sprinkler system had triggered, but the water that sprayed from ceiling nozzles sizzled as it hit the wall of heat coming toward us.

The walkers I tried to raise from Her Majesty's kills didn't last much longer than that. Even their bones crumbled to ash in the Black Hat's flames.

Maybe Ishmae could have stood against him, if she'd stayed at the Academy and learned to control her power, but we sure as hell couldn't.

I really fucking hated Pyromancers.

CHAPTER 59

If you can't fight, run.

Neither Her Majesty nor I were in good shape. I was bleeding like a stuck pig and she was still performing her one-woman impression of a chimney, but our legs worked just fine as we sprinted down the hall away from Red Dragon.

If he'd wanted to, he could have filled that entire hallway with fire. Maybe Her Majesty would have survived, but I'm pretty sure I'd have been ash just like my walkers.

The fact that he didn't told me he, at least, believed Tyrant still wanted me alive. How long that thought would remain at the forefront of his mind was anyone's guess. Fire has a way of leaping beyond the constraints set for it.

Regardless, we made it to the far stairwell with some room to spare. I hurtled down two flights of steps while Her Majesty just hopped the railing and dropped to the basement floor.

As we reached the basement, we again caught sight of the stragglers of our human convoy. These were the weakest of the survivors... the ones who could barely walk on their own. Each was being supported by someone else, but the pace had slowed to a crawl.

"Is anyone even in the tunnel yet?" I asked through gasps. Whatever energy I'd stolen from both the Lightbringer and Titan was long gone.

"They should be. I showed them the way before coming back for you."

I coughed, clearing smoke from my lungs, and ducked into the closest office, looking for anything to block the stairwell door with. "Thanks for that, by the way."

"No point being owed a favor if the man who promised it dies." She shook herself, almost like a wet dog, and more smoke filtered out. "If I'd known we were going to get barbecued, I might have decided otherwise."

"Turns out prison breaks are a bitch," I admitted, "even when the prison's not the Hole."

We wedged a few desks into the hallway, but the bright light under the stairwell door warned us of the approaching Pyromancer.

"Got any bright ideas?" I asked her.

"Shit no. I'm the muscle, remember?"

"I've got one," said a weak voice behind us.

One of the prisoners had been left behind, propped against the hallway wall. The shriveled state of his left leg made it clear why he'd been at the back of the crowd.

"Where's your travel buddy?" Her Majesty's question was met with a look of confusion. "The person who was supposed to help you get to the tunnel."

"She could barely keep herself upright, let alone the both of us. I told her to go on ahead." His face and mostly-naked body were both dripping in sweat, but his eyes were steady. "No reason we should all die down here."

I was pretty sure that was *exactly* what was going to happen, but kept that part to myself. "You said you had an idea?"

"Yeah. I used to be an engineer. Buildings like this rely on structural beams to stay upright. Pretty sure they're fireproofed to delay their collapse but if you pull the right beam, whole thing should come down.

The stairwell door started to glow. Red Dragon had arrived.

"That's great, but…"

"I'm also an Earthshaker."

All those prisoners in cells next to the dampeners, and I hadn't even thought to ask how many were Powers.

"How long do you need?" asked Her Majesty, watching the door go white-hot.

"Started before you folks even got down here. Won't be long now."

"Let's get you to the tunnel then," I said, hoping Her Majesty would have a better idea how than me. She was still hot to the touch, and I was down to one halfway-functional arm.

"I'm a High-Two," said the man, waving us off. "Power enough for a Three, maybe, but none of the control. Closer I get to the tunnel, the further I am from the support beams, and the higher the chances I bring the tunnel down on us instead of the building."

A blast of heat reached us as the door melted to slag, showing Red Dragon standing in another stairwell of fire.

"Five seconds," the unnamed Earthshaker told us. "Go."

ooo

Her Majesty and I hadn't quite reached the storage room when the foundation that the Earthshaker had been chipping away at tore free, bringing two vertical struts and the structural beam on top of them crashing down. If the whole building had collapsed, we'd have died then and there.

Well, I would have anyway. I wasn't so sure about Her Majesty.

Instead, the building fell in stages, almost like it had been planned that way. The loss of one structural beam caused the building to drop, putting pressing on other beams. Most of the building might have even stayed intact, if it weren't for the fact that Red Dragon had been marching through, burning everything in his path.

Inadequate support beneath. Weakened structures above.

It came down in stages, but it did come down.

By then, we were in the storage room. I had one old woman over my shoulder, and Her Majesty had another in her arms, and if the mercenary's still-hot leather was giving the other woman contact burns, it was still better than dying.

We pushed into the tunnel as the earth shook around us and a building that had been around since the Break finally fell, burying Red Dragon and anyone else who'd still been inside.

One more enemy dead and buried. Can't say I minded.

The trek through the tunnel was hell. The lights had gone out when the building collapsed and twenty-seven of us were packed into a tight, serpentine space. Someone up ahead was a Lightbringer, but their light was swallowed by darkness with every successive twist and turn.

The fact that so many of the prisoners had made it even this far was nothing short of miraculous. I kept expecting my power to alert me to a new corpse, somewhere in the tunnel ahead, but so far, everyone was holding on.

I don't know how long the journey took. Thirty minutes? An hour? All I knew is I was putting one foot in front of the other, still carrying a woman old enough to be my grandmother, doing my best not to bang her head on the tunnel wall.

I ran right into the back of one of the prisoners ahead of me, the man Her Majesty had tasked with carrying Amos' body, before I even realized they'd stopped. "What's going on?"

Nobody back here seemed to know, so I handed the old woman off to another prisoner and made my way forward, Her Majesty on my heels. Within minutes, we were at the exit. The Lightbringer was at the front, his aura flickering.

"Why'd you stop?" I asked him.

Before he could reply, I heard a familiar voice. "The brother bird can't fly so it crawls instead. But is it then really a bird at all, or just some sort of feathered worm? Who can say says the who?"

The wound in my shoulder had finally stopped bleeding, but I could feel my weakness even through the blanket of emptiness. Playing rear guard had left me exhausted and drained the well of my power down until I could almost see the bottom. Maybe I was stronger than Jimmy Taylor but I sure didn't feel like it.

"Wait until the action starts," I told the Lightbringer and those around him, "and then get everyone out and deeper into the city. Do what you can to find somewhere to hide."

"But what about the Crow?"

For a brief, insane second, I thought he was asking about me, not Jimmy. I blame the blood loss.

"If anyone wants to help, they can, but the Crow is mine."

No walkers. One hand. No armor and no weapons except for the knife I'd pulled from my shoulder.

But fuck if I didn't have a smile on my face as I left the tunnel and entered Reno for the second time that night.

It was time to make the asshole pay. For Bakersfield. For John and Mama Rawlins. For Nyah.

CHAPTER 60

"Plan?" murmured Her Majesty, the sole Power who'd joined me as I left the tunnel.

"Same as always, I guess."

"Kill 'em all."

"Damn fucking straight."

The last vestiges of night were melting away beneath an uncaring dawn as I stepped onto the dirt-caked streets of Reno. Jimmy Taylor waited in the middle of the road, surrounded by a dozen walkers in varying states of decomposition.

He wasn't alone either. A Titan stood to one side, this one male, beefy arms crossed in front of him, the bandana on his head an unfortunate reminder of Backstreet from the Bay Side Brawlers. A Mineral Shifter had already taken her gemstone form, shining prettily in the early morning light, and there were another dozen normals, all armed with assault rifles.

The last group wasn't much to look at, even dressed up in tactical gear, but I knew from painful experience that a bullet could kill me just as easily as a superpower.

A smile, greasy and wild, lit up Jimmy's face as I came into view. He opened his mouth and let the words spill out, full of rhymes and repetition, just to demonstrate to the world how very crazy he was. Maybe something he said even made sense for once, but I wasn't listening. The time for villain monologues had ended weeks ago in my cell.

This was a time for retribution.

All night, I'd been using my power like a hammer. Kill this. Raise that. The endless effort had left me drained, so this time, I took Alexa's advice and tried to wield it like a scalpel instead. I sent a single pulse out with my breath, hunting for corpses in the surrounding buildings, like radar seeking a ping.

I didn't expect to find anything, not with another Crow in residence, and the results sadly met those expectations. No dead anywhere around us, except for the dozen walkers Jimmy had already raised.

But that's where things got interesting. Because I could feel each of those walkers, the emptiness that animated them almost a match to what I carried inside me.

And if I could feel them... maybe I could make them mine?

As Jimmy's monologue came to a close, I let my power trickle into the walkers around him, a small seed burrowing into the other Crow's emptiness.

It wasn't enough, on its own. If we'd been closer to Tyrant's lair, maybe I could have pulled on the energy of all the people who died when the building collapsed. Maybe I could have even raised some of them as walkers. But the escape tunnel had taken us blocks away, and all I had to rely on was the power inside me.

And that wasn't enough.

Until the Queen of Smiles went to work.

A storm of shrapnel hurtled out of a building further down the street. It ignored the three Powers, the twelve walkers, and instead tore through the first squad of armed normals. Barbed wire and steel and half-melted rebar shredded the soldiers like tissue paper, and just like that, I had walkers to raise.

I only managed four, because two of the instant corpses were too shredded for even my power to raise. If I was a hammer, then Her Majesty was a blender.

I dove to the side as a hailstorm of bullets from the remaining squad of soldiers chewed up the street behind me. Her Majesty had moved on Jimmy, but the Shifter had interposed her bulk between them, and the storm was striking sparks off a hide that was literally harder than stone.

That left the other Crow to send his walkers against mine, while the men with guns continued to fire.

Maybe a Stalwart or a Jitterbug could dodge bullets forever. Hell, some Titans didn't even have to dodge.

But me? I wasn't so lucky.

I got the hell off the street, running for the safety of the nearest building, letting what remained of my power fill me, eking out every last drop of speed from a body that should have collapsed hours earlier.

Somehow, I made it to cover, but that was the only bit of good news. I was already down to two walkers, and had only taken out one of Jimmy's in the process. Worse, Her Majesty wasn't making any headway at all with the Shifter. I couldn't help but think that had something to do with her almost dying to Red Dragon, with the storm she became having almost melted into scrap.

Bullets were still pinging off the stone around me, and I had no clue where the Titan had gone.

Not until he kicked in the wall I was hiding behind.

Drywall exploded inwards, showering me in dirt and plaster, throwing me onto my back where some sharp piece of discarded rebar tore into me, just barely missing my spine. Then the Titan was looming over me, one foot raised to smash me into paste.

I rolled, pulling myself off the rebar that had impaled me, just in time for the foot to come crashing down on it instead. As tough as the Titan's skin, the rebar didn't even make a dent, but I didn't care about that. I reversed direction, and wrapped myself around that leg.

And when he reached down to pull me off...

Well.

A trickle of energy washed through me, healing aches I'd been blocking for over an hour. I brushed off the dust that had once been yet another of my enemies.

If I could have, I'd have killed the Titan some other way. Not just because I was running empty on power, but also because a raised

Titan would still have at least some portion of that same strength and armored skin.

And that was the sort of walker we really needed right then.

But life doesn't give a shit what we need. I'd have to settle for not being dead.

One down, too damn many to go.

A peek out into the street showed me the rest of the battle wasn't going any better. With the storm stymied by the Mineral Shifter, Jimmy Taylor and his eight remaining walkers were headed my way, and the last six soldiers were flanking my position. Whatever healing I'd gotten from death touching the Titan was undone in an instant when a bullet ricocheted off the rubble around me and embedded itself in my hip.

The emptiness shattered, and I nearly collapsed from all the pain I'd been ignoring. My back and my shoulder. The burns on my arms and hand. The hole in my back. And now this.

I desperately reached for the emptiness, even though all my time at the Academy had taught me that was *not* the way to call on my power. Predictably, the more I strained, the more elusive it became, as Jimmy closed in on me, as the armed soldiers took up firing positions.

Then the world went white.

Sheltered in the ruined building, I actually missed the worst of it, but the single burst of light still left an afterimage, an echo of brightness that was there even when I closed my eyes.

The cries of pain and anger from the street told me Jimmy and his troops had gotten it way worse than I had.

I blew out a breath, ignoring how badly it hurt, and let the world go with it. Opened myself up to the shallow pool of emptiness left at my core.

And then I was on my feet and out in the street, scooping up the knife I'd dropped during the initial assault.

Back toward the tunnel, the people Her Majesty and I had released were slowly retreating deeper into the ruined city, but the Lightbringer was facing us, only now lowering hands that still glowed like neon torches. He looked exhausted, like that one flare of light had taken every ounce of energy from him.

Another Two then, at best. Much like the Earthshaker who'd given his life to stop Red Dragon.

Fuck anyone who sees those Powers as lesser than the rest of us. Maybe they'd never have the strength or the control to be Capes, but they were both heroes in my book.

Jimmy and the remaining six soldiers were stumbling about, rubbing their eyes, or pointing their assault rifles in random directions, all temporarily blinded by the Lightbringer's display, but the walkers didn't need eyes to see. One shuffled toward the distant Lightbringer.

The other five turned on me.

I stretched out again with my power, but the seeds I'd planted in Jimmy's undead minions remained just that, and there wasn't enough emptiness left in me to water them.

So I charged the nearest soldier instead, ducked under his flailing rifle, and drove my knife into his throat. As he fell, I pulled the gun from his hands, turned, and shot two more soldiers, twenty-two rounds expended in a matter of seconds.

It wasn't how Jessica Strich had taught us to shoot, but fuck if it wasn't still effective.

Three more dead, but now the walkers were on me, rotting hands squeezing with a strength just bordering on superhuman.

I didn't bother trying to death touch them. They were already dead, after all. I didn't bother raising the soldiers I'd just killed either. Three versus eight was horrible odds, and there wasn't a chance in hell they'd be able to keep the walkers from tearing me apart.

Instead, I thought back to the vision I'd had out at the Hole, the ocean that was not ocean, and the pools of darkness drifting in to replace the light.

I breathed out again, not even hearing my own scream, and opened myself, like unlocking a door. Opened myself to the three soldiers I'd just killed. To the two Her Majesty had shredded too badly for me to raise, even to the Titan I'd death touched just a dozen feet away.

What seeped into me was cold and dark and thick, polluted by the last moments of fear or regret or rage, but beneath it, encapsulated within it, was an emptiness I recognized. Six dead men, and I ate that death like it was one of Winter's brownies, filtering through their final gasps of emotion and pain to harvest the emptiness that lurked beneath.

And then, as something gave in my shoulder—in both shoulders, damn it—I sent that energy into the walkers around me, like a rainstorm in the desert.

It took a second, a second that I didn't have as another part of me twisted and tore, but with my eyes closed, I felt the change when it happened. Saw that seed I'd planted in each of them finally take root, finally grow and spread, snaking through the iron grip of Jimmy Taylor's control, shattering it from the inside out.

Just like that, the walkers were mine.

Now the fun could really begin.

CHAPTER 61

My walkers obliterated the remaining guards, and I ate those deaths too, feeling the emptiness rise inside me like a black-watered tide. Jimmy was babbling something, but I still wasn't listening. I buried the fucker under a wall of dead, heard the bones in his arms and legs break as my minions dragged him to the ground, pinned him there with limbs outstretched.

Maybe I should have taken his hand, like he'd taken mine. Just carved off pieces of him, one at a time, watching the life trickle out of him, smiling as each new cut took him closer to the edge.

Fuck if that didn't sound appealing, after all those weeks in my cell, after what he'd done in Bakersfield. Half-brother or not, I wanted him to suffer.

But desire and hate are just emotions, primal though they might be, and I was floating in the void, free of such human concerns.

I drove my knife into his eye instead.

And then, as he fell back against the dirt-covered street, I ate his death too.

A scream sounded from down the street as the storm finally found a way past the Mineral Shifter's gemstone shell and then there was silence. I could feel Her Majesty take shape, a gleaming ball of energy that didn't conform to anything human. In the opposite direction, prisoners continued to flee into the night, like flickering candle flames I could track without looking.

Out of nowhere, I found myself scowling. Those lights offended me, gnawed at me like ants under the skin, or a dream I couldn't quite remember. The city was blessedly silent but for these heartbeats, these breaths, the figurative and literal stench of humanity that filled the air.

And I wanted it gone.

I was on my feet, my walkers already turned to hunt down the prisoners I'd just risked my life to save. I'd like to say I don't know what would have happened if I hadn't been interrupted. I'd like to say it but the fact is, I do know, and unless you died before me, you do too.

That shit's still coming, sorry to say.

But not quite yet. Not in Reno, where my attention and killing intent were pulled away from the fleeing prisoners as something soared into the air, several blocks away from us, with a roar that shook the streets.

Turned out not even five floors of concrete was enough to stop a dragon.

○○○

Her Majesty's sigh was almost entirely free of metal. I couldn't help but notice that the smiley-face decal on her visor was less melted than it had been. "Have to say, Bakersfield, I'm starting to think taking your job was a mistake."

I shook my head, banishing the inexplicable urges that had put me on the very cusp of sending my walkers to murder civilians. "I think you might be right."

Red Dragon hovered fifty feet in the air, slowly rotating until he spotted us. The aura of flame intensified around him, and he started to drift our way.

I left my knife in Jimmy Taylor's eye where it belonged, and grabbed one of the remaining assault rifles instead. The magazine was more than half empty, but beggars can't be choosers.

He didn't even try to dodge, and when I ran out of rounds, I could see why. None of the bullets had made it through the inferno surrounding him.

"You should go," I told the mercenary by my side. "Maybe my walkers will be able to hold him down long enough for me to touch him."

"And maybe pigs will fly out of your sweet little ass," she shot back. "He's strong, but he's not fast. If we can get to my bike, we might be able to make a run for it."

"And what about the people we freed?"

She shrugged, the leather of her jacket creaking with the motion. "You can be a dead hero or a live asshole. If you think anyone up there's watching or judging, you're a bigger fool than I thought. God doesn't exist."

"And Dr. Nowhere?"

"*Him* I have words for."

I grabbed another assault rifle and spread my walkers out in a half-circle as Red Dragon finally neared us, plumes of smoke rising from his oversized nostrils. Maybe Her Majesty was right about me being a fool, but I didn't give us a chance in hell of making it to wherever she'd stashed her electric motorcycle. And if I died, I wanted it to be on my feet, with blood on my hands, and a hearty *fuck you* on my lips.

The Black Hat's aura devoured my bullets just like it had the first dozen rounds. My walkers didn't fare any better; skin cracking and melting away, bones crumbling to powder like mundane corpses at a crematorium.

I charged in anyway, because why the fuck not?

It was like stepping into a furnace. More than a furnace. The mouth of hell itself. My hair ignited. My skin started to blacken just like my walkers'. I was still at least ten feet away, and wouldn't survive another two.

And then the fire vanished, revealing the naked and doughy-faced bald man who'd been standing at the center of the blaze. Red Dragon clutched his chest, smoke still trailing from his nostrils, and then fell to the street with an impact that shook the nearby buildings.

And floating in the air above him, exactly where the Black Hat's heart had been when he was upright, was a tiny sphere of hyper-compressed darkness.

Turns out Alexa had gotten Sally Cemetery's message after all, although it had taken even longer than for Her Majesty, taken days of wailing from an inmate in a bayside asylum to convince the staff to actually look for the individual their patient was screaming for. As far away as Los Angeles was, it would have taken just as many days to get to Reno, but she hadn't come alone.

Next to her stood Door, in his trenchcoat and fedora, closing the portal he'd made out of two fragments of wood hanging from a hinge.

I finally let my power go, and slid bonelessly to the street.

ooo

When I woke, I was on a gurney in a room I knew by heart. I could hear Gladys shuffling about, but when I opened my eyes, it was Alexa standing there next to me.

"I hope you haven't been there the whole time," I managed, voice dry and spent. "It can't have been too much fun."

"Gladys sent word that you'd be regaining consciousness soon." Alexa looked tired and drawn, even paler than normal, but her lips quirked in that almost-smile. "I'm not sure if that's standard Healer's intuition or if she's just had to heal you one too many times."

"A bit of both," declared the old woman in question, before fixing my therapist with a hard eye. "I'll leave you two to talk, but don't take too long. The boy needs more sleep."

"Yes, ma'am." There was nothing but respect in Alexa's voice. Smart woman. She waited for the door to close behind Gladys and turned to me. "Your friends and classmates are waiting to see you, as are at least a dozen people from different government agencies, but as the one who found you, I pulled rank so I could talk to you first."

"The prisoners?"

"Healed, if possible, and resting in hospitals around Los Angeles," she said. "And next in line to be debriefed, no doubt."

"Tyrant?"

She shook her head. "Showed up with a dozen Powers to defend an installation in Fresno. He was gone again before Dominion could arrive. Left a lot of dead in his wake too, but we got more information on him in that one fight than in the past decade. I suppose you already know he's a Pyromancer? Titan too, though you'd never expect it, given his size."

"He's a lot more than just that. And a lot worse."

Black eyes darted back to the med ward door and then met mine with sudden intensity. "Tell me."

So I did. I told her everything, from the night on the Academy wall all the way to my early-morning showdown with Jimmy Taylor.

"Was he right?" I asked her. "Is Tezcatlipoca really expanding his domain? Is Dominion really dying?"

"I haven't heard anything about Dominion or cancer, but..." She nodded. "The research team Tyrant told you about really did exist, and their findings with Tezcatlipoca have been confirmed. The government has been quietly moving people north and away from the border for years now."

"And what happens when it hits San Diego?"

"I don't know. We're all looking for answers, Damian. Once you graduate, maybe you can help us find them."

"Maybe."

"I can't help but notice one hole in your story," she continued, voice still gentle. "A hole that's conspicuously six feet tall and wears a motorcycle helmet."

I scrunched up my face, as if trying to remember. "Doesn't ring a bell."

"Really."

"Really. I did take a few blows to the head. And lost a hand," I added, waving my stump around as if she hadn't already seen it. "But if there was such a person in Reno, maybe they were the reason I survived. The reason all those other prisoners made it out. Whoever they are would deserve our thanks."

"If there was such a person."

"Exactly."

Alexa sighed. "Well, it might interest you to know that this person that wasn't there was gone before we started triage. Slipped away even as Red Dragon died."

I couldn't quite hold back my smile.

"Damian, whatever experience you may have had with her, whatever debt you may feel you owe, you have to believe me when I tell you this: the Queen of Smiles is dangerous."

I thought back to that moment of utter inhumanity I'd felt after killing Jimmy Taylor, that urge to wipe Reno clean of life. I hadn't told Alexa about that either. Wasn't ever going to. Instead, I was going to find out where it came from, crush it, and then live my life... and fuck what had happened to all the other Crows before me. I was stronger than Jimmy, stronger than Sally even. I had to believe that would be enough to keep me sane.

I felt my smile shift to something cold and hard.

"So am I."

EPILOGUE

There were less than a hundred people at Amos' funeral, but the quality more than made up for what I saw as an insulting lack of quantity. Dominion. Kodiak. Paladin. The Scarlet Dynamo. Bard and Alexa in her guise as Midnight. And every Cape student and graduate that could make it. Because Alicia had been buried in Santa Barbara and that whole city had fallen into the ocean, Amos had requested in his will that his ashes be cremated and spread above that same ocean.

Dominion did the honors himself. On any other day, I might have spent that whole time watching him from the ground, wondering if the great Cape seemed a little more worn than usual, wondering how much time he really had left. At Amos' funeral, I only had thoughts for the old history teacher himself.

I never saw Amos' ghost, not then, and not in all the time since. I like to think there wasn't enough of him left behind for that; that every part of him was somewhere else, with the love of his very long life.

Can't say I truly believe it, but it's a nice damn thought.

○○○

I know. That's not what you want to hear about. Dead professors and Crows, madness and revenge, favors owned and paid. All that shit's just icing, isn't it? Just something to taste, to sink your teeth into while waiting for the real meat of the story.

I know what you want.

You want to know if I made it to the Remembrance Day dance with Poltergeist.

Fair enough. And the answer is yes. I'd been gone for a full month, spent a week being debriefed by a succession of people from agencies whose names I never learned, attended a funeral, and missed the vast majority of the Graduation Games—again—but when Remembrance Day rolled around, there I was in my tailored suit and an emerald button-up shirt that matched Tessa's strapless dress perfectly.

She and the rest of Team Five had survived the assault without a scratch, and we all made it to the dance. Even Muse, whose future at the Academy was now very much in question.

We danced. We ate. We drank. Tessa and I spent time with Silt and Cynthia, with Vibe and Paladin, and even London and Olympia, who'd decided, to the disappointment of a huge number of men, to attend as each other's dates. Nobody commented on the way my sleeve dangled off the end of my right arm, and Tessa didn't complain when I stepped all over her toes, although she did start using her telekinesis to move my feet into their proper place.

The end of the night found us on the bench in the clearing on the west side of campus, the ocean still achingly beautiful despite the recent reminder of the many horrors that it hid. Tessa's lips were soft and cool, the curves of her body blending with the straight lines of mine, my arm—my left arm—holding her snug and tight against me.

Remember that moment. Thousand stars in the sky. Crash of waves on the distant shore. The warmth of being with someone who cares.

Remember it. Hold onto it.

You're going to need it where we're heading.

AUTHOR'S NOTE

Thank you so much for reading!

Sequels are strange. Second books in a trilogy are even stranger. With the first book being the setup and the third book being the payoff, that middle book is left to do a lot of the heavy lifting in getting the plot where it needs to go. *Red Right Hand* was a first for me, and I honestly wasn't sure if it had come together or not until the very last page.

I hope you enjoyed it and that you're as excited to read the last book in the series as I am to write it! Damian's journey (figurative and literal) is not over yet and the Free States' future now hangs in the balance. Tyrant may have seen another of his plans go up in flames, but the Black Hat is far from defeated. Tezcatlipoca is growing in power to the south. And then there's the little matter of that favor the Academy's only Crow now owes the Queen of Smiles.

It all comes to a head in *One Tin Soldier*, the final book in Damian's story, which will release in fall 2021. I can't wait to share it with you!

In the meantime, if you're looking for something a little different, please check out *Investigation, Mediation, Vindication*, the first book in my other series, The Many Travails of John Smith. It's a humorous urban fantasy, starring a San Diego slacker who quickly finds himself in way over his head.

Last but not least, if you enjoyed *Red Right Hand*, please consider leaving a review. As an indie author, my books depend heavily on word of mouth and the feedback of readers like you.

Thank you!

ABOUT THE AUTHOR

Chris began life as a gleam in someone's eye, but birth and childhood were quick to follow. He's been fortunate enough to live in Spain, Germany, and all over the United States of America, and is busy planning a tour of the distilleries of Scotland.

A graduate of the Johns Hopkins University's Writing Seminars program, he put that degree to ill use for twenty years as a software engineer, but has finally circled back around to the idea of writing for a living.

Chris currently lives in Nevada with his angelic wife and ever-expanding whisky collection and occasionally ventures outside to peer upwards, mutter to himself about 'day stars', and then scurry back into the house.

Red Right Hand is his third novel and the second in the Murder of Crows trilogy. Chris frequently shares updates and new content on his author website at https://christullbane.com.